THE WOLF AND
THE RAIN

TANYA LEE

ISBN 978-1-7753929-1-0

The Wolf and the Rain is a work of fiction. All names and characters are products of the author's imagination or are used fictitiously. Any resemblance to actual events or persons, living or dead, is entirely coincidental. Except for Frank the Cat. Frank is real.

Please note that this work contains mature themes.

Edited by Melissa Frain

Cover design by Lena Yang

Visit Tanya Lee's website at: Tanya-Lee.com

For A.M.

"I am no bird; and no net ensnares me"

Charlotte Brontë, Jane Eyre

1

The North

SAM WOKE INTO NOTHINGNESS. Panic washed the remnants of the dream away as she reached outward, searching for something tangible, something real—found blankets, the cold hard metal of her baton, the shirt she used as a pillow. Next, the slow, practiced exhale.

I am Samarra. I am in my bed, in the factory, in the Barrow, in the North. A second exhale.

He'd been alive this time, his head resting on a pillow, a grin on his face. *What had he just said? Or maybe he was about to say it.* Then footsteps, the sound of the door opening.

That was all she remembered; that and the look of betrayal. It wasn't how it had happened—just a projection, not a memory. A third exhale.

The sun would be up soon. She changed her clothes under the blankets to keep the chilly air at bay, slid down the ladder, and walked softly down the stairs and across the factory floor. Most of the other residents were still asleep, though she could see Ava bustling around in her shop, her dark skin and short black curls already streaked with flour.

Sam paused, watching for a moment as Ava dug a knuckle into her hip and grimaced. It made her seem older, the pain. *Or maybe that's the grief.*

Sam's eyes shifted down to her new boots, the previous night's discomfort returning. She didn't like gifts. They made her feel guilty.

Why? This one isn't on you. Not like—

Enough. We don't think about that anymore.

Ducking a clothing line, Sam made for the door.

The guilt was misplaced, unnecessary. Ava's daughter had died before Sam had even arrived in the Barrow.

So you take her mother, her job, her room, and now her boots? There's a term for that in the North—they call it grave robbing.

Stepping outside, Sam pulled the roll that Ava had given her the night before from her pocket and took a bite.

The dead girl had no need for boots. Sam did. It was practical.

And you didn't know how to refuse Ava.

She shoved the memory away. She didn't want to remember the look on Ava's face, didn't want to think of her loss. She had enough of her own.

Sam took a deep breath, willing her thoughts to quiet, and bit into the roll again.

Taste the bread.

Chilly air filled her nostrils, masking for a brief moment the stench of burning plastic. *Inhale. Exhale.*

She let out one more slow breath, and then set off down the trash filled street.

It took her three quarters of an hour to reach the Vaun compound. Jackal, of course, was already waiting. The first thing she noticed every morning was his silhouette. Against a backdrop of electric lights, the only ones she had ever seen in the Barrow, his shadow stretched skinny fingers from the spiked fence down the muddy path all the way to her feet. The man himself leaned against the bars, weight on one boot, hatted head bent forward so that his chin rested on his chest.

Every day she arrived before the sun and every day he was waiting, head bowed, eyes closed, more scarecrow than man.

"Good morning," said Sam, as she did every day.

"Almost," said the shadow.

They waited in silence. Crouching down low, Sam leaned back against the fence, resting her arms on her knees. It was a view she loved, looking from the compound across the field out toward the woods. Eventually some new pest would descend on the area, reducing the trees to dry, brown husks; they always did. For now, though, the trees were young and thriving and green.

Sam snuck a peek at Jackal. Even half asleep, tension lined his frame: square jaw, broad shoulders, wiry limbs; muted energy pulled inward like a spring. Sam couldn't tell if it was violence he was harbouring or grit, but she had the sense that he was waiting for something. *Not straw, then. Steel.*

As the sky began to brighten, a murder of crows circled overhead, cawing noisily as though they owned the skies. *Of course, they do.* Not many species of birds had survived the Decline. Crows had learned to avoid diseased food sources, it was believed. Or perhaps they hadn't —perhaps those that survived had become resistant to the diseases themselves. *Meaning the weak died out.* That was how it had happened with the original West Nile virus, at least. All of the species that could be killed by the virus, had been. Those that remained were immune. Even subsequent mutations of the virus hadn't touched the crow population. *Now they just spread it to the mosquitoes. Who spread it to us.*

Sam craned her neck to watch as they flapped over to one of the guard towers behind her, perching like gargoyles on an upper parapet. She wondered if they ever dared approach the compound proper; she had yet to witness it, but then only a small fraction of the heavily fortified edifice was visible from the front entrance. *A murder of crows. What an ominous title for a categorical grouping.*

A high-pitched voice broke the silence, singing out, "Good morning, good morning, to you!"

Two slim, willowy figures were approaching. Cassio rolled his eyes at his twin, pulling up his hood as though to block out the sound.

3

Excepting the fact that he was as dark as she was fair, Cassio's face was identical to his sister's, producing a multi-coloured mirror effect: Black eyes to jeweled greens, dark brown hair to white-blond.

Xenia skipped over to plant a kiss on Jackal's scruffy cheek and swing herself up onto the fence, hooking her feet in the bars and dangling upside down. She swung forward lightly, touching her nose to Sam's and earning a smile in return. It was difficult to remain aloof around Xenia.

"New boots!" She pointed at Sam's feet. "Nice, nice—fancy ladki."

"Thanks," said Sam. Xenia continued bobbing, her upside-down eyes locked on Sam's. Clearly, she was expecting more from the conversation.

"They were...they were Raina's." The name felt clumsy in her mouth, like she'd just uttered her first word in a new language.

What, becoming a superstitious northerner are we, scared to call on the dead?

Obviously not. It's just...Ava never says her name.

"Ah." Xenia blew a strand of white-blond hair out of her face. "Just keeping 'em warm for her, then."

Sam stared at Xenia. She must have mixed up her Northern idioms.

"What—What do you mean?"

Xenia looked puzzled at Sam's confusion.

"Well, she'll want them back, no? I don't remember Raina being overly charitable."

"But—"

"Somebody shoot that monkey before it gives that girl monkey rabies." Hakuund's deep voice bellowed from across the field, drowning out Sam's question.

Xenia gracefully pulled one long leg off the fence and kicked backward, the momentum flipping her around so that she could stare Hakuund in the eye as she proffered a deeply insulting hand gesture.

"Are monkey rabies different than other types of rabies?" Cassio drawled out, looking up from where he now leaned, hands in pockets, against the fence.

"Yep," said Hakuund as he clasped hands with Jackal. "Monkeys give 'em to you."

The latest arrival was powerfully built, as tall as Jackal and twice as bulky. Sam suspected Hakuund was the younger of the two, though probably even they didn't know. There were no record keepers in the North.

Hakuund certainly looked younger; his dark skin was smooth and unmarked where Jackal's was weather-beaten. Exposure to environmental toxins, poor nutrition, the remnants of old illnesses and injuries that had been endured rather than cured: hard living left its mark in the Barrow. It did not always correspond with age.

Xenia hopped nimbly back down to the ground and bounded over to Hakuund, who pulled her into a one-armed hug. He rubbed the top of her head with one of his gigantic hands, eliciting a squawk of protest from Xenia, and nodded at Sam. He didn't give Cassio his usual crushing hug. Not that he hugged Sam, either, but then she was still new.

Wanting to continue their conversation, Sam tried to catch Xenia's eye. Xenia, deep in discussion with Hakuund, didn't notice.

"Busy night?" Jackal asked Cassio, who was trying and failing to hide a yawn.

"Alright," Cassio said. "Late start. Barely made it home before dawn." Cassio's eyes, Sam noticed, never left Hakuund.

Jackal gave a wry smile. "Better you than me. I'm too old for that shit." He reached into his pocket and dug out a small bag, which he passed to Cassio.

"Got your bonus."

Sam gave up trying to attract Xenia's attention and slumped back against the fence, watching out of the corner of her eye as Cassio opened the bag and pulled out four small, bright orange bits.

"Amazing man, where the gods did you get these? Xen!" Cassio called to his sister. "C'mere, Jackal brought Christmas early."

She turned away from Hakuund and walked over to her twin. He passed her one of the orange pieces.

"Brilliant," she said. "You are wondrous, Jack."

The twins pocketed the gifts before Sam could get a better look. She noticed Jackal watching her and quickly dropped her eyes. *Sloppy, getting caught staring.* It was probably okay though; based on the twins' reactions the items were rare, even in the North.

If it even mattered. Ava was always so worried about someone finding out that Sam was a southerner. But then, Ava worried about a lot of things. In the months she'd been in the Barrow, Sam had rarely heard anyone so much as mention Seira. It was as if the world ended at the southern wall.

Hakuund gave a low whistle and the five of them turned toward the compound, watching as the gate rose and a slim figure dressed in white stepped out onto the causeway.

Benison followed the raised concrete platform to the fence where they waited in silence. The puddles were relatively shallow today; he could have walked across the yard if he'd wanted to. Sam suspected he preferred to keep his shoes clean.

Benison passed their scrolls through the fence, watching with narrowed eyes as they read through the information and handed them back to him.

Only Sam was allowed to keep hers. Most days she received a map and a list of items to obtain, unimportant odds and sods such as herbs or oils. Perhaps the other drudges carried out similarly petty errands, perhaps not. She would not find out. A shred of information divulged and employment would be terminated, along with the indiscreet party. They were warned regularly.

Benison had given a small bag of xots each to Jackal and Hakuund, coins of varied size forged of steel and plated with copper, bronze, or nickel, yet somehow all endowed with the same value: the unit of one. Xots were used only for high-end transactions. Local trade was typically conducted using sack—small cloth bags filled with grain, usually rice. It was somewhere between four to seven sack to a xot, depending on the weight of the grain and the avarice of the parties involved. Sam found dealing in sack to be inconvenient and had often wondered whether anyone had considered re-valuing the xot.

She leaned in for her own bag of coin and caught a whiff of Benison's breath, sickly sweet like maple milk that had begun to turn sour.

Benison merely stared at her. "They're expecting you." She nodded, asking no questions, as she'd been instructed.

Benison unlocked the bicycles one at a time, waiting until each rider had exited the compound grounds before unlocking the next one. Sam waited as Jackal's wiry frame disappeared from view. Hakuund, the giant, followed, then the twins, slim and graceful. *It was like releasing animals into the wild, if the animals needed to be discouraged from forming illicit assemblies.*

"You can't go on bicycle," Benison said, once the others had vanished from sight. "And when you get there, take the path straight down to the bridge."

This was unusual, but again Sam just nodded. After one last glance at the map, she pocketed the scroll and headed off on foot. A fat raindrop thunked off her shoulder, and then another. She pulled up on her hood and quickened her pace.

Today's map led her eastward, almost to the overflow. *Well, one of the overflows.* Half of the city was permanently flooded, neighbourhoods of vacant homes rotting in the polluted run-off. Even the plant life had been displaced in these areas, choked out by the phragmites that were slowly invading the city.

Sam didn't mind walking. The woods were beautiful, though the trees were too sparse to offer respite from the rain. *Damn pests.* She didn't even know what they were called, not the current mutation. There had been the mountain pine beetle, of course. It had decimated the west and then turned eastward when the temperatures rose.

Then there was a mutation and the beetle's appetite expanded to include other types of softwoods. Then came a second mutation and the hardwoods began to die. *Smart of the beetle to diversify its food source.* Survival went to those who adapted.

Still, she hated the thought of those beetles swarming the trees, picking them clean. There was altogether too much death in the North. Dead trees. Dead crops. Dead livestock. And the people...

Like Ava's daughter.

Sam's thoughts drifted back to her conversation with Xenia. Did Xenia not know that Raina was dead? It seemed unlikely. They'd worked together, after all. Perhaps it was yet another strange Northern custom, speaking about the dead as though they were still present. Sam continued to mull it over until she recognized that her thoughts were circling: Xenia's words, baseless theories. She needed a distraction.

There was a story she often thought of when she was alone in the woods, a Northern fairy tale that Ava had recounted for her. Folk and fairy tales fascinated Sam. She found them to be magnetic, if horrifying.

The story centered on a little girl who is walking to her grandmother's house when she is intercepted by a wolf. The wolf is hungry, but the child refuses to share the food she carries, provisions intended for her grandmother. The wolf takes revenge by rushing off to the grandmother's house and eating the old woman. When the little girl arrives, the wolf pretends to be the grandmother, luring the child closer and closer to the bed where he lies, ready to pounce. The child becomes suspicious and flees, finding a woodcutter who helps her kill the wolf. The grandmother is miraculously alive inside the wolf and the child gains a new fur coat.

According to Ava there were alternate versions of the story. Sometimes the child and the grandmother are both eaten, a tragic end to a bleak tale. In other interpretations the child and the grandmother cut their way out of the wolf's stomach and fill the wolf back up with heavy stones.

"How would a wolf sleep through that?" Sam had asked.

"He's in a deep sleep from overeating," Ava said. "Also, it's just a story, don't go ruining it with your logic."

Stories for children, whether in the South or the North, were always intended as a lesson. What was the lesson here? Sam couldn't decide. *Always share your food with hungry strangers, lest they eat you and your loved ones instead? Lock your door in case a wolf thinks to barge in uninvited? Keep a small knife on your person at all times in case you need to cut your way out of someone's abdomen? Don't overeat because you might not notice someone stabbing you?*

While the wolf was the obvious villain of the story, Sam had trouble identifying the hero. The grandmother was the victim; the woodcutter, when he appeared, played only a supporting role. Ava thought it was the child, but Sam disagreed. The girl was complicit in her grandmother's death. The wolf was charming, true; but wolves were well-known predators. She should have been able to recognize the threat. *Instead she leads him to someone that she loves.*

Sam heard a rustle in the bushes and reached down for her baton. A gigantic rat darted out, chittered wildly at her, and raced up a tree. Sam let out a deep breath, suddenly very glad that her team did not work in pairs. The last thing she needed was a witness to her suddenly overactive imagination.

The baton slid easily back into her boot. Concealed weapons were safest, according to Ava. Exorbitant prices meant that carrying a crossbow or visible blade made you a target for thieves. In the Barrow, there were a lot of thieves. One of the things she hoped to purchase, once she had a bit of coin saved up, was a small, easily concealable knife.

"So," Sam said when she finally reached her destination. "This is why I couldn't take a bicycle."

The road, marked innocently on her map with a solid line, looked to have seen a mudslide. Heavy rainwater had formed into rivulets, pushing through the trash to race in muddy streams down the steep hill toward the lone building. The earth at the bottom of the hill had been dug out, allowing the dirty water to pool below the big, dilapidated house, which rose like a mountain from the swamp.

A wooden plank served as a bridge, connecting the base of the hill with the front stoop. *Of course, I'll have to get to it.* Sam sighed, and eyed the land in front of her, which amounted to a muddy slide. Mudslide, muddy slide, an etymology she had never taken the time to consider in the dry lands of the South. She would have to be strategic.

Amidst the slippery plastic bags and food waste, a clump of chunky garbage, including an old tire, stood out. It was about three feet down from where she stood. She half walked, half slid down to it. From there she slid to a pile of bricks. Bit by bit, she made her way down to the makeshift bridge. The residents here clearly did not relish visitors. Either that, or this was their idea of entertainment. Sam scanned the building, almost expecting to see a crowd of onlookers munching on groundnuts and placing bets on when she would fall.

Phragmites grew thickly around the base of the swamp. It made Sam think of a siege, the reeds pushing inward, surrounding the old house. At least the phragmites provided her with some traction, though she didn't like that they obscured her view of the ground.

Sure enough, near the bottom of the hill she tripped and narrowly missed falling into a large pit. It wasn't a natural pit, but one dug by human hands. Sam leaned forward to look inside. Sharp sticks pointed upward with obvious intent. She glanced back up the hill and realized with a chill that there were dozens of these pits. The only section that had been spared, besides the cliff edge behind the house, was a thin strip of land leading straight down to the bridge and the front door; one way down, one way up. *Take the path straight down to the bridge, indeed.*

She crossed the bridge and made her way up the stairs to the door. A metal hammer was hanging by a string from the handle. Sam picked it up and stared at it for a moment, then gently tapped it against the door. A few moments later a tiny old woman opened the door. A few tufts of grey hair sprouted from the sides of an otherwise bald head.

"I'm here for the Vauns," Sam said.

The old woman stared at Sam, and then turned and walked back inside. Since she had not slammed the door in her face, Sam assumed that the woman intended for her to follow. Cockroaches skittered ahead of her down a hallway that smelled like mould and rust and something Sam couldn't place, something that made her want to complete her task as quickly as possible.

The old woman led Sam to a sitting room where a small man sat on a dirty chair. A massive black dog sat beside the man, its jaundiced eyes fixated on Sam. Behind them stood an enormous bookcase, once pink, now blackened with soot, housing dozens of dolls with chipped faces and frilly dresses.

As the woman bent forward to whisper in the man's ear, the dog let out a low growl. Though she was several feet away, Sam gagged at the smell of rot emanating from its mouth.

The woman left silently, and the small man turned to Sam and smiled, revealing a set of rotten teeth. A few greasy strands of hair that might once have been blond had been draped over his scabbed head, as though to hide the bald spots. His eyes were red and weeping, and his fingernails, Sam was shocked to see, were several inches long, yellow and twisted. He in turn seemed to be studying her.

"You're new," he said. "I can smell it on you." He leaned forward. "Like honey." His smile twisted into a leer.

Sam looked down at her feet, a behaviour she hoped he interpreted as diffident. This man was a compound contact; throwing him out a window would undoubtedly be a bad idea. The dog untangled his long legs and lurched toward her. Sam purposefully slouched lower in a display of submission that brought her right hand closer to the baton stashed in her right boot. Standing, the dog's head was level with her shoulders. He circled her, bringing his foul mouth in close to sniff at her. The smell intensified with the dog's proximity. Sam lowered her hand another inch, breathing through her mouth.

"Will you stay to tea?" the man asked. "Or something stronger?"

"I am required back at the compound," she said, the dutiful drudge. *Is he armed?* She could fend off the dog, but not if she was ducking crossbow bolts at the same time. There could be other guards nearby as well—just because they were not visible did not mean that they were not present. All in all, she would prefer not to fight her way out.

Sam heard the click of his fingernails tapping on wood, and then a loud sigh. The old woman, who had been hovering at the doorway, shuffled into the room carrying a small package. She had wrapped the item in an old piece of cloth, and Sam could feel the firm edges of a wooden box underneath the musty fabric. She bowed low to the man, slowly, so as not to incite the dog, and, avoiding his eyes, followed the old woman back outside.

The rain had stopped. As Sam retraced her steps back across the bridge, she couldn't help wondering if he would have let her leave so easily, if she wasn't a drudge. Compounds were as feared as they were hated. Sam may be complicit in the Vauns' affairs, but she also reaped the benefit of their protection.

Kicking the toes of her boots into the mud for traction, Sam made the slow ascent back up the hill, pushing the thought away. She wished the rain would start again—as though a downpour could wash away the stench lingering in her memory.

2

The South

I WAKE before the bells chime. Lily is still asleep, her arms splayed out across the rumpled blankets. I lay still a moment, listening to the breathing around me, savouring the familiarity. Tonight, I will sleep in a different bed, in a different city. I know this, but I cannot picture it. All of my memories live in this place.

Turning to look at the clock, I catch movement out of the corner of my eye and duck just in time to avoid being hit in the face with a rolled-up sock. Iris grins at me from the next bed. "I knew you were awake. Let's go look around," she whispers.

We slip on light canvas shoes and pull sweaters over our matching white nightgowns. I shut the door quietly behind us. Iris grabs my hand and we run down the hallway on the pads of our feet. I am faster than her and reach the end of the hallway first.

I peek around the corner. The coast is clear. We race over to the utilities closet. Iris watches behind us as I crouch down and slide the small metal pin into the lock on the door, pressing my ear to the catch and listening until I hear a click.

She pushes in ahead of me. By the time I lock the door behind us she is already standing on the uppermost shelf, her hands pushing up the ceiling panel. She hoists herself up and disappears into the ceiling. I scramble up onto the shelf in turn and reach through the open panel to grasp the metal rafters above the vent. My arm muscles tense as I lift myself up and swing my legs into the opening. I shimmy forward into the duct and then flip from my back to my stomach, pulling the panel back into position behind me. Feet first, I make my way forward. My shoes touch Iris'; she waited for me. We inch our way through the passage like a creature with two heads.

We follow the vent for several minutes. When I feel sweat start to trickle down my temples I know we're almost there. Sure enough, the vent widens and I can finally turn around. Careful not to make a sound, we approach the grate and gaze down into the hall.

Several medics mingle below us, talking amongst themselves. Not all of them belong to our division; some of them I do not recognize at all. Our designates, plain in their grey uniforms, hover around them. Neither group attempts to interact with the other.

Iris points directly beneath us, where a woman and a man are entering the room. Rich, dark green cloth hugs the woman's slim form, and white stones shimmer from around her neck. The man is wearing a scarlet suit. The fabric is beautiful. It flutters as they move, seeming to catch, hold, and then absorb the light. My gaze drifts to the tops of their heads. I wish they would walk farther into the room, so that I might see their faces. Both of them have black, oiled hair. I wonder who they are.

The room's occupants have turned to greet the newcomers, hands pressed together across their eyes in deference. The courtesy is received but not reciprocated—the man and woman merely nod and turn from the attention, speaking together in low voices. Designates and medics alike fade into insignificance.

"...flowered, though some of the others have," the man says to the woman.

I frown at the odd personification of the word, and strain to hear her reply.

"...No perfect time." She sounds irritated. I catch the words "precautionary" and "false positive," but the rest of the woman's response is drowned out by the hum of voices.

Faintly from behind us, I hear the bell. Reluctantly I turn toward Iris, who is still staring, rapt, at the scene below. I tap her on the shoulder. She starts and I see her hesitate for a second before she turns and follows me out.

We took too much time. Back in the closet we listen at the door for a full five minutes before there is a break in the patter of footsteps. I nod to Iris and she slides the door open carefully, takes a peek, and then sprints off down the hallway.

I lock the door from the inside and shut it behind me before following my friend down the corridor. Finding our room empty, we grab our towels and hurry to the lavatory. Luckily, the rest of the girls are still bathing.

They have laid out the shaving tools today. Standing in front of the mirror, I run the blade over my scalp. The hum of a dozen other shavers buzzes around me, like bees though much less precious. The stubble on my head is longer than usual; it has been a full five days since our last shave. They want us to look our best today.

When I have done all that I can, Iris steps behind me, practiced hands catching the bits I missed. I do the same for her, staring at the freckle on the back of her right ear: another insignificant fragment of familiarity.

Back in our room a basket of meal replacement bars and small cups of prickly pear juice have been laid out for us. I eat and drink mechanically, in silence. We all do. The weight of imminent change has stamped out our desire to converse.

Finally, Designate Lews arrives. She looks us over critically and then nods. We line up and follow her outside in silence. Designate Lews does not permit chatter, even were we so inclined.

Lily reaches her hand back and I take her fingers in mine. I feel Iris take my other hand. We are led down a hallway to a secured door. I can feel the excitement bubbling up around me now as we transition from waiting for change to actually moving forward. Designate Lews stops in front of the medic wing to scan her card and we follow her inside.

The cold cement floors have given way to grey tiles and bright lights. We pass steel doors with symbols on them, symbols whose lines and curves I have long since memorized but never deciphered. At the end of the hallway we are led into the waiting room. Designate Lews leaves and is replaced by one of the medics I do not recognize.

Olive is the first to be called. She stands slowly, hesitates, and then follows the medic through the door. We wait in silence. Even Iris, forever being punished for her inability to hold her tongue, is quiet, staring at the door ahead. Beside me Lily wipes her palms on her smock and I think I can hear her heart racing. I stare at the ceiling, counting the tiles, making patterns. I wonder if any of them are loose.

The medic returns almost immediately and collects two more girls. There must be more than one station set up today; the examination itself could not have finished so quickly. It is several long minutes before more girls are summoned: three again, including Lily this time. She stares at me for a moment, uncertain. I nod and do my best to give a reassuring smile, which does not seem to reassure her. Regardless, she wipes her palms one more time and then follows the medic out of the waiting room. When it is Iris' turn she squeezes my hand and walks quickly away, not turning once to look back. Holly follows her and then Hazel. Only two girls are called in the next round and the pattern changes from threes to ones and twos. The last two girls are called together, leaving me alone. I trace patterns in the ceiling tiles again, then the floor tiles. It will not be long now.

The medic leads me to a small examination room. I take off my clothes, put on a robe, and lie on the table, feeling the paper crinkle underneath me. It is warm in the room but I shiver anyway. The medic looks at my eyes and in my ears and puts a cuff around my arm that expands and tightens and then loosens again. She puts an earpiece to my back and listens. She then covers my face with a mask and tells me to name our country's council members. The edges blur and I fade into darkness.

3

The North

SAM ARRIVED BACK at the compound to find a produce cart parked beneath one of the towers. A heavyset woman picked a potato up off the cart, scanned it for rust and mould, and passed it to Benison through a panel in the fence. The vendor hovered beside the woman, speaking animatedly. About his wares, Sam assumed. She was too far away to hear the conversation.

Looking up, Sam spotted two guards, guns trained on the vendor —or the woman, perhaps. Like Benison, the woman wore all white, the uniform of a domestic servant. Sam had never seen one outside the gated area before.

Based on the stack of empty baskets on the ground beside Benison, Sam suspected she might be waiting some time for him to sign off on her package. She didn't mind, though. She was enjoying the woman's systematic selection process.

She noticed one of the guards watching her and gave what she hoped was a courteous, but not inviting, smile. He continued staring at her, completely deadpan, until she looked away.

"If you're hoping for a response, you're wasting your time."

Sam turned to see Jackal behind her. *Of course. Who else could have snuck up on me?*

"Maybe somebody should try to keep them from going mad with boredom," Sam said. "Nobody likes a lunatic with a gun. Except maybe other lunatics with guns. Or, I guess, anyone that wants to instigate general mayhem. You'd just call them General Mayhem, I guess." *Jit, I'm rambling.*

Something about Jackal made her uncomfortable. Most of the time when she was uncomfortable she turned conveniently taciturn. Why he induced awkward babbling, she couldn't say. "They should pay me by the joke." *Taow jit.* This was worsening by the minute.

"Okay," he said after a moment. "Let's hear one then."

Sam blanched. "A joke? Uh...ok. Um. How do you know that witches have the best vocabularies?" She waited, but Jackal did not look remotely interested in guessing the punch line.

"Because they're the best at spelling bees!" Sam finished, inwardly cursing herself. It seemed in her panic she had mixed northern lore with a very Seiran educational tool, creating a wholly untranslatable joke.

"Do you know what a spelling bee is?" she asked after a moment.

He raised his eyebrows and gave an "obviously not" shake of his head.

"In Kanlan, they will gather a group of children who can read and write and give them words to spell aloud." Kanlan was the neighbouring town she pretended to hail from, chosen because it was close enough not to raise questions but far enough that she doubted many people had ever travelled to or through it. "It's a contest. As soon as you spell a word incorrectly, you're out. Whoever can last the longest, wins. So, it's vocabulary spelling, whereas in old fairy tales witches cast magical spells... This may be a better joke to tell in Kanlan."

He nodded. "Yeah. Maybe."

They stood in silence a moment and then turned in unison back toward the grocery cart.

Rain started and then stopped, and then started again, so light that Sam didn't even bother pulling up her hood. The cold was worse than the wet. She dug her hands farther into her pockets.

At the first drop of rain Benison had flipped up a small awning, secured to the fence above the panel: shelter for one. Sam was surprised that the compound had gone to so much trouble for his comfort. He was a domestic, after all, albeit one with a small degree of authority. *A slave with power over the other slaves is still a slave.* Perhaps the awning was not for his benefit. Perhaps it was for theirs. *To remind us that we're less valuable than he is.*

When the baskets were full, Benison passed a small bag of coins to the grocer, who pocketed it without counting the contents. Sam supposed that with a pair of rifles pointed at your head, it probably was not worth causing a fuss if you were shorted a xot or two.

Not until the grocer was halfway across the field did Benison unlock the gate and gesture for the domestic to re-enter the compound. Once the woman was back inside, two guards proceeded to examine her. Sam wondered what they could be searching for. *Knives hidden in her hair? Treasonous messages in her undergarments?*

The rain began falling in earnest, forming puddles on the ground around them. Sam gave in and pulled up her hood. *At least I have boots now.* She looked down at them, frowning slightly. *Raina's boots.* Xenia's words from their conversation that morning popped back into her head. What was it that the other girl had said, exactly? *Raina will want them back. She said that Raina will want them back.*

Sam glanced over at Jackal, who was watching Benison, his grey eyes unreadable.

Sam opened her mouth and then shut it again. The question sounded incredibly stupid in her head, any way she phrased it.

Cringing inwardly, she cleared her throat. "Xenia—" Her voice cracked. *Bav jit taow.* "Xenia said something about Raina coming back."

Jackal made no response. *Of course he hasn't. I haven't asked a question.*

"But she's—I mean, she's...dead."

She had his attention now.

"Ava, her mother—"

"She said that Raina's dead?" Jackal's eyes were boring into hers.

"I—well..." Sam stopped. Had Ava ever actually said the word "dead"? Sam wasn't sure. "I don't know," she admitted. "But she thinks that Raina is gone."

Jackal looked bewildered. "Gone, sure. But gone and dead ain't the same thing."

"So...is she? Coming back, I mean."

Jackal's focus had already shifted back to Benison and the guards. "Most folks that leave on the solstice plan to come back. Some do, some don't."

"Leave...on the solstice." Sam tried not to look as confused as she felt.

"Look," Jackal said, turning back to Sam. "I didn't know Raina that well. Or Finlay even."

"Finlay." She had heard the name before—he had been a drudge with the Vauns before Sam moved to the Barrow.

Jackal was staring at her as though she was particularly stupid.

"Raina's boyfriend," he said. "It was him that got Raina hired."

"Oh," she said. "And he also...left?"

Jackal shrugged. "Guess so. Again, it was the solstice. Not like anyone says goodbye." He paused, and his dark brow furrowed.

He seemed about to say more, when Benison turned towards them, his eyes seeking out Jackal. He jerked his head toward the grocer, and Jackal turned and walked silently and quickly after the cart.

Benison then unlocked the panel in the fence and gestured impatiently for Sam to pass him the package.

"Let's see it."

Sam passed the rag-encased box through the fence. Wrinkling his nose at the musty wrapping, Benison took the package and walked back toward the compound proper.

Sam glanced out toward the woods. Jackal was searching the grocery cart. She wondered absently what he was looking for.

It may be emotional self-preservation on Ava's part, assuming the worst-case scenario. After all, Ava had never struck Sam as an optimist. With an inward shrug, Sam pushed the thought of Raina from her mind. It was Ava's business, how she chose to think and speak about her daughter. She would not thank Sam for prying.

Sam continued watching Jackal until footsteps signaled Benison's return. The package was gone and he was holding a bag of coins. She noted the pained expression on Benison's face as he pulled out a xot and dropped it into her outstretched palm.

"Can I be of further assistance today?" Sam asked, as she did after each mission.

"It's unclear at this time. I suggest you wait."

Sam nodded. It was the response she received most days. She hadn't determined yet whether it was a lie intended to test her patience, a power play to remind her that she served at his behest, or an honest answer.

She settled back against the fence to wait. Jackal was on his way back, the grocery cart gone from sight. A flash of white-blond emerged from the woods and raced toward Jackal. Xenia leapt onto his back with a high-pitched ululating cry. He broke into a rare smile as she planted a kiss on the top of his head. They continued toward Sam, Jackal dumping Xenia unceremoniously on the wet grass beside her.

"Hi, love," Xenia said, brushing her sopping blond hair out of her eyes. Somehow the rain on her cheeks only made her eyes shine more brightly. "Good day?"

"Good day," Sam said with a smile.

"Is the big bad B around?"

"You just missed him."

"Sadness! You got anything more today?"

"It's unclear at this time. It has been suggested I wait."

She heard a tsk and looked up. Jackal was staring at the compound. Sam glanced over her shoulder and saw that Benison was returning. He beckoned for Xenia to approach.

"I'm gonna head out, but what are you doing later tonight?" Xenia asked Sam after she had signed off with Benison.

"I'm not sure," she said, as though she ever engaged in anything besides working and hiding in her nest.

"We're going to the Hive tonight. You should come."

Sam couldn't be sure she hadn't imagined it, but she thought Jackal's face darkened at the suggestion...not that Sam felt any more pleased at the invitation herself.

She had heard of the Hive; it was some kind of party spot for people who were much more socially inclined than she was.

"Come on," Xenia said, "I've been stuck with just these wretched boys for ages."

She smiled and Sam felt herself relenting. There was something about people with unfaltering conviction. *Perhaps when you can't imagine yourself failing, nobody else can either.*

Xenia must have read the surrender on her face, for she gave a victorious grin. "We usually meet at the night market an hour before midnight. We'll wait for you, so if you flake out and stay home we'll all have a terrible time and be horribly cross with you tomorrow. Okay? Lovely!"

Before Sam could respond, Xenia blew her a kiss and bounded off.

4

―――――

The North

SHE HEARD THE DRUMMING FIRST, and then some shouting that did not quite pass as singing. It seemed the whole of the Barrow was here, spilling out of the Hive in a drunken tangle of bodies that smelled of sweat and unsavoury habits.

There was so much trash surrounding the Hive that Sam was unsure at first whether to walk atop or wade through it. She settled for the former, hoping it would not lead to misstep and injury. *Or worse, misstep and ridicule.*

Three middle-aged men were trading blows near the front entrance, staggering to find their balance after each slow and inaccurate punch. The balcony above them, filled past capacity with dancing women and men, sagged dangerously under their weight. Judging from the blank expressions on the faces of the dancers and the discarded blue cloth bags at their feet, dust was circulating. Xenia took Sam's hand and gave her a big grin.

"This is what fun looks like, see?" Xenia flourished a long, graceful arm at the scene around them, accidently swatting a tattooed woman on the arm in the process. "Oops, sorry." Xenia flashed her usual charming smile.

The woman looked like she was about to swat Xenia right back when she jerked to a stop, hunched over, and began projectile vomiting.

"Poor thing," said Xenia, dancing sideways to avoid stepping in the pile of sick.

They joined the throng crowding the front entrance. Sam, thinking longingly of orderly Seiran queues, squeezed up close to Xenia. At least it was warmer, huddled together.

An old woman stood in the doorway, a crate of sack by her feet. "Is she the owner?" Sam asked Xenia.

"Owner?" asked her twin, who had overheard. "No one owns the Hive."

"Whoever gets here first can take a fee for cleaning up that night," Xenia said.

"What if they just take the sack and leave?"

"Finlay tried, the jit."

Sam looked up at Hakuund, who had wedged his gigantic form between the twins. He slung a dark, brawny arm over Cassio's shoulder and grinned down at her.

"When he came back, the clan—"

"The what?" asked Sam before she caught herself.

"The clan!" shouted Hakuund, as though her hearing was the problem. He was so loud that he startled a nearby group of adolescent boys. Macho posturing fell away as several of the boys jumped. One even let out a small shriek.

"Oh, right," said Sam, as though yes, in fact she had been struck by momentary deafness.

"So, the clan, the clan tied him to a tree, left him for a week. Gave him plenty to eat and drink, so by the end of the week he was nicely marinated in his own piss and dung."

Barbaric. Outwardly she just said "hmm," and tried to appear both uninterested and unimpressed. Judging from Hakuund's grin, she failed.

"There's a saying in the Barrow," said Jackal. It was the first time he'd spoken since Sam had met up with the group a half hour ago. "Kids say it, even: 'Don't piss where you play.' Considering Fin was here most nights, well..." Jackal shrugged.

He looked unconcerned. So did Cassio, Sam noted. Hakuund was actually chuckling, and Xenia had an oddly satisfied look on her face. Sam was getting the distinct impression that Finlay had not been overly popular amongst the other drudges.

They had reached the front of the crowd. Sam watched the old woman at the door. She'd only collected two sack in the time that they had been waiting; two sack for about two dozen people. *Perhaps the cost is per group, not per person. Or perhaps most people just don't pay.*

The woman coughed and spat blood onto the ground. It was a common enough sight, but one that still unnerved Sam. *Bronchitis maybe. Lung cancer more likely. Possibly both.*

Hakuund flicked the woman a xot, gesturing back at the five of them. She caught it in a gnarled hand, her face brightening into a toothless grin, and waved them through.

Sam glanced down at the crate of sack as she passed, each small dirty bag representing a morning's labour for the average person. No wonder so many people hated drudges. The handful of xots that Sam had managed to stash away over the past three months felt pitifully small, especially when she considered her lack of job security, but in the Barrow any surplus of coin was rare.

Inside, the stink of wet clothes and the suffocating press of bodies were enough to make Sam turn right back around. Unfortunately, she turned directly into Hakuund and Cassio. Fear of social shaming prompted her to turn her head upward, as though she was intentionally walking backward in order to get a good view of the wall above the door.

Fortunately, there was actually something in her sightline to examine. Torches had been placed high above the entranceway. Spinning, she realized that they ringed the entire room. Sam found this comforting. *Unless a bunch of drunkards or dustheads start climbing the walls, we will at least be safe from fire.*

Slowly they made their way through the crowd, Sam crammed between the twins. Hakuund and Jackal seemed to have disappeared entirely. Cheers and sloppy kisses greeted Xenia and Cassio wherever they went. Even being near so much attention was overwhelming. Sam started to feel like she might be sick. They reached a bar and found Hakuund. He grinned at them and pressed a dented metal tankard of moonshine into Sam's hand. She sniffed it and gagged.

"Skol!" he roared, smashing his cup into hers. He swallowed the mess in one monstrous gulp.

"You're going to kill her," said Xenia, who took Sam's drink and poured half into a second mug for herself. Winking at Sam, she plugged her nose with one hand and took a small swallow.

"Whew, terrible!" she said, wrinkling her face. "Okay, your turn!"

Sam plugged her nose and took a sip. "Acchh, why do you drink this?"

"Oh, and I suppose the brew in Kanlan tastes like strawberries," said Xenia.

"Well, it's better than this!"

"You got a problem with the drink, you can go—"

Hakuund laughed and clapped the huge, hairy barkeep on the back. "It's okay, mate, she's a foreigner, doesn't know any manners yet."

Sam wondered how she had failed to notice him standing there. Perhaps even more surprising was the fact that she had failed to smell him.

Hakuund's comment caused the barkeep's eyes to narrow even further. "Foreigner, eh? Where from?"

Sam might have been imagining it, but it seemed as though other heads turned toward them at the word.

"Not that foreign, just Kanlan," said Cassio.

"Kanlan!" His face broke into a grin, revealing a set of chipped, yellowed teeth. "I got cousins there, maybe you know 'em?"

Luckily, at that moment the drumming intensified and Sam was able to point to her ears in the universal gesture of *Sorry, can't hear you!* She looked at Xenia and pointed upstairs with a questioning look.

"Yeah, c'mon! Cass? You coming?"

He shook his head and pulled one of the small orange bits from his pocket. After a quick twist, he stuffed one into each ear. Sam turned to Xenia, mystified, and saw her do the same. *What is this? Some kind of inner-ear drug?* Though it looked foamy it didn't seem to be disintegrating. *Is it blocking sound? That would be a mercy indeed.*

A young girl had approached Cassio. Before Sam realized what she was witnessing, coin passed from the girl's hand to Cassio's, and a small blue cloth bag from his hand to hers. Cassio pocketed the xot and glanced up. Her heart racing, Sam shifted her focus to the staircase behind him. *Did he catch me staring?*

Xenia tapped her shoulder, pointing at Sam's cup as she drained her own. Sam plugged her nose and did the same, grateful for the distraction. *Are the others peddling dust as well?* She pushed the thought from her mind. Curiosity was not a virtue, not here, not anywhere. She wondered again whether Cassio had noticed her watching, and if so, whether he would report her. She pushed this thought away too. What would happen would happen. She could only wait and see.

Placing her empty cup back on the bar, Sam followed Xenia up the crowded staircase. She saw hands reaching at skirts, pants, shirts, wallets, to be slapped away or grabbed in returned. Xenia reached for Sam's hand, pulling her along like a child.

Feeling unsteady, Sam grabbed at the railing, only to feel it give way beneath her. A chunk of rotted wood fell away and landed on a man standing below, smashing into his shoulder and knocking his drink to the ground. Without so much as a glance upward he let out a roar, spun around, and punched the man behind him.

Sam hurried after Xenia, who had reached the top of the staircase. Short, squat tree stumps served as tables, most littered with pipes made out of old bottles. Around them, women, men, and children sprawled on cushions, some gazing dazedly about in the dim lighting, while others were talking or chuckling to themselves. A few lay unmoving on the floor, asleep presumably, although dead was not an impossibility. The only signs of life were the small, dark shadows that moved across their exposed flesh. Cockroaches, Sam realized as she got closer. She shuddered and looked away.

Her eyes landed on a group of children, not much older than

twelve or thirteen, sniffing up lines of white powder in a corner. The matching burn marks bubbling at the backs of their necks suggested they too had recently joined one of the many gangs operating in the Barrow. *Baby huaina.*

"Angie, darling."

The woman Xenia approached was standing near the banister, her back toward them. A flat piece of wood had been nailed into the railing, creating a counter. She stiffened and slid a small pile of xots from the counter into a cloth bag, which she quickly tucked into her vest before spinning around, a big smile on her face.

"Xenia! Hello, gorgeous."

Xenia gave the woman a kiss on each cheek before turning back to Sam.

"I need to chat with her, private matter. Do you mind? I'll just be a minute."

Sam shook her head and forced a smile.

"So, my brother says he talked to you..."

The women turned away, and Sam took another look around, at a bit of a loss. Colourful sheets had been hung on the walls, bits of shiny scrap metal sewn into the patterns to produce a disorientating effect. There had to be other rooms connected to this one—the downstairs had been far larger and there was no other staircase. *Is that a ladder, resting against the back wall?*

It was, and a pair of heavy black boots was descending from the ceiling above. Jeans followed boots, black jacket followed jeans. The wearer stepped off the ladder, the movement oddly fluid for someone so heavily muscled. The man crossed the room to the far wall and disappeared. Sam squinted in the feeble light but could not make out a doorway.

Her eyes drifted upward. Curious, she walked over to the ladder, took a step up onto the bottom rung, and paused. Faint moans and groans drifting down told her exactly what activity was taking place in the attic. She dismounted and wandered over to the far wall, stopping where the man had disappeared. Reaching out a tentative finger, Sam poked the cloth wall hanging. *Wood. Solid wood.* She walked slowly to the right, dragging her hand along the fabric. Wood gave way to empty air. Pushing the cloth hanging aside, she crossed into a new room.

Like the last room, people sat on cushions, but in large, open circles this time, facing one another. They looked to be playing dice, perhaps with a gambling component, as in the middle of each circle was a pile of goods made up primarily of sack, though Sam spotted a few xots, weapons, items of clothing, and random personal items such as mirrors and cups.

Large, scarred men stood along the back wall, a few of whom turned to glance at Sam as she entered. She could feel them sizing her up and then immediately dismissing her. Thanks to her small stature and lack of tattoos, she didn't tend to register as a threat. This was exactly how she preferred it.

A few onlookers clustered along the wall opposite the men. As unobtrusively as she could, Sam joined them. In the circle directly in front of her, the man she had followed was hunched over, whispering in the ear of one of the players. The player passed him something— coin, she assumed.

The man clapped the player on the shoulders and straightened, his gaze landing on Sam's spying eyes. He was handsome, with a square jaw and pleasing, symmetrical features, and short blond hair that had been carefully oiled. His clothes were well made and Sam didn't see any tattoos. *Not a huaina, then. Or at least, not your typical huaina.* A dimple emerged as he smiled at her and winked.

Sam quickly shifted her gaze, observing the players next to him with feigned intensity. Feeling discomposed, Sam willed herself to focus for real. *Look, a whole new set of rules to learn. Learn them.*

Each player had a cup containing a single die, which they shook and then upended on the ground. Next, they slid their chosen currency forward into the middle of the circle, after which they were allowed to peek under the cup at the outcome of their roll. Working clockwise around the circle, each player either added to the pot a second time or tipped their cup sideways to signify withdrawal. At that point anyone who had bet would lift up their cup to reveal the die beneath.

In the first round Sam watched, the player with the highest

number took the winnings. In the second round, however, two players had the same highest number, and both lost. One of the losers took offense and elbowed the other player, unluckily seated beside her, in the face.

Two of the large men stationed along the wall intervened, grabbing the women, who were now screaming curses at each other, and pulling them apart. Sam felt the crowd stir around her and got the horrible impression that this was the reason that they had come to watch.

Out of the corner of her eye, Sam watched the blond man make his way back toward the door. When the fight was under control, Sam too slipped quietly out of the room. The man was nowhere to be seen.

She wanted some air. There should be a balcony somewhere— she had seen it from the grounds, hadn't she? *There.* A slight flutter behind one of the wall hangings caught her eye. She stepped past the unconscious body of a teenage girl and slid the wall hanging aside.

Sam's sense of direction seemed to have failed her—rather than the balcony she had found a small, smoky room. A row of large barrel drums had been set up along the far wall, two or three musicians to a drum. They struck the skins with their palms in perfect unison, beating out the simple, repetitive rhythm that Sam had been hearing since she had arrived.

Sam felt someone squeeze her hand and turned to see Xenia beside her. She passed Sam a mug. "I'm okay, thank you but—"

"Drink!"

Sam took a reluctant sip. *Horrible. Even more horrible than the brew we had downstairs. Didn't think that was possible.* She passed the cup back to Xenia, who drained it.

"Do you want to play?" she asked Sam, gesturing toward the drummers. "We're no good at it, but I love watching Hak!"

It was only then that Sam noticed that one of the large, shirtless, sweating musicians was indeed Hakuund. He was one of the few people who had a drum all to himself. Perhaps nobody wanted to be within flailing distance of his trunk-like arms. She caught his eye and he grinned, gesturing for her to approach.

"Go on!" Xenia said. "But wait, first—"

Xenia handed her another cup. Resigned, Sam took a sip, grimaced, and headed over to Hakuund. She passed him her drink, which he accepted with a grin, drinking with one hand while the other continued to beat out the simple pattern. *Excellent. That was mutually beneficial.*

She observed Hakuund, waiting until she had memorized the pattern of strong and soft beats to join him at the large barrel drum. She touched the skins lightly at first, then striking out with greater force as she became more certain of the rhythm.

A new melody sounded; someone was blowing into a woodwind instrument. The two patterns snaked together, the new line reinforcing rather than confusing the main rhythm.

"You're doing good, girl!" Hakuund shouted at her.

The ding of something hard striking metal; Hakuund moved to the drum beside them. A new man took his place across from Sam. The stranger's hands were a blur. He was striking the same beats as the others, but the movement was larger, radiating through his legs, spine, shoulders.

Glancing up at Sam through a fringe of black hair, he nodded toward her left. She stared at him a moment, confused. He gestured again to her left. Continuing the rhythm, she stepped tentatively to her left. The man grinned and copied her. She took a few more steps, circling the drum, and again he followed her.

Gaining confidence, she began to move in time with the music, her steps easing from a mechanical march to a dancer's sway. She switched directions and the stranger reversed step without missing a beat. Her hips, she realized; he could see the motion building.

They continued around the drum, eyes locked together. Her arms and shoulders were aching and sweat dripped down her face like rainwater, but she found she didn't want to stop. It was loud and damp and bordering on painful, but it was beautiful, and beauty was rare. Sam knew enough to hold the moment and linger.

He switched to a different rhythm, following the woodwind instrument rather than the main drumline. Sam moved back to her original position. Her partner continued to dance. She closed her eyes, inviting the music in.

The sudden feel of a man's chest against her back sent an ugly jolt through her body. Sam froze.

The man's hands, playing on either side of her, slowed. Skin pulled away from skin. He was moving away from her, a confused expression on his face.

She licked her lips, wanting to rectify the situation. *It's me,* she wanted to tell him. *It's what I did. I'm poison.* The metal ding sounded a second time.

"What, you tired?" Hakuund was back, the stranger gone. Sam forced a smile and picked up the rhythm again. The room was suddenly overstimulating. She wondered when she could leave without giving offense.

"Louder!" shouted Hakuund with a wide grin.

Sam obeyed, increasing the strength of her blows. It felt good. She struck down harder still, the music rising to a crescendo bordering on frenzy. Tension in her jaw, neck, and shoulders moved down her arms and out her fingertips as though the violence of the blows were driving the paralysis from her body. Louder and louder still, until the music from her drum was the only thing she could hear.

Eventually her arms gave way and she collapsed backward against the wall in a breathless heap. Hakuund broke away a moment later. He slung his arm around her neck in a sweaty one-armed hug and led her back to Xenia.

"Who's this girl?" a familiar voice shouted, and Sam looked over to see Cassio passing her a drink.

"Transformed, my love!" Xenia's voice sang out. "An animal after all!"

Sam took a sip. It didn't seem to taste so terrible anymore. She grinned up at the twins and saw that Jackal was there too, watching her with a curious expression on his face.

Feeling bold, she smashed her mug into his, shouted "skol!" and drained her cup. *Like a true Northerner.*

The twins and Hakuund all burst out laughing. *Perhaps not, then.*

It was not malicious laughter though, and Sam laughed with them. Jackal even let out a small smile before draining his cup.

The smile froze on his face. His head snapped back toward the door. "Do you smell smoke?"

Xenia and Cassio glanced at one another and followed Jackal as he exited the room, Sam and Hakuund close on their heels.

Outside, the pounding of the drums was no longer loud enough to block out the sounds of panic. Below them, on the ground floor, people were screaming, yelling, fighting, and pushing past each other. In the confusion, some even seemed to be shoving their way farther into, rather than out of, the building. On the staircase, terrified people pressed forward, crushing those on the bottom steps who were trying and failing to force their way onto the ground floor.

Sam could not only smell the smoke now, she could see fire. Flames licked at the wall across from where she was standing, creeping from the first floor up toward a section of the balcony that Sam was fairly certain had been intact an hour ago. The three torches that had hung on the wall beneath it were missing.

Jackal gestured back toward one of the sheets. "Outside!" he yelled, and then, looking around at the mess of drugged bodies slumped forward on the low tables or leaning sluggishly against the walls: "Grab someone if you can!"

Sam squinted through the thickening smoke and ran toward a child, maybe eight or nine years old, asleep on one of the cushions. The child was so grimy she couldn't tell if it was a girl or a boy.

"Hey!" The child was warm and breathing but completely unresponsive. She folded the skinny body over her shoulder and straightened up slowly, scanning the room. *Where is the sheet Jackal pointed to?* She pulled her shirt over her mouth, trying to keep the smoke out of her lungs.

She made it to one of the sheets and pushed, only to feel solid wall behind it. *It would be a waste of time to panic. Just try the next one.*

"Sam!" It was Jackal. As she stumbled toward his voice, something grabbed her foot. She looked down to see an old man, coughing, reaching up a hand toward her.

"Get up! Get up and follow me!" He lay back down, coughing harder.

"Sam!" It was Jackal's voice again.

Sam hesitated, but she was starting to run out of air. *What can you do? You going to carry him too?*

A few more steps and a beautiful blast of frigid air hit her in her face. Out on the balcony, Jackal pulled the child off her shoulders.

"Gods, Sam! I meant pull someone along, not kill yourself trying to carry dead weight!"

Sam coughed in response, trying to pull as much oxygen into her lungs as she could. Jackal leaned over the balcony and dropped the child.

Sam let out a scream and lunged forward, only to see that Hakuund and Cassio, ten feet below them on the ground, had caught the child in some kind of net. Clothing, she realized; they were holding clothing taut between them.

"You're next!" Jackal shouted at her.

Sam swung her legs over the railing, lowering herself as much as possible before jumping onto the grass. She leaned to the side as she landed, rolling off the impact. Pulling herself gingerly to her feet, she picked a slimy piece of plastic out of her hair. *Good old trash, helping to break my fall.* She felt jarred and bruised but nothing was broken.

Sam limped over to her companions, who stood clumped together, eyes on the smoke pouring out from the Hive. Sam tried not to think of all the people who were likely still inside.

With sudden horror she realized that they hadn't warned the people they had been drumming with. She tried to pick out their faces in the sea of bodies around them but it was too dark and too crowded.

A profile half seen caught her eye. She squinted in the dark, uncertain, and then the crowd shifted and she lost sight of him. Sam took a step to the right and spotted him again, weaving his way through the horror-stricken onlookers. His body was already familiar somehow, the way he moved gracefully like a dancer, like water. She took in the square jaw, the oiled blond hair; it was the man she had followed into the gambling den. As he passed by, Sam saw that he led a young teenage girl by the hand. A thin, short dress was all that covered her scrawny frame. *Isn't she cold?*

The girl slowed, turning her head upward to gaze at the sky, and was jerked forward by the blond man. Her head bounced limply, and Sam caught a glimpse of the girl's little face: thick, black kohl lined unfocused eyes. *Dust, of course. Always dust.*

He tugged at her hand again: protective, or perhaps possessive. Predatory, anyway.

A big, wet raindrop hit her nose. A few cheers went up but Sam doubted even a heavy storm would help at this point. It might salvage some of the structure, but it wouldn't save the people trapped inside. They would have suffocated by now.

The adrenaline brought on by the drumming and their hasty escape was fading, the cold setting in. Sam pulled up her hood and crossed her arms over her chest in a futile attempt to stay warm.

She realized that she was waiting for the authorities to arrive. To douse the flames with sand and search for survivors, administer medical attention to the injured, and interrogate the able-bodied.

"Let's go," Jackal said to the group, "before they start looting."

Sam stared at him. He raised his eyebrows slightly, as if to say that exploiting tragedy was perfectly normal.

Sam looked up at the fire one last time and then began picking her way through the crowd, alone. Jackal was right. It was time to go home.

Away from the Hive, the streets were empty. Sam fought the urge to glance back over her shoulder. *It's the hour, that's all.* She had never been out so late in the Barrow before. The heavy rain washed out the sound of her lone footsteps, enveloping her in a muffled quiet that left her deaf as well as blind in the dark, foggy streets. She wished the downpour would wash away the stink of smoke that clung to her.

The rain really wasn't so unbearable now that she had proper boots. *Raina's boots. Did she walk this same route, in these same boots? She must have done, many times.* Sam wondered if the other girl liked solitude, or whether she found the long trek back to the factory to be lonesome.

Were the streets truly as empty as they appeared to be? Sam gave her head a shake. There was always reason to be watchful, but it would not do to spiral off toward improbabilities. Hyper vigilance was understandable given the night's events. Who wouldn't be shaken? The fog didn't help either, nor the rain.

A low hum caught her ear, sending a chill down her spine. She darted into the shadows, ducking behind the rusted shell of an old car. She sank into a fighter's stance, ready to reach for her baton if necessary. The humming grew louder, overbold. Soon a hulking shadow came into view, a large someone with a very confident stride. A familiar stride.

"Hakuund?" Sam straightened up.

"Ah! There you are," a booming voice said, the cheerful tone cutting through the murk and swatting dark imaginings back to the shadows. "You are surprisingly hard to track."

"You were tracking me, then?" asked Sam.

"Jack sent us off in groups. You snuck off before we had a chance to tell you."

"Oh," said Sam, hoping her relief wasn't palpable. "Is that...normal?"

"Not really, but sometimes it's needed. Nights like these, it's not a bad idea. Especially when we have newbies." He grinned at her.

"Well, thanks. I hope I'm not out of your way."

"Can't say that until I know what way's your way. So lead on, little bird."

She hid a smile and stepped out of the shadows. Hakuund fell into step beside her. She was perfectly capable of handling a few stray miscreants on her own, but it did feel nice to think that someone else might be looking out for her.

The humming started up again. *Perfect. Maybe he won't even expect me to talk.*

"This is it," she announced a half hour later.

"Hmm," he said, eyeing the factory. "Wouldn't you rather be in the main hub, where all the festivals are? It's pretty quiet in this part of town."

"I like the quiet," Sam said with a smile.

"Huh, yeah, I can see that." Hakuund chuckled. "Okay, goodnight, kid." He gave her shoulder a squeeze. "See you in the morrow."

Sam waved and watched him stride off into the night. "Kid," she scoffed. *Like a baby goat.* The big bear couldn't be more than a few years older than her.

5

The South

SHOULDER STRAPS HOLD ME UPRIGHT. Forcing open gritty eyes, I realize that I am seated on a bus. I look around frantically for Lily or Iris, Holly, any of the faces I have grown up with. There is no one here I recognize. I share my seat with another girl who looks to be near my age. "Where are we?" I ask her in a whisper.

She turns slowly to face me. Her eyes, which seem to be having difficulty focusing, are green. "They haven't said." Her voice is slurred. "Sometimes we stop and a new girl or boy is brought on."

I start and scan the bus around me. Sure enough, there is a row of boys at the front of the bus. I stare at them. I have never seen a male child before, only middle-aged or elderly male designates or medics. I stare around at the other occupants of the bus and realize that everyone is wearing the same clothing—long-sleeved shirts and pants in the same olive green. Most of the others are sleeping. The few that are awake are sitting in silence. I look down at myself and I see the same uniform. My feet feel like they're suffocating in thick black shoes that extend up to mid-calf.

"So nobody here knows anybody else?"

She shrugs in response. Then suddenly it hits me.

"Have—have we *left* my division?" I ask. "What, but we..." I stop when I realize heads are turning toward me. I am being overloud. I hold the words in and feel my breath catch in my throat. My friends' faces flash before my eyes and I can feel myself starting to hyper-ventilate.

A medic hurries toward me, murmuring, "Not possible, another hour at least."

She holds a dropper up and I automatically open my mouth. It tastes like oranges.

I thought we would have time to say goodbye. I feel my breathing slowing down. Slowly in and slowly out. I count the windows on the bus. There are fifty-four. My face feels heavy. Everything is fine. There are ninety-two of us on this bus. Everything is fine.

THIS TIME when I awaken the moon is high above us. We must have arrived, for the vehicle has stopped and everyone is standing. I stand as well and follow the green body in front of me. When I get to the door I realize that we are at a train station.

A medic is waiting; she hands me a sweet. Another woman takes my hand and flips it over. I look confusedly at the number scrawled on the inside of my wrist. When did that happen? She points me to a train car with the letter A posted above the entrance.

I have never been inside a train before. It looks the same as the bus, only smaller. There are a dozen seats and half as many children.

I sit on a plush blue seat. A voice comes onto the receiver and tells us to relax, enjoy the sweet, and prepare for a pleasant journey. I chew mechanically, staring at the thin biodegradable plastic wrapper: purple, my favourite. My eyelids grow heavy again and I feel the wrapper dropping from my fingers onto the floor.

SUNLIGHT PULSES BEHIND MY EYELIDS. Fighting the urge to slip back into unconsciousness, I force my eyes open and peer out the window. The landscape is golden brown, as dry and barren as the land we have left behind. My head is foggy and I cannot stop yawning. When the girl beside me wakes, a different girl from the one on the bus, we do not make conversation. Somehow talking seems like too much effort. They bring us rolls and date palm juice.

I must have fallen asleep again, for the next time I open my eyes it is night and the train has stopped.

When we step off the train a guard with a gun is waiting for us. We follow her across a dusty field to a gated base. I count seven more guards with guns at the base, patrolling the grounds or watching us from the rooftop. Looming high above them is a tower. This information is important, I suspect, but I cannot seem to remember why.

A woman checks the numbers on our wrists and then leads us down one corridor, and then another, and another. I lose track of the twists and turns. I feel my feet dragging and wonder when I will be able to sleep again. We enter a room with several rows of beds.

"This is your dormitory," the woman says. "Choose a bed. The lavatory is across the hall. I will come for you twenty minutes after wake-up tomorrow. I expect you to be dressed and ready when I arrive." She turns and exits.

Like a choreographed dance, the other children step forward, falling into the closest bed: right, left, right, left, right, left.

Fighting my fatigue, I force myself to walk to the end of the room and claim the corner bed near the windows, skinny strips of glass that stretch from the floor to the ceiling. I barely manage to crawl onto the mattress before I slip back into sleep.

6

The South

I WAKE ABRUPTLY. Was there a bell? I do not hear one now. Black curtains are rising, high over my head. The sunlight is bright, almost blindingly so. I look down at myself and see that I am still fully dressed. I turn my hand over; the number is gone. Had there truly been a number? The previous night and day are hazy. I am not even certain that it has only been one day and one night since I left my division. I scan the room around me. There are eleven other beds, eleven other children of a similar age. Some of them are boys.

I think there were fewer of us yesterday. Perhaps more children arrived in the night.

Along with a bed, my station features two wall hooks and a small chest of drawers. I find two more sets of clothing inside, identical to the ones that I am wearing except that there is a number stitched onto the front of each shirt in yellow thread—the number three. There is also a cotton nightshirt and pants, some clothing made of light, stretchy material, a lighter pair of shoes, and a body towel. All of it is in the same olive green colour and looks clean, though not new. There is a laminated card atop the dresser depicting a child garbed in three different outfits, the words "morning", "afternoon", and "night" written above the corresponding image. A second card illustrates how our stations should look, complete with instructions on how to properly make the bed. It is unnecessary—the folds used for the bed sheets and covers, none of this is new.

The others are getting out of bed and pulling off yesterday's clothing. Some wrap their towels closely around themselves while others undress openly and unashamedly. Conscious of the males in the room, I slip under the blankets to remove my clothing. Tying my towel around myself, I join the jagged line and file out of the dormitory across to the lavatory.

The row of toilets is on my right, shower stalls on my left, just as they were in the lavatory in my division. The standard large, navy-coloured buckets are clustered in the middle of the room beside a large metal tap. After the strangeness of the previous day, I appreciate the sameness of the room. The familiarity is comforting.

I wait while the girl in front of me picks up a pail and places it under the tap. She pushes a large button and I count as the water streams out into her bucket: ten seconds. I follow suit, as do the others after me. When I step into a stall with my bucket I find body and face soap bottled in the usual packaging, the Administration's promise of health and hygiene circling around each cylinder in thick, reassuring black font. Lightly dampening my skin, I lather on soap, happily breathing in the familiar scent of earth apple. I rinse myself with the water in the bucket, top to toe, careful not to waste any. Back in my division we each received fifteen seconds of water. We only bathed every third day though—I wonder whether we are expected to bathe more frequently here.

I pull my towel back on and walk shivering to the toilets. I wish we had been given sandals or slippers. The porcelain hole at the center of the toilet stall looks clean, but I am careful to place my feet outside of the footholds, just in case.

Bladder emptied, I take a gob of sanitizer and return to the dormitory. I change under my sheets into fresh clothing and am just tying the laces on my heavy shoes when the woman from last night enters the room. She is not a designate, and yet I do not know how else to classify her. She stands at the entrance a moment, watching us watching her.

"Each time I enter a room you will stand at attention," she says, walking slowly down the center aisle between the two rows of beds. Her voice is stern, but not cross. "This means: backs straight, eyes forward, feet together, and hands down by your sides. In here, you will stand at the foot of your bed. In the classrooms, on the right side of your desk."

By the time she has finished speaking we are all positioned as instructed, bodies rigid, breathing hushed. Out of the corner of my eye I watch her stare intently at each child in turn, listening as her footsteps draw closer. I am last. She is older than I had assumed at first. She moves gracefully, her arms and shoulders toned with muscle, and her hair is black and shiny, but her skin suggests that she is well into middle age. Her clothes, though green like ours, are made from a different fabric and follow different lines. I cannot help it—my eyes flicker over to hers. Blue eyes, and there is something off about them. A small line rings the iris. Is she wearing contact lenses? It is hard to imagine why anyone would choose such an outdated technology.

"Eyes ahead," she says in a low voice. My eyes snap back. I feel a flush creeping up my neck and am annoyed at myself for having failed to follow this first, basic command.

"The next several days," she says, walking back toward the front of the room, "will help us to assess your strengths and to identify how we may support you to better thrive. Do not worry about forming bonds or familiarizing yourself with the base; there are many bases along the border and we will determine which environment will be most suitable to your growth once we have a better understanding of both your needs and capabilities. Enjoy this time as a period of reflection. There is no need to speak unless spoken to directly by myself or another one of the P2s who will be directing your activities." She speaks mechanically; I wonder how many times she has given this same speech.

"You may now follow me to breakfast," she says by way of conclusion, and turns and strides off down the corridor. We form a queue and trot out after her, determined not to fall behind.

7

The South

MY FIRST IMPRESSIONS of the base are slipping away. There were towers, I think, and guards, but I am not certain. My memories are muddy. The fragments that remain leave me with the assumption that the base houses hundreds of people. I am surprised to find that the canteen is nothing more than a small, plain room, empty except for two long tables.

We take the bench on the right side of the room and wait while other children file in after us. They look to be of a similar age and wear the same clothing that we do, yellow numbers bright against the muted green fabric. There must be a second dormitory; I wonder where it is located.

On the table I spy familiar items such as corn bread and sorghum porridge. I sniff my cup: prickly pear juice. The small, cream-coloured dish beside my plate holds three vitamins, two small and one large. I take a small sip of juice and swallow the vitamins. Same cup, same contents, which I take in the same order that I always have: first small, then large, and lastly small again, for symmetry.

When the meal ends we bring our dishes to one of several bins filled with sand. I scrub mine clean, dip it in disinfectant, and stack it before following my group out of the canteen and into a large classroom.

A few dozen desks have been arranged in rows, a porta on each one.

"Choose a seat," the woman who is not a designate says, "and begin answering the questions. You have two hours and there will of course be no speaking."

I touch my thumb to the porta and the screen lights up, the number three appearing and then disappearing. The test opens automatically. There are pages and pages of questions on topics varying from mathematics and vocabulary to history and ethics, two dozen possible answers listed below each one.

Some of the questions are easy, covering the hierarchy of virtues or the Administration's official mandate, or demanding formulas and dates that we were required to memorize this year or last. Other questions, however, cover topics that are completely new to me. Some seem to be logic or morality based, but others demand knowledge that I simply do not have. I feel panic beginning to crawl upward from my belly and I cannot help but wonder if the other children are faring any better than I am. Useless reactions, both; I am wasting time. I take a deep breath and think.

I have always understood curriculum to be absolutely uniform, without variation from one division to another. If this material is not covered by the standard curriculum, I reason, none of us will have the answers, which means that I should not waste time on these questions. Hitting the "pass" button, I search for topics that I know or questions that I can reasonably solve. Hopefully there will be time to cycle back to the others at the end.

By the time the second hour ticks to a close I have completed barely half of the test. Perhaps the intention is to teach us humility, by reminding us of how much we do not know. Or perhaps the intention is to cause anxiety, to reveal how we perform under stress. Or perhaps I have failed.

Next she leads us back to our dormitories and instructs us to don

46

a set of the light clothing and shoes. She then brings us outdoors to a large field. A man and a woman who introduce themselves simply as protectors indicate that we are to follow them in a slow run around the field. This too is familiar; we ran daily at my division.

I long to sprint ahead of the group. Instead I hold back, keeping to the middle of the pack. Without knowing what activities will follow, it is wiser to preserve my strength. They lead us through a series of stretches—many familiar, a few new. Next, they line us up at one end of the field.

"When I blow my whistle," the female protector says, "run as quickly as you can to the line at the end of the field. When I blow the whistle again, run as quickly as you can back to this starting point."

When the whistle sounds I leap forward, pulling ahead of the group. A tall girl and a boy with tanned skin pull up beside me. We cross the line at the same time. On the way back the boy and I gain slightly, finishing before the other girl. The whistle sounds again and we sprint off to the far side of the field a second time. The boy and I are neck and neck again. On the way back he gets a faster jump. Halfway across the field, however, he starts to slow—I suspect he is tiring. I gain on him and we cross the finish line together again.

The whistle sounds and we continue in the same pattern. While our overall speed decreases each time, neither of us gains the advantage over the other. The other girl, who began so quickly, is near the back of the pack now, while others who started more slowly have pulled ahead. They are all far behind the two of us when the exercise finally ends. Most of the others collapse on the sand, but I lean over into a stretch, breathing deeply. The pain in my legs and my lungs is a good pain—it makes me feel strong.

For the next activity we are shown a few different types of movement, each one labeled with a number. I create a picture in my mind, organized and clear.

"ONE!" shouts the male protector as we sprint backward; "TWO!" as we run forward; "THREE!" as we jump high into the air, tucking in our knees; "FOUR!" as we push ourselves up from the ground with our hands; "FIVE!" as we run sideways with one leg crossing over the other. Then he begins mixing up the numbers:

"TWO! FIVE! THREE! ONE!" I push myself to remember each movement, to respond quickly and with confidence each time. I suspect that what they are watching for is the delay from when we hear the number to when we react. I feel sweat dripping into my eyes and shake my head.

When the drill is finished, the woman pairs each of us with a partner. The boy across from me looks vaguely familiar. I wonder if he is housed in the same dormitory as I am. She then gives each pair a set of wooden cylinders. Each cylinder is attached to a piece of rope.

On the woman's command we swing the cylinders first toward the left side of our partners and then the right. The boy I have been partnered with dodges right, then left, the cylinder swinging harmlessly through the empty air. We switch directions. I hear the whoosh of breath as cylinders sink into stomachs, the rap of wood bouncing off rib bones like mallets striking xylophones. I notice my partner improving with practice and hope that I will do the same when it is my turn.

Once we have mastered this, the male protector adds a third task, one that entails swinging the cylinder toward our partners' feet, forcing them to jump.

The three types of swings are numbered. Like he did during the earlier drill, the protector calls out the numbers in different orders: "ONE! THREE! TWO! TWO! ONE! THREE!" Again I am forced to remember which move corresponds with which number, but this is different in that confusion on my part, a false start, a hesitation, carries consequences not only for me but also for my partner. My arms become tired and my mind wants to wander. I push myself harder, focusing intently on the task at hand.

When the protector finally calls an end to the drill, I collapse onto the dirt. My partner gives me a tentative smile and does the same. Looking around, I notice that he seems to be one of the few not nursing a bruised shin or shoulder.

The male protector leads us through a set of stretches, and then bids us sit cross-legged, our hands resting in our laps, our eyes closed. I settle into the familiar pose, following his voice, soft and soothing, as he guides us through relaxation one body part at a time, from our toes to the tops of our skull; knees, shoulders, eyes, discard tension on command.

Rather than leaving us alone to meditate after relaxation, though, he continues speaking. "Hold your hands out in front of you, close to your face, elbows relaxed. Within your hands I want you to visualize a ball of light. Feel the warmth on your palms and on your face. Your skin absorbs the light, is nourished by it. Now take the ball of light and expand it: bigger than you, bigger than the field. All of these individual lights now merge to create one giant sphere: it is ours to share. You would no more divide it now than you would separate the atoms in your body. The warmth caresses your face, just as it did before when the sphere was small. The light continues to sustain you. Feel the light press into your bruises, your cuts; feel your body heal under its care. It permeates your skin, devouring unpleasant thoughts. You feel clean and cared for. Now, with your mind's eye, look around yourself, above and beside the sphere: you see the sky. You, like the other children around you, are planets. There are so, so many of you, and yet the sphere gives each one of you a path so that you may move, circling its warm, beautiful light. There are no collisions and you never lose your way; the sphere keeps you safe."

When we emerge from meditation, the protectors pass out midday meal bars and small flasks of water sweetened with dried dates. We eat and drink slowly, in silence.

Once we have finished eating they lead us to a shed filled with large, green bins. On top of each one is a long, skinny rectangle of black fabric.

We carry the bins back to the field, where the protectors explain that the pieces inside fit together like a puzzle.

"The task is direct, but not simple," says the male protector. "We will give you step-by-step instructions that will enable you to complete the puzzle."

"However," the female protector adds, and I think I can detect a hint of a smile in her voice, "first you must tie the black fabric over your eyes. You must tie it so that not a speck of light is visible to you. You may begin now."

I pick up the fabric, fold it twice lengthwise, and fasten it over my eyes. I tilt my head upward, downward, and side to side, until I am satisfied that I have indeed been rendered sightless.

"Raise your hand if your blindfold is not yet secure," the male protector says. There is silence. I think I hear footsteps, but the dusty ground absorbs most of the sound.

"For this activity it is mandatory that you remain silent, avoiding not only words but also sounds," the woman says. "Take a nice, deep breath, and listen to my voice."

I breathe in and count to six before releasing. My shoulders drop; I feel relaxed and ready.

"Reach into your bin and find a hollow cube. There are grooves on one side. Place it on the ground, with the grooves facing up. Next, find two isosceles triangles and click them into the grooves. There is a hexagonal piece with a single groove. Lock it onto one of the triangles. Then locate the octagon piece that is closest in size to the hexagon and lock it onto the other triangle."

She is speaking quickly, too quickly. It is not possible to complete each task as she describes it. I am still looking for the octagon when she moves onto the next step.

Don't worry, I tell myself. *If I do not forget the instructions, it will not matter if I fall behind.* I find the octagon and place it on the ground beside my small structure, and move onto the next step. Soon I have three structures instead of one, placed in sequence for the two times I fell behind, each comprised of two to three pieces.

I am slightly ahead of her now, however, and take the time to slide the second structure onto the first. As it clicks into place some kind of projectile strikes me in the jaw. It is not painful, merely distracting. I purse my lips, suppressing all sound, and continue listening.

Another one hits me in the forehead; I ignore it. *What did she ask for?* A waved rectangle piece. I search the bin and find it quickly. *Now, how did she say it would attach...the side, she said at the side.* It clicks in easily. She pauses. I take advantage of the brief respite, picking up the third structure and attempting to slide it onto the base that I have created. I cannot find the groove she described.

As she moves onto the next step I put the third structure back on the ground. *I can come back to it,* I remind myself. There are three more steps that I manage to complete in the allotted time. She begins describing the next piece and I take a risk, picking up the third structure again. This time it clicks onto the base. I rush to the bin in search of the next item: a sphere. It is the last piece in the box. I fit it onto the top of the structure and stand forward at attention.

Only now do I let myself reflect on the exercise, the purpose of which must have been to determine how we react when we fall behind. The distraction, I suppose, could have been to determine whether we could maintain focus when faced with interference. Alternately, it could have been to determine whether our blindfolds were properly attached. Testing for focus or honesty then. Maybe both.

"Remove your blindfolds and pack up your bins."

I sneak a peek around as I disassemble my structure. Stray puzzle pieces litter the dust; few of the others managed to complete the task.

Next they lead us to an active play area. There are the usual rings and horizontal ladders to swing from, rows of tires to step through, and narrow planks to balance upon. The key difference is that there is not one but two identical sets of equipment, raised in parallel a good twelve feet above the ground. There is also a line of small platforms, raised at a distance from one another that would permit jumping, but not stepping, from one to the other. It's a race, they explain.

The first three times we race against an opponent, but the protectors record our individual scores. I am faster than my opponents, but then they do not seem to be particularly fast.

The platforms have a significant influence on the outcome of each race. What I did not anticipate was the instability of the platforms; each time someone lands on one it sways under their momentum. Some of the children are visibly frightened of heights. The fear makes them hesitate, and the hesitation makes them lose.

"For the next round," the male protector says, "the winner of each race will return to the back of the line to race again, while the losers assemble at the benches below."

I win my race three, four times. The crowd at the benches grows. The protectors seem to have given them a filler task in the meantime, for they jump and run in place, though their eyes stare upward at the few of us still racing.

I stretch out my shoulders as I wait for my turn. The boy I ran alongside out in the field was eliminated quickly; he does not like heights, I suspect. He watches me now from below. I catch his eye accidentally and look away.

Only two of us are left now. My shoulders are aching and blisters bubble on the palms of my hands. I race across the beam, leap for the ring in front of me, and my hands slip. I remember to bend my knees before landing, shielding my face with my arms as I roll sideways.

Shaking off the ringing in my arms and legs, I race back to the starting line. Though my opponent is nearly done, I start the course again at top speed, as though I can still win. I cannot, I know, but what I do not know is whether they are still recording my time or what variables they will use to calculate my overall score. I finish quickly, joining the others on the ground before folding over into a stretch. No one makes eye contact or offers a sympathetic pat on the back. We understand that the ban is not restricted to speech; communication of any kind would be frowned upon. I feel grateful for the compulsory isolation. Condolences would have been a waste of time.

My body is sore from the day's exercises and from the fall, and my stomach gurgles with hunger. They usher us back to the field and begin to lead us through a series of poses.

The routine is familiar except that the protectors leave us in the poses for minutes at a time, far longer than I am used to. I can see that the others are struggling as well, slipping out of the postures briefly, shaking out shoulders or hips before sliding back into position. The tremble in my arms becomes a visible quake, but still I hold on. *I can hold on for twelve more breaths,* I tell myself. I reach twelve and the protectors have not yet called for a new pose; *six more breaths,* I tell myself. I can go another six.

The field grows steadily darker around us. I find that I am waiting, expecting every pose to be our last, or barring that, for the fixtures that loom above us to replace the sun's light with electric illumination. I wait but nothing changes.

In the dying light I observe the children next to me giving up on poses more and more quickly. As my legs throb with pain, I wonder whether I am being unreasonable in my expectations. It is almost pitch black now. Can the protectors even see us? I shake off the feeling of doubt. If we have been told to hold a position, then we must hold it until we collapse or until we are relieved. Obedience is the highest virtue.

I hear someone approaching. A metallic face ringed with specks of green light crosses into my line of vision: the female protector wearing some kind of face shield. Night vision goggles, I imagine, though when we studied this technology last year the goggles in the photographs were different—more like a helmet than a mask. Perhaps the textbook is now outdated.

Finally, they give the command to relax into a comfortable seated position; deep breaths, they say, as slowly as we can, and at last the closing directive: pull focus from the internal eye back out to the field where we sit.

Then we are on our feet, stumbling in the darkness as we follow the protectors back to our dormitories, where they allot five minutes to apply cleansing powder and change into fresh clothing.

Too tired and too sore to be self-conscious, I douse myself in powder and change my clothes in the open space beside my bed. Fighting an overwhelming urge to lie down, I force myself to hang my dirty clothes on a hook and use the spray bottle on the sweatiest patches.

In the canteen I pour myself a small glass of prickly pear juice and dish a slice of gourd, some potatoes, and a scoop of pine nut and soybean salad onto my plate. For the second time today, I find that I am grateful for the obligatory silence. I can barely muster up the energy to eat—expectations of polite conversation would have been too much.

As we finish our meal, the designate appears at the end of our table.

"After you have cleaned your dishes," she says, "you will follow me back into the classroom."

I see looks of desperation on the faces around me and struggle to keep my own expression smooth and pleasant.

We file into the classroom for the second time today. The designate enters after us and walks to the front of the class, holding up a small book. "You will read one page and then pass the book to your left," she says.

I frown. We have been tested countless times on our reading skills throughout the years. Can they really think it worthwhile to do so again?

As soon as the first child starts reading, my mind begins to wander, my body urging me to lay my head upon my arms and rest. I straighten up and focus on what the girl is saying. She is describing a battle, the positions of opposing sides. They are going to test us on this, I realize.

Blinking my eyes aggressively, I force myself to actively listen to the names, places, and titles she is rattling off. When I feel my attention wandering, I push my thumbnails into the soft skin under each fingernail; the pain pulls me back into the room. Even with these measures I wonder how much information I am actually retaining. I wish I had a porta or a slate to take notes on.

Once each of us has taken our turn at reading, the designate beckons for the last child to bring the volume to her. She finishes the chapter and asks a few children seated at the front to pass out portas.

"You have sixty minutes to map out two moments in the battle, key strikes or turning points. In a few concise paragraphs you must explain what made these two moments critical to the outcome. You have one hour beginning now."

My maps may not be beautiful, I decide, staring down at them at the end of the hour, but at least they are clear.

I bring my porta to two older youths who have appeared and are now flanking the designate like olive green leaves around a stern, sharp blossom.

They stack the portas and pass around a bag of sweets before leading us back to our dormitories. I chew the soft, squishy candy as we pad along behind them, enjoying the exotic flavour. Blue, like the purple sweets, are a rarity, a treat.

In the lavatory, I gargle a minty dental solution, staring at myself in the wide mirror as I start the obligatory count from one to sixty.

Leaning forward until my face is scant inches from the mirror, I come to the conclusion that I look exactly as depleted as I feel. I give my head a shake and then stretch my eyes wide open and cross my pupils.

A gentle cough sounds behind me and I quickly refocus my eyes. As the lines of the lavatory unfurl and swing back into place I catch sight of a pair of huge, grey eyes in the mirror. They crinkle before we both look away. After the isolation of the past few days, the shock of human contact sends little electric jolts dancing through me. For a split second the haze of exhaustion clears. Though my eyes are lowered now, I smile back. Perhaps she sees, though probably she does not.

My minute is up; I spit the solution into the washbasin and make my way back to the dormitory. I have only just reached my bed when the room fades to black.

The next day follows a similar pattern, as does the day after that, and the day after that. Written and oral tests morning and night, physical contests in the afternoon; it has become routine, as constant as the exhaustion I fight from wake-up until lights out. I keep expecting my body to adjust to the pace, but every night I crawl into bed feeling more exhausted than the night before. How many nights, how many days, I cannot say. My brain seems to be too tired to hold the moments, to file them into memory. Come morning, the trials of the previous day seem to have simply faded away as though they never happened at all.

The specific tests we undergo change each day, along with the protectors who instruct us. At least, I think the protectors change—I cannot seem to bring any faces to mind for comparison. After the first day we are given fewer individual tasks. Sometimes I have a partner; sometimes I am part of a group of three or four.

My performance grows weaker each day. At least I am not the only one; glazed eyes and sluggish bodies walk with me from the dormitory to the canteen, to the classrooms, to the fields. I wonder how well they are scoring, how I stack up against them. I am too tired to take in anyone else's struggles or successes.

8

_____

The North

SHE WOKE UP ON FIRE, sweat pooling from her body in spite of the cold. *Exhale.*

I am Samarra. I am in my bed, in the factory, in the Barrow, in the North.

She exhaled a second time, her breath shaky. Had he been alive at the start of the dream? She couldn't remember. At the end there had been flames, smoke. Did she find him? Did she give up and run for the window? She couldn't remember that either. It didn't matter. It was another lie, the fire at the Hive intruding on her past, distorting the memory. *Exhale.*

C—

Don't say his name.

She had to fight all day to stay awake. Though two nights had passed since their near-death experience at the Hive, she still felt exhausted. The nightmares didn't help, of course, nor the cough that had woken her up twice—a little leaving from all the smoke she'd inhaled.

Usually she hoped for long days—more missions meant more coin—but it was with relief, not disappointment, that she took the day's early dismissal. It was all she could do to drag her tired body home from the compound.

She was halfway to the factory when the storm began. Peering through the rain, she found a doorway with an awning and stepped out of the downpour. Her hands were numb and clumsy as she pulled out her flask, took a small sip of water, and then carefully stowed it back in her jacket pocket. *Always small sips.* It was hard to kick the habit of rationing. She pulled the flask back out and took a long swig this time. She needed to work on these little tells when she was alone; otherwise someday they would give her away.

Not all of the after effects of the other night were unpleasant: she'd gotten a rib-crushing hug from Hakuund the morning after, and Jackal had become discernibly less curt with her. He was still as quiet as always, but it seemed a friendlier silence between them. It was as though she had passed probation. It should not matter, but it felt good, being treated like an insider.

A forlorn meow brought her attention downward, where an enormous orange cat was sitting, staring up at her.

"Oh. Um, hello," Sam said. "What do you want?" Haughty eyes met hers and did not look away. "I guess...food? Sorry, I don't have anything for you."

The cat meowed again. This time the tone was decidedly belligerent.

"What do you even like to eat? Apples? Small children?"

The cat stood up and started brushing against her ankles. She bent down and touched its coat gently with the back of her finger. It started to emit a deep rumbling sound, and Sam pulled her hand back quickly. *Is it going to attack?*

The door swung open. "What do you want?" a gruff voice demanded.

Sam turned to find an old man with dark brown skin and meticulously brushed grey hair glaring down at her.

She jumped up to respond, but instead erupted into a coughing fit. "Sorry," she said, once she could speak. "I just wanted out of the rain for a moment."

"Humph." Suddenly he cocked his head to one side, his bright blue eyes narrowing as he looked her up and down. Sam frowned.

"Can I help you with something?" she asked.

His expression changed from suspicious to thoughtful. "Maybe, maybe. Can you climb?"

"Oh," said Sam. "Um, well, yes. Why?"

"Me and my wife, there's something in the rafters we need. Can't get up there anymore. Lazy grandson was supposed to come by, but we ain't seen him in weeks. Can't pay you, but there's dinner."

Sam's first instinct was to help. Servitude was a virtue ground rather vigorously into you in Seira. *Are instincts of obedience a good instinct, though? Also, this is probably a trap.* Sam considered this last argument for a moment. The man didn't look cruel, just grumpy. He was also leaning on a walking stick. Unless he had a band of bruisers or a very elaborate booby trap behind that door, Sam would be perfectly safe. She waited to see if the cynical voice in her head had a counterargument. *Nothing? Alright.* She shrugged and gave the old man a nod.

Once Sam was through the doorway, the man pulled a heavy bolt back over the door. Sam followed him down a short hallway and through a second heavy door, one that required multiple keys for multiple locks, and into a small kitchen.

The first thing that Sam noticed was that it was warm, wonderfully warm. She felt a tingle in her fingers as they began to thaw. The second thing she noticed was that the apartment was pretty. The furniture was well made, and it was clean enough that Sam wondered if she should take off her boots. She might have offered, except that her socks were only marginally cleaner.

Then they turned the corner and Sam gasped. The walls were lined with bookshelves, big, floor-to-ceiling bookshelves filled with hundreds of books. Unable to stop herself, Sam started toward the nearest one.

"You read," a soft voice said behind her.

Sam whipped around, startled, to find an old woman watching

her. She was tall, taller than the man, and wore her long, white hair braided around her head like a crown.

"I, uh..."

"It's okay, dear, nothing to explain." The woman approached, smiling at her. She moved gracefully. *Like a dancer.* "Obviously we can too, so we're all among likeminded people." Something was off about this woman, but Sam couldn't determine exactly what it was.

It's her teeth. The woman had a complete set of teeth—white, even teeth. In the North, most people's teeth had yellowed by early adulthood; few had a full set by middle age. Sam had been making a conscious effort to smile, on the rare occasions she felt like smiling, with her lips closed. It was a small thing, but a telling one. Toothpaste, qualified dentists, braces, none of that existed here. *Could the woman also be from Seira?*

"I'm Geo," she said, and offered her hand to Sam. "My husband probably didn't introduce himself. His name is Jem." She hadn't let go of Sam's hand. "Will you stay for supper?"

"Uh, thank you," said Sam. "That's very kind."

"I thought she could get those boxes out of the rafters," said Jem.

"Darling." Geo laughed without turning her head toward him. "We can offer a guest a meal without asking for a favour in return. Honestly," she winked at Sam, "you're losing all of your manners in your old age, my dear."

"Oh, but—no, I mean, I'm happy to help, really."

"Good," Jem said from across the room. "We got a ladder under here, come get it out. Please," he added after a stern look from his wife.

A moment later Sam was sitting in the rafters, looking at three identical boxes. "Which one would you like?"

Jem pointed to one, and Sam picked it up gingerly. It wasn't heavy. Beside the boxes was a length of rope. Sam tied it securely around the box, which she then lowered to the ground before climbing down the ladder after it.

Geo and Jem approached, opened the box, and surveyed its contents. Not wanting to snoop, Sam backed up a few feet, gazing at the titles in the bookshelf opposite her.

"Lovely." Geo beamed at her. "Thank you, my dear. Shall we eat now?"

Sam was expecting the usual fare—rice, lentils, possibly cabbage or potato if she was lucky. But along with the staples there was a purple root vegetable she didn't recognize, cooked apple, and a delicious yam and potato dish in which the roots had been smashed up and flavoured with butter and salt. Their daughter, they told Sam, had named it "yamashed".

There was a subtle shift in tone when they spoke about their daughter—traces of old grief, Sam suspected. She wondered if the girl had even made it past childhood. Most children didn't in the North, hygienic conditions being what they were. In truth, Sam found it surprising that anyone at all survived infancy, considering exposure to contaminated food, contaminated water, and contaminated air, not to mention the diseases, pervasive and ever-evolving, that were spread by the city's thriving population of rats and mosquitoes.

"We usually sit and read after dinner," Geo said once they had finished eating. Sam started to jump up to help Jem with the dishes, but Geo took her hand once more, keeping her at the table. "Would you care to join us?"

Sam tried not to appear as excited as she felt. There were textbooks and works of fiction, biographies and children's books; some she even recognized. Gingerly, she slid out an old, well-worn volume of plays written by a man named John Patrick Shanley and flipped open a page at random. *Oh, words, words, delicious words!*

Sam was about to settle down on a floor cushion with her find when a thought occurred to her.

"Do you have a dictionary?" she asked.

Sam slid the heavy, musty, burgundy-coloured book that Geo pointed out onto the floor, and flipped to the letter 'S'. *There it is.* The solstice, she learned, marked both the shortest and the longest days of the year: a winter solstice, and a summer solstice. The dictionary description noted that some cultures celebrated the solstice, but did not elaborate further.

"Did you find what you were looking for, dear?" asked Geo.

"Yes, but, well, I was hoping for more," said Sam. "Are there any books about special days, festivals and such?"

Geo furrowed her brow gently. "I think so. Which festival were you interested in?"

"The solstice," Sam said. Jem turned from the sink where he was washing dishes, a frown on his face.

"The solstice?" asked Geo. Sam thought she might have stiffened ever so slightly.

"Yes, I just... A little girl at my factory asked why we celebrate the solstice, and I didn't really have an answer," lied Sam.

"Oh, well, that is a good question indeed," said Geo. "I don't know if there are any books on Northern festivals specifically, but there is a volume on ancient religions and myths, which I believe many of our rituals are descended and adapted from."

Geo pointed out a massive tome on the bottom shelf of one of the bookcases. The tension, if it had even truly existed in the first place, had dissipated.

It was still raining outside when Sam left, the downpour so aggressive now that Sam could see raindrops bouncing off a patch of pavement. Was it raining harder than usual, she wondered? Or was it simply rare to have found a few feet of city street where the pavement was both intact and free of debris? She pulled her hood over her head and stepped out into the rain.

Sam had not spent long with the book on ancient religions and myths. It was exceedingly dry and made no mention of the solstice. Instead she had returned to the book of plays. Sam had rolled the words back and forth in her mouth as she read, savouring the syntax.

"I am not the hero of this play. I am not the hero of any play I could be in. Except a play I wrote."

I am not the hero of this play.

She wanted to read the whole thing again, from start to finish. *Maybe I will.*

Geo had invited her to visit anytime. "For a meal, to read, or just to chat," she'd said. "Knock six times so that we know it's you."

Sam had stuttered out an awkward thank you. She'd sounded formal, she knew, and stiff. She'd sounded Seiran. Geo had just smiled graciously in response. Even Jem had given a wave and twisted his scowl into something that may have been intended as a smile.

A loud meow pulled her attention downward. "You're still here. Well, goodnight, cat," Sam said, and resumed walking. A few moments later something orange flashed at the edge of her vision. It seemed the cat was following her, dashing through the rain to crouch in doorways or beneath abandoned packing crates, anything that could offer some amount of shelter from the sky's onslaught. *Is this normal cat behaviour?* She would have to ask Ava.

Thinking of Ava, Sam slowed, and impulsively ducked down a side street. Though it was only a block from the factory, Sam had visited the local market just a handful of times.

The entranceway was crowded. Sam squeezed past a pair of very young, very pregnant girls, trying not to stare at their large, round bellies, and entered the dank room beyond. *Growing a child in uteri. Such an absurd concept.*

Vendors leaned or crouched against walls, wares proudly displayed on old blankets. Homemade scales and the bags of rocks that served as counterweights sat atop wooden crates, within which they placed any sack they earned.

Leathery old men loitered in the corners, smoking and socializing while their grandchildren peddled frayed sweaters and jeans, worn bags and hats, chipped dishes and faded blankets.

The smoke triggered yet another set of hacking coughs, earning Sam a dirty look from an old woman. Her grey hair hung down her back in greasy clumps, and she was sucking on a homemade smoke, an assortment of maps and batteries arranged carefully on the dirty blanket at her feet.

Beside her a pretty girl with long, wavy auburn hair winked at Sam, nodding toward an assortment of combs. Sam was fairly certain that Shale had been selling tools the week before and socks the week before that. Rumour was that she would sell you more than a comb or a sock if you had the coin, though she might pick your pockets in the hazy aftermath. "I'm a business woman," she had told Sam when they first met, "I follow opportunity."

"How's business?" Sam asked.

"Slow." Shale's voice was low and sultry, unapologetically sensual.

"Well, it's uglier than usual outside," said Sam. "Bet a lot of folks are staying cooped up tonight."

"And you? Are you feeling cooped up? I could help with the cabin fever."

Sam laughed and rolled her eyes at Shale. "I'm on a mission," she said. Auburn eyebrows lifted with interest.

"Have you been to the east corner?" Shale asked after Sam had explained what she was looking for.

Sam shook her head. "I've only ever bought spices here, and oil. For Ava."

"She's still sending you out, huh?"

"I don't mind."

"It's not that. It just worries me that she never leaves the factory anymore."

"Well, she doesn't need to, I guess. I mean, I can..." Sam trailed off mid-sentence. Shale was looking at something behind Sam, her lip curling ever so slightly.

Sam looked over her shoulder, wondering what could have prompted a slip in Shale's carefully crafted façade. A child was tugging something small away from another child. One of the pregnant girls had wandered in and was haggling loudly with a skinny youth selling underwear. A handsome man with short, oiled blond hair and an easy smile was helping an old woman lift a burlap sack...

"Do you know him?" Sam asked in a whisper, flushing slightly. "I saw him at the Hive and—"

"I'd steer clear, girl," Shale said.

"I—what? Who is he?"

"Maddox."

Sam frowned. Shale's response was hardly an explanation. "So why—"

"Just steer clear," Shale repeated.

She watched the man whisper something to the old woman, who laughed. The two pieces didn't fit: the scene in front of her was incongruous with Shale's warning. Then an image flashed before Sam's eyes, forgotten in the midst of the horror of the fire: the charming blond man, Maddox, leaving the Hive with a young drug-addicted girl in hand. Sam opened her mouth to probe further, but then stopped. She didn't know Shale very well.

"So, east corner?" she asked instead.

Sam followed Shale as she weaved through the maze of vendors and their displays, though she hesitated when the redhead disappeared behind a curtain. A pale hand reached back through the curtain and grasped her wrist, pulling her forward.

Gone were the dirty blankets and cheap goods. Higher-end items were spread out on tables. Sam saw fur pelts, pots and pans with minimal dents, and little vials filled with bright and smelly liquids.

Shale scanned the vendors, and then pulled Sam into an unlit corner.

"He has a few," she said, pointing at a skinny man with black hair pomaded into spikes. He reminded Sam of a picture she had once seen of a prehistoric lizard called a stegosaurus. "Or at least he did a few weeks ago. Nasty piece of work, though. Tell you what." Her big brown eyes locked on Sam's. "Wander past, see if he has one that you want. I can do the haggling for you." When Sam raised her eyebrows, the redhead winked.

"Seeing as it's for Ava."

Sam walked slowly past the man's table, feeling particularly awkward. Chest out and arms crossed, he leaned back against the wall, eyeing her suspiciously. *There.* She wandered past a few other tables, feigned interest in a particularly fine metal tankard, and then snuck back to where Shale waited.

Whispered instructions, the passing of coin from Sam's hand to Shale's, and the redhead was soon strutting up to the spiky man. He straightened up when he saw her coming, fleshy lips parting slightly like a dog anticipating leftovers. They began chatting, voices too low for Sam to follow. She waited, eyeing the merchandise in question. Heads were shaken emphatically, voices were raised and then lowered again, and twice Shale started to storm off.

Eventually, though, Shale's prowess paid off. Trying not to look too pleased with herself, Sam followed the other girl back through the market, tucking her purchase into her coat.

When she reached the factory, the cat was sitting outside the door, staring expectantly up at Sam. "How did you know...? No matter. You're not coming in, so, again, goodnight, cat." She squeezed through the door, shutting it quickly behind her.

It was late, but the factory was still buzzing. Sam hurried to the far wall and the dilapidated staircase. At the top of the stairs she turned sharply toward the right, edging through the shadows on her way to the north wall. Feeling around in the dark, she found the end of the ladder she had painstakingly knotted together from mismatched fabric scraps.

Hanging from the rafters above the second floor was an old metal lift, just big enough for one person. She could easily spot anyone trying to approach and could pull the ladder up at night. She loved her bird's nest and lived in constant fear that someone would try to commandeer it.

Stepping around the rough blankets that served as a bed, Sam reached up and pushed on a metal pane in the ceiling. The bucket she had placed on the roof the night before was full of rainwater. She carried the bucket down into her nest, tied a knotted length of fabric to the handle and lowered it down to the second floor, following a moment later on her ladder. Sam then lugged the fresh water down the staircase and over to Ava's shop.

"Thought you'd forgotten about me," Ava said, taking the full bucket from her and passing over an empty one. "It's chana boil tonight."

"Actually," said Sam, filling up a mug with hot water and settling down in her usual spot, "I already ate."

"Humph," Ava said, once Sam had filled her in on the night's events. "They could be spies, you know."

Sam rolled her eyes. "They're elderly. Even if they were spies once, which I doubt, they certainly aren't now. They're probably just, you know, like me."

"Maybe. But still, be careful—"

"—and don't tell them anything," Sam repeated in unison with her friend. "I know. I'm being careful."

Ava stared suspiciously at her. "Hmm. Okay then. Can we work? Or you still too tired?"

"Oh." Sam thought about it for a minute. In the excitement of the evening, she seemed to have forgotten her earlier exhaustion. "No, I can work."

Along with containing one of the factory's few crude chimneys, Ava's living space was unusually roomy.

"The trick," she'd explained to Sam, "is to move in when a place is near empty and use all sorts of boards, crates, and curtains to give it a disorderly look. Nobody figures out that all these bits go together, or even guesses how big it is."

There were two whole rooms: one with a fire pit for heating water and a barrel big enough to bathe in, and a second with two beds and a few locked trunks that served as tables as well as storage units.

In the second room, they pulled out cushions and settled around one of the trunks.

"I brought you something." Sam pulled out her purchase and laid it beside the board they used as a slate. The corners of the book curled up slightly. Sam tried to flatten them back down to no avail.

"What's that?"

"Try reading the title." Ava had mastered the alphabet and could sound out a variety of words. They were starting to work on her spelling now.

Ava glared at the booklet. Sam knew not to take it personally; Ava always glared when concentrating.

"Ee-easy...Soups...and...Ste—ews." Ava paused. "Is this a—a book for food?"

"It is. I thought it might be nice to have a book to work from, and since you like to cook..." Sam trailed off, feeling self-conscious.

Ava's brow unfurrowed, and Sam could have sworn that the corners of her lips switched upward ever so slightly. "Hmm," she said. "It's nice to see a practical use for all this nonsense. How'd you get this? Fool thing to spend money on."

"Shale helped me."

"So, she'll be wanting a favour then."

"What, you don't think she was just helping me, you know, for fun and friendship?"

Ava shrugged. "Isn't friendship just a lot of favours owed and given?"

"Are you implying that you would like to do me a favour?" Sam asked, searching around the base of the trunk for the piece of chalk they used for writing on the slate. Ava shot her a dirty look and then snorted.

Getting down onto her stomach, Sam poked her head under Ava's bed. There it was, beside a lonely cockroach that fled at the sight of her. When she returned to the table, Ava had the booklet in her hands. Ever so gently, she turned the stained cover page and peeked at the first recipe.

Pretending not to notice, Sam picked up the slate and began writing out a list of words. Ava was a fast learner, if an impatient one. She was stubborn too, complaining bitterly every time a word was not spelled phonetically.

It was Ava who had insisted the lessons take place in private.

"But why?" Sam had asked. "Some Northerners can read—I thought you said it even gives you status." Ava had sighed, looking at Sam the way you might look at a child who has not yet learned to reason.

"Yes, it's not a problem, but status means attention, and questions. You really want people talking about you, asking you questions?" Sam had shaken her head and dropped the issue. She knew that she was not a particularly accomplished liar. *Not yet anyway.*

Ava had placed the booklet on the ground and was opening the trunk. She rummaged for a moment, dumping out a blanket and some candles, before removing a dusty box. Ava laid the box on the ground and pried off the lid. Inside were small, soft clothes. Baby clothes, Sam realized. For some reason it always made her feel sad and a bit confused, these symbols of motherhood, of family.

Beneath the clothes was a small children's book. Ava picked it up and laid it down beside the cookbook, as though to compare the two. Peering over Ava's shoulder, Sam caught sight of a long, hairy snout.

"It that the story of the wolf and the child with the red cape?"

67

Ava jumped, as though she had completely forgotten that Sam was in the room with her.

"I didn't know you already owned a book." Sam leaned forward to get a closer look, but Ava snatched it back off the floor, hugging it to her chest as though she feared Sam might try to take it.

"Got it for Raina. When she was small."

"Oh," said Sam. "But you couldn't...how did...did she read it?"

"And how would she read it, huh? Use your head, Samarra. This ain't Seira. Kids don't read here."

"I, well, I mean—Raina did," said Sam. "Didn't she? She must have, to work as a drudge."

"That was later," said Ava.

"Oh."

Ava scowled at her, though her expression softened when she looked down at the book. "I knew the story anyway. So, I'd tell it, and she'd look at the pictures."

"Did you—did you want to work with that book? Learn the words?"

Ava shook her head and placed the book gently back into the box. She layered the baby clothes back on top of the book, closed the lid, and placed the box back in the trunk. "No reason to."

Sam wasn't sure how to respond. Something in Ava's expression warned her to tread carefully.

"It was that fool boyfriend taught her," said Ava after a moment, closing the trunk.

"Taught her to read, you mean?" asked Sam.

Ava nodded.

"Her boyfriend Finlay."

"Yes, Finlay."

"And...he is...I mean, he..."

"Spit it out, girl, you're irritating me."

"The other drudges think that Raina, and Finlay too, of course, left on the solstice, that they're, or they might, come back." She blurted it out all in one breath, her eyes on the slate as though it could provide her with answers.

Silence.

Might as well keep going now. "But you think—I mean, I have been under the impression, anyway, that Raina is, well, that she's...dead." As soon as the words were out, Sam wished she could take them back.

Still more silence. Sam snuck a peek at Ava and wished that she hadn't. The grief on her face was terrible to see.

"Yes, Samarra. I think she's dead."

"But...she might not be? How did she—when did you see her last?"

Ava waited a very long time to speak.

Eventually she took a rag out of her pocket and began pulling at a string. "Summer solstice last year. She came home in the afternoon—brought me an apple tart. Left before dinner though, another late-night mission with that bav compound. Was planning to go straight from there to some fool party."

"And—"

"And that was the last I saw of her."

"So why do they think she skipped town?"

"Because, well, she talked 'bout it, didn't she? Always said she was going west, talked about it ever since she was a little girl. Convinced there were jewels in the mountains out there, thought with all the quakes, the earth would just spit 'em out. Yeah, she was..." Ava trailed off. She'd completely unraveled the rag.

Sam waited for Ava to continue. When she finally spoke again, something had softened in her face. "She had this way of screwing up her mouth when she was real set on something. Made me laugh, which made her real mad. Her little face, so mad. She was always tiny, you know. Tall, but with these little bird bones. Not much like me at all."

"And the solstice?" asked Sam after a moment.

"We got a tradition, here," Ava said. "Night of the solstice—summer or winter, don't matter which—you need to do something big, say, leave town maybe, take a new lover or leave somebody, you do it that night. It's blessed, you see. Lucky. And if it's leaving you need to do, you just do it. No goodbyes, no nothing. And the folks that are left behind, well...you wait. That's all. And then one day the person you love comes home. Or they don't."

"But you don't think she left."

Ava's eyes drifted over to Raina's old bed. She looked suddenly tired and old, and horribly, unsettlingly vulnerable.

"Didn't say that. Just know she ain't okay. Can't say why I know it. I just do. It's—you don't have mothers, in the South, do you?"

It was Sam's turn to shake her head.

"When it's your babe, some things you just know. Don't need nobody to tell you. Mother's instinct, they call it."

Sam started to speak and then stopped. Ava was right. Sam didn't have a mother, would never be a mother herself. These were bonds that she could not understand.

"Here." Ignoring the list of words that Sam had written on the slate, Ava picked up the booklet again. "What's this fool word? Zuh—chee—nee?"

Taking her cue from Ava, Sam turned her attention back to the lesson. She scanned the faded page, looking for the offending word. "Zucchini. You pronounce it like a 'k'."

Ava looked as though Sam had just suggested they sashay topless through the import market. "Pronounce it like a 'k' when it's spelled 'cch'? Why the jit don't they just use a damn 'k' then?"

"Here, don't forget this," Ava said as Sam left an hour later, passing her a roll. "Or the bucket! You shoulda put it outside earlier, you know—what is that?"

Sam turned and groaned. "How did you get in? And how did you find me? Are you some kind of demon cat?"

"Hush, girl. There are way too many fanatics here for you to be going on about demons—you want them to come over and start talking to us? This is the biggest cat I've ever seen though."

Sam cocked her head at the cat. "How big are they supposed to be?"

"Oh, maybe a quarter that size. Hmm, here, you wait one sec." She rummaged around in her shop for a moment, and then came over with a small bowl of water.

"Lots of rats to catch, once you're done," she informed him.

"Is that what they eat? Rats?" asked Sam.

"Yup, rats, roaches, the usual. You never had a cat?"

Sam shook her head. "I'd never even seen one until I got here."

"It's why folks keep 'em, mostly. To catch pests. How this one got to be so fat though...I wonder where it came from?" Ava bent down and started petting the cat. "No fleas even, that's weird." The cat started emitting the rumbling sound again.

"It followed me home after dinner," said Sam. "Although actually I saw it before dinner. Is it growling?"

Ava snorted. "I guess you've never heard a cat purr before. Means it's happy. Actually..." She flipped the cat over. "He's happy. We shouldn't turn him out, plump prize like this one, he'd be a nice meal for a stray pup or a coy dog. You can stay in my shop, mister, as long as you keep your dirty paws off my counters." She scratched under the cat's chin, causing the rumbling sound to deepen.

"What?" she asked Sam, who was staring at her in shock.

"You're just—you're just never this nice."

"Not nice? Really? Who has been taking care of you, little gull?"

"Oh, you're kind, you're just not nice."

Ava shrugged, clearly trying to hide a smile.

"See, you pride yourself on it."

Ava put the cat back down. "Hakka, he's heavy. Anyway, it's bedtime. Go away." With that she disappeared back into her room, leaving Sam alone with the cat, who had started to rub his face against her leg.

"Okay, well, you have somewhere to stay. Good job."

She reached down and petted him gently. Dried out, his fur was quite soft.

"Well, goodnight, cat," Sam said again, securing the board across the front of the shop before leaving.

It was late, far later than Sam usually went to bed. She swung open the ceiling panel and pushed the bucket out as quickly as possible to limit the amount of rainwater that fell onto her bed. She hung up her coat and snuggled under her damp blankets.

Raina, who had been hovering at the back of Sam's mind all evening, pushed her way to the front. Sam's mental image of the girl was growing clearer: tall and thin, Ava had said, and strong-willed. Did she have her mother's smooth, dark skin? From what Sam knew, children often, though not always, resembled their parents. Finlay she couldn't picture at all. Her tired brain kept bringing to mind the man from the Hive. Maddox, Shale had called him.

She was fading into sleep when something landed on her feet. She sat up with a start, reaching for her baton, only to find herself staring into a pair of bright green eyes—green eyes on a fluffy orange face.

"How did you even get up here?" She stared up at the rafters and then over to the beams and pipes that crisscrossed the walls beside her nest, looking for a plausible pathway. The cat sat down and started licking himself, clearly uninterested in further conversation.

"Ugh, okay, fine. I give up." Sam nestled back under the blankets. A few moments later the rumbling started again.

9

The North

SHE DREAMED of Raina that night, late in the night, after she'd paid homage to her shame. It started with an old dream, one she'd dreamt many times before. Corvus lay dead on the bed they'd shared, scarlet liquid dripping from a syringe on the bedside table the only splash of colour in a white, sterile room. It wasn't how it had happened, of course. Even when she slept she lied.

In the dream she left the room and stood in the hallway, unsure of where to go. Usually this was when the dream restarted. Cue, repeat. Except that this time Ava was watching her from the end of the hallway. This Ava was young, though, with long hair and a smile instead of a scowl.

The girl turned and fled. *Raina.* Sam's whisper echoed down the long empty hallway. She started to follow her and the dream ended. *Exhale.*

She closed her eyes and listened. It was her trick: *feel the blankets, taste the air, listen, smell, see...*

And?

It's quiet today. There were no raindrops clunking on the roof above her head. She kicked the blankets off and heard an indignant meow. The cat turned around and glared at her.

"Sorry. I forgot about you."

The cat only glared harder. She reached out hesitantly and he lumbered up to rub his face against her hand. *Touch the cat's fur.* That was a new one for her.

She dressed and climbed down the ladder, the cat watching her descent from above, paws tucked beneath his heavy body. He had gotten up into her nest, but could he get down? Maybe she needed to carry him. That might be difficult, unless she could pop him into a bag, perhaps? She might need to ask Ava. When she was halfway to Ava's, something darted around her feet, nearly tripping her.

"Oh, well, clearly you don't need my help then." She switched direction, heading for the door instead.

"I'm serious, you can't come to work with me."

The cat continued to trot along beside her.

"You see?" she said when they reached the end of the trail and the compound came into view. "This is clearly not a place for cats."

She leaned down and petted the top of his head, then stepped onto the grounds. She waited a few minutes before glancing back over her shoulder. Luckily, the cat had turned around and was heading back toward the factory. Or perhaps other popular feline haunts—how was she to know? Relieved, she continued on, settling down in her usual spot.

"Good morning," she said to Jackal.

"Almost," he responded, as per their script.

Hakuund and Cassio arrived together, talking animatedly in low voices. The boys clasped hands with Jackal in greeting, while Hakuund gave Sam a hug and Cassio squeezed her hand. Xenia appeared a moment later, giving kisses all around.

"How are you?" she asked Sam, with an extra squeeze. "Are you up for something tonight?"

"What kind of thing?" She had a feeling that her dream of a nice, quiet reading party was unlikely to come true.

"Low key," said Xenia. "Cass and I thought we'd get some cards going tonight, just the team."

Sam thought fast. She enjoyed games—games were structured and had clear rules, what was not to like? She didn't know any Northern card games, but she could probably evade suspicion by saying that her friends back home didn't play. She brushed off the voice in the back of her head that was reminding her she should limit social interactions with the other drudges. *If it is a team activity, my participation is linked, albeit informally, with my work.* The voice in her head thought that this was a fairly weak argument.

"Sure," she said before she could change her mind.

Xenia drew out directions to her and Cassio's factory in the grass. "We usually do dinner together when we play, lots of picky food. Everyone brings something to share."

Sam nodded. She'd noticed that sharing food was at the core of most relationships in the North.

"A family," Ava had told her once, "are people that eat from the same pot, whatever their blood."

Sam had found this horribly confusing. "But blood is important here."

"Yes," Ava had said, "until it's not. Then it's those you have history with."

Sam had found herself leaving this particular lesson more bewildered than she had been when she arrived.

As usual, Sam was the last one to leave the grounds. She pedaled south, cutting through the trails until she came out onto a back road she'd found the previous week. Picking up speed, she had to fight the impulse to close her eyes; this road had fewer potholes than most but that was not exactly a high commendation. Haste was encouraged, of course: The faster she acquired the day's goods, the higher her wages. Her team had also emphasized speed as a good tactic for deterring any huaina that thought to profit from robbing a compound. *Mostly though, going fast just feels good.*

Did Benison give her this same bike to ride? Did she race down this road?

There were three possibilities concerning Raina: either Raina had left the Barrow and was living somewhere else; she had left the Barrow and then something bad had happened to her; or something bad had happened to her in the Barrow last year during the summer solstice. The first option seemed the most likely. How much stock should she put in Ava's maternal intuition?

Breathing hard, Sam hopped off her bike and pulled out her water flask. She took a sip, her eyes on the chaos below. The first time she'd come to the import market she'd felt so overwhelmed that she'd had to retreat with only half of the items on her list acquired. She had stumbled into a quiet alley and had spent a good half hour with her head between her knees before she had been able to muster up the fortitude to head back in.

It wasn't just the number of people that was overstimulating—there were plenty of crowded markets in the area, oft frequented by the strange and the dangerous alike. It wasn't the profusion of shops either, though they seemed to lie atop one another like morning glory attempting to strangle out the competition. It wasn't the way the vendors shouted at customers, trying to entice, guilt, or bully them into purchasing their wares, or even the stray dogs that roamed in search of a handout. For Sam it was the smells.

The perfumes, the plants, the animals, the food; there were a million different fragrances in the air. That first time, she had been worried that she might vomit from sensory overload. The second time, she'd left with a migraine. Today the smells were making her hungry.

Pressing a hand to her grumbling stomach, Sam took another sip of water. Her eyes drifted past the market, to the contaminated waters beyond. There at least was one smell that she wouldn't have to deal with. They were just far enough from the dead lake that the stink of rot didn't pollute the market. *To think that people used to eat meat from lakes and rivers.* The thought was nauseating.

Rumour was that if you followed the street downward into the lake, you'd find the original market, lost during the Decline when the waters had risen high enough to devour whole city streets. Sam had no intention of investigating further; she hated the water. There was no reason to go down there, anyway. Polluted water and phragmites —it was not a place for humans anymore.

It was time to move: the sweat was cooling on her body and soon she'd be colder than she had been before the ride. She pulled out the scroll and examined the map at the top corner. After taking a few minutes to commit it to memory—it wouldn't do to pull out a map in the middle of the market—she took her bicycle by the handlebars and commenced threading her way down into the throng.

"Dried basil! Dried basil and rosemary!"

"Cabbage and potatoes! Clean—no rust, no mould!"

"Corn kernels, popcorn!"

"Hey ladki, bad luck lately? One of these beside your bed turns that bad to good."

Sam jerked sideways as the man shoved a fist-sized spider in her face.

"What, you scared?" He sneered at her. "Don't let fear make you turn down this chance. Everyone who buys says that one, maybe two days later, something incredible happens!"

Sam just shook her head, holding tightly to her bicycle as she skirted past him.

"One found ten xots just lying on the ground! Another met his long-lost brother!"

The smell of meat cooking caused Sam's stomach to gurgle a second time. She caught sight of a skinny goat rotating over a spit. Meat was a delicacy in the Barrow. Most livestock only lived long enough to reproduce once or twice before dying of disease or heat or drowning in a flood. Sam had only eaten artificial goat before. *Maybe I'll buy some today before I leave.*

Just then the front of her bicycle bumped into something. Sam looked down to see the carcass of a stray dog, covered in oozing red sores. *Then again, maybe not.*

"Need to forget? Old love, old fight, maybe? One drink of this and it's gone, gone from your memory, gone forever!" A woman brandished a dirty cup at the crowd. "Something bad done to you? Something bad you done?" She caught Sam's eyes and bared her yellow teeth in a grin. "Three sack and you're fresh as a baby."

It was a scam, Sam had no doubt. Best-case scenario it only gave the drinker giardiasis; worst case it killed them. *Which technically does rid them of the memory, I suppose. And even if it did work...guilt shouldn't be cast off. Not if you've earned it.*

"Hey!"

"Sorry, sorry." Distracted by the woman, Sam had accidentally bumped an old man with her bike. He gestured rudely at her and sped up.

"Not getting excited anymore? No matter what age you are, dandelion liqueur will rouse up even the saddest serpent! It is inside you, you just need to wake it up!" The man was making lewd hip gestures and winking at anyone who met his eye.

Sam looked down quickly, just in time to see a small hand reach toward her bag. "Hey!"

A small child darted away through the crowd. Sam was still not used to seeing children working as pickpockets or branded with gang insignia; they hardly seemed like children at all. She wondered if they had parents or if they lived together in packs like wild dogs.

"Teeth rotting? Don't suffer! Get 'em pulled, a tooth for a sack or three teeth for two! Pull 'em before they rot you from the inside out!"

Sam could see it now: the image of a book carved into a wooden signpost. Two older men sat on cushions, wrapped in fur blankets. Their eyes were glazed over and they sat perfectly still—the telltale signs of long-term dust use.

"Readers! Real readers here!" A young girl with an unusually deep and raspy voice hustled the crowd. "Anything you need to read, or get writ, get it here! Here for one week only! We even got messengers to carry letters, as far as you need 'em to go, we'll get it there!"

A few hulking huaina lurked in the shadows behind the readers: hired muscle. Readers were so valuable that they inevitably ended up affiliated with one gang or another, usually the same gang that got them addicted to dust.

Sam stopped. She could see the narrow pathway leading down behind the stall, just as Benison had drawn it on her map. She looked over at the readers, then back down at the path again. *I should really complete the mission first.* Yet she found herself wheeling her bike over to the small tent.

"Need something writ, lala?"

"Er—I'm actually more interested in the transport," said Sam.

The girl looked at her, mystified.

"You said you have messengers?"

"Ah, yeah! Where you want it to go? Elwood? Yehnt?" The girl named two neighbouring towns.

"How far west can you go?"

"As—as far west as you want, ladki! Cost you though." The girl's voice had risen to a discernable falsetto. *She's lying.*

Sam nodded at the girl, and then wheeled her bicycle around.

"Okay, okay, we'll cut you a deal! C'mon back, lala, c'mon back!"

Sam turned down the narrow pathway. Shops backed onto the path from both sides, giving her the impression that she was sneaking a peek at the market's unmentionables. She wondered if someone was going to come shoo her away.

At the end of the walkway a small tent had been erected. The signpost displayed a white flame inside a black one. Sam pulled open the flap and stepped inside. Though the lighting was poor, she could see that boxes had been arranged in neat rows on the muddy ground. *Hardly an efficient use of floor space.*

A small shadow jumped up and darted out the back of the tent, leaving Sam alone. Peering into the closest box, she saw a metal cylinder marked with symbols.

A hoarse voice broke the silence. "You here to snoop or buy?"

Entering through the back flap was a woman in her early forties, skeletal with curly blond hair. She wore an accusatory expression, as though Sam had broken into her home instead of wandered into her shop. *Clearly she doesn't get customers too often.*

"I need a cylinder of QX787," said Sam.

The woman continued to glower at her. "Fifteen xots," she said, coughing as she spoke.

"Eight," said Sam, fighting the urge to look away from the woman's hostile eyes.

"Twelve, lowest offer."

"Eight," Sam repeated, crossing her arms in what she hoped would be perceived as an authoritative posture.

"Fine, ten, but that's it."

"Eight," said Sam a third time, her eyes beginning to water. She gave herself a mental shake and blinked. *Being resolute does not necessitate a staring contest.*

The woman stared at her for a full ten seconds before spitting on the ground between them. Even in the dim lighting Sam could see that there was blood in her saliva. "Eight," she agreed.

Sam pulled eight xots from her jacket pocket and placed them in the woman's outstretched palm. The woman stared at the coins for a long minute before stashing them securely inside her oversized, raggedy vest. She then knelt and carefully pulled a metal cylinder the size of Sam's forearm from one of the boxes, wrapping it in an oily rag before placing it gently in the basket of Sam's bicycle. Producing a piece of cord from her back pocket, she then proceeded to thread the top of the basket, forming a cover over the cylinder. When she had finished, she looked across at Sam.

"Don't drop it," she said, without a twitch of a smile.

Sam nodded in reply. Turning away from the woman, she peeked over her shoulder and began slowly backing her bicycle out of the store.

"Don't drop it," the woman repeated, reaching out to grab Sam's handlebars. "It's not just you, girl; anything within half a mile will blow."

Sam stared at the woman for a moment, trying to decide if she was kidding. It seemed impossible that this woman would tolerate, much less venture, a joke. It seemed comparatively more plausible that Sam was actually about to take a two-hour bike ride across a bumpy, smashed-up road carrying an explosive; an explosive that her warm and caring employers hadn't bothered to warn her about. She supposed that for the Vauns, a drudge who dropped their property, be it a bag of potatoes or a bomb, was not worth retaining anyway.

Sam nodded again and continued to back her bicycle out of the tent, the woman's eyes following her until the tent flapped closed behind her.

At least Benison had seen fit to give her the appropriate information on how to haggle with the vendor. Every single aspect of that
exchange had been inconsistent with the typical Northern bartering
culture.

Sam walked her bike back up the path toward the main market,
trying not to envision her own fiery death. *Wait, would it explode with
fire? Or just shrapnel?* She should have asked more follow-up questions. Either way, death would be quick. *Unless of course I'm horribly
maimed but somehow survive.* She did have a knack for surviving.

Sam was knocked abruptly out of her morbid reverie by the
unpleasant sensation of someone grabbing her arms from behind. A
large someone, she guessed, probably similar to the longhaired troll
of a man who had grabbed her bike at the same time. She stomped
down, her boot colliding with her attacker's in-step. With a roar of
pain that told her that her assailant was indeed male, he jerked
forward, giving Sam the opportunity to slam her head backward into
what she hoped was his nose. It seemed he was even taller than she'd
thought, for her head only thudded into a meaty chest.

Okay, plan B. She rocked her weight forward and then quickly
back, kicking her boot upward, over her shoulder and into her attacker's face. Based on his cursing, she had hit her mark, though the blow
was not enough to make him loosen his crushing grip on her arms.

The second huaina was already moving through the crowd with
her bike. On the plus side, this left some nice empty space in front of
her. This time she leaned back first and then flung herself forward,
managing to flip her attacker over her and onto the ground. *Hmm,
that's quite a bit of blood. I may have actually broken his nose.* What was
really lovely, Sam noted with satisfaction, was that the blood seemed
to have gotten into his eyes. Taking time to aim, Sam reared back and
then swung one booted foot into his genitals. As he screamed, she
sped off after the other huaina.

She could see the back of his head, a hand higher than everyone
else. He was going against the current, barreling forward as quickly as
his bulk allowed. Though the crowd was scrambling to get out of his
way—the benefit of being a giant, she supposed—it was only a
matter of time before he collided with someone or something.

She was not a giant and no one moved out of her way. What she was, was slim and fast, and very good at weaving her way through a crowd. It didn't take her long to catch up with him. Seeing that he held the right side of her bike, she slipped over to the left side, sliding her baton out of her boot as she approached. As quickly as she could, she jabbed the baton at the huaina's large, beefy neck. At the same time, her left hand reached for the bike handles.

"Taow!" He aimed a left-handed hammer strike at her face.

Sam ducked, all the while maintaining a firm hold on her bike. She dodged the blow that followed as well but was starting to have misgivings about her ability to fight a man three times her size while keeping her bicycle upright.

As she spun away from a third punch, something knocked her attacker backward. A slight, dark-haired man Sam didn't recognize followed his first hit with a second and a third. The giant crashed backward, seemingly stunned. This was excellent timing, as the first huaina had reappeared, covered in blood and looking exceptionally angry.

"Hold this," Sam said to the stranger, thrusting the bike at him. "Drop it and we all die."

Trusting in the newcomer's sense of self-preservation, Sam spun around and kicked giant number one in the knee. He buckled forward and she aimed a kick at his face. Her boot collided with his temple. He tottered and then collapsed onto the muddy ground. Sam spun around frantically and nearly crashed into the stranger, who was luckily still holding her bicycle.

"Thanks." Sam took the handlebars back from him, trying to catch her breath.

"No problem." He smiled at her. He was close to her age and dressed, like every fashionable northerner, in artfully ripped black clothing. It was a craze Sam would never understand. His skin was light brown and his eyes were a bright, piercing blue. He looked like trouble, she decided.

"Uh, yeah, thanks," Sam said again, struggling to hold her bicycle steady against the onslaught of oncoming traffic. She needed a way out—out of this crowd and away from the huaina—and she needed to find it quickly. *There.* On the raised road running parallel to the main throughway, a stream of people was headed toward an exit.

Hugging her bicycle close to her body, Sam shouldered her way through the oncoming crowd until she reached the muddy ground beneath the road. There was a stone-strewn ramp that led from the main path to the upper road, but it was about a hundred feet behind her. Not wanting to risk another encounter with the huaina, she pushed her bike up the short, very steep and very muddy slope. *It's only a few feet, shouldn't be a problem. Just one big step.*

In the midst of transferring her weight onto her front foot, she felt the ground slip beneath her boot. With mounting horror, she slid downward into a graceless, mucky split, both hands stretched upward in a desperate attempt to keep her bicycle upright.

"Get back!" she cried out. "Everyone get back!"

In the madness of the market, nobody seemed to hear her. Out of the corner of her eye she saw someone vault up the hill beside her. Her bicycle was lifted up out of her hands and placed onto the upper bank. Caught off guard, she somersaulted backward into the pile of muddy refuse at the bottom of the hill.

"Thought you might have needed some help with that," the blue-eyed man called down to her.

"Yep," she said, looking up at him from where she lay, limbs in a tangle. "Thank you. Again."

"Again, no problem." He waited while Sam got to her feet, picked a slimy piece of plastic out of her hair, and climbed back up the hill.

Sam took her bicycle, which she was feeling rather a lot of loathing toward, nodded at the man, and continued onward. Once submersed within the crowd, she glanced back to check that the huaina weren't following. This was when she noticed that the man was still beside her. He smiled at her again.

She frowned. "Are you following me?"

"I'm following the crowd," he said, clearly unperturbed by the hostility in her voice. "Tell me more about yourself and I'll decide if you're worth following." This earned him another frown from Sam. *What an annoyingly cheerful man.*

"I'm Adder," he continued. "And yes, I do spend much of my time helping strangers. They actually call me Saint Adder. It's a burden, really, all the adoration. I try to dispel all the myths that have since sprouted up about me, but once one has a following, really, what is one to do?"

Standing above them atop wooden crates, several men in dirty white robes were shouting down to the crowd.

"Man sinned! Woman sinned most of all! And the world ended. We said it was coming and it came, it did! Now we live forsaken as the floods rise and winds, oh the winds! Hurricanes have ripped apart man's work in the east and the earth has shaken it all to rubble in the west. We are forsaken! We were forsaken because of arrogance, because of blasphemy! Our only chance to come back to the light is worship, worship! Join the Sinners Reborn; give us your xots, they mean nothing! Join us in a life of purity, a life of worship!"

The speaker finished by reaching out his arms imploringly to the crowd as his converts moaned and chanted behind him, shaking jars filled with coin.

"Join! Join! Join! Join!" Their voices grew louder with each beat.

"I feel like you're new in town," Adder shouted above the noise. Sam made no response.

"Where are you from?" he asked. "Wait, let me guess. If I can figure it out in three guesses or less then you have to tell me, okay? Let's see...Gronnsia!"

Sam shrugged and quickened her pace. "Okay, then...Yehnt? No, not Yehnt. I take that back. Kanlan!"

Sam gave an inward groan. Somehow, she resented this Adder knowing anything about her—even the fabrications she'd created. She supposed she could lie—people lied in the North all the time. She suspected, however, that if she denied it he would continue to follow her, shouting out the names of various Northern towns.

Sam gave what she hoped was a vague and noncommittal expression. He seemed to take that as agreement.

"Don't worry, I won't ask why you left. Wouldn't want to be nosy! Good on you for being so adventurous, though. Everyone here talks and talks about seeing the world, but most people, they never leave the Barrow. Are you trying to send a letter home, then? I saw you over at the readers' tent." He gave her a wide grin. "I mean, had to be shipping you were looking into, right? Obviously a drudge doesn't need help writing a letter!"

Sam stopped short.

"Oh, sorry, was that supposed to be a big secret?" It wasn't said in an antagonizing or threatening manner—on the contrary, he was still horribly chipper. "Because if so, the Vauns should probably splurge on a new style of bike."

Sam sighed. It wasn't a secret, not really; most people she had any kind of regular interaction with knew she worked for the compound. Still, she generally tried to avoid broadcasting this information; it only served to attract unwanted attention. The idea of a complete stranger being able to deduce that she was a drudge on sight alone... it rankled. Adder was right, though—the bicycles they used were distinctive, not only because they were all the same beautiful, cobalt blue, but also because they were clearly well made and maintained.

Sam veered off the upper road onto a small trail that looked like it was rarely used. A deserted path was generally a bad idea, but then she didn't generally carry around explosives. She also didn't fancy returning within easy reach of the men who'd been chasing her.

"Anyway, what's your name?" He had followed her onto the trail. Sam eyed him. She doubted he was planning to rob her, having in all likelihood saved her life a moment ago. *Twice. Unless he dispensed with my attackers in order to claim the goods for himself?* Though it was possible, she thought it unlikely; he could have made off with her belongings while she was busy fighting the second huaina. He may well be self-serving, but what exactly he was hoping to obtain was less clear.

"Sam," she said at last.

"Sam. I would like to formally welcome you to the Barrow." He stopped to inflict a theatrical, sweeping bow upon her.

"Uh, thanks," she said. "Although I have actually been here awhile now."

"Well, you are still welcome." He eyed the trail in front of them. "This path is probably fine, but it has on occasion been used by huaina looking to hijack nice folk such as yourself. But hey, if you give me a ride around to the west entrance, I solemnly swear to help you defend your strangely dangerous bicycle against anyone that tries to divest you of it. Plus, I'll help you watch out for sinkholes."

Sam turned her face away, but not in time to hide her smile. "Fine," she said, swinging a leg over her bike.

"Brilliant," he said, and settled onto the seat behind her.

10

The North

"*Everyone here talks and talks about seeing the world, but most people, they never leave the Barrow.*" Adder's remark had stuck in Sam's head. When it came down to it, unless Raina showed up at the factory one day, it would be near impossible to determine if the girl was living, or had been living, outside the Barrow. If something had happened to Raina while she was still in the city, though...

Wait. Stop. You have one objective, remember? Stay safe, stay hidden. Don't look for trouble. Raina was not her problem. Ava had not asked her to look into her daughter's disappearance. *Plus, the trail is long cold.*

Sam spotted the shop she had been looking for. She had noticed it during her last few visits to the local market, though she had never before stopped to make a purchase. It seemed frivolous, buying snacks and treats when Ava always gave her dinner. She also wondered whether it might insult her prickly friend. Carrying rice, lentils, or cabbage across the Barrow to Xenia and Cassio's factory, however, seemed logistically problematic.

You don't have to go, the sensible voice in her head cautioned. *Stay home.* If Sam was being honest with herself, though, she craved the companionship of people her own age. *What, you can't be alone?* The voice had taken on a mocking tone. *Southerner.*

She was also feeling particularly flush with coin. Apparently, her morning mission had been deemed worthy of danger pay, if not informed consent.

Shale was chatting with the vendor. She ducked under the counter to greet Sam with a kiss on each cheek. "Hello, lovely," she said.

Something in Shale's voice reminded Sam of the cat. It was the rumble; Shale rumbled when she spoke.

"How goes the drudge life?"

"I fought a muddy hill today."

"Did you win?" Shale raised one auburn eyebrow prettily.

Sam thought about it for a moment. "I did not."

Shale let out a laugh, light and twinkling like a set of wind chimes, very different from her usual throaty chuckle. Sam had often wondered if the chuckle was fake. Despite Ava's cynicism, Sam chose to believe that their exchanges were legitimately friendly.

"Dirty business," said Shale, shaking her head at Sam. "You should look for some more elegant work." Both girls laughed at this.

"I need a shareable snack for tonight." Sam gestured at the treats on display. "We're playing cards. Suggestions?"

Shale twisted her lips to the side, gazing at the options. "Groundnuts or dried soybeans are a good option; that or the fried potato slices. Of course..." She sighed with feigned wistfulness. "On a drudge's pay you could get all three, even add a dessert if you're in the mood. I would avoid the apple sweet loaf though, there's a pinch of dust in most batches. Although," she said, looking sideways at Sam through her long eyelashes, "you could bring one and just not eat any yourself—if you want a little advantage."

"Hmm." Sam tried not to look shocked and appalled. "I'll probably skip the dust—tonight's more about the camaraderie than the pot."

Shale rolled her eyes but pulled her into a one-armed hug. "Lover, I forget sometimes you're new to the Barrow."

11

———

The North

"DARLING!" Xenia gave her a kiss and pulled her inside. "Finally, we're all here."

"Am I late?" asked Sam, who was absolutely certain that today, like every other day, she had arrived early.

"No, no, but Hak's been here since the afternoon and Jackal came by to talk to him hours ago, and then, just, nobody left, you see. So, I've been terribly outnumbered for ages."

Xenia and Cassio's quarters were not what Sam had been expecting. Everything was beautiful, from the wall hangings and the glossy wooden furniture to the intricately painted screens that separated the main area from the bedrooms. Even the kitchen was aesthetically pleasing—the pots smooth and shiny, the fire pit decorated with painted tiles. Ava's set-up, which had always seemed palatial to Sam, appeared suddenly small and drab by comparison.

She was surprised to see that a shrine had been set up in one corner, complete with candles and incense, as well as a small brass statue that Sam didn't recognize. She hadn't pegged the twins as religious.

The boys were at a low table, sitting on cushions. Judging from the half-empty bottle of moonshine, they had already started drinking. Cassio was carefully filling small squares of paper with herbs from two different containers while Jackal rolled them into cylinders.

Hakuund whooped when he saw her. "Finally, we can start! Also, I'm famished. What do we have?"

"Well," said Xenia, "we have your contribution of...nothing, and Jack's moonshine. Cass and I have apples and rolls, so by the gods, Sam, tell me you brought actual food."

Sam held up her offerings—she'd splurged, buying groundnuts and soybeans as well as fried potato pieces. The roar of approval she received made her feel much better about the coin she had begrudgingly given over to the vendor. She made a mental note to thank Shale.

"Newbie comes through!" Hakuund was even louder than usual —Sam wondered how much they had already had to drink. *I may stand a better chance at winning tonight than I thought.*

They filled their plates and settled around the table. The three men had already started smoking.

"Ah." Hakuund let out a satisfied sigh. "Best thing to come out of the South."

"Straight smoke or hasha for the ladies?" Cassio asked, holding out the pre-rolled options. Sam really did not relish the idea of filling her lungs with carcinogens, however Ava had warned her that there were certain social situations when it was expected.

"Aren't people worried about lung cancer?" Sam had asked.

Ava had simply stared at her with exasperation.

"Oh right," Sam had said. "The pollution. Everyone already gets lung cancer."

Xenia opted for hasha, a blend of tobacco and cannabis, while Sam took a regular smoke. The last thing she needed was to relax and potentially become over-talkative.

The smoke tasted foul. *It's no worse than what you breathe in walking down the street every day.* Sam took a second drag and then twisted the end against her plate. She had noticed that it was common to consume a smoke slowly, extinguishing it after a drag and lighting it up again at a later point.

"It's because it's so goddamned expensive," Ava had told her. "Although why the jit poor people waste the bit of coin they have buying that poison is beyond me."

Sam had to agree. She picked up her apple, inspected it for rust and mould, and took a big bite, hoping to wash the taste of tobacco from her mouth. She noticed Jackal watching her. *Damn.* She had probably made a mistake—used the wrong fingers, held the smoke in for too long, or maybe not long enough.

"Five by five?" Cassio asked the group, starting to shuffle the cards. "Sam, you familiar?" She shook her head, relieved when no one commented.

"It's really simple. I'm going to give you two cards. Don't show them to anyone. Next, I'll cut the deck and flip over the top card. If one of your cards matches the one I flip over, your card is now null. Worthless. It's called a 'Kill Card', and I'll flip over three more of them. The fifth is different—this is an automatic trump. If one of your cards is the same as this fifth card, you win. On the off chance that one of the kills matches the trump, it stops being a kill card. Trump trumps it—get it? At the end, whoever has the highest card wins. And if two people have the same highest card, trump or not, it comes down to the suit: spades is highest, then hearts, followed by clubs, and lastly diamonds. We'll bet each time before I flip a card over." Xenia was passing out colourful plastic chips. They were old and faded, but they looked like they had been properly manufactured at one point. "For your xot, you get one hundred points in chips. The black ones are worth ten, the green five, and the blue one. Whoever wins all the chips at the end wins the five xots."

Sam nodded. Compared to the complex games she had learned growing up, this was extraordinarily simple. The betting, though, was new to her. Xenia and Hakuund often bet large amounts even if they had bad cards, in the hopes of scaring off the competition, whereas Cassio was more likely to pull out of a game at the start. Jackal was impossible to read. His betting style changed each round, and his face never gave the slightest hint as to what type of cards he held. Even when she had a strong hand, Sam felt reluctant to bet a large number of chips. She had known when she agreed to play that the night would be expensive—the cost of food and the cost of playing. She certainly did not expect to win her money back. Still, she had a hard time parting with those chips.

An hour later, only Sam, Xenia, and Jackal remained in the game. Sam glanced at her cards: she had a king of hearts and a three of spades. It was a risky hand—if the king showed up among the first four cards, she was left with nothing but a three, an almost certain loss. Trailing in third place with only ninety points in chips, one bad round could knock her right out of the game. Jackal had close to one hundred and fifty points and Xenia had the lion's share with well over two hundred; they could easily outbid her.

For the first round of betting they each contributed twenty points. Xenia, the dealer for the round, flipped over a jack of diamonds. Another twenty chips went into the pot from each of them, leaving Sam with only fifty. A nine of hearts was flipped over. *Two more to go.*

"All in," she said, sliding her meager remaining stock into the middle of the table. The next card flipped was a five of clubs. Jackal and Xenia raised the bet even higher among the two of them. Xenia flipped over the last of the Kill Cards: a king of diamonds. *Damn.* Sam tried to keep her face blank, although at this point it made no difference. She was out. Xenia raised the bet again—and Jackal went all in as well. She flipped the trump card: a three of hearts. Sam could feel her face starting to glow. She flipped her cards over.

"Are you kidding me?" Xenia brandished an ace of spades, the highest natural card. Sam tried not to grin as she pulled the chips toward herself. Jackal was already pushing the secondary pot toward Xenia.

"What did you have, Jack?" Xenia said to Sam. He smiled but said nothing, already shuffling his cards back into the deck. "Typical. Always have to be a bloody mystery, our Jack."

"Let's go all in, shall we?" Xenia said to Sam, as Jackal wandered over to join Hakuund and Cassio.

They pushed both piles of chips into the middle and Sam began to deal out the cards—face up this time. She gave herself two jacks, spades and hearts, and Xenia a queen as well as the jack of clubs. She turned over four kill cards—including the queen of hearts. Highly improbable though it was, the trump turned out to be the remaining jack. Sam, with the highest jack, was declared the winner, apparently validating some ridiculous cultural superstition entitled "beginner's luck". She slid one xot back to Xenia.

"Second place gets their buy-in back." Hakuund and Cassio booed her loudly from the corner where they'd been drinking steadily since they'd stopped playing cards.

"What kind of garbage is that?" Hakuund asked.

"She's messing with our system," said Cassio.

Xenia gave Sam a big grin. "I think it's lovely."

While Xenia settled down with the others, Sam wandered over to the stash of food, tore off a piece of bread, and took a small handful of groundnuts. *Delicious.* She wished they hadn't added so much salt, but then they always seemed to in the North. *Someone needs to explain to them the link between excess sodium and hypertension.*

"Oh gods, not again. This is your worst argument, darling," Xenia was telling her twin as Sam joined them.

"Just because it vexes you doesn't mean it's a bad argument, sister dear." Cassio had taken off the heavy silver ring he always wore and was rolling it between his thumb and forefinger.

"Why don't you walk up and offer yourself to them, then?" Xenia asked.

"Xen! Don't give him bad ideas," said Hakuund. He'd had so much to drink that he was starting to slur his words.

"I'm not talking about me, or us, or anyone that has a decent living," Cassio said. "But what about people who can't get work? Or who are sick? Are you telling me free meals, medicine, somewhere safe to sleep wouldn't be a step up?"

"It's not free," Jackal said, lighting up a second smoke. It smelled of tobacco, no trace of cannabis.

At least I'm not the only one who didn't take hasha.

"Well, yeah, your labour pays for it, but beyond what you get that day, it pays for the permanence. No worrying about the future, mate."

"Right." Xenia rolled her eyes. "Because when you're old and sick, they definitely keep paying for your rice and potatoes."

Her twin shrugged. "Ever met anyone they've kicked out for being old or sick? I haven't."

"Well, obviously not. A bunch of senile old domestics spreading their secrets? I'm sure your years of service are rewarded with a pat on the bum and a hemlock surprise."

"Hemlock?" Hakuund waved a large, meaty paw at her. "Girl, that's just wasteful. Compounds'll never just throw away an investment. There's always some profit to be had."

"Yeah, I dunno," said Cassio, frowning slightly as he eyed a cockroach, the empty moonshine bottle held aloft in one hand. "I think if it was that bad, there'd be breakouts, rebellions and all that." The cockroach ran forward toward Cassio, seemed to sense the danger, and switched directions.

"Maybe there have been, how would you know?"

"Yeah, man, there are a lot of guards with guns behind those bars. Think it's only to keep intruders out?" said Hakuund.

"And that's another example," Cassio said, trying and failing to crush the cockroach with the bottle. "Guards ain't domestics, they're born free like all of us, without some of our advantages, of course. They choose the compound. Of course, they get let out sometimes..."

Hakuund snorted and brought a heavy fist down on the cockroach. "For a couple of hours, maybe, when a vendor needs a spanking." He scraped the remains from the blade of his hand. "They don't have lives on the outside."

"Yeah, and they 'choose' it when it's the only way to pay off gambling debts or hide from some gang or other that wants 'em dead," said Xenia. "Or worse, they're recruited when they're, what, ten years old? Eleven? Is it even fair to ask a kid to commit their whole life to something?"

"Same age as kids are when gangs start recruiting 'em," said Hakuund.

"Hmm, I always forget that huaina were people once too," said Cassio, grabbing a handful of soybeans out of Hakuund's bowl.

"Well, they're so charming," said Xenia.

Cassio winked. "As delightful as old Fin." He tossed up a soybean and caught it in his mouth.

"So, Finlay..." Sam trailed off as four heads turned toward her. Based on their expressions, they had forgotten she was there. "He... It just seems that you weren't...close."

Hakuund let out a snort. "Close? Who in their right mind would want to get close to that jit?"

Well, Raina. Jackal was watching her, a closed expression on his face. She did her best to appear nonchalant.

Cassio took a long, deep puff of hasha. "He's just...he'd take a xot over a friend any day. You know the sort."

"Probably explains why he had so many," Xenia said, pulling a smoke out from behind her ear and twirling it in her long fingers before inhaling, slowly. Sam wondered if the twins realized how often they mirrored one another's actions. "Had a few huaina sniffing around for him here one night last year, decidedly unfriendly they were. The ones with the stupid-looking burn marks on their chests— skulls or whatnot. What do they call themselves again? Is it the 'Haunted'? Or, hang on, is it—"

"Wait...they were looking for him here?" Sam asked.

"We were, unfortunately, neighbours," drawled Cassio. "And they're called the 'Hunters'. Why would they be the 'Haunted'? Not threatening a name at all, sis."

"Do any of his friends live here still? Or family members?" asked Sam.

Cassio shrugged. "Only people I noticed him spending a lot of time with were girlfriends. He only lived here for a few years though."

"Girlfriends...other than Raina, you mean?" asked Sam.

"Well, yeah," said Cassio. "I mean, not at the same time, if that's what you're asking. One appeared, disappeared, new one appeared—"

"You know, I was pretty close," interrupted Xenia. "With that whole skull and death thing they have going on."

"Nope, not close," said her twin. "Even the 'Haunters' would have been better. The 'Haunted' sounds like the name of a troupe of musicians. Mournful ones. Lots of string instruments and no drums."

"How did you see the marks?" asked Hakuund. "Were they just walking around shirtless?"

Cassio chuckled. "Don't get too excited, lover, it was the solstice."

Hakuund put a hand to his chest in a display of indignation. "Over a bunch of huaina? Lowest of the low, kid, you couldn't pay me to touch one."

"They're rough, but they have it rough," said Xenia.

Cassio snuffed out his smoke. "That they do. Domestic life's a fair shot more comfortable, wouldn't you say?"

"Well now, that's the heart of it, ain't it? Cassio likes to be comfortable," Jackal said, gesturing to their posh surroundings with a rare grin.

"And Xen," said Cassio, but without much conviction.

"Oh yeah, this is all for me."

"Whatever." Her twin scowled at her. "You enjoy it."

"Well, of course I enjoy it, but it wasn't me that found and dragged all these beauties back. You're basically a dragon, roosting over your treasures."

"Yeah, well, you live here, little ladki, so lore says you're a big, greedy reptile by now too," Cassio said, tossing a soybean at her. She caught it in her mouth, eliciting big cheers from both her brother and Hakuund.

"Don't waste food, sib," she said with a grin, crunching away.

Sam didn't get home until close to dawn. Ava was already up baking the day's bread.

"Well, look at you!" Ava laughed upon seeing her tired face.

"What's—" Sam cleared her throat. The tobacco smoke had left her throat raw. *Foul stuff.* "What's a dragon?"

"A giant lizard with wings who hoards coin and jewels and breathes fire."

"Really?"

"Only in children's stories."

"Oh. Can I have a roll?"

Ava scowled but tossed her one before turning back to the oven. Surprised, Sam fumbled the catch, knocking the bun back into the air before she managed to snag it with her left hand. It was warm and soft, and only increased her desire to go to bed rather than head to the compound. She trudged up to her nest, where a sleepy ginger cat lay sprawled out on her bed.

"Well, you look rested," said Sam. He poked up his head and gave a strange cooing meow, not even bothering to open his eyes. "No, you sleep. One of us should."

Sam switched to her other shirt and spare pair of jeans. They weren't any cleaner, but at least they didn't reek of smoke. She hung the night's clothes on a nail, hoping they would air out a bit. It wasn't raining yet, so she pulled herself out through the ceiling panel and up onto the roof.

Along with Ava's buckets, Sam kept a small washbasin on the roof. She shivered as she splashed icy water on her face. Patting herself dry with a rag, she eyed the thick rain clouds overhead. Though the sky was brightening by the minute, it was going to be a dark day.

It was odd to think that a year ago it would have been Raina, climbing from the metal lift onto the roof to fetch water. *Did Raina call it a nest too? Probably not.*

Ugly black smoke pumped into the cold morning air. Someone must have set fire to one of the nearby trash heaps.

It surprised her that Raina had chosen a partner as decidedly unpopular as Finlay. *Why be with him, if he's such a bad guy? And was it a coincidence, huaina looking for Finlay the night he and Raina disappeared, or was he involved in something dangerous?*

She could smell the putrid odour of burning plastic now. *So much for clean rainwater.* She'd thought they were above the contamination of the city here, but clearly the roof of the factory wasn't high enough.

She tried to picture them: Finlay and Raina. She knew Raina was tall and thin with dark skin—but beyond that the image was hazy and confused, Ava's face and then Sam's flittering in and out by turn.

And Finlay. She couldn't bring a man to mind, only yellow eyes and a long, hairy snout. A smile and lies. *Her lover or the wolf?* Sam pressed a thumb into her temple. She couldn't seem to stop her brain from working the problem.

The smell was becoming unbearable. She pulled the collar of her shirt up over her mouth and nose and headed back inside. *Okay then. There's only one logical thing to do.*

12

The North

SAM RUSHED home from work the next evening. If she hurried, she could fetch the bucket of rainwater and get to Ava's shop before the dinner rush. Shale always came by Ava's for dinner, though timing varied greatly one day to another. As long as Sam got there early enough, she would be guaranteed to see her at some point that evening.

A small crowd of people huddled around the entrance to Ava's shop, mostly children with the exception of one slim redhead. *Well, that is convenient.* The commotion, she realized once she got closer, was being caused by the large, orange cat. He was lying on his back in front of Shale, enjoying a vigorous tummy rub. Sam had had no idea that cats liked being petted on the stomach. She was actually surprised he was allowing it—it seemed an undignified sort of business.

"Not mine," Ava was saying, "hers."

"I love him!" a little girl roared at Sam. "What's his name?"

Sam stared back blankly. *A name? You were supposed to name a cat?*

She thought quickly. She should pick a very standard, conventional Northern name.

"Frank." She saw Ava grimace out of the corner of her eye.

"Frank?" Shale asked, looking at her with a puzzled expression. "The cat is named Frank?"

"Yes," said Sam. "Frank, the cat."

Shale gave a shrug and resumed petting the cat, who had been gently bopping her with a large, velvety paw since she had stopped. "Okay. I would have thought Pumpkin, or Peaches or something, but I guess Frank is a good name."

Sam mentally kicked herself. *Of course cats don't have people names. Why did I think that they would have people names?*

"Frank the cat! Frank the cat!" The little girl was shouting.

"He's so fat! I love him!" said a boy who looked to be her brother.

Well, there is no going back now. The cat was, and would always be, Frank.

"It's good for Ava, having something soft and cuddly around," Shale said to Sam, squeezing her hand. "She's been a bit more like her old self of late." One more squeeze, and Shale turned to leave.

"Um, actually, I was going to ask you..."

Shale turned, ginger eyebrows arched, full lips curved into her usual half-smile.

"Have you already eaten?" Sam asked. *Stupid question. Obviously she has, or she wouldn't be leaving.*

Shale nodded slowly. Though she continued smiling, the expression seemed forced. An odd look flashed in her eyes.

She's used to people wanting things from her. "I just wanted to ask you a question," Sam said. She glanced over at Ava. Her friend was busy serving the queue of customers that had formed.

Shale crossed her arms, watching Sam expectantly.

"Um, I was wondering if you could tell me about Finlay."

"Finlay?" Shale asked, none of the usual sultry notes in her voice. Sam realized that her question must have caught Shale by surprise. "What on earth do you want to know about Finlay?"

Sam flicked her tongue against her lower teeth, deliberating over her next move. She didn't know Shale very well. *Does anyone know*

Shale very well? The woman was smart, though, and she had known Raina since Raina was a babe. *Is she trustworthy? Perhaps not. But she is clearly attached to Ava.* "You know Ava thinks Raina is dead."

Shale shrugged her petite shoulders. "Yeah, but Ava always expects the worst," she said with an airy toss of her red hair.

"Do you think she's wrong?"

The flippant expression faded from Shale's face. She stared at Sam for a moment, and then her eyes glazed over in a visible shift from outward to inner focus. Whatever she was thinking or remembering, Sam was not privy to. Finally, Shale shook her head. "No. She talks a lot of shint but her instincts are good. So what, though? You planning to track down Raina's killer?"

Sam started. "Uh, just keeping my eyes open," she said, trying not to sound as disconcerted as she felt by Shale's choice of words. *Why does she assume Raina was killed?*

"No, you're asking questions."

"Should I not be?" asked Sam.

"As a rule?" Shale flashed her a crooked smile. "No. But me, you can ask me all you like, honey. I'm very friendly."

"So...you think someone killed her?" asked Sam.

"Well, she wasn't sick, now was she? Or with child. Least as far as I know. And no body turned up, and we did look. Which means that someone killed her on purpose or killed her by accident and hid the body."

"Or she left."

"Or she left." Shale nodded. Her eyes drifted toward the exit, and Sam got the feeling that she had limited time left to get the information she needed. "Course, it's the Barrow, and Raina was young and pretty. Very pretty—did anyone tell you?" Shale's smile was bitter this time. "Lots of nasties in the Barrow target the young and the pretty."

"And Finlay?" asked Sam. "Did he 'target' Raina?"

Shale ran a hand through her wavy tresses and sighed. "Finlay was a creep. Anyone could tell you that. I never got why Raina liked him, but she did. And he seemed to like her. But I did wonder...Raina..."

Shale stopped and for a moment Sam thought that she wasn't going to continue.

"Yes?" asked Sam.

"It's just something Raina said once, something about another of Finlay's ex-girlfriends having disappeared."

"What do you mean, disappeared?"

"I don't know. Raina said it off-hand, a joke about how she didn't have to worry about him going back to his ex because she was gone. I didn't think anything of it at the time, but when Raina went missing I thought maybe Finlay...but then he disappeared, too, so it's probably nothing."

"Right, of course," said Sam, though her mind was already whirring.

"I didn't tell Ava that bit. Didn't think she needed more to worry about."

"Okay, I—"

Shale took one of Sam's hands. "I still don't think that's something she needs to know."

Sam looked into Shale's large brown eyes. "I understand."

Shale nodded and let go of Sam's hand.

"Do you know where I can find any of their friends?" asked Sam.

"Raina's friends? Well, there's Megan and Isla: you know them, those two sisters that never stop talking? They live just there." She gestured toward the far corner of the factory. "But Finlay? I never met any of his friends." She paused. "If he even had any."

Sam nodded, trying not to show her disappointment. Shale gave an apologetic shrug and turned to leave.

"Oh, wait!" Sam remembered, calling after her. "The Hunters—those huaina with the skulls on their chests—do you know where I can find them?"

13

The North

THE DREAM BEGAN the same way: his body cold on the bed; then the hallway, and Raina disappearing around a corner, Sam in pursuit. This time, though, the chase continued: down one hallway and then another; down a flight of stairs, then a ladder; down, down to a city below the city. It was a perfect replica of the Barrow on a moonless night. Unless you looked closely you might not even notice that you walked beneath a ceiling of dirt and tree roots instead of the night sky.

Raina stood at the window of a small house, peering inside. She looked back to where Sam was standing and waved her forward. "See?"

When Sam got close, she realized that Raina was looking at her own reflection.

Not her reflection. There's no glass in the Barrow.

It was another Raina. She was standing inside the room, looking outward. Behind her were three other girls, all young, all pretty. They were setting a table for a meal.

"Look again," said the Raina outside the house.

That was when Sam noticed the strings. Fishing line, actually, pulling the girls upright like marionettes: arms, chins, eyelids, even the corners of their lips. She looked down to their feet: heavy chains anchored them to the floor.

Just then the cold steel of a crossbow bolt pressed against the back of Sam's head. And she woke up.

The dream had stuck with her while she changed her clothes and left the factory. *Look again,* Raina had said. The words echoed in her ears while she walked through the city streets and the trails to the compound. The world felt over-bright and distant, as though her dream was refusing to give her up.

When she reached the compound she crouched down, her back against the fence, and closed her eyes.

Smell the grass. Touch the fence. Hear the crows.

The silence helped. She snuck a peek at Jackal, leaning against the fence, eyes closed.

Smell the grass. Touch the fence. Look at the scarecrow.

By the time Hakuund and the twins arrived, the last dregs of her dream had faded.

"It's not that hard. It's really just about your posture," Xenia said, demonstrating the headstand a second time.

"Upside down posture," said Hakuund.

"Well, yes. Also, if you start to fall, don't flail about trying to over-correct."

One eyebrow raised, Hakuund turned to Cassio. "How long can she do this?"

"Gods, I don't know. An hour, maybe? One time she tried to read a book like this. She kept calling me over to turn the pages for her."

"It makes you smarter, see, all that blood rushing to your head," said Xenia.

"Ain't your hands cold?" asked Hakuund.

"Oh, it's nothing. Hey you." Xenia grinned, her eyes on Sam. "C'mon, ladki, give it a try!"

Sam was saved by the sound of the compound gate opening. Benison appeared in time to catch sight of Xenia's long legs flailing as she rushed to flip back over. He walked down the causeway to them, his scowl even deeper than usual. It seemed he did not hold with acrobatics on compound grounds. Not that Sam had reason to believe that he might approve of them off of compound grounds, either.

He cleared his throat and glowered at the five of them. As if on cue, the rain started to fall. Sam pulled her hood up over her head and pushed her hair back, tucking it into her shirt.

Without looking up, Benison moved ever so slightly to the left so that he stood underneath the small awning. He then turned his attention to Hakuund, whom he beckoned closer. They spoke in low tones for a few minutes while the others waited. Xenia especially seemed to be having a difficult time standing still. Sam noticed her starting to sway, lips moving subtly to some song only she could hear.

Benison beckoned for Jackal to approach next. Sam stared at Xenia's white-blond locks, watching the beads of rain collect. Though she, too, wore a hood, the other girl never bothered to tie her hair back or tuck it in when it rained. *Is it odd, that I do this? Is this Seiran fastidiousness, another tell?* The rain escalated into a downpour, and the individual drops disappeared.

Benison cleared his throat again, though this time he addressed the lot of them. "In addition to your tasks today, there will be a group mission tonight." He grimaced, as though even the thought of collaboration pained him. "You will meet here a half hour to midnight to receive instructions and equipment from Jackal, who will be the lead. In light of today's double mission, you will," and here his face twisted into the deepest scowl Sam had witnessed from him yet, "be permitted to take tomorrow off. Now, line up for the day's assignments. You're already late."

If anyone had thought the day's workload might be light, allowing for the drudges to rest before the night's mysterious task, they were sorely mistaken. Sam's list that morning consisted of three different stops in three different corners of the Barrow. None of them, unfortunately, were located anywhere near the Pike.

Not that Sam would have had time to track down and question a Hunter between missions, especially as "near the Pike" was as much information as Shale had been able to give her. *Well, that and a lot of reasons why meeting with a Hunter is a stupid and dangerous idea.* Sam waved the warning away. She could take care of herself.

In truth, though, she didn't know how she would identify a Hunter when she got to the Pike. *Perhaps a climatically improbable heat wave will descend upon the Barrow, prompting shirtless frolicking through the streets? Or I could simply ask men at random: "You! Stranger! Will you please disrobe?"*

At least she knew to look for male huaina. The Hunters, like most gangs, permitted only members from a single sex.

"All boys," Shale had told her. "And mean. You gotta go through someone, a contact, and still answers'll cost you, even if it's not information they care to keep secret. And even if you do pay, they...well... If I were you, I'd find another way to track down Raina and Finlay."

It was a risk, Sam knew. The safest bet would be to start by speaking with Raina's friends: the sisters. *If they know something you might not even need these huaina.* Sam had found their sleeping quarters the previous night—a makeshift tent that was small, musty, and at the time had been empty. It was reasonable to think that as Raina's peers they would have information that Shale and Ava did not. *About Finlay's missing ex-girlfriend, for example?*

From what Ava had told her about the solstice, it wasn't statistically impossible for two of Finlay's girlfriends to have gone missing. What if there were others, though? Cassio had said that Finlay had had a steady stream of girlfriends. After her conversation with Shale, Sam had been unable to suppress a horrible image of Finlay hiding out in some bunker with a harem of female prisoners. *Which means that they're still alive. Otherwise the wolf would have emerged to look for new prey.*

It was a fourth scenario and one that Sam hadn't originally thought of. The idea of Raina, not killed and buried in the Barrow, not free somewhere in the intangible west or dead in the pursuit of a new life, but trapped somewhere in the city, suffering daily, needing help... It gave Sam a panicked feeling, and panic was a useless emotion; it left her scattered, as though she were about to fly off in a million directions at once. What she needed was logical, concrete action. *Just follow the leads. Leads are clues, and if Raina is still alive some-*

where in the Barrow the clues will lead me to her. She could start that evening by speaking with Raina's friends. *Assuming they're home this time.* She just had to get through the day.

It took Sam nearly two hours to reach the first destination by bicycle. She could have made it in half that time if the streets between the two points hadn't been flooded beyond use. Sometimes it felt to Sam as though the Barrow was nothing but a giant obstacle course, a maze where every wrong turn ended in an overflow of greasy, polluted water.

The building reminded her of the Vaun compound, though it lacked the compound's scale and grandeur. She supposed the similarity lay in the fact that it was fenced in and patrolled by men with crossbows.

Benison had given her a password, a dozen numbers and letters she was expected to repeat in a specific order. He had made her repeat it several times before leaving, ripping the code off the bottom of her scroll and tearing it into tiny pieces once she had the code memorized. "Don't get it wrong," he'd said.

She approached what looked to be the front entrance. One guard took her bike away while another proceeded to search her. She looked away as his hands passed down the front of her soaking wet shirt, then up one leg and down the other. When he gestured her forward she saw that another man had approached the gate.

"Password."

Sam rattled off the alphanumeric code, as though afraid her recall might fail if she delayed a minute longer. Fortunately, he nodded and the gate swung open.

The man ushered her through a side door. Sam stepped into an ornate room, her eyes moving immediately to the ceiling. It had been painted in the style of old churches. There were birds flitting past waterfalls and deer nibbling at fruit trees. Lovers embraced as children with wings—cherubs, she thought they were called—bobbed in the air above them. Whereas the paintings in the book had been beautiful, though, this was garish. The people were crudely drawn in jarring colours with thick, uneven lines.

"Beautiful, isn't it?" A woman in a tight pink dress beamed at

Sam. A black apron with deep pockets was tied around her waist. Sam tried to smile while breathing heat into her frozen hands. She felt suddenly very aware of her clothes, plain at the best of times and now stretched out from the rainwater, and the hair that was clinging to her face in wet clumps.

"We had a whole troupe of artists in, they got it done in just a week. This one madman gave us the idea—of course he wanted us to hire him alone and give him half a year to complete it. Many hands make for quick work, though. That has always been my philosophy. Now, what can I get for you?"

These codes had been much easier to memorize. "An R80 and a V70," she said. As usual, she had no idea what type of product she was requesting, only that they were expensive, as per the heavy bag of coins tucked securely into her jacket.

The woman's eyes opened wide. "Ooh, yes, of course! But we were expecting... No matter. We'll have it ready in a flash."

The woman sashayed over to the side of the room where a group of young teenage girls were waiting. She gave instructions to one of the girls, who scurried out of the room, and then turned back to Sam.

"Shall we take care of the boring details?" Seeing Sam's confusion, the woman clarified: "Payment, dear."

Sam pulled a bag of coins out of an inner pocket and handed it to the woman. Without glancing at its contents, the woman dangled the bag behind her back. One of the girls stepped forward, took the bag, and proceeded to count the coins.

"I had assumed the other girl would be back—but of course, it's not for us to question how the Vauns operate. You'll see her, though, yes? I have a little something for her."

"Something for...for Xenia?"

The woman frowned. "No, it was a different name. River? Forest? I can't remember. Pretty girl with dark skin and long hair."

"Raina?" asked Sam, her heart thudding. "It's a gift for Raina?"

"Ah, yes, Raina. We don't deal in gifts, though, dear." The woman winked at Sam. "She ordered it last time she was here. It arrived months ago, actually."

"Oh," said Sam. "But she's...I mean, she's not...with the Vauns anymore. But here, I can..." Sam slid a hand into her jacket pocket, looking for the small stash of personal coin she carried. "How much is it?"

The woman chuckled. "Oh, we don't deal in promises either. She paid already, of course. Oh, thanks, dear." The first girl had returned, clutching a large basket in her skinny arms.

Raina prepaid...and then skipped town? Now that seems unlikely. "When did she make the order?" Sam asked the woman, who was pulling items out of the basket and laying them on a table: a large plate with squares of different coloured powder, several jars filled with liquid, and a thin black tube. From a table drawer she pulled out a few sheets of purple paper and proceeded to wrap the items, all except the black tube.

"Hmm...April or May last year? She did know that it would take a few months," she said, as though Sam might accuse her of having dallied on the order.

Sam watched distractedly as the woman pulled a small glass vial from her apron and shook a few drops onto the paper before sliding the packages into a sheath of plastic. A flowery scent wafted over.

"Here." The woman pressed the small black tube into Sam's hand. "Bring it to her, will you? Lovely. Now," she said, without giving Sam a chance to reply, "I think you deserve a little bonus, something for you." She took a step closer, studying Sam's face. Moving even closer, she pulled a long, thin object out of her apron and poked it toward one of Sam's eyes.

Sam jumped backward, her hands flying up to guard her face. The woman giggled. "It won't hurt you, darling." Sam looked down at the object. *Right. Just a brush. A makeup brush.* It looked different than the products Sam had seen and used in Seira: different, but properly manufactured, not homemade.

Feeling embarrassed, Sam closed her eyes. The woman drew a wet line across each of her eyelids, close to her lash line.

"Keep your eyes closed for another few seconds," she said.

Sam could hear one of the girls whispering to the woman, assumedly confirming that payment was sufficient.

"There, that should do it. Why don't you take a look at yourself?"

The woman snapped her fingers and a girl appeared with a large, gilded hand mirror. She offered it to Sam, who lifted it hesitantly to her face.

When was the last time I looked in a mirror?

Dark hair, small features, light brown skin: she looked exactly as she remembered. A little mangier, perhaps, but otherwise unchanged. *What, you thought five months of living in the Barrow would transform you into someone else?*

The woman coughed gently and Sam's eyes snapped to the black line drawn thickly across her eyelids. The eyeliner did not seem to be of very high quality, though it was certainly better than the home-made kohl that was popular in the Barrow. She wondered whether it would even last the night.

Sam forced a smile and passed back the mirror. The woman beamed at her.

"Oh, well, we just want to give everyone an experience, you know? It's part of my philosophy too." She handed Sam the package and gave her a wet kiss on the cheek.

Only when the door shut behind her did Sam lift the tube up to her face for a closer inspection. It looked similar to the product the woman had just smeared onto Sam's eyelids. Such a small, unimportant item; yet it must have cost Raina a xot, if not more. It was possible that Raina had simply forgotten about the order. *Or maybe this is evidence, tangible evidence, that Raina didn't just leave. Which means that, dead or alive, she's still in the Barrow.*

Back in the yard, a guard returned her bicycle. Sam had expected she would be searched a second time, but nobody stopped her as she wheeled her bicycle out of the gated area and back into the rain.

14

The North

SAM DIDN'T GET BACK to the factory until late that evening. Though her stomach was growling, she did not go immediately to Ava's shop. Instead she picked her way toward the far corner where the two sisters lived. She was in luck this time: candlelight flickered from behind the thin, cloth walls and she could hear two voices. They seemed to be arguing.

Sam raised her hand as though to knock, remembered that the entire place was made of fabric, and called out instead: "Hello?"

The voices stopped. A section of the curtain was yanked back and a dark, frizzy head poked out. "What?"

The girl, who was certainly Megan or Isla, though Sam wasn't sure which, squinted at Sam. "I know you. You're Ava's.... uh..."

"Friend?" said Sam at the same time that the girl suggested: "Helper?"

Both were correct, though neither was quite right, Sam realized. A second frizzy head popped out. "Oh. You. What do you want?"

The sisters, though not twins, looked very similar. They shared not only the same hair but also the same inky black eyes, both pairs of which were staring piercingly at Sam.

"Um, I..."

The first sister rolled her eyes. "Spit it out girl, we've—"

"Got places to be," said the second sister.

"I wanted to ask you about Raina."

"Raina?" asked the second sister. "Why? Is she back?"

"Er, no. I, uh...actually, I am trying to find her... Do you happen to know anything about where she went or who she saw the night she left?"

The two sisters stared as Sam as though she had sprouted antlers.

"It was the night of the last summer solstice," Sam said.

"You want to find—"

"Raina? Good luck, I mean, I don't even know where—"

"Would you even start?"

Sam wondered if the sisters always hijacked one another's sentences. The effect was rather dizzying; she couldn't seem to keep track of which of the girls had said what.

"So," she tried again. "Did you see Raina the night—"

"Of the solstice? Ladki, we ain't see her for—"

"Weeks before—"

"Months even."

"Months? Maybe a month...or maybe it was months, I think—"

"Last time was maybe that night—"

"At the Hive, not that she stuck around, took off with Finlay like—"

"Even then, it's been years since we really—"

"Not years...a year maybe."

"At least since Finlay, and then she got that compound job, never had time, did she?"

"Not that we ever—"

"Good for a laugh, right, but otherwise?"

"So," said Sam, determined to pull facts from the fragmented phrases she was hearing. "You used to be friends with Raina, but hadn't seen much of her since she started seeing Finlay? And you had no contact with her in the weeks before she disappeared?"

"Yeah, pretty much."

"Not that we were ever—"

"I mean friendly, maybe, wouldn't necessarily say friends, though—"

"We went out together, but couldn't exactly count on her, could you?"

"Is there anyone she did spend time with before she left?" Sam asked. "Besides Finlay?"

"Well, she talked to everyone, I mean, go out with the girl, and you'd see—"

"But didn't *talk*, you know, just blah blah, chit chat. If you're asking if she had—"

"Other friends? Nah. We're probably the closest thing."

"I see," said Sam, her heart sinking. "Well, do you know any of Finlay's friends, maybe, that I could talk to?"

The sisters shook their heads in unison.

"Not exactly our favourite—"

"Sleazy guy, didn't know much about him."

"Kinda a good riddance situation, y'know?"

Sam nodded, and thanked the two girls before extricating herself from the conversation. As she made her way toward Ava's she could not help but feel disappointed. It wasn't just that the sisters had been unable to help—what was bothering Sam the most was their apparent lack of interest in Raina's welfare. "Northerners won't give yesterday's trash to a stranger, but they'll leap into the flames for their own," Ava had told her once. The sisters were clearly an exception.

Ava greeted her with raised eyebrows. "Long day."

"It's about to get longer," Sam said, plopping down in her usual spot. "We have a night task."

A soft, orange ringtail flicked against her knee. "Hi Frank," she said. He meowed loudly and rubbed his face against her left boot.

"What, you peddling dust now?" asked Ava.

Sam started to roll her eyes and then stopped. Benison had given them no information on the evening's mission—for all she knew, he would be asking her to sell dust. She was not even sure how she would respond if he did. At the end of the day, jobs were scarce, and almost none paid a fraction so well as the compounds did.

Ava didn't press the matter, thanks to a steady stream of customers demanding her attention. Sam ate her boil in silence, watching Frank. He had turned away from her and was busy grooming himself. From this angle his backside made a perfect circle.

"You look like a ball," she said. He stopped for a moment to stare insolently at her, and then returned to his grooming. She had to admit that it was nice to have someone waiting for her when she got home at night, especially someone who didn't care in the slightest where she came from or who she worked for. *Easy companionship: always a rarity.*

15

The North

"Okay, it's time," Ava was saying, shaking her awake an hour later. Sam rolled over and nearly squished something furry, eliciting an indignant "Meow!"

"Sorry, Frank. Hey, you let him sleep in your room?"

Ava ignored the question and tossed Sam her jacket.

"Thanks." Sam rolled out of Raina's old bed and put on her boots and jacket. She gave the cat a pat on the head and made her way out of the factory. She had hoped the nap would energize her, but so far she just felt groggy and confused. *Am I forgetting something?*

The wind had started up again, grinding the cold down into her bones. At least the rain had stopped.

A torch; I should have brought a torch. The wooden path was darker than the city streets. She squinted at the dirt in front of her, trying to remember where she usually skirted pits and exposed roots.

She was the last to arrive.

"Okay." Jackal started speaking as soon as she reached them. "We're going into the Dens. Hakuund is meeting with someone. Our job is security. Discreet security—this is supposed to be friendly, so Hakuund's going in alone. We'll post up nearby but out of sight, in case it goes sour. Questions?"

Sam had several questions, in fact, but she kept her lips closed and nodded with the rest of the group. She had heard of the Dens— nothing detailed, but also nothing good. From what she knew, it was a hot spot for gang activity and featured some high stakes gambling.

"Do we get toys?" asked Xenia. Jackal reached into a large bag and pulled out a crossbow. Xenia's eyes brightened.

"For me? Darling, you shouldn't have." She took the crossbow and a few bolts, humming happily to herself.

Jackal passed a pair of hatchets to Hakuund, a second crossbow to Cassio, and pulled out a longbow for himself.

He looked at Sam next. "How are you with knives?"

"I would find them to be helpful, yes," she said.

"Good." The knives he gave Sam were beautifully crafted, with perfect balance. They had also already been sharpened.

"We are expected to return these at the end of the night," Jackal said, looking at Sam. "So if you're gonna throw something, make sure you can retrieve it."

Sam had always found it interesting to observe how people behaved in the moments leading up to a test or a trial. The twins chattered nonstop about trivialities, while Hakuund was distracted and withdrawn, a stark contrast from his usual loud exuberance. Jackal's demeanor was unchanged; he broke his habitual silence only to indicate a meeting point, a small clearing about ten feet from a fork in the wooden path where they would reconvene if they became separated.

"Well, that's stupid then," Cassio was saying to Xenia. "Why would she think that mattered?"

"I didn't say she said it mattered, I just said that she thought that he…"

Sam tuned out the twins, focusing on the task at hand. The other three had ranged weapons; her knives, though, would only be useful if she was close to the action. *Will the room be crowded? Will there be many non-implicated bystanders? Do they know we're coming? Are we recognizable targets?* She looked at her team. Though he was quiet, nobody would dismiss Jackal. Skinny he may be, but he looked strong; he looked like a fighter. If she were working as a guard, she would take note of him. The twins, tall, beautiful, and electric, could not have attracted more attention if musicians heralded them into every room. Hakuund, always the loudest, always the most energetic, was not a man that you could meet and then forget. In short, the group was about as inconspicuous as a troupe of players dressed in motley. *Except for me.* She quickened her pace to match step with Jackal.

"I was thinking, since nobody knows me here, would it make sense for me to stay closer to—"

Jackal was already nodding. "Drop back and enter after us. Get as close to Hakuund as you can. We'll be posted up on opposite sides, wherever we can find a vantage point."

They continued in silence, though Sam could feel Jackal watching her out of the corner of his eye. *With suspicion or approbation?* She had such a hard time reading him.

Their destination turned out to be a big warehouse set in the middle of a bare earthen field ringed by forest on all sides.

As her teammates stepped out from the cover of the trees, Sam fell back. A group of women soon appeared, too busy talking amongst themselves to notice the slight, dark-haired girl following behind them.

Near the entrance, several men and women had positioned themselves atop plastic crates. One of them was shouting down to the crowd. Something was wrong with their faces, but Sam was too far away to see details.

"The fires to the west burn! Burn without stopping! They are coming for us, like the rains came for us! Don't make the mistakes of our forebears—Give her what she wants! Purity in strength! Give us the sick, give us the crippled, give us the lame and the deaf and the dumb! They are an affront to her greatness. We will spill their blood and she will rejoice and forgive us our sins! The rains will slow, the fires will die out, and seas will roll back." It was blood on the preacher's face, Sam realized, down his cheeks and around his eyes. "Let us bleed them! Let us bleed them! Let us bleed them!" The man's followers, all similarly lined with blood, were chanting along with him.

No one else in the crowd was taking note of the cult. Sam looked straight ahead, trying to act as though she'd heard all this insanity before.

Two large men were flanking the doorway. They had metal wires woven through their earlobes and the hair on one side of their heads had been shaved off. Their eyes scanned the crowd, categorizing each person as they entered: by tattoos and gang insignia, by size, by visible weapons, by level of threat.

They gave Sam the barest cursory glance and gestured her toward a third man who was taking payment. She tossed the man a sack and pushed her way inside.

She'd been expecting a multitude of small gambling rooms. What she found was a stadium, with three floors overlooking a central arena. While the main floor was packed with people pushing and jostling, she could see that the upper floors held seats. There were even attendants circling with food and drink.

Sam sifted through the press of bodies, squeezing between an old man and a young girl with comprehensive neck tattoos, to peer over the ledge at the flat, muddy field below. Dark reddish-brown stains coated the arena walls. She shuddered. Hopefully she would be gone before whatever contest was to take place got underway.

It didn't take her long to spot Xenia's white-blond head on the other side of the pit. She was leaning on the railing, her eyes fixed on the north side of the room. Sam followed her eye line, squinting in the semi-darkness until she found it: torchlight glittering off the axes strapped to Hakuund's back.

Sam turned away from the pit and began making her way over to him. Being small had its advantages: for one, she was good at weaving through crowds. It also had its disadvantages, such as elbows swinging unintentionally at her face.

She reached the north end a few bruises the richer but otherwise unscathed. In case someone was watching, she cheated her face and body toward the pit, all the while keeping Hakuund in her peripheral vision. He was leaning against a pole about ten feet to her right, his arms crossed in front of his massive chest. His eyes glanced lazily over the crowd, seemingly disinterested. There was a raised platform just past him, equipped with a barrier to keep unwanted persons from approaching. Four huaina were sitting inside, a few jugs of liquor on the table beside them. *Is this where the meeting will take place?*

"Wagers! Wagers are open! Five to one against the Hand! Don't be a jit, leave here rich!" A group of children, maybe ten to twelve years old, were waving tickets and jingling boxes of coins. Their heads were shaved on one side, matching the men who had been controlling the entrance. The piercings in their ears looked fresh, and a few were showing signs of infection. Someone pushed in front of Sam, making their way toward the children. She reached out to grab the ledge for support and found herself pushed forward a second time. *Oh, well, may as well swim with the current.* She would watch Hakuund just as easily from his right side as his left.

She drifted forward, slipping past the bookies...and found herself facing an onslaught of people coming from the opposite direction. *I clearly didn't think this through.* A beast of a man came roaring toward her, lifting one hand above the horde to flash some kind of note. His T-shirt, cut so widely around the armholes that it barely counted as a shirt at all, swung to the side, giving Sam a glimpse of his bare and branded chest. The image was crude and the proportions wrong: the skull stared vacantly at her, twisted and misshapen.

Sam ducked her head and brought her forearms up, protecting her face against the man's flailing tree trunk of an arm. If he had noticed that someone hovered at elbow level, he gave no sign. After a quick and loud discussion with one of the bookies, he turned around and strode back the way he had come. She spared a glance at Hakuund. He hadn't moved. Sam hesitated, but only for a moment. *I won't go far.*

She dove through the space that his departure had opened up, and soon found herself somehow, miraculously, outside the madness. The man came to a sudden, abrupt halt, forcing Sam to swerve to the left of him. He had stopped, she saw, because they had reached the ledge. Bringing her arms to rest on the railing, she stared down at the pit, no clear idea of how to broach the topic of Finlay with this stranger. She had been so focused on finding a Hunter that she had never actually considered what she would say when she did track one down.

The pit was no longer empty. A group of women and men were rolling a massive barrel into the center of the arena.

"I, uh, was wondering—" Sam said, turning to face the man, only to break off when she realized that he was locked in conversation with someone else, someone hidden by his hulking frame. She quickly turned her gaze back to the scene below.

"No Jayce?" a man asked, mock surprise in his voice. "What, Axel didn't trust him after last month?"

Down in the pit, the women and men flipped the barrel upright and dashed from the arena.

"Jayce is an idiot." The rasping bark belonged to the huge man she had followed: the Hunter.

"See you bring this straight to him," the first voice said. "I'll be watching you. Go anywhere near a bookie and I'll—"

The big man growled something under his breath, too quickly for Sam to hear, and stormed off.

Someone slammed into Sam's left shoulder, pushing her straight into the man's companion.

"Hello," he said, smiling at her as though they were old friends. It was the man from the Hive, the man that Shale had warned her to stay away from. He had shaved both sides of his head since she had seen him last, though the line of blond hair at the top was still slicked back with oil. His eyes were dark brown, almost black. Sam felt her cheeks redden.

"Hi," she said, and looked back to the arena. *Did he notice me eavesdropping?*

"What's your wager?" he asked. Despite her best efforts, she found herself turning back to look at him again.

"I, uh, haven't decided yet."

"Well, you better hurry," he said. "Bets'll be closing soon." He continued smiling at her. "Have I met you before?"

Sam shook her head mutely. His voice had become soft, caressing. *Is he flirting with me?* He had a sort of sloppy sensuality about him.

She was not actually certain it was being directed at her—she might have simply stumbled into the spill zone.

"I'm Maddox," he said, holding out a large, callused hand.

"I..." *Oh gods, where is Hakuund?* "Have to go. Place bets. Like you said." Sam spun around and began pushing her way back toward Hakuund. *What was I thinking? How much time has passed?*

With relief, she spotted Hakuund's huge, dark frame, a head above the crowd. A huaina approached him. Though not one of the men who had been at the door when Sam arrived, with his half-shaven head and wire ear adornment he clearly belonged to the same gang.

Hakuund followed the man, stopping automatically in front of the platform. Sam followed, an eye on Hakuund, while angling herself toward the pit as though looking for a better vantage point.

What kind of dealings does Maddox have with the Hunters? She spun out of the way of a troop of female barkeeps with heavy makeup and matching black T-shirts, narrowly avoiding crashing into a particularly angry-looking girl with a tray full of empty mugs balanced in her arms.

Sam managed to stabilize the tray with one hand, catching a large steel bottle with the other. The girl grabbed the tray back with both hands, glared at Sam, and strode off. Sam wheeled around in time to see Hakuund disappear up a back staircase.

"Damn."

The sight of three huaina standing guard at the bottom of the staircase told Sam that the upper floors were off-limits to the average viewer; either that or admission was expensive. Since Sam had neither an invitation nor the inclination to hand over her well-earned xots, she was going to have to sneak through. She needed a diversion. Considering the chaos that already surrounded them, she would need something big. She looked down suddenly at the steel bottle still clutched in her hand. *Well, that's a terrible idea.*

Sam ducked behind the pole that Hakuund had been leaning against earlier. She pulled off and stashed her jacket, wondering if it was naive to think that it might still be here when she returned. It would be a cold walk home without it. She plucked a few cat hairs off the black shirt she was wearing underneath and ran a hand through her hair. She was suddenly very glad that she had been too tired earlier to wash off the cheap eyeliner.

With a deep breath, she picked up the jug, and stepped out from behind the pole. *Walk as though you have no fear of being stopped.*

She tossed her head back and adopted what she hoped was a look of mild irritation and boredom. The three men were chuckling together as she approached, watching but not challenging or denying her entry. In fact, they did not speak to her at all, nor acknowledge her presence with so much as a wave or a nod. They simply stared at her as she passed them and started up the stairs. She felt lucky. She felt like an animal on display. She felt like kicking all three of them in their stupid faces.

The stairway ended at the second floor. High, round tables dotted what seemed to be a gambler's lounge. At the center of each table candles floated in bowls of water, casting a low, flickering glow. Attractive young barkeeps passed with food and drink while patrons milled around the tables, talking, laughing, consuming. Others circled with coin boxes and tickets. *No sack up here.* They, too, were dressed in black, though red flashed from ribbons tied around arms or woven through hair.

Chairs had been set up in front of the ledge in two rows, the second row raised up on thick boards to ensure that all guests were able to enjoy an unobstructed view of the night's spectacle.

It was busy, but not crowded. Sam ducked down and left the empty jug under a table. She knew far too little about Northern hospitality customs to impersonate an active barkeep.

Hakuund she had spotted immediately. He was to her right, speaking to a woman at one of the high tables. Two male huaina sporting the same insignia as the men posted downstairs and at the entrance watched from a few feet away. The woman, who looked to be in her mid-forties, was attractive and nicely garbed in a black dress and high-heeled boots.

Sam wandered over to the ledge, glancing casually down at the crowd on the main floor. She found Xenia again, and soon picked out

Jackal and Cassio. All three of them were scanning the room; they must have lost sight of Hakuund.

Sam leaned her arms heavily on the railing and stuck her head out as far as she could.

Even if they spotted her, she suddenly realized, only Xenia would have a clear shot. From where they were standing, Cassio and Jackal were effectively out of range. Sam brought her wrists together, crossing them in what she hoped was a perceivable x. Eventually Jackal looked up and spotted her. He stared at her for a moment, and then started making his way through the crowd. Toward Xenia, she hoped. Cassio had disappeared; hopefully he was doing the same. As long as nothing overly dramatic happened within the next few minutes, she would have backup.

A roar from the crowd below pulled her attention to the pit, where two men, naked and armed with spears, had entered the arena. One sported a large blue 'x' on his chest; the other was marked in red.

In stark contrast to the ground floor, where voyeurs were pushing and shoving to get a better view of the arena, most of the chairs around Sam remained markedly empty. The second-floor guests continued to circulate, seeking a better drink, better odds, a better companion.

Long, wriggling serpents were making their way out of the barrel. One reared up, snapping forward at the man in blue, who jumped back, nearly tripping over his spear. The men looked terrified. Sam had a sinking suspicion that these were not thrill-seeking volunteers, entering a contest for gain or glory. The man in red managed to stab a snake. As he pulled his spear back to strike again, three serpents fell upon him at once, snapping and biting. The man in blue tried to help, stabbing and slashing at the serpents that were pooling onto the other man. He was so focused that he did not notice the largest snake of the bunch sliding up behind him. By the time the man realized what was happening, he was already ensnared. He tried in vain to free his arms, screaming as the snake tightened its grip. Beside him, the other man had completely disappeared under a mass of snakes.

Sam pushed back from the ledge, sickened.

"Thirty-five seconds for the red, forty-six for the blue!" a voice called out behind Sam. A handful of groans and a few celebratory shouts went up from patrons who had clearly bet on, though not condescended to watch, the murder taking place below.

Sam swallowed, fighting to keep her expression bland. She turned to face the bookies, who were laughing and joking with patrons as they doled out and received coin.

To the right of them, Hakuund was handing the bag he had been carrying to the woman. Without looking inside, she tossed it to one of the huaina. While he was examining the contents, she gestured to the other man to approach. She leaned in and whispered something in his ear, after which he left quickly through a side door.

The woman smiled at Hakuund, reaching out and taking his hand in hers for a moment. She said something in a low voice that prompted him to throw his head back and let out a bellow of laughter. *Hmm, maybe tonight's going to be easy after all.*

Sam glanced back over her shoulder at the pit below. As far as she could see, no efforts were underway to remove either the snakes or the bodies of the two men. She feared the snakes would soon have more 'opponents.'

Back at Hakuund's table, the woman had stood up and was bestowing a kiss on each of his cheeks, her hands on his broad chest. He must have said something flirtatious in return, for the woman gave a mock gasp and wagged her finger at him, a coy smile on her face. They laughed again, and then she turned and swept out of the room, just as her companion returned with a bag and two additional men. When Hakuund accepted the bag, Sam saw her friend's smile fade slightly. She wandered slowly toward the bookies, watching out of the corner of her eye as Hakuund placed the bag on the table and took a quick inventory. He looked up at the man, a forced smile on his face, and asked him a question. The man just shrugged in response.

"Four to one? Come on, it's got to be six at least!" the woman in front of her was arguing.

"It's three downstairs," a man told her. "I'm giving you the best there is."

Still trying to smile, Hakuund was pointing at the other huaina, who was holding onto whatever goods Hakuund had brought with him. This man shook his head. Hakuund took a slow step toward him, offering up the bag he'd been given.

In one synchronized movement, all four men pulled out weapons. The huaina Hakuund had been approaching lashed out with a long, ugly blade; Hakuund jumped back, narrowly avoiding a slash to the throat and causing the club aimed for the back of his head to connect with his shoulder instead. A roar of pain escaped him, eliciting laughter from the man wielding the club. The laughter was cut off abruptly as the huaina glanced down, puzzled, to see the handle of Sam's knife sticking out of his stomach.

As Hakuund pulled his axes out, Sam raced forward, jumping up to stab one of the men in the neck as he lunged toward Hakuund. She pulled out the knife and slid toward the first man she'd attacked, slashing upward with one blade while she pulled her other knife from his belly. As he toppled backward, she spun back to see that Hakuund had taken down one of the men. The last one was slumped on the ground, a crossbow bolt through his throat.

"Come on!" Hakuund roared. Sam snatched the bag from the hands of the man she'd killed and then she sprinted down the stairs. Hakuund blew through the huaina at the bottom, knocking them into a heap. They were back up within seconds, pushing their way through the crowd after him.

Sam started to follow, and then spun around and dove behind the pole where she'd stashed her jacket. From her hiding spot she watched as a group of men thundered down the stairs. They looked around wildly for a moment and then split into two groups and ran off in opposite directions. Zipping up her jacket, Sam tucked the bag inside and slid the two knives up her sleeves. She wove through the crowd, keeping the huaina in her sightline.

She heard the screaming before she even reached the doorway. A woman with a shaved head was chopping at the bloody-faced preacher with a big, ugly piece of serrated metal.

"Heathens!" she shrieked. "Bloody scum! The blood you spill must be your own! For Ba'al!"

There were others, similarly shorn women and men echoing the cry: "For Ba'al." The woman held the makeshift knife up above her head with her right hand. The other members of the cult followed suit, the conviction on their faces steadfast and terrifying.

"The blessed! The blessed!" Their left hands, Sam realized with horror, had been cut off at the wrist.

Sam looked around wildly for her team. *Have they already fled?*

"Transform!" The woman was shouting again. "Transform and weed out the unworthy! Worship Ba'al and he will stop the grounds from shaking! He will calm the winds! He will douse the fires!"

Huaina seemed to be everywhere. Sam saw one watching her and drifted into a crowd of youths. She followed them to the edge of the forest, and then skirted around to the path they'd taken earlier. As she entered the woods, a bolt thudded into a tree near her head. She ducked behind the tree and glanced out. The man who'd been watching her was reloading his crossbow.

The woods behind her were dense. *Should I try to hide?* In the split second she considered it, another handful of huaina joined her attacker, all laden with weapons and torches. Hiding from one person was a lot easier than hiding from a half dozen. Sam turned and sprinted down the trail.

The first part of the path was open and straight, leaving her exposed. Luckily, she had a head start of about a hundred feet. If she could reach the first bend, the twists and turns that followed would offer her some protection. About twenty feet from the bend she heard a shout. She'd been spotted. Fear and adrenaline propelled her forward; she was flying now.

She felt it hit, felt the pressure, but no pain. She stumbled for a quick second, and then picked up her pace. *Where is the pain?*

She kept running. *An arrow that goes clean through is better.* Her brain shared the fact calmly, as if from far away. *Why is that again? Oh, right. That way it isn't necessary to draw the arrowhead back through your body. They can just hack it off instead. Lovely.* There was a fork, she remembered. She had to find the fork.

She heard a war cry. *They must be close. Excited for the kill.* She waited for impact. Someone was shouting, somewhere. A bolt thudded into a tree ahead of her. She heard more screaming. *Did the cultists follow too?* She shook her head. That did not make any sense.

She wondered how much blood she had lost. *The fork. I'm looking for the fork.* She pictured herself searching the trail for an eating utensil and let out a breathless giggle. Then, as she sprinted around the next corner, she saw it.

Sam leapt off the trail, stumbled around a tree, and scrambled noisily over a fallen branch. *Stealthy. You have to be stealthy.* If they could pinpoint where she'd left the trail, she was dead. Worse, she would be leading them to her team. She steadied herself, slowing her breath.

The pain hit her suddenly, so intensely that she retched.

"There you are," Sam said, as the night darkened around her. "Was wondering when you'd show."

16

T he North

"Bav Jit. Is she dead?" *Sounds like Cassio. Hmm, maybe there is life after death after all.* She found this to be surprising, but uplifting.

"She has a heartbeat," someone else said after a moment. *Xenia too?* She thought it a pity that both of the twins had come to this, but at least she would have some company in the afterlife.

The right side of Sam's stomach exploded in pain. The scream boiled out of her before she remembered where she was. She clapped a hand over her mouth and looked up frantically.

"It's okay." Hakuund's face appeared above Sam. "We took care of your friends."

"Hakuund," a voice called out—Jackal's voice. Hakuund's face disappeared and was replaced by Xenia's.

Cassio was speaking. "We need to get the bolt out."

"No—" Sam started to respond, but the movement brought on a fresh wave of nausea. She closed her eyes and tried to focus on breathing.

"He's right, Sam." It was Xenia's voice again. "It has to come out."

Sam took a careful breath and forced her eyes open. *You can do this.* "It stems the blood. Leave it in until it's time for the adhesive."

The twins exchanged baffled expressions. Sam closed her eyes again. She reached down and her fingers touched metal, not wood. *Bolt. It was a bolt, of course, not an arrow.* So much for not having to pull the head back through her body.

"They're never going to go for it," Sam could hear Hakuund arguing. "There's no chance. Let's just take her to a stitcher."

"It's their mission, they're obliged," said Jackal.

"Only if they say they are."

"Go convince them, then."

Footsteps approached. "We gotta get the arrow out."

"She won't let us. Says it's keeping the blood in."

"Is it?"

"I don't know. But she said to leave it, so I'm leaving it."

Sam opened one eye. Jackal was crouching down beside her head. "We need to get you to a stitcher. Can you walk?"

"Yes," Sam said. *I hope so.* She was shivering now, sweat pooling and then cooling on her clammy skin.

Jackal placed his hands under her armpits and lifted her, slowly. The forest spun, pain shooting out from her side into her stomach, chest, hips, even down to her toes. Heat swam over her, and black spots danced around the edges of her vision. She gritted her teeth, willing herself to stay conscious.

Xenia took one side, placing her arm around Sam's waist, and Jackal slid over to support the other side. One step, and then another, and then Sam felt herself sinking down.

Sam found it rather touching, her teammates working together, trying to keep her alive. Ava's prejudices were perhaps just prejudices. *And if they despise Finlay, he probably is despicable.* She saw it again, yellow eyes and a hairy snout. *With long, sharp fangs, too? Well, of course! Can't be a wolf without teeth, can he?*

Maybe that's where she's hiding. Maybe he gobbled her up. Sam giggled at her own joke, and then gasped as a fresh wave of pain shot through her.

The next thing she knew, one pair of hands was lifting her by the shoulders, another by the knees. *I must have blacked out again. How delicate of me.*

"What about Hak?" It was Cassio's voice again.

"He'll catch up with us before the turnoff," said Jackal.

"Melena's?" asked Xenia.

If there was a response, Sam missed it. The pain was constant now. She focused on her breathing, counting each breath in, each breath out. *How long will it take to reach the stitcher?* She needed a timeline. If she made an assumption, say an hour or so, the journey would take her somewhere between seven and twelve hundred breaths; breathing slowly, more like seven to nine hundred. She'd take nine hundred as her estimate, to be conservative. *Okay*, she told herself, *nine hundred breaths.* All she had to do was get from nine hundred to zero.

Sam had counted down to four hundred by the time Hakuund caught up with them. She opened her eyes, squinting in an effort to bring his face into focus. He looked past her and shook his head.

"What did he say?" Jackal's voice sounded behind her. He must be the one holding her shoulders. Looking down, she saw that it was Cassio holding her knees.

"He said their policies are non-negotiable."

Sam felt her body being transferred from one set of arms to another. A gentle pat on the knee told her that Xenia had relieved Cassio as well.

Sam had a hundred and fifty breaths remaining in her count when she heard knocking. They were outside a building and a strange woman was speaking. She could hear someone wailing and another voice screaming. *Is it me?* She breathed in—*one hundred and forty nine*—and out again. *Nope, not me.*

There was a powerfully sour odour. Through the smoke she identified urine and feces, vomit, blood, and beneath it all, rot. She was lowered onto a dirty blanket and turned gently onto her left side. There was a fire beside her, making it hot, far too hot. Something touched her hand, and she pushed open her eyes. A dog was sniffing at her. There were open sores along his back.

"Shoo!" Xenia scolded the dog, who turned and slunk away. His genitals had been sliced open, the two bloody halves trailing behind him.

"...not happy we lost the product, either. They want to talk to you."

The product, there was something important about the product. Sam tapped the leg closest to her left hand. Xenia bent down.

"Hey, my love, Mel's coming, she'll sort you out."

Sam shook her head. "My jacket." Her teeth were chattering, making it difficult to speak. "It's inside my jacket." Xenia looked confused, but proceeded to undo Sam's jacket. She pulled out the bundle.

Sam could hear talking, but she couldn't seem to make out their words anymore. She started a second count. *In thirty breaths the stitcher will be here. I just have to get to thirty.* She wished she could stop shivering.

Someone was forcing a piece of leather between her teeth. It tasted like it had been marinating in a latrine. A woman had taken hold of the back of the bolt and was slowly pulling it out. Sam screamed into the leather, trying not to vomit. She felt someone's hand in hers and gripped it so tightly she would wonder later if she had bruised them. Sam could feel the wet spreading down her stomach. The woman pushed something rough into the wound and then laced a needle through the skin on her stomach, and then her back.

When she had finished, Sam watched her move to another woman, who had a long gash down one arm. Beside the woman, a teenage girl was lying in a pool of dried blood. Based on the blue tint to their skin, both she and the babe that had been laid on her chest had died hours ago. They were alone too. No lover grieved by the woman's side, no parent or friend. *Does anyone even know she's here? How will they find out that she died?* There would be no record, not here. Even if the stitcher was literate, which Sam strongly doubted, there were too many patients, too little time, not enough light to see by. No, there would be no trail to follow.

Images of mass graves flashed through Sam's mind. She pictured the girl and the baby entombed in the mud, then her own body, cold and blue.

The black specks returned to hover on the edge of her vision. She was tired, so tired. *Don't black out. Hold on. Don't black out.* She took a slow breath, trying to re-establish control. Her mind drifted, a third girl appearing in her vision: dark skinned, tall, pretty. *Is Raina buried somewhere, nameless and forgotten? How would we know?*

Sam's attention snapped back to the stitcher, who was using the same needle she had just used on Sam on her new patient. Fear coursed through her like an injection of epinephrine.

Sam looked around frantically for her friends. They stood huddled together, too far away to hear her. Then she realized that she was still holding someone's hand.

"I have to disinfect it," she said, looking up into Xenia's green eyes. There was fear there, and pity.

"I don't know what you mean."

Sam looked around again. She didn't see any medicine, or even any water. She looked back at the fire beside her, and shoved the metal crossbow bolt into the flames.

"Knife—in my boot," she said to Xenia, trying to speak calmly despite the waves of pain and panic crashing around inside her gut. "Place the tip in the fire for a minute, and then cut my stitches."

"What?" asked Xenia, moving to pull her hand away.

"Do it. I know what I'm talking about. My mother was a stitcher," she lied.

Still looking uncertain, Xenia found the knife and placed it in the fire. Sam gave herself fifteen breaths, and then nodded at Xenia. Taking off her jacket and wrapping it around her hand, Xenia pulled the knife from the fire and cut Sam's stitches, first in the front, and then in the back. Blood began surging out again.

Sam reached down and felt the tip of something rough. With a sickening tug that made her wonder if she'd grasped a vital organ by mistake, she pulled out a small, dried flower.

She retched. "Get the bolt. Touch it to the wound."

Xenia froze, her hand midway to the bolt, staring at Sam as though she had just asked her to pluck out an eyeball and eat it. Jackal turned toward them, a look of concern on his face. *I'm losing too much blood.*

Grabbing the jacket from Xenia, Sam reached over and pulled the bolt from the flames.

"Put the leather back in my mouth."

Biting down into the sour skin, she took a deep breath and pressed the sizzling metal to the open wound on her stomach.

It was pain unlike anything Sam had ever imagined. It felt as though the fire was devouring her skin, her organs. Without waiting, she pressed it to the open wound on her back.

She dropped the bolt and curled onto her side, struggling to breathe. When she was able to speak, she turned to her team. The men had come over and were standing behind Xenia, matching expressions of horror on their faces.

"Wire," she spat out. "Two pieces."

Twenty breaths, she told herself. *Just get through twenty breaths.* Thankfully Xenia returned by the time she was halfway through her count. Without speaking, Xenia grabbed two crossbow bolts, lay the wire across them, and pushed the contraption into the flames. She seemed to have grasped Sam's strategy of heating everything before it touched her skin. Once the wire was burning hot, she began weaving it back through the exit point on Sam's stomach. She then did the same for the wound on Sam's back. Sam was fading in and out of consciousness by this point. She noted someone bringing over a pair of wire cutters, and saw Xenia purify the ends in the fire before using them to cut the excess wire.

"What the jit are you doing?" The stitcher had returned. "Let me see that."

Sam tried to speak, but only managed a garbled moan. Xenia stepped in front of her and handed the woman a xot. "Thanks for your help, Mel, we'll take it from here."

"Can you help me get home?" Sam whispered when Xenia knelt beside.

Xenia took her hand and gave her a weak smile. "Of course. Where do you live?"

"I know," Hakuund answered from somewhere above them. "You don't worry about a thing, little bird, we'll get you home."

17

The North

THE PAIN HIT her as soon as she opened her eyes. She could hear herself screaming, a hoarse, shrill sound she couldn't seem to cut off. She felt something being pushed against her lips.

"Breathe in," a voice instructed. Sam took a shallow breath in. "Again."

Sam breathed in deeper this time. Smoke surrounded her, dulling the pain. She breathed in once more and felt herself falling. There was a rabbit hole, she remembered. Maybe this was the rabbit hole.

There were birds circling, watching her. She was so thirsty. It was dry, everywhere, barren: a desert. The land was flat. She could see for miles in all directions, no splash of blue or green to break the monotony.

The birds began to caw. She hit the ground, covering her neck as one dive-bombed her. She felt its beak digging into her back. It was eating a hole right through her. She tried to roll away but couldn't move. Wings stretched out, covering her. Scales, the wings had scales.

She looked up at the bird and saw huge yellow cat eyes staring back. The reptilian face opened, and Sam caught fire.

Children surrounded her. She was sitting in the blackened ruins of the Hive. A little boy passed her a pipe. She tried to push it away. Her hands were being tied together. Someone was covering her nose. She had no choice but to breathe in.

She staggered to her feet and wandered past a curtain. There was drumming. It was a simple pattern, just two beats over and over again: the heartbeat of the Hive. She saw Hakuund and Cassio, and waved. They didn't see her. Hakuund had Cassio's face in his hands, their noses almost touching as they whispered together. She felt a hand slide around her waist. Xenia was smiling at her.

"It's not what it looks like, see?" she said, pulling her shirt up to reveal a mark branded into her stomach. "It's time for you too, now."

Jackal appeared with a metal bar. "I'm sorry," he said, and pressed the branding to her skin. She screamed. The drummers stopped playing, their eyes on her.

"Ssshhh, shhh my love," Xenia whispered in her ear. "Embrace the pain. You deserve it, don't you? After what you did?"

Sam started to slump to the ground but found that Jackal was holding her up. Xenia lifted Sam's chin and pried her mouth open. She pressed her lips to Sam's, blowing smoke down her throat.

The ground was damp under her; it smelled of pine needles. She lay on her back, her hands locked casually behind her head. *Am I resting?* She thought there was something that she was supposed to be doing, but she couldn't remember what it was. She stared up at a tree, high overhead. She could see it clearly, the trunk and the branches, even though the sky above her was black. There was no moon tonight, and smoke obscured the stars.

She looked to the side and her heart skipped a beat.

Corvus lay beside her, a grin on his face. "I meant to tell you—"

Sam blinked and the scene changed. Raina lay where Corvus had been a second ago.

"It's okay," she said. "I'm fine with it, really. He never leaves my side. Well, except to hunt."

Looking past Raina, Sam saw a figure walking away from them.

There was a bow on his back, and his bare arms shone like moonlight. He looked back at Raina and smiled.

"Corvus?" Sam asked.

Raina looked confused. "Finlay," she corrected Sam.

Her face brightened and she leaned in toward Sam as though to share a secret. Just as she opened her mouth to speak, the ground shuddered.

Sam blinked again and Corvus lay beside her once more. They were alone. Raina was gone, so was Finlay. Corvus reached out a hand toward her, a look of terror on his face.

"Help me," he said, before the earth swallowed him up.

"No!" Sam dove after him.

Dirt rushed up, pushing into her nose, her mouth. Her lips tightly shut, Sam raked the earth with her hands, desperate to carve out a place to breathe.

The dirt turned to mud, the mud to water. A current grabbed hold of her, pulling her toward the surface and life, or the ocean floor and death, she didn't know which. She couldn't hold her breath any longer. Seawater started to flood her nose and mouth.

Suddenly, she was ripped from the water, flung up with the spray and thrown down on cold, wet rock. Water poured out of her lungs. *Something hurts.* Sam looked down and saw a shiny metal fish poking out of her stomach. The fishing line hung limply behind her; it must have snapped. She grabbed the line and pulled. The bait ripped backward through her stomach, leaving a small hole in her midsection. Sam couldn't scream, couldn't even breath.

Smoke, heavily perfumed with incense, tickled her throat and made her cough again. The pain subsided, enough for her to take in her surroundings. She was in a cave, dank and dark and empty except for her cold, bleeding presence. A flash of motion—long, wavy dark hair disappeared around a corner.

"Raina," Sam said.

She stumbled shakily to her feet and followed in uncertain, jerking steps. Her boots didn't seem to be connecting properly to the ground. *Like a marionette. Except the string snapped, didn't it?*

Light gleamed through the rocks: there was a small opening.

Without considering where it might lead her, Sam wiggled face first through the hole and landed with a thud in a dark hallway.

She smelled it first; its foul breath made her retch as she stumbled to her feet. A low growl followed. Sam took a panicked step to the right, then the left. She couldn't tell where the sound was coming from.

The thud of paws hit the floor, and suddenly he loomed behind her, his yellow eyes hungry. Sam turned and ran.

An angry snarl sounded in her ears: he was close, too close. Every second she expected to feel his teeth tearing into her neck. Someone, somewhere was laughing. Sam ran down another hallway, and another. Too many. *The house can't be this big; I saw it from the outside, didn't I?*

The hallway ended; there was only one door. She yanked it opened and found herself facing row after row of cheap, ugly dolls. A sick feeling in the pit of her stomach, Sam stepped away from the dolls and their glassy, black eyes. She had known all along that the dog would chase her here.

"Been waiting for you," he said from the center of the room.

Sam spun around. The man had a rifle this time; it lay across his lap like a pet. He reached out a small, red hand and grasped the barrel lewdly. "Shouldn't 'ave kept me waiting, little girl," he said, curling his foul, scabbed mouth into a pout. "This is where you belong. This is where we keep the guilty."

Something moved out of the corner of her eye. The dolls were growing, their faces becoming more and more life-like until the dolls were gone and a row of women knelt in front of the bookcase, naked and chained and terrified.

Sam turned back, but the dog was there, waiting. She scanned the room desperately. *The window.* Not caring how badly the fall would hurt her, Sam ran toward the open window and dove forward.

She woke up in Ava's room, in the bed that Raina had used as a child. She sat up gingerly and checked the blanket for blood. It looked like the wire had held. She hissed as the wound began to throb. A loud meow sounded on the other side of the door. "Frank?"

Her voice came out a thin rasp. "Get Ava, please." *Wow, I truly have gone mad.*

Ava must have heard her through the door, because she burst in a moment later, the fat tabby plodding along at her heels. "Getting yourself stabbed! By the gods, Samarra, what is wrong with you?"

Sam's temples exploded in a headache. "Yes, I am alive. Hurrah," she said as Ava stormed back out of the room, returning a moment later with water, tea, and rice porridge.

She leaned over and sniffed at Sam's wound. "At least I don't smell rot. You're lucky, you know, most end up in the ground with far less than this."

"Luck," Sam whispered, reaching for the water. Ava swatted her hand, glared at her, and held the cup up to her face. Sam had to stop herself from guzzling the entire glass. She didn't think Ava would appreciate her vomiting in her bed. *If I haven't already.* "Do people here not understand about sanitation, disinfectant?"

Ava just stared at her blankly.

"It's not chance," said Sam. "Well, it's some chance, but mostly it's clean hands, clean bandages...cleaning instruments properly with chemicals or boiling water."

Ava shrugged. "I never heard that before," she said. "Are you sure that's right?"

"Of course. It's not belief, there's evidence...data. It's science." She gave a weak laugh. Talking about science in the North was akin to preaching about gods in the South.

Ava held up the mug, and Sam took a tentative sip. It was willow bark tea, with a hint of something else. She looked questioningly at her friend.

"It's valerian. Not that you're worth it. Foolish girl."

Sam raised her eyebrows and took another sip. Valerian was extremely rare—either Ava was wealthier than she let on, or she had a good friend somewhere.

"None of your business, nosy." Ava glared at her. "It was a long time ago."

Sam heard an indignant meow and turned her head to see Frank, also glaring at her. *Can cats glare?* It seemed this one could. He turned his back on her and stalked out of sight. A moment later she felt him jump up and plop himself down at her feet.

"Goodnight," Sam whispered. Her eyelids were already drooping.

"Not yet, you lightweight, I want to get some food into you."

Sam tried to respond, but she couldn't seem to convince her face to comply.

"Fine, sleep," Ava said with a sigh.

Sam felt a light kiss on her forehead, followed by footsteps. The sound of the door closing told her that she was alone again. *Well, not quite alone.* She could hear Frank rumbling at the foot of her bed.

18

The South

I WAKE IN FULL DAYLIGHT, as exhausted as if I had not slept. The curtains are already raised. Was there a bell? I can never seem to remember. It is certainly later than usual. I sit up and realize that the bed across from me is empty. Not only is it empty, it has been stripped. Glancing around the room, I count a total of five empty stations. Six other children stare around the room, bewildered. If I am late, at least I am not alone.

I am pulling the sheets taut when I hear the click of her boots. We stand at attention as she walks slowly up and down the room, inspecting us, our stations. I am conscious of my nightclothes, the fact that I have yet to bathe or clean my teeth. I also need to urinate, badly. Had she expected us to be ready when she arrived this morning?

"Pipit." Her voice rings out across the room. "Your station does not meet standards. Are you careless or defiant?"

The room is silent. I try, without moving my head, to see whom she is addressing. The others look as confused as I do.

"Pipit," she says again. "Are you careless or defiant?"

Is it a name? I know the word. It's a bird, I realize, though the image brought to mind is not one of wings and feathers but the imprint of words on paper. It must have been included in a lesson: spelling, perhaps, or diction. Certainly not biology, or there would be a photograph to conjure to mind.

I see them now, small birds, one above each bed. I frown. Have they always been there? I do not think so. There is writing beneath each one, but the letters are so small that I cannot make any of them out. I switch to looking at the stations themselves. One of the boys has left yesterday's clothes on the floor. I look at the image above his bed—is it a pipit? It is certainly not a sparrow or a robin or a lark.

I catch the boy's eyes and glance pointedly down at the puddle of clothes near his feet, and then past him toward the bird. His eyes shift upward to a point above my head, and comprehension dawns on his face.

He straightens his shoulders. "Careless, Designate, and I apologize." His face is red.

My pulse races as she appears in my line of vision. Her eyes hover on me for a moment before moving to the boy. Did she notice our exchange?

"It is Protector Nem," she says. "P2 specifically, but in addressing the person, 'Protector' will suffice. You may correct yourself."

We wait in silence while Pipit hangs his clothes on the hook beside his bed, his small, protruding ears and the back of his neck flushing pink. I have heard this code, P2, before. If the P stands for protector, then this woman falls into the same category as the women and men who have been leading our physical tests. Are they also P2s? Or are they P1s or P3s? I wonder whether P1 is the top or the base of the hierarchy.

"We have completed the assessments," Protector Nem continues once Pipit stands again at attention. "Based on an evaluation of individual strengths and areas for further development, each child has been matched with the instructors and infrastructure best suited to their optimal growth. It has been decided that the seven of you are best suited to the program here, at this particular base."

Her speech has become mechanical again, another recitation well practiced.

"Feel welcome to relax, and treat this as your new, permanent home. The rest of your cohort is arriving as we speak. After breakfast, you may relax, or explore the base. I will show you the layout so that you may see which areas are accessible to you. The base qualifiers are tonight, which I am sure you will enjoy watching." She looks at each of us in turn, standing bleary-eyed and rumpled at the foot of our beds, and gives a small, tight smile. "You are welcome to speak now, as much or as little as you desire. Work together, eat together, play together—your cohort, the other first-year cadets, or C1s, is your new family."

One is a low rank, I conclude. If we are C1s, there must be higher-level cadets—the older youths I have seen.

"To preserve the sanctity of the assessments, however, it is forbidden to discuss what you have experienced to date here at this base, either with each other or the new arrivals. Nor should you focus on the past. Today you begin your training as a cadet. Look only to the present and the future. In the interest of optimal health for you and your cohort, this is an order.

"Now," she says, glancing up at the window, "you may bathe and ready yourself for breakfast. For your convenience a dispensary has been installed here in your dormitory. Log in with your assigned name to receive your customized vitamins every morning and your evening sweet. I will return in thirty minutes."

I wait until she leaves the room and then turn to stare up at the bird above my bed. Perhaps today I will look for a library—I would like to know exactly what kind of bird a sora is.

I gather my towel and head to the lavatory. A girl catches my eye and smiles. I smile back, but after so many days of silence I feel reluctant to speak. The others, I assume, feel similarly, as voluntary silence reigns as fully as had the obligatory.

I bathe quickly. When I am stacking my bucket neatly in the pile that sits beside the communal tap, a glint of metal catches my eye. Shavers have been laid out in front of the mirrors.

I run the blade over my skull, and then reach back to feel bits of longer fluff, stray hairs that have gone neglected since my arrival. There are only two of us shaving right now; the other, a boy, finishes and lays down his shaver.

"Would you..." My voice croaks, hoarse from disuse.

He cocks his head at me, and then flashes a strange sort of smile. "Sure," he says, his voice equally raspy.

I hand him my shaver and he runs it gently over the back of my head. His other hand he places on my shoulder. I shiver slightly despite the warmth of his fingers, oddly intimate after so many days of social isolation. I watch him through the mirror, and note that he is not much taller than I am.

When my head is fully shorn I offer to return the favour.

"No, thanks," he says with another strange smile. "I'm trying for stripes."

He turns his head and I see lines of dark stubble. He has missed hairs on purpose. He moves toward the door and I follow, bewildered. Consciously inviting a reproach—are all males so peculiar? I suppose I will find out.

I stop in front of a familiar-looking black box that has been installed beside the door. I touch the screen and a series of letters appear, the instruction: *State your name.*

"Sora," I say. The sounds are clunky on my tongue; we are as yet unacquainted. I hear the sound of pills falling into a cup, of liquid pouring. A panel opens to reveal a small dish containing the usual colourful assortment of vitamins and a small cup of juice. I swallow each pill and then place the containers back into the dispensary and shut the panel door. The words *Thank you, Sora* flash across the screen.

I pick up my new clothing—and pause. Why did I call it new? It looks the same as the clothing I wore yesterday and the day before. I stare at the long-sleeved shirt and pants, rubbing the material gently between my thumb and forefinger. I cannot pinpoint what is different. The others are nearly dressed; I am falling behind. I pull on my changed but unchanged uniform and am just tying the laces of my boots when Protector Nem returns.

I see it as we line up. Our individual numbers are gone, replaced by the alphanumeric C1. Of course, I do not need the number three anymore. I am Sora and I am a C1.

We take a new route today, I think. Somehow, I have not been able to hold the twists and turns of the various corridors in my mind long enough to organize them into any kind of mental map. A low hum at first, the buzz of indistinct conversation builds to a crescendo as we turn the corner.

The real canteen is much larger. Rows upon rows of tables seat people of all ages, many garbed in the now-familiar olive green, though smatterings of yellow, red, blue, and violet break the monotony.

We are led to a table at the very front of the room, where several other children wait. I wonder if they are the new arrivals Protector Nem spoke of—the remainder of our cohort.

In the front of the room, long tables are set perpendicular to the rest, one empty, the other occupied by several older women and men. They sit on the far side of the table, facing the room rather than each other. At the center of the group is a woman with spiked red hair and the alphanumeric code P5 stitched onto her jacket. Perhaps it is her straight, hooked nose that brings to mind a falcon. I read a book once by an author who claimed that in olden times falcons were trained to hunt alongside humans. None of the falcons in the illustrations had been red, though. I wonder if it is disrespectful to compare her to a bird, when this is the species used to identify the newest cadets. Of course, we are not birds of prey.

The room becomes suddenly and abruptly quiet. Footsteps sound, overloud and out of place: a small group of women and men are entering the canteen from a side door near the front of the room. They are not wearing boots or soft shoes meant for running—the heels of their shoes are sharp; some are even raised. They settle at the empty table as a group of children descend on them, carrying cups and platters. The children, garbed in green, look drab beside the newcomers, whose dress is bright and elaborate, extravagant; they remind me of the strangers that Iris and I spied on...one week ago? Two? My throat tightens at the thought of Iris. I relax my face into a smile and take a slow, deep breath: in through my nose, out through my mouth.

More children enter the canteen, passing out food to each table. No one is speaking and no one is eating.

It dawns on me suddenly: they must be from the Administration. A shiver of excitement darts up my spine. I do not recognize any of them from official broadcasts, but that does not signify anything.

"The Administration is an efficient machine fuelled by the labour of many," Designate Lews used to say. Only the council members ever appear directly onscreen.

The silence is finally broken when the falcon woman rises to her feet. In near perfect unison, the cadets and protectors follow suit. As one, the women, men, and children around me raise their hands, pressing them together in front of their eyes: the sign for deference. We copy them, just a split second behind. My back is straight, my eyes forward. *Downcast eyes have things to hide*: the old adage.

"My fellow Seirans, it is my pleasure today to welcome several delegates of the Administration to our base." Her voice is warm and serrated, like sand passing over a rock in the midday sun. Not a falcon after all. Not feathers, but scales; sun and sand and scales.

"Their presence today is an honour. Such is the richness of our nation, that the highest leaders invest in each and every Seiran. Please join me in welcoming them today."

An older man with broad shoulders and a long blond ponytail rises from the table and crosses over to the center of the room. I like the colour of his suit: a rich, bold purple. We remain standing and press our palms together over our eyes a second time.

"Thank you, Grand Neilem, for the kind words of welcome," he says, nodding at the red-haired woman, who bows her head and returns to her seat. His voice is clipped, his tone formal. He turns out and faces the room. "The Administration sends thanks and greetings to you, our esteemed protectors, and welcomes our newest cadets to the base." He looks directly at our table and smiles, projecting assurance if not warmth.

"The Administration has supported you, fed you, and invested in you, and as of today you are given a great opportunity. For the next five years you will learn, grow, and flourish here at the border, under the wings of your elders. The lessons you learn will enable you to take your final place within our ranks, as not only recipients of, but also contributors to, this bountiful largess that we are privileged to serve. Today, as you begin this journey, you are born anew. We welcome you to shed your old selves, old lives, and old attachments. The past is over; leave it behind and look now to your present and our glorious future. Beholden, duty-bound, in gratitude."

"Beholden, duty-bound, in gratitude," I repeat, one voice in a large chorus.

Protectors and cadets alike take their seats and breakfast begins. I chew on my oats, mulling over the man's words. Something about his speech rankles, but I cannot decide what, so I dismiss the thought and focus on the food before me.

I am finishing my porridge when, for the third time today, everyone rises and presses their hands together in front of their eyes. The representatives from the Administration are leaving.

A few minutes later the adults sitting at the head table file out as well. The protectors follow in shifts, some kind of predetermined order they can see that I cannot, and then the older cadets. I notice that only the two head tables remain laden with dishes; the other groups all return their own plates and bowls, giving them a cursory scrub with sand before leaving. Soon only the youngest cadets remain. Some clear or clean tables or wipe floors, though the majority of them are dipping the scrubbed dishes into an antiseptic solution before drying and stacking them in a metal cabinet. I wonder whether I should be helping.

"Tomorrow after breakfast you will take over this task from the second years." Protector Nem has returned. "Today, however, is for resting, and for getting to know your new home. Please scrub your dishes and then follow me outside."

I try not to stare at the second-year cadets as we exit. They appear busy, but several take the time to smile and wave at us as we pass.

We follow her in silence down a seemingly endless number of corridors. Finally, she leads us through a set of double doors into a large, indoor square.

Instead of the basic cement flooring that I am used to, we walk upon natural stone tiles. Long steel planters run from the outside of the room to the center, slicing the courtyard into eight long, skinny triangles. I peer into one of the planters and see smooth, round stones. I wonder if they are real or synthetic. The ceiling is transparent, allowing sunlight to beam down upon the green roots and cacti that have sprouted from the rocks. Tables dot the courtyard, along with benches and loungers, a few occupied, though most are empty.

In the middle of the square is a large screen, currently displaying a woman's face. She looks to be middle-aged, and has a friendly smile and long blond hair streaked with both green and grey. *Atalet,* the screen reads, *P3, inventor of the somnac, five-time base representative at the contests, silver medalist nationally in 324 Adm., we thank you for your contribution.* A new face appears on the screen, an older man with lightly tanned skin and a very wide grin. *Jenner,* the screen notes.

Protector Nem gestures at the screen. The man's face disappears and is replaced by a diagram depicting an assortment of boxes. She holds her hand above one of the boxes and the words *Tranquility Square* appear. Small dots begin to materialize as well, mostly green at the center, though I see bits of colour along the periphery. I frown at the screen for a moment, and then scan the room. The men and women scattered about the square are not all wearing green: one woman is wearing a scarlet dress, while the man beside her sports a yellow shirt and black pants. The dots represent people, I realize, fascinated.

Library, Armoury, Training Ring One, Training Ring Two, Canteen, Medical Ward: markers appear and disappear as Protector Nem waves her hand along the screen. Most of them appear to be west of us. She was speaking, it seems, while my mind wandered. I wonder what I have missed.

"...for protectors only, however cadets are welcome, in fact encouraged, to watch matches in their spare time. Training Ring One is where you will actually practice."

A tentative hand rises up in front of me.

"Yes, cadet?"

"Are there specific hours for each of these rooms?" a boy asks. I think it is the same boy Protector Nem called out for carelessness this morning: the pipit bird. He is tall, the tallest of the group, and the skinniest too.

"Good question." She gives him a nod of approval. "Not for protectors or fifth-year cadets, however for cadets who are levels one through four, 2200 is lights out. You are expected to have returned to your dormitory by that time and to remain there until morning. Except for visiting the lavatory, you are not permitted to wander about after hours.

"The medical wing," she points at a block, which swells and pulses in response, "you should never enter unless you have an appointment or are requested to do so by a P3. The kitchens are also forbidden unless a higher rank cadet or a protector gives you permission. This wing," she points to a long hall to the west of us, "houses the library. You are welcome to visit—the P2 in charge will point you to the sections that first-year cadets are permitted to access. The east wing, however," here she points to the area east of our dormitory, "is off-limits to all cadets and level one, two, and three protectors.

"There are outposts here and here." She taps the screen with a finger. "They are not relevant to you now, but once you become protectors you will be able to use your stipend to purchase whatever goods you desire."

She gestures at the screen again. The boxes fade away and are replaced by Jenner and his grin. *P1, obedient, model protector, we thank you for your contribution.*

"You will assemble at the canteen at 1300 hours for the midday meal. In the meantime, please feel welcome to explore or to rest. First and second-year cadets are typically only excused from lessons and duties on state holidays, so this is a rare treat. I suggest you take advantage of it."

With this statement she sweeps out of the square. I stare at the others: my cohort, my new family. A few of them return my gaze, but the majority stare at the screen, the skylight, the plants, or the floor, anything but their fellow cadets. I have never had to begin a friendship before; the girls in my division were a part of my daily life for as long as I can remember. This is different: odd, uncomfortable, and yet intriguing.

A girl turns and follows Protector Nem's quickly fading footsteps out of the courtyard. A boy follows her, and others him. Back to the dormitory, I suppose. Soon only two remain: Pipit and the girl who smiled at me this morning.

"Are you exploring?" the girl asks. She has big grey eyes; they light up when I nod.

"I'm a Starling. What are you?"

"Sora. And you're Pipit, right?"

Despite being mid-yawn, the boy nods his head vigorously. "I want to find the library and the training rings. Will you look for them with me?"

"Sure," I say, glad for the company.

"I'd like to find the rings too," Starling says. "Ooh, and the armoury!"

I emulate the gesture that Protector Nem used to bring forth the map and am rewarded when the bright, smiling face of *Jrani* disappears and the blocks return. "So the library, the rings, and the armoury...I'm interested in the armoury too... Okay, I think I've got it. Anything else to check?"

I turn around and find the other two staring wide-eyed at the screen.

"How did you do that?" Pipit asks. "I just figured, you know, cadets weren't allowed... Or at least, not us."

"Oh." I had not considered that screen usage might be restricted. "I just sort of..." I hold my hand out toward them and flick my wrist and fingers in imitation of what the protector had done.

"Wait, can you do it one more time?" Starling asks. I show the gesture to her again, slowly this time. She copies it once, twice, and then turns to the screen and repeats it a third time, more quickly. Nothing happens. She tries again with no results.

"I wonder..." I repeat the gesture at the screen. It returns to Jrani and her feats. "Now try," I say.

She looks puzzled, but complies, and shoots me a big grin when the map reappears. I catch her hand as she moves to close the map.

"Wait," I say. "I want to see something." I gesture at the screen. Nothing happens. "Now try."

The map disappears. "I think that whoever opens it has to close it."

"Huh." Starling stares at it, transfixed, and then turns and smiles at me again. "Neat."

"Do you want to try?" I ask Pipit, who is watching us with a horrified look on his face.

"Can we just go find the library?" he asks. "Please?"

"Yeah, okay." I step around a planter and head for the northwest exit. "I think it's this way."

The library is enormous. It dwarfs the square, even, in height if not in square footage. The bookshelves reach to the skylight, accessible by means of the many balconies that orbit the room. I imagine that from the top platform, the distance between feet and floor is staggering, the sunlight blinding. Not that I am able to find out firsthand; Cis are limited to the first floor. Perhaps they visit at night, whoever has access to that top floor, or maybe they wear sun goggles.

"Yes, it's very nice, but I'm trying not to fall asleep," Starling is saying to Pipit, who sits huddled under a pile of books.

There is so much to see that I cannot seem to settle on a single book. I will have to return soon.

"Sora." Starling interrupts my reverie. "Rings?"

"Rings, yes. Pipit, are you coming?"

"Yup, right—right behind you." He painstakingly separates two books from the pile—the daily limit for Cis—and returns the remainder to the shelves behind him.

The P2 in charge of the library reluctantly glances up from his book when we approach. Without standing, he picks up a porta and waves it lazily in the direction of Pipit and the books he has clutched to his chest. "Pipit, Dorm B, *Drought-Resistant Agriculture* and *Seiran Birds: Ornithology in the New World*."

Starling raises her eyebrows at Pipit as we exit the library.

"I don't like fiction," he says. "I like facts."

"Will you look up soras for me?" I ask.

He nods, brightening at the request.

We follow the clang of metal. Pushing open the heavy door, we find that Ring One is packed full of bodies, mostly older cadets, though I do see the odd protector. Some are training with blunted blades and wooden sticks; others are practicing hand-to-hand combat or wrestling.

"Maybe the stands would be better," says Pipit.

I nod, gratefully turning away from the clamour. After so many days of silence, I find it overstimulating: the noise, the smells, the sheer number of people. We retreat into the corridor, wandering the halls until we manage to track down a staircase.

"Much better," Starling says as we enter the arena seating area.

Rows of simple metal chairs circle the ring, nailed to an angled floor to allow even those in the back rows an unobstructed view of the grounds below. The stands are empty this morning, except for one small figure seated in the front row.

Recognizing the lines on the back of his skull, I make my way down to him. His head is cushioned on his arms, which rest casually on the railing, though he turns his face toward me when I sit down beside him. "Hi," he says with a sleepy smile.

"You're Vireo, right?" Pipit asks from behind me. "I read your bird. I mean your sign. The bird sign."

The boy nods, still looking at me.

"Sora," I say. "She's Starling, and he's Pipit."

"We thought everyone else had gone to bed," Starling says, settling onto the seat behind Vireo. "Have you been here the whole time?"

"Mostly," he says. "I looked for Ring Two first, but it was closed, even for viewing."

"For the...the qualifiers, maybe," Pipit says. "I bet Ring Two is bigger, if it's where the protectors train." He furrows his brow. "Do any of you know what the qualifiers are, exactly?

All three of us shake our heads.

"We'll find out tonight, I suppose," I say.

Vireo yawns widely and looks back out onto the training grounds.

"Hey, what's over there?" Starling asks, pointing to the far side of the ring.

"I think it's for ranged weapons," Pipit says as we make our way toward them.

He notices the confusion on my face. "Guns, bows, weapons for shooting something from far away. I read a book on it."

I realize as we approach that he is correct. Each long room, enclosed within transparent walls, features a single cadet. In the first room there is a girl firing a gun at a target. She looks a fair bit older than us: probably a fourth or even a fifth year. Her ears are covered.

Farther along we see a cadet shooting long bolts instead of bullets. Another cadet is throwing knives at her target.

"Do you think we're going to learn all this?" Pipit asks, staring down, wide-eyed, at the cadets below.

"I hope so," I hear Vireo say, more to himself than to Pipit.

"We are going to find the armoury next," I tell him. "Maybe we'll get to see some of these up close. Want to come?"

We make our way out of the arena and down not one but two flights of stairs. The subterranean floor is cold and dark. The few lamps that line the walls do not illuminate until we approach, their bulbs casting a thin, sickly light that fades before we reach the next set. Most of the rooms are unmarked, and locked, we learn as Vireo casually twists each door handle we pass.

The armoury, when we find it, is small and cramped. Shelves of wooden staves, metal poles, and blades leave little open floor space. Well-worn pads and helmets hang from the walls, making the stuffy room even stuffier. Though we are allowed to be here, we creep forward like thieves.

As I lean forward to peer more closely at a broad metal blade, a face appears inches from mine. I am not the only one to startle. Behind me I hear someone bump into a shelf. The clang of metal shatters the silence.

A tiny old woman stands glowering at us, her hands on her hips. "What do you want?" Her head is as closely shorn as a child's, an odd contrast against her skin, which is weather beaten and lined as though she has spent the past seventy years exposed to the hot midday sun, stubbornly refusing to apply her daily ration of sun-saving lotion.

"I, uh, we—we—" Pipit's face is red again.

"You're the new group, I suppose," she says. "You want some kind of tour, do you? Fine, fine—but do not touch anything!" She glares with particular animosity at Vireo. To be fair, he does seem the most likely to misbehave.

Vireo holds up his hands, a gesture of innocence or perhaps submission.

"Okay then," the woman says, pursing her lips. "I'm Protector Gin, P2, of course. These," she rests her hands against a large wooden staff, "are pretty much the only things in here you'll be getting this year. Well." She cracks a rusty smile. "That and a lot of bruises."

I catch sight of Pipit's face and wonder if I look as startled as he does. I have never heard an adult speak so informally before.

She waves dismissively toward the swords and then starts picking her way toward a particularly crowded corner of the armoury. "Nope, you won't touch a blade until you master wood." She gestures at us to follow her and I realize that what I had assumed to be a dead end actually houses a small passageway. A passageway, it turns out, lined by knives in every style and size.

"These are fun. You will probably get them second year, depending."

"Begging pardon, Protector, but what does it depend on?" I ask, hoping the question does not antagonize her.

"On you, of course! It's obvious, really."

"But I don't see—when would we use staves or blades?" Vireo asks. "The tech we have is a thousand years past all this."

"First of all," Protector Gin says, "the Administration has tech. You, bird, have nothing. Second of all, do you think the Administration is just going to give guns to a bunch of children? Do you have any idea how foolish that would be?" She snorts and picks up a knife, tossing it gently into the air with one hand and catching it with the other.

"Spend a year showing us you have the discipline to master a wooden staff, and then maybe you'll see steel. Maybe. Prove that you can be trusted with a blade, and maybe you'll get a projectile. And always, always, hand-to-hand, skin-to-skin, because thirdly, you're only as good as the weapon you hold. Signals get blocked, toys get stolen, and then what do you have left?" She jabs a skinny finger at my chest, as though it were me, and not Vireo, who had questioned the Administration's training process.

"Me," I say.

She rewards me with a wide grin. "You. So you better be a well-trained weapon. Now, do you want to see the range weapons or what?"

After the armoury we head back to the canteen for the midday meal. The first-year table is empty when we arrive. "I wonder if they're all still resting," Starling says, to no one in particular.

"Maybe." The head tables are also empty. I pour watermelon juice from the steel carafe that is on the table into four cups and pass them around. Pipit mumbles a thank you, fluttering a hand over his face to cover a yawn. Vireo takes one sip of juice and then crosses his arms atop the table and lays his head upon them. I feel something pushing into the side of my shoulder. Starling opens one eye, offers up a lazy smile by way of apology, and then continues to doze against me.

A large bowl is placed between us.

"Come on," I say with the limited energy I can muster. "Food first, then sleep."

It's stew, hot and fragrant, with gourd and potato, tomato and pepper. There is also millet flatbread to accompany it. We eat slowly and in silence, a sharp contrast to the rest of the room, which buzzes with talk of the qualifiers. From the occasional phrase overheard and deciphered by my tired brain, I understand that they involve physical tests of some sort.

Vireo finishes first and starts to rise with his dishes. He looks over, surprised, to find that Pipit has grabbed a fistful of his shirt. A half-formed memory from the morning pokes through the haze.

"Ah...order," I say from across the table. "Protectors first, then senior cadets, then last is us."

"Right, okay. Wake me up when it's our turn." With that Vireo lays his head on the table and, to all appearances, falls fast asleep. Starling has reoccupied my shoulder. I hear a gentle snore bubble up. I will have to remember to tell her to visit medical and have that fixed.

We wait; the time drags. This meal seems endless. I look over at Pipit, who, like me, seems determined to remain alert or at least upright. We need a game.

"One, three, seven, fifteen." I have to speak slowly to keep from slurring my words.

He stares at me blankly for a minute, and then breaks out into a smile. "Thirty-one," he says. "Double and one."

He tips his head back, eyes on the ceiling, his brow furrowed in concentration. "Nineteen, fifteen, eighteen, one."

Nineteen, fifteen, eighteen, and one: What pattern can he possibly have made? I might have expected nineteen, fifteen, eighteen, and fourteen, to be followed by seventeen, thirteen, and sixteen: down four, up three. Unless...has he switched from numbers to wordplay? I run the alphabet through the set of numbers and laugh. "My name."

He nods, grinning.

I lean my elbows on the table, and Starling starts to slide off my shoulder. I lunge back and manage to grab hold of her before she can tumble completely off the bench. She inhales with one loud finale of a snore and opens her eyes.

"Did I fall asleep?"

I nod.

"Can we go now?"

I look around. The protectors have left, and the older cadets. The last few stragglers seem to be making their way up, dishes in hand. "I think so."

The curtains have been lowered in our room. I stumble past eight sleeping bodies to reach my bed. Without undressing, I crawl under the sheets. I realize that I have no system in place to wake myself in time for the qualifiers; I acknowledge this but can do nothing before I fade from consciousness.

19

The South

I WAKE TO DAYLIGHT. Have I overslept or under slept? No, not daylight: electric light. The familiar automated tone bubbles up from a receiver: "The qualifiers will begin in thirty minutes. Please make your way to Ring Two. Punctuality is a matter of consideration for your fellow protectors and cadets. Latecomers will not be admitted."

We exit en masse, a stumbling, blurry-eyed procession of first years. I wonder whether those at the front of our cluster even know the way. Perhaps they are simply walking toward the common areas in hopes of finding someone to follow. We soon merge with another stream, although I think they are first years as well. Their faces mirror the same fatigue that I feel dragging at my leaden limbs.

The protector's arena is large enough to hold Ring One four times over. The grounds themselves are shrouded in darkness, though the stands are brightly lit. The star-like bulbs scattered across the transparent ceiling look to have been installed for aesthetic rather than practical reasons. Created to uphold the illusion of an outdoor stadium, I assume—all the appeal of nature without any of the inconveniences of an uncontrolled environment. I wonder if there are quiet nights when one can walk into Ring Two and see real stars, or whether the electric lights are always lit.

A large screen is descending from the apex.

"Firsts to the back rows!" An older cadet waves to us to the back. "Once protectors and older cadets are seated, you may move forward into any vacant spots."

We shuffle along to the top of the arena.

"Sora!" Starling is calling me from several seats over. I step down into the row below, cutting across a dozen empty seats until I stand just below her. Vireo is there as well, and Pipit. They extend their hands and pull me up onto an empty seat.

"Thank you," I say, settling down between Starling and Pipit.

A spotlight appears front and center, revealing a small, rectangular amplobox. Red hair flashes under the sudden illumination: Grand Neilem. She sits in the center of a group of women and men, those who occupied the head tables at breakfast.

I hear familiar notes, though the sound is richer, closer. Real violinists, I see them now, in the corner of the amplobox beside a grand piano.

Grand Neilem stands to begin the words of thanks. The screen high above us flickers on, projecting the Grand's face in minute detail.

> The rains pulled back
>> From our lands
>> Drought swept sea to sea
>> We would have perished, all
>> But you delivered us

It is as though she stands behind me, leaning forward to speak quietly in my ear. The intimacy makes me shiver as I repeat the leitmotif at the end of each stanza, one voice among many.

> Fruit withered on the tree

Crops failed one by one
From the brink of famine
You delivered us

Generation zero
No child was born until
You pushed the bounds of science
And delivered us

Fear led to violence
As rule of law grew weak
To a greater order
You delivered us

Beholden, duty-bound, in gratitude

The choreography is unchanged, notes flowing in between the verses, instruments respectfully silent during the speaking of the words. It is the same perfect synchronization I have always known, not a breath of overlap. What I listened to every morning at my division, however, standing with my hand on my heart and my eyes on the receiver, cannot be compared to what I am not only hearing and seeing, but feeling now. The words sink deeper, notes springing off my ribs and through my veins. It is more than words. I feel the glory.

We were taught to remain silent afterward: a sign of respect and a time of reflection. There is no silence here.

A roar is building, stoked in individual hearts but spilling out through hands, feet, and mouths into the collective air. It takes my breath away. The noise seems to be gaining mass, pushing upward with so much force that I imagine it popping the glass from the top of the arena like the cork from a bottle.

I have never seen anything so passionate, so uninhibited. It would almost be disorderly, were it not unified. Then suddenly the resonance comes to an end: release, then inhalation, now the collapse.

"We are here today to select one team of protectors and one team of cadets to represent our base at this year's contests." Grand Neilem is speaking again. "As usual, the top four teams in each category have been preselected to compete against one another in a variety of matches, the details of which are unbeknownst to the competitors. They know only, as you do, that we will test their strength, their stamina, and their strategic thinking, not as individuals but as a group. It is teamwork that makes our country strong: teamwork, discipline, and obedience. We have an additional surprise for you this year, one that only further demonstrates the bounty of our leaders in Ankev. It is my privilege to welcome an honoured delegate of the Administration to share the exciting news with you."

The man in violet who had spoken at breakfast stands, nodding to the Grand. My eyes flicker upward, from the man in the box to his image on the screen.

"My fellow Seirans," he begins, staring solemnly into the camera. "Since inception, the annual contests have been held in our great capital and broadcast to all our cadets and protectors. The true beauty of this competition, however, cannot be fully captured on a screen. The live event is undeniably more powerful than the broadcast. As such, the Administration has decided that this experience should no longer be restricted to Ankev.

"Considering that this base has produced the greatest number of winning teams, it has been determined that the upcoming games shall be hosted here. At the end of the year all competitors, the broadcast staff from Ankev, and many key members of the Administration will therefore join you here, in this arena, for the annual contests."

The stadium is silent, though the air seems to pulsate with suppressed acclamation.

"Fellow protectors, dear cadets." Grand Neilem steps up to the front of the amplobox a second time, a large smile on her face. "You may join me in thanking the Administration for this generous gift."

For the second time tonight, the arena around me erupts with noise. The excitement in the air is palpable, and contagious. Though I have only just learned of the existence of the contests, I too feel the thrill, racing staccato-like up the vertebrae in my spine. I feel a hand squeeze mine and look over to see the same fever in Starling's eyes. I want to shout along with the crowd, but I cannot seem to work out how. The air catches and dies in my throat. Never mind, I tell myself; you can learn.

"Now, to introduce our competitors, please welcome Protector Djie."

The spotlight grows and splits; one eye continues to light the amplobox while the second floats downward, illuminating a single man standing atop a cylindrical platform. His hair, the same dark blue as the cloak he wears, has been swept into a ponytail.

"Welcome to the qualifiers!" he bellows, in a voice that is more music than speech. "Four teams of protectors and four teams of cadets are competing for the chance to take part in this year's contests. You know their faces. You have watched them sweat and bleed and fight to be faster, stronger, better! I give you...your contenders!"

As his hands sweep outward, light floods the base of the arena, revealing sixteen protectors, each dressed head to toe in one of four colours: black, blue, white, or gold. Even their hair has been dyed to match. The crowd cheers them on and I realize now how many of the protectors in the crowd have dressed themselves in one of these same four colours. To show support for a particular team, I suppose.

In the center of the ring, eight freestanding wooden walls tower above the contestants. They are maybe twenty feet high and about six feet across. The narrow strip of wood at the top is only two or three feet thick, though it widens to three times that size at the base.

A spotlight moves toward the far side of the arena, still shrouded in semi-darkness. I follow its trajectory with my eyes and spy a host of structures covered in rings, ladders, poles, and wire. Metal glints from the wall behind them. Weapons.

The light settles on a large entranceway as cadets burst out from the darkness, racing four abreast to the center of the ring. Each row forms into a tight cluster that allows the crowd to distinguish among the sixteen matching green uniforms and bare skulls, the four competing teams. The cadets appear to be nearly as tall and as strong as the protectors. I wonder if they are all fifth years.

Protector Djie gestures now toward one of the wooden frames. "The first task is simple. Each team must work together to bring all four teammates up onto the wall. The first team to complete the exercise will receive four points, while the second place team will receive two points. No points will be awarded to the third and fourth place teams." Protector Djie stops to wink at the camera. "Sounds easy, doesn't it? Now, at the top of each wall sit two of the key virtues that our great nation is founded upon: optimism and perseverance."

The screen zooms in on one of two small, diamond-shaped figures that stand atop each of the wooden structures. A hollow must have been carved into the top of the wall to hold the virtue steady, for the glass figure stands upright, the word "optimism" emblazoned upon it.

"Knock one of the virtues over and the entire team must return to the ground and begin afresh. Knock it off the wall entirely and the team receives zero points for this round. Knock both of the virtues off the wall and the team is eliminated from the qualifiers. No attempts may be made to catch or steady a virtue that has been compromised.

"As we must select both a team of protectors and a team of cadets to represent our base in this year's contests, there will be two rounds of each task: one round for our protectors and one for our cadets.

"As usual," he says, turning to face the contestants, "we will begin with our protectors." In unison, the cadets bow to Protector Djie and march over to the sidelines where four benches have been set up.

Though he continues to address the contestants, Protector Djie shifts his energy back to the stands. "No equipment may be used beyond your hands, your arms, your legs, and your brains. Protectors, you may begin on my count: three, two, one!"

There is a flurry of movement and colour as the contestants sprint toward the wooden structures. My eyes flit from one team to the next, unsure of where to look. Choose one, I tell myself, or you risk missing everything.

I see a body in gold flying upward. Her teammates have executed the throw perfectly, for she lands, feet first, atop the wall. She does not stop to celebrate, but turns, braced, to assist the man that follows. Her teammate lands dangerously close to one of the glass figures. He dances to the side, flinging his hands outward in an attempt at stability. My heart is in my throat as he sways forward and then backward. For a moment I think he will fall, but then, beautifully, he regains his balance.

A flash of brilliance to their right pulls my attention: four protectors dressed in blue are staring, horrified, as a virtue rocks back and forth atop their wall. Three of them are standing on the wall, while one sits half draped over the ledge. It looks as though he had been trying to swing, rather than pull, himself up to join them. I cringe as the glass figure rocks one more time and then topples from the wall.

Behind them, three shapes in white slide from a wooden structure and rush to form a human pyramid.

My head swivels back toward the gold team. The largest of the four, a male, crouches on the ground, arms braced against the wall, weight shifted forward. A woman climbs up his back until she can place her feet on his shoulders. She, too, crouches, while the man slowly straightens. Once he is upright, she starts to stand herself, reaching her hand forward toward the waiting hands of her teammates. The distance is too great—they cannot reach her.

Cheers resound. I look over to see the team in black standing atop their wall, hands clasped and raised as one in victory. Both virtues stand upright and untouched beside them.

The gold team is not distracted. The man at the top of the wall now holds the female protector by her ankles. She reaches down and grasps the forearms of the woman below her. She shouts something to the man on the ground and he begins to climb carefully up the bodies of his teammates.

The human ladder works. The remaining teammates successfully scale the wall and cheers once again fill the stadium. They have obtained second place and two points.

"Isn't it thrilling?" Starling whispers from beside me. I look over and see that she is staring, transfixed, at the scene below.

I nod, though I know she is not watching me. A thought sparks like a match and I catch my breath. "That could be us, someday," I whisper.

She turns to me now and grins, her hand gripping mine tightly. The protectors are leaving the arena; it is time for the cadets to march forward and take the stage. All around us, the stands reverberate once again with cheers and stomping feet.

I wonder why we whisper.

20

The South

I LIE in my bed in the dormitory that night, counting. How many courses did each team complete? How many weapons did each contestant draw? I want to remember each match, each trial. The others have been asleep for hours, but though I want to be well rested for the start of training in the morning, I cannot convince my mind to slow.

I sit up and lower my feet onto the cold floor. On my way to the lavatory I stop and glance down the empty corridor. I wish I could wander about a bit. For a fleeting second, I wonder if there are vents or passageways through which I could pass undetected, as Iris and I used to. Then I remember that I would still appear, one small green dot, on the big screen in Tranquility Square.

I frown at the thought. How did I become a dot? I look up at the ceiling, searching the bare cement in vain for a camera. Perhaps we are only captured in public areas—the square, the canteen and such. I continue on to the lavatory.

If the screen relies on camera recognition, does it perceive only that we are, in fact, uniformed cadets or protectors dressed in green? I wonder if it can distinguish between us. The uniforms are similar but not identical, matching in colour and fabric but not in cut. Perhaps the uniform itself is inconsequential, and the cameras register simply the alphanumeric codes. If I had zoomed in closer, would I have seen a mark signifying rank? Beyond that—if I looked more closely still, would I see a name?

I walk across the empty bathroom to the washbasins and the wide mirror that stretches out horizontally above them, remove my shirt, and lay it on the narrow ledge. I examine my arms, my stomach, and then turn around, peering backward over my shoulder at my neck, my back: nothing. Running my fingers along the backside of my ears I feel only soft, smooth skin. I pick up my shirt, and then pause. Leaning in toward the mirror, I raise my right arm, and see it. There is a tiny red mark at the base of my armpit: a line barely three millimeters across and perfectly straight.

With my left hand I touch a finger gently to the cut. I can barely feel the ridge, it is so slight. It has been a few years since I have needed a medic to close a wound but the mark is unmistakable. I push against the red line, wiggling my finger in small circles. It does not sting—it must have been several days since they operated. I push harder but cannot feel the tracker with my finger; they must have buried it deep. I catch sight of myself in the mirror and smile politely, as though my reflection were a designate that had caught me misbehaving.

It is a relief, I tell myself, knowing that they can always locate me. The grounds outside are uncontained; if a sandstorm were to blow through when I was outdoors one day it would be easy to get turned around and lose my way. I pull on my shirt and return to the dormitory. I feel that sleep will come now.

21

T he North

"WE'RE NOT GOING to bother her, we're going to bring her joy and entertainment." *Is that Xenia's voice?*

"Fine, you can go in." Sam recognized the warning tone in Ava's voice. "But what you're gonna bring her is some jook and more tea. And you're not going to tire her out."

Something heavy shifted and then jumped down from the foot of the bed.

"Oh, hello, you handsome fellow."

Sam peered out of one eye and saw Xenia scooping Frank up in her arms.

"That cat's a beast! You can't just lift him up like a baby." Cassio followed his sister into the room, a mug in one hand and a small bowl in the other.

"But he wanted me to! I could feel it. You just wanted a snuggle, didn't you, plumpy?"

"Hey," Sam croaked.

"She *is* alive!" Xenia plopped down on the bed beside Sam. "How you feeling, lala?"

"Like I was gutted and burned alive."

Cassio brought her the tea and rice porridge and then took a seat on the crate beside the bed. "Sounds about right." He shook his head. "Cooking an open wound like that... You got bones. I mean, I think maybe you're crazy, but you got bones."

"Ooh, you should have seen Benison's face when Hak gave him the goods the next day," said Xenia. "He was so relieved, he almost smiled. His eye actually started twitching."

Sam's smile turned into a grimace as her lips cracked and bled. *I'll have to ask Ava for fat to rub on them. Of course, I could just be dehydrated.* She took a sip of her tea. Miraculously, it was not scalding hot. It also tasted normal. Ava must have run out of valerian. Relieved, Sam took a bigger mouthful. She preferred pain to narcotics.

"How long have I been out for?"

"Five days," Cassio said. "We came by earlier, but you were out cold. We brought Ava supplies, though. She's snappy, I like her."

Sam wasn't sure what Cassio meant by supplies, and she was too tired to ask.

"Eat," said Xenia, taking the tea and placing it on the floor. "Snappy's orders. Also, you're kind of a skeleton."

Sam took a closer look at her hands. Xenia wasn't exaggerating. The skin was stretched taut over bone; she barely recognized them as her own. She stirred the jook and tried a spoonful. It too had been cooled. *Ava must really want me to eat.*

"And Benison..." she asked between mouthfuls. "...has he...? Am I fired?"

"Of course not!" Xenia said quickly. "You've got a good stash from that night too, Jackal's keeping it for you. Benison hasn't pushed for you to come back yet, either."

"Yet," Cassio repeated, earning a glare from his twin.

"Jack should be by tonight or tomorrow, actually. We've been taking shifts, darling," she said when Sam gave her a puzzled look.

Beneath the fatigue and the throbbing pain, Sam felt touched. She started to say something, but found her eyelids closing.

"Hmm? Oh right, yeah, we drugged your tea. Have a good sleep, lala."

Sam felt someone take the half-finished bowl of jook from her hands. The door closed a moment later.

22

The North

SAM HOPED she didn't look as relieved as she felt to see Hakuund's wide frame follow Jackal into the room the following evening. She didn't have a problem with Jackal, but neither did she particularly enjoy the long awkward pauses the two of them tended to lapse into.

"Here's my hero." Hakuund bent down and planted a kiss on the top of her head. She looked up at him and grinned.

"How're you feeling?" Jackal asked, settling down on the crate that Cassio had dragged over the day before.

"Better," Sam said, declining to describe the constant, burning pain. She hadn't woken up screaming that morning, so technically she was doing better than she had been.

"Holy jit, this guy's fat." Frank had emerged from under the bed and was watching Hakuund.

The cat turned his back on Hakuund, offended, perhaps, by the comments about his girth, or perhaps by the sheer size and volume that was Hakuund. He wandered over to Jackal, who stretched out a hand for him to sniff. Frank complied, and then settled down by Jackal's feet with a loud and belligerent, "Meow!"

"He was like this when I met him. Also, I like him this way." *I can't believe I'm defending a cat.*

Sam started to reach for the tea that Ava had brought her earlier and let out an inadvertent hiss as the movement set her side on fire. She counted backward from twelve, waiting for it to pass. The pain soon settled back down into the low, constant throbbing she had grown accustomed to.

"Taow, kid, you need something for that?" Hakuund asked.

"I can manage it," she said, though she was unable to keep the strain out of her voice.

He shrugged. "I guess when it comes to stitching, you know best."

"Xenia said your mom was a stitcher," Jackal said, passing her the mug of tea. "I reckon we could learn a thing or two from you."

Hakuund nodded vehemently. "There's nobody outside the compounds can stop infection. Every stitcher in the Barrow is the same as Melena. They can cut and sew, sweat out a fever maybe, but you're as likely to end up in the ground as you are to walk out again. That's why nobody sees a stitcher unless they have to. You know that cult, the one that worships Ba'al? They say it's the ghosts of the dead that hang around, trying to infect the living."

"Course," Jackal said, petting the cat absently, "they're bav jit crazy."

Hakuund shrugged. "What, because they say you can cure a toothache by cutting off a finger? Or better yet, somebody else's finger?"

Sam hid a smile and took a sip of her tea, wondering if it was drugged. You could plead your case with Ava from dawn until dusk; the woman would do as she pleased. From the way Jackal was eyeing her tea, Sam could tell he was wondering the same thing.

"Before I forget." He pulled a bag out of his jacket and passed it to Sam. "Your cut from the Dens."

Sam took the bag, surprised. From the weight of it, she was holding several weeks of pay. Hakuund leaned in and winked at Sam.

"Old Jack bartered you some damage pay."

Sam looked at Jackal, who shrugged.

"Figured you'd need some time to mend. No point you starving to death before you have a chance to get back to work." He stood up, brushing off Sam's thanks. "We'd've been down one member permanently if you hadn't played it like you did. Plus, the value of the goods—they owe you a lot more."

Sam didn't know how to respond.

"We should head out," Hakuund said, before the awkward silence could stretch on for too long. "Send word if you need anything." He stood and tussled her hair in a manner similar to the way he had tried to pet the cat.

Jackal just nodded, and the two men turned and left. Sam took another sip of her tea. The visit, short as it had been, had managed to tire her out. Either that or her tea was drugged after all.

The pain, her fatigue, the drugs she assumed were in her tea, gave the days that followed a surreal quality. Later she would remember moments, visits, conversations, but the time between them seemed to drop off and disappear. Each time she woke up, she had to ask whether a minute had passed or hours or days.

Invariably, when she slept, she dreamed the same dream: Corvus poisoned or shot or suffocated in their bed; leaving and running through the hallways; finding the underground city and the house where Finlay had imprisoned Raina and his other ex-girlfriends, now strung up like marionettes. The only thing that ever changed was the chase. Sometime she was following Raina and sometimes it was Corvus. It didn't matter: they led her to the same place.

It was a week until Sam stopped losing time, until days became days and nights became nights. Even then she remained bedridden.

It was Ava who suggested they begin her lessons again.

"I don't know why 'ph' makes the 'f' sound, it just does," Sam said from Raina's old bed, where she sat propped up on pillows.

"Well it's bav."

"Okay, that's fine, but you're learning a written language, not creating one. You have to follow the rules, even the ones you think are stupid."

Ava glared at the slate in front of her and then grudgingly crossed out "farmacy" and wrote "pharmacy".

"I don't even know this word, why do I have to know how to write it?"

"It's a place that sells medicine," Sam explained for the second time that afternoon. "In Seira, the government takes on that role."

"Exactly. It's some fool Southern word I won't ever use."

Sam sighed, began to explain again why language should not be limited to words you already know, gave up, and filled her mouth with onion loaf.

Frank chose that moment to burst into the room, a half-eaten rat carcass dangling from his mouth.

"I was wondering when you'd make time for us." Ava heaved herself up off the crate she was sitting on and disappeared into her shop, returning a moment later with a dish of water. Frank dropped the rat remains and half waddled, half ran over to her. Sam eyed his merrily jiggling paunch and ripped off another piece of the onion loaf. "I wish you'd let me pay you for this."

"You're giving me lessons," said Ava.

"It's not enough."

"What, you wanna throw coin away? Foolish girl."

"I thought the whole point of becoming a drudge was so that I'd have a few xots saved up in time of need. Isn't that what you said? Sell your soul but you'll never sink to taking a debt?"

Ava sighed and sat down on the bed near Sam's feet. "This ain't debt, you and me."

Sam eyed the other woman out of the corner of her eye, unsure how to respond. "Well," she continued after a moment, intent upon her argument, "you hate the Vauns. I thought you'd love the chance to spend their money."

"You act like your place with them is permanent."

"Isn't it?"

"It's as permanent as they say it is."

"That's illogical. All that damage pay? They've invested in me."

Ava stared at her, a mixture of exasperation and pity on her face.

"Come now, girl," she said. "Damage pay is a unicorn. Everybody talks about it, ain't no one ever seen it."

"What are you talking about? I've got it right here." Sam pointed to the trunk where they had locked up the bag of coins. "And what's a unicorn?"

"It's a magical horse with a horn that everyone goes mad for."

Sam frowned, puzzled.

"It don't exist! Look, you did a big job and I'm sure you got a good haul, but all that didn't come from them."

"What, do I have some mysterious benefactor then?"

"You got a few."

Sam stared at her blankly.

Ava sighed. "Your team, you gull, they padded it."

"No. They can't have. I wouldn't take coin from them."

"Which is why they lied."

"Well, I'll give it back to them."

"No, you won't. You'll just do the same for them, if the chance comes up." Ava sighed again and stood back up, rubbing a calloused knuckle into her right hip. "This is how it works in the North. I just didn't think a bunch of drudges would follow code."

"And why is that?" asked Sam, too tired to pretend that she wasn't bothered by Ava's comment.

"Don't expect a drudge to care much about anything besides coin. Not you," she added, noticing the look on Sam's face. "You ain't a real drudge."

And Raina? Sam opened her mouth, wanting to make a point, wanting to know; she closed it again. *What would it profit? Nothing for Ava. Just you.*

She recognized in herself a morbid curiosity. She wanted an excuse to talk about Raina—not only about how she disappeared, but the little details: how she thought; things she'd said. It was as though she hoped to recreate the girl from memory alone. *I've too much time alone of late, that's all.*

She could feel another headache coming on. With a sigh, she picked up the slate, erased "pharmacy" and replaced it with "phase".

Instead we'll just sit here, both thinking about her, saying nothing.

23

The North

A MONTH later her injury had mostly healed, although Ava declared her to be "as weak as a toddler with the sweats."

She could hobble around Ava's quarters, but her nest was out of the question, and Ava vehemently opposed her leaving the factory for any reason.

"You walk like you were born yesterday. Who *wouldn't* rob you?"

Sam thought Ava was probably exaggerating, but humoured her nonetheless. *For now.*

It was odd to have no structure to her days, to wake up when she pleased and shape each moment on a whim. Perhaps it would have been pleasurable, if she were whole and healthy. As it was, she missed her independence; she missed being productive; she missed the distraction of routine.

At least she had daily visitors. Hakuund and Cassio usually came together. Hakuund had even taken to bringing her treats—a small pastry, a honey stick. Sam was touched that he thought her worth his time and coin. They typically visited in the evening after supper, chatting about nothing for a few minutes and then heading out on mission or to a party. She was fairly certain the two of them never slept. Xenia often arrived with Jackal in tow, although he never had much to say and tended to bow out after a few minutes.

Ava had been standoffish with the drudges at first. Xenia won her over slowly with her charm and infectious smiles, Hakuund with maple loaf. Cassio she actually seemed to approve of from the start. It was Frank that finally quelled her misgivings about Jackal. He seemed to favour Jackal above everyone except Sam. "If the cat vouches for him, I suppose he's alright," Ava had eventually concluded, glaring at Frank as though the cat was actively trying to vex her.

The visitor that surprised Sam most of all was Shale. The redhead stopped by every day or two, her visits often coinciding with Xenia's, with whom she had become fast friends while Sam was drifting in and out of drug-induced sleep. Sam was not sure what had prompted the visits—pity? Curiosity?

Whatever the motivating factor, Sam was grateful for her company. Shale always had stories to share, tidbits of information she collected from all over the Barrow. Sam spent most of her time listening, which suited her perfectly.

Both Shale and Xenia had dropped by that evening. Xenia had even brought an activity: goopy paint. It was a special type of goopy paint, she had explained. When it was applied to skin, the designs would last for weeks. It didn't take long for Sam to realize that painting with goop was not a skill that she naturally possessed.

"There isn't really a trick to it. You either have a steady hand, or you don't."

"So, I don't then," said Sam.

"Nope, not at all," said Xenia. "She does, though."

Shale flashed them a coquettish smile. "I've always been good with my hands."

"Here, I'll draw over your...attempt." Careful not to smudge the intricate lines she had painted on the back of her own hand and wrist, Xenia popped a pillow under Sam's elbow and started spinning the goo around in a web-like design.

Shale had finished designing her own left hand: a mass of swirls and leaves. She watched Xenia for a minute and then took Sam's other hand in her own and started painting a vine.

"So, when do you wash the goop off?" Sam asked.

"You don't. In an hour or so we'll brush it off and wet it with sugar water."

"Why, so I can attract my very own mob of flies?"

Xenia stuck her tongue out at Sam. "It helps the dye set."

Sam watched in silence for a few moments as the two women worked. It felt strange, as though she were a queen with hand-maidens waiting on her. *If the handmaidens far outshone the queen.*

Xenia had drawn a bird on her wrist. Sam traced the shape with her eyes. She found it strange that the symbol still remained in the North, long after the birds themselves had gone extinct, dead from disease or heat or environmental contaminants. *At least we've still got the crows.*

Around the painted bird, brambles jutted out, seeming to meld into—

"Is that fire?"

"It is. A battle scar."

"Oh, good. It can go with my actual battle scar."

The designs had reached her forearms, Xenia humming away while Shale was working in focused silence. Sam wondered if they were consciously racing each other.

"So—"

"Nope." Xenia's eyes remained fixed on the thin line of goop that she was applying to Sam's arm. "I looked for him yesterday, but if he was there, he wasn't selling in his usual spot. I'll check again next week."

"How did you know—"

"It's your tone, darling. You ask the same way, every time."

"Oh. What about your contact?" Sam asked Shale. "The girl you said used to date one?"

Shale shook her head. "Haven't seen her."

Sam nodded, trying not to let the disappointment show on her face. "Thanks for looking, anyway."

Now that she was feeling stronger, she itched to leave the factory and track down Hunters. The ticking of time irked her; she felt the trail growing colder every day and couldn't suppress the feeling that she had missed out on her best opportunity the night at the Dens. *Patience is a virtue,* a small voice in her head reminded her. Sam shoved it away. She lived in the North now. Seiran morality could go hang.

She had been reluctant to involve Shale and Xenia, but the alternative of waiting until she was well again to resume the search had seemed unbearable. They had both agreed to help her look for Hunters, albeit only by asking within their personal networks—a painfully slow process that had yet to yield any results. The only time Sam had met with outright refusal was when she had asked Shale to make contact with Maddox.

She hadn't given a reason, and at the time, Sam had let it go. Shale really seemed to despise the man. As the weeks passed without further leads, though, Sam began to regret her earlier decision not to press the matter.

Sam's restlessness was worsened by the fact that the Hunters were a weak lead at best. Members of the gang had had some kind of dealings with Finlay, true, but there was no guarantee that they knew anything about Finlay and Raina's disappearance, even if they were willing to speak with her. Unfortunately, they were also the only lead.

Brainstorming with Xenia and Shale had not led to any new insight. Xenia had indulged Sam by walking through the scant details she could remember of the couple's last weeks at the compound, even bringing her twin in for similar questioning, but the sad fact remained that neither of them seemed to have known Raina or Finlay very well at all. Despite living in the same factory as Finlay, they couldn't point her towards a single contact or provide a name or even a good description of any of his previous girlfriends.

"Is there a place he spoke about? Somewhere he might have gone if he wanted to hide?"

The bewilderment on their faces had been tinged with pity, as though they thought Sam might have suffered some minor brain damage when the huaina shot her in the gut.

If the Hunters were a dead end, Sam wanted to know as soon as possible. It could be that the Hunters had come looking for Finlay last year because they had been involved with his plans to kidnap Raina and other women. *And it's equally possible that their interaction had nothing to do with Raina.* Sam waved the thought away. She had to pursue all possible leads.

Why? Why do you have to pursue any leads at all?

Sam waved this thought away, too. It was the right thing to do.

Is that it, then? You're just a kindly citizen, doing a good deed?

A stupid criticism. There were no citizens in the North. How could there be citizens without a state?

Sam's suggestion that they go down to the Pike and ask people at random if they knew a Hunter had been strongly vetoed by the other two girls.

"But why?" Sam had asked. "I'm going to offer to pay for information. Why the secrecy?"

"It's just not how it's done here," Shale had told her. "Publicly calling them out...they'll take it as a hostile move. You need to find someone you know who knows them."

Sam thought that Shale was being overcautious, but she hadn't argued the point. Certainly, she did not want the other two to do anything that they were uncomfortable with. Besides, once she was back at full strength, she could go track down the Hunters herself.

Sam stared at the bird on her wrist. "And when you do make contact, remember not—"

"We won't mention Raina," Xenia said, repeating Sam's words back to her. "We'll only say that we've a friend who has coin in exchange for information on Finlay."

"And arrange a meeting," added Shale. "During which they will rob and then murder you."

Ignoring the last comment, Sam pressed a finger into her brow, willing it to unfurrow, and took a slow, deep breath. *Let it go until tomorrow. There is nothing you can do today.*

Xenia, who had reached Sam's elbow first, paused as though wondering whether to take her design right up to Sam's shoulder.

"Uh, I think that's probably good, right? My shirt sleeves cover from here anyway."

"Well, only when you're clothed," said Xenia.

"Uh, yup. Only, only when I'm...clothed."

Xenia looked at Sam with a big smile, seeming about to say something when she interrupted herself with a loud "oh!" She opened the paper tube that held the goopy mixture.

"We almost forgot the dip. Okay girls, if you need your hands for anything, do it now."

Shale got to her feet and sashayed out of the room, offering no explanation. The other two girls looked at each other and shrugged. They had grown used to Shale flitting in and out.

Xenia rubbed the mixture onto the ends of Sam's fingers, up until the first crease.

"What is this for?" Sam asked. "Besides making it more difficult to keep the dye from getting all over our clothes, beds, food..."

"For beauty," Xenia said, as though it was obvious.

"Oh."

"Where's Jackal tonight?" Sam asked when the silence had gone on too long.

"He had some special task but said that he might drop by later."

"He's been with the compound a long time, huh?"

"Actually, not really. Maybe two years? He was still pretty new when we joined up. Hak, now, he's been with them for ages."

"Oh. I assumed—"

"That because Jack is lead, that he's the veteran? Nah. Hakuund can just be...unreliable. He'll take off for days sometimes, no warning. We never know where he's gone or if he's okay. It drives my brother crazy."

Xenia had just finished dying her own fingertips when Shale reappeared, cradling a large jar of liquor. Sam hoped it wasn't moonshine.

"Sikera?" asked Xenia, her green eyes lighting up. "Lovely, darling. Do you brew?"

"Gods no. I am, however, the recipient of many useful gifts." Shale set the jar down on the floor and knelt in front of Xenia, offering up her fingertips.

"Okay," said Xenia, once she had finished. "I'm gonna go beg sugar off Ava."

Shale watched her go, and then shook her head at Sam. "Now that is a woman who is very good at getting what she wants."

Sam raised her eyebrows.

"I'm not being nasty. That's praise, girl. She may actually be better at it than I am."

"Well, that is praise indeed."

Shale laughed.

"Lookie what we get!" Along with the sugar water, Xenia returned carrying a plate loaded up with rolls.

She placed the bread beside Shale's jar and began sprinkling the sugar water onto Sam's hands and arms, careful to coat all of the meticulously drawn lines of goop. When she moved on to Shale, Sam lifted herself gingerly to her feet and hobbled off to find cups.

"You can take those three jars there," Ava said over her shoulder, dishing out boil to a group of customers. "What'd Shale scrounge up for you?"

"Sikera."

"Pulling back then, huh? Smart." Ava turned around to grab more bowls and noticed the confused expression on Sam's face. "Gods, I still forget that you don't know anything." She filled up three more bowls and passed them out to the remaining patrons. Once she'd tucked their payment into the box she kept under the counter, she settled down on the crate across from Sam.

"Okay, little stray. So, for a group of friends, or if you're with family or a lover, you drink sikera from the same jar. Getting separate cups, it's...it means there's no trust. Doing it to an old friend or lover..." She whistled. "Well, that's a sign of breaking. With new friends, it's plain as telling them you don't want to get to know them any better."

"Why is everything so complicated here?" Sam said. She looked at the cups in her hand, looked at Ava, looked back at the cups, and sighed. She turned toward the door, took a step, and then turned back and placed the cups on the shelf. Avoiding Ava's eyes, she hobbled back to her friends.

Why do all of the social bonding activities in the North have to be so damn unsanitary?

She entered the room to see Shale trying to pick up a roll using the insides of her wrists and turned and walked back to the kitchen.

"Brilliant," Xenia said, stabbing a roll with the metal skewer Sam had brought her from the kitchen. Sam smiled and took another sip of sikera, which had surprised her by tasting of apples. It was also delicious. *Why does everyone drink moonshine when there's sikera?* It also seemed to be dulling the pain in her side, which usually worsened as the evening wore on.

Jackal walked in just as the three women finished the last roll.

"Perfect timing, handsome." Xenia giggled at him, earning a raised eyebrow in return.

"Xen's a harpy," said Shale. "I'd have shared with you."

"Begrudgingly," Xenia said, ducking as Shale threw a metal skewer at her. "Sikera?"

Jackal accepted the brew, looking at the three of them. "Obliged," he said, and took a long sip.

With his usual spot on Ava's trunk inaccessible by reason of dishes and leftover goopy paint supplies, Jackal seated himself at the foot of the bed. A loud "prow" sounded from underneath the bed, preceding the emergence of the fat orange cat.

"Were you here this whole time? You sneaky beast." Xenia reached out a hand to scratch under Frank's chin.

"Late night," Shale said to Jackal.

"It's been busy." He looked at Sam, who felt a stab of guilt. She knew they had been picking up her slack. "Actually." He cleared his throat. "I have some bad news." Panic started to prickle up Sam's spine. She wondered if he was about to tell her that she was fired.

"They want you back day after tomorrow," he said. "I told them you can barely walk and that for certain you can't ride. Benison said that it wouldn't inconvenience them if you took twelve hours to complete each task, so long as it got done." He looked at Sam, an unusually sympathetic expression on his face. "I tried."

"That's bav!" said Xenia. "She'll get mobbed by huaina, going out like that! They can't ask this!"

"It's fine," Sam said, relieved that she hadn't been dismissed. "I'll go slow, and it'll be okay." She smiled at them. "I'm grateful for the time I've had."

"Don't be a martyr, girl," Xenia said with a frown. "You can fight this."

"Fight a compound?" Shale raised her eyebrows.

"It really is okay," Sam said, looking at Xenia. "It'll be good to be doing something useful again."

Xenia glared at Jackal, as though it were his doing—the usual price of carrying someone else's bad news. Shale passed the sikera around again. They each took a swig in silence, the mood considerably less merry.

24

The North

THOUGH SAM HAD LEFT for the compound a half hour earlier than she was wont to, as she hobbled down the trail the next morning she realized that she had overestimated herself. Even beyond her injury, which was already throbbing, the muscles in her underused legs were aching and her breath was coming out in gasps. At least she wasn't cold—the seasons had sped along while she had been hauled up in the factory. It was a transformation she welcomed, until the mosquitoes descended.

It wasn't the bites that she minded so much, though the welts itched and stung. Every bite was a roll of the dice.

Not that she was a vulnerable demographic; the very young, the old, and the sickly, they were the ones who usually died from the sweats, as locals called the various fever-inducing diseases spread by mosquitoes.

Malaria 2A, Zika 2B, West Nile 3A, Dengue 2C, Chikungunya 1B— before the Decline, they had coded the mutations. Now nobody even bothered differentiating between them. Though they still had their unique symptoms, the later mutations were uniform where it counted. A high fever, chills, profuse sweating, flushing... *And sometimes you die. Sometimes you're young and healthy and you still die.* There was no prevention, no treatment. Northerners prayed. Sam killed mosquitoes, one at a time.

It hadn't always been this way, she had been taught. The deadly strains of mosquitoes weren't actually native to the North. It wasn't until the temperatures had risen that they had begun to make their way northward, bit by bit.

Bite by bite, rather.

By the time she arrived, Benison was already making his way down the causeway. With no time for a proper greeting, her friends each touched her shoulder or arm briefly as they passed by.

Benison curled his lip when he saw Sam approaching, last of the litter. "I understand you can't ride."

Sam shook her head. He opened a panel in the fence and passed her a scroll and a very small bag of coin.

"If you can only complete half the work, you can expect half the pay."

Sam scanned it quickly. The items were low-end, the type of products she had been tasked to obtain when she had first started working for the compound. Perhaps it was a coincidence. Or perhaps he shared Ava and Xenia's opinion that anyone who looked as infirm as Sam did was likely to be jumped.

The market was one she had been to before. Maybe an hour away by bike. On foot, the trip was going to take her close to four hours each way. She had wanted to go by the Pike after work to look for Hunters. At this rate, it would probably be dark by the time she finished the day's mission.

She looked up and nodded to Benison, trying not to show her disappointment, and started off across the field. *Straighten your back, lengthen your stride,* she told herself, unwilling to reveal to Benison or anyone else who may be watching the true extent of her discomfort. When she reached the first bend in the trail she collapsed against a tree, hissing with pain. She allowed herself a moment's rest, swatting at the mosquitoes that buzzed around her face, and then began hobbling down the path.

It was evening by the time she arrived back at the compound. Her shoulders ached under the weight of her pack, filled to capacity with items that were far heavier than they were valuable. The grounds were empty, barring the guards standing at their usual spots inside the fence. She slid the bag slowly off her shoulders, managing, despite her best efforts, to trigger a stabbing pain so sharp she had to bite her cheeks to keep from crying out.

Leaning carefully against the fence, she turned her face upward, letting the rain cool her flushed cheeks. She would have given her day's pay to be able to collapse onto the wet grass. Considering she barely had the strength to lower herself into bed at night, she doubted she would be able to make it to the ground and then back up again. Sam shuddered, picturing herself floundering like a beetle on its back, Benison and a pack of armed guards staring down at her with mockery in their eyes.

It was fully dark by the time Benison emerged from the compound. He took a look through her bag, wrinkling his nose as though her presence somehow sullied the goods. *Stab wounds are not contagious,* she wanted to snap at him. Instead she told her face muscles to relax, her jaw to soften. Pain made her peevish, a self-indulgent attitude she could ill afford, especially in front of Benison. She struggled to maintain a pleasant expression as he passed over her day's wages, a fraction of what she usually earned.

Turning toward the woods, she hesitated. She was exhausted, and the pain in her side was so bad that she was having trouble thinking straight. *Are you really in the best shape to deal with a bunch of violent huaina?* She supposed it wouldn't be the worst thing to wait a few days, just until she was feeling stronger.

Choking down her disappointment, she made for the trail that would lead her home to the factory.

25

The North

"So, you're not dead." Jem greeted her with a glare the following day. "Just forgot all about us?"

Sam lifted the corner of her shirt to show him the scar. "Got stabbed."

"Humph," was all he said, although Sam could see him softening. "We've got chana balls and rice globes and sugar dots cooking. Don't know why everything has to be round tonight, but you may as well come in and help us eat them."

Geo greeted her with a hug and a kiss on each cheek. "Please tell me I misheard?"

"I'm okay now, it was just a long recovery."

"Let me see."

Sam showed Geo the marks.

"All the way through?" Geo hissed in sympathy. "How did this happen? Please tell me you didn't see some horrible stitcher. Actually, is this a burn mark? How on earth did you get burned? Never mind, you don't need me prying. I'm just glad that you're okay."

Sam shared a heavily edited rendition of the incident, admitting she had caught a huaina's bolt and detailing the bloody aftermath, but omitting the series of triggering events. Overall, she gave the impression that she had been caught in the middle of someone else's fray. Geo and Jem knew that Sam worked for the Vauns and never pressed her for details related to her work.

"...the same needle, without a drop of water or disinfectant."

"But how did you know to burn it?" Jem asked. Sam thought she could detect a trace of suspicion in his voice.

"My mother was a stitcher," she said, the lie rolling more easily off her tongue with each repetition. "But a good one. She taught me that you must keep everything clean, washed with boiling water or burned. Otherwise rot will set in."

"Hmm," said Geo. "Well, maybe Kanlan is better, but the stitcher you saw was standard for the Barrow. How can there be better, when they can't pick up a book and learn?"

It was a good point. She supposed there could be oral traditions of medicine, but literacy made the transfer of knowledge much easier, and knowledge was power. Being able to read and write was the reason she was able to scrape a better living than most. If she didn't want to be a drudge, she could also work as a reader. She pictured Raina and Finlay, working as readers a town or two over. *It wouldn't be such a bad life.*

"Anyway, dear, the second batch of sugar dots should be ready in a moment. Can you stay long enough to sample a piece or two?"

26

The North

SAM HAD TAKEN to haunting the streets underneath the Pike between missions, though she had yet to approach anyone. As loath as she was to admit that Shale and Xenia's worries might be well founded, the women, men, and children who hung around the Pike seemed a dangerous lot. Piercings, ink, presence or absence of specific colours: it seemed a dozen gangs consorted in this neighbourhood. She stared at the faces—guarded, defensive, cocky, and scared—and wondered which of them, if any, were Hunters.

Eager to avoid conflict in her weakened state, Sam found small nooks and crannies where she could watch, unobserved, their comings and goings. The rain thundered down, slowed, and then thundered down again. Pigeons strutted about. Huaina boasted and traded and occasionally fought. Above all, the Pike towered up, thousands of feet high, the broken tip pointing upward at the sky as though in accusation.

It was another few weeks before she felt well enough to ask Benison for a bicycle. She knew she was ready when she managed to complete her entire morning exercise routine—a set of moves that required balance, flexibility, and strength—without pause. As the sight of Sam moving slowly from one pose to another sent Ava into shrieks of laughter, Sam was glad when she was finally able to return to her nest with only Frank for company. He judged her, she didn't doubt, but silently.

Sam climbed onto the bicycle that Benison had unlocked for her. Trying to reassure her skeptical self that neither Benison nor the compound guards on duty were watching, she pedaled tentatively forward, relieved to find that the motion didn't pull too badly at her injury. Picking up a bit of speed, she tried and failed to suppress a huge grin as she made for the trails.

The spice market was still coming to life when she arrived a few hours later. It had rained on her twice during the ride: intense downpours that lasted only minutes and then vanished, leaving behind battered skin and flooded streets. Sam didn't mind. It was hot, finally; let the sun dry her.

She settled down on a packing crate and watched as vendors assembled their makeshift tables and unpacked their wares. A young man was artfully arranging a selection of fresh basil and mint on a table nearby, biting his tongue in fierce concentration as he fiddled with the aesthetics of the display. A girl not much older than him soon arrived with a second box of plants. Rolling her eyes, she whacked him on the back of the head and barked out something that Sam could not quite hear, but which was undoubtedly along the lines of: "Stop wasting time, you lazy jit." The gesture he made once she had turned her back was not one that Sam had ever seen before, but it too needed no translation.

Someone was plucking lazily at a string instrument. Maybe she would wander over later to listen. She was in no hurry to return to the compound. If she arrived back early in the day, Benison would be sure to assign her a second task. While she did not want to overexert herself, it was never wise to refuse a mission, regardless of how badly one had been skewered and roasted. *Better to just avoid him.*

Sam would enjoy the market, maybe even splurge on a sweet bread in celebration of her return to cycling—after she had completed her tasks, of course. After all, how relaxing could a spell of self-indulgence really be when she still had work to do?

Customers were starting to filter into the market. Sam got up from her crate, pulled her bicycle upright, and looked to the items on her list.

She found pine pollen first, sold by a tiny old woman wrapped in an enormous pink shawl.

"Yes, dear, lots available this time of year." She held out a box filled with glass jars, and beamed when Sam selected three.

"Enjoy," she said. "It really is the best. Why, you could get an erection out of the limpest zucchini!"

Sam stared at her for a moment, certain she must have misheard. The old woman adjusted her shawl, which was threatening to slide off her petite shoulders, and gave Sam a tiny wink.

Sam turned away, trying to fill her mind with the symbol for hyssop. Hyssop, hyssop—she was looking for hyssop next.

An hour later, her basket filled to capacity, Sam stood captivated before an array of sweet breads. There were loafs glazed with maple or apple syrup or filled to bursting with cherry paste, even baked in swirls and coated with sugar and cinnamon.

"If you can't choose, gimme three sack and I'll fill up a big bag with a bunch of 'em," the young salesgirl offered.

"How about two sack for a small bag?"

The girl gave Sam a blank stare. "One sack for one or three sack for a big bag. So two sack is two breads."

Spending three sack on sugar and flour was absurd, Sam told herself, ripping off a piece of the cinnamon loaf first. *Completely impractical. Paying two sack for a meager two pastries though, that would have been robbery.* She wasn't a fool. She licked her fingers and wandered toward the music.

The song was quite lively. It still amazed Sam how the simple homemade instruments she'd seen in the Barrow could produce such a variety of sounds. A group of young children had gathered and were jumping up and down, kicking their legs out and flailing their arms wildly. Raindrops started clunking down. A little girl pointed at the sky and shrieked with laughter.

"River, come on!" An older girl was tugging on her hand, pulling her back into the dance.

The girls had matching brown, frizzy hair: sisters, probably. They held hands and spun in circles until the little one collapsed, giggling, on the muddy ground. Instead of getting up, she waved her little arms and legs back and forth, leaving an imprint in the sludge. Above her, the air was speckled with mud as the dancing children splashed the rainwater at each other, at the crowd, at the sky.

They reminded Sam of the sisters at the factory. Raina's friends, if they could truly be labeled as such. It bothered her still, when she thought of them and their indifference. Did nobody miss Raina, aside from Ava? What a horrible thing to be gone and to be missed by so few. What a horrible thing for Ava, to be so alone in her grief.

A few more days, that was all Sam needed. A few more days and she would seek out a Hunter to question. *And if that's a dead end too? What then?* She waved the thought away. There had to be something there. *Why? Because you've been building this up in your mind for so long? That's on you.* She didn't expect them to have all of the answers, but surely they would know something—something small, even, a tidbit of information that would lead her to Raina and Finlay. She'd dreamed of the house in the underground city so many times that she had started to take for granted that they were still in the Barrow, hidden away somewhere.

The musician was crouched down low, eye level with the tots as they giggled and shook their dirty hair at him. Laughing, he stood back up, catching Sam's eye and flashing her a huge grin. It was the man who had helped her when the two huaina tried to steal her bomb-laden bike at the market that time. The one who wouldn't stop talking. What was his name again? She tore off a piece of the maple loaf and took a bite. It was an odd name, one that smelled of sun-baked rocks and perfidy. *Adder, like a snake.*

Sam crammed one more piece of cinnamon loaf into her mouth and turned away from the crowd. The rain was already slowing. *Such a fickle sky today.*

She was wedging the bag of pastries into the basket on her bicycle when a pair of unnecessarily stylish black leather boots wandered into her sightline. Up past torn black jeans and a dark green shirt, a hand stretched out toward her: a lightly tanned hand gripping a pear.

"I'll swap you fructose for sucrose," he offered with a wide smile. Bright blue eyes sought hers, and she was reminded of her earlier impression of him as highly educated and annoyingly cheerful. She looked skeptically at the pear.

"No rust, I checked."

Sam hesitated.

"Do you think I've poisoned it?" Adder asked, raising a hand to his chest in a dramatic display of indignation. "Here," he said, and took a large bite.

"So, now you're offering me half eaten food."

He reached into his satchel, pulled out a second pear, and held it out. "I promise it's just a pear. You won't turn into a donkey or spontaneously blurt out all your secrets."

Sam was starting to feel ridiculous. She took the pear and passed over the bag of sweet breads.

Adder plopped down on a tree stump and examined the contents of the bag. Tearing off a piece of apple loaf, he looked expectantly up at Sam. With an inward groan she walked over and settled herself on another stump, as far from his person as she could without giving offense.

She turned the pear around in her hands. *No rust. He was honest about that, at least.* She wiped it with the inside of her shirt and took a bite. It was delicious, truly delicious.

He tore off a second piece of apple loaf and grinned at her before stuffing it into his mouth. "No bombs today?"

"Nope," said Sam, her mouth full of pear.

"No? What about firecrackers?"

"Nope."

"No explosives at all?! How terribly dull."

Sam finished the pear and looked expectantly at the bag of sweet breads.

To her dismay, Adder reached into the bag a third time and tore into the maple loaf.

"I, for one, love firecrackers. What better way to celebrate the solstice than with party favours that can blow your face off?"

"How—" Sam stopped. The last thing she wanted was to prolong this conversation. *But how does he even know what a party favour is?* It was a dead expression. Sam had only stumbled across it by chance when she was flicking through an old dictionary at Geo and Jem's.

"How do I like to celebrate the solstice?"

"That's, no—not what I was—"

"Usually a small, intimate affair. The Barrow is known for them. Classy, elegant—just a few hundred people and a mountain of moonshine." Adder licked his fingers, cocking his head to the side as he watched her face. "How about yourself?"

"I, uh—"

"Going to party with the twins?"

Sam froze. "How do you know…"

Adder winked. "Everyone knows the twins. And who they work for."

Sam scowled.

"Well?" asked Adder.

"Well, what?"

"You going to ring in the solstice all together? One big, happy drudge family?"

Sam's scowl deepened. New to the Barrow she may be, but she could tell when someone was prying.

Adder gave her another one of his irritating smiles.

Say anything. Just end the conversation. "Maybe."

"I guess you've got a month to figure it out."

Sam gave a noncommittal shrug and looked pointedly at the bag of pastries, hoping he would take the hint. He shuffled the bag to his other hand and continued to smile at her.

"I should get going," she said, getting to her feet. Was she going to have to ask for her food back?

"Back to work?" he asked, standing up as well.

"Hmm," was all she said.

He watched her for a moment, and then passed over the sadly depleted bag of sweet breads.

"Have a safe ride. Hope I'll see you again soon."

"Sure," she said in a tone that offered no encouragement, and pushed her bike past Adder, toward the exit. Once she was past him, her polite expression gave way to a scowl. The whole interaction had been decidedly unpleasant.

27

The North

"YOU GULL, he was trying to flirt with you," Ava said, looking up from the steaming pot that night.

"Well, if he was, someone should tell him that he's doing it wrong. Soap?" Ava tossed her a bar and Sam started lathering her hair. "He just wouldn't stop talking."

Ava snorted in response. "With you so mum, guess he had to. This one's boiling finally—you want another pot of hot in there?"

"Yes, please."

Ava slowly added scalding water to the bath, turning the tepid water instantly, gloriously hot. Sam gave a sigh of deep contentment and sank into the water. After so many sponge baths, this tub was heavenly. Distantly, she heard Ava set the pot back onto the fire pit and bustle out of the room.

"You're being oddly nice today," she said when her friend returned a few moments later.

"I'm always nice, you little jit."

Ava glowered at her when she laughed. "It's because I shared my apple loaf with you, isn't it? Is apple loaf the key to your affection?"

"You're like a parasite I've got fond of. Probably because you've infected my brain."

"That old nest of wires and rags? Yech, I wouldn't go near there."

Ava let out a loud bark of a laugh. "Least you're a funny little parasite. Had no idea you'd end up so saucy, quiet thing you was when you got here."

"I'm only like this with you, A," Sam said.

"Well, I'm glad to hear it." Ava lowered herself onto a crate with a groan, pushing a hand into her lower back. "Don't trust—"

"Anybody, especially a drudge," Sam finished for her. "Yeah, yeah."

"Humph. If you'll shush for a minute, I got something for you." Opening up her hand, Ava dangled a necklace from her fingers. There were two charms on the end, both made of copper: a rectangle and a bird. It was the only piece of jewelry that Sam had ever seen Ava wear. Sam frowned. *She used to wear it every day. When did she stop?*

"But...why? I mean, thank you, but..."

Ava shrugged. "Would rather you have it. Don't need it, do I?"

"But—"

"Fine, if you don't want it." Ava pocketed the necklace, looking hurt.

"No, it's beautiful," said Sam, because it was. "But don't you want to wear it?"

Ava shrugged. "I'll leave it on your clothes," she said, heaving herself back up.

There was an odd feeling in Sam's chest. She looked at Ava, really looked at her, as she ambled over to where Sam's clothes lay folded in a neat pile and laid the necklace on top. Was it her imagination, or was Ava looking shabbier? Her clothes looked like they could use a wash, and there was a hole in her apron that needed mending. Worry: that was what Sam was feeling.

"I mean it," Ava said, turning around. "'Bout how you talk. 'Specially at the compound. Get to know them, talk with them, go out with them, but don't trust 'em. You can't trust a drudge."

"I'm a drudge," Sam said with a sigh. She was sick to death of this cyclical conversation. She stared at her friend's face. *She looks older.* Was it grief? Grief took many forms, she had heard. Could it age someone prematurely? Yet Ava's grief would have been freshest when Sam arrived. *She should be healing, not deteriorating.* "And you like them—the twins, Hakuund, Jackal—you like all of them."

"You're an exception. As for the rest of 'em, sure I like 'em, but they're all owned by the Vauns. Domestics inside, drudges outside, but they all belong to the Vauns."

"It's not the same thing. It's a job, being a drudge, that's all. Domestics are different."

"If you can't wake up one day and say, 'hey, I'm sick of this, so thanks boss, but this ain't for me' without getting your throat slit, you ain't some free worker, Samarra. You're a slave."

Sam thought on Ava's words for a moment. She'd heard the stories, of course; everyone had. "But compounds are not some all-seeing, all-knowing powers. Skip town and you're safe. How would they find you?"

Ava shrugged. "Either way, drudges are—"

"And there is no way he was flirting with me. He's probably just a spy." She dunked her head under the water before she could hear Ava's response.

28

The North

SAM FROWNED AT HER SCROLL, looking from the rough map to the warehouse she had ridden two hours to reach. She wasn't actually certain that it was a warehouse. The trash piles reached so high that the building itself was barely visible. *This is bad. Even for the Barrow.*

What could the Vauns possibly want from a place like this? She wiped the sweat from her face, pulled out her water flask, and drained it. The exercise felt good; she felt strong. She doubted that any of the others could have gotten here faster. Well, in terms of pace, anyway—she'd gotten lost on the way from the import market, so the journey itself had taken twice as long as it should have. Her pace, though, that was on point. *Okay, onward.*

Someone had shoveled a skinny path to the entrance. Sam looked at it and hopped off her bike. She didn't dare ride—an accidental swerve to either side and she would trigger her own burial. As she walked her bike forward, rats the size of pigeons raced around her feet, not the least bit wary of her.

Sam had thought there was nothing worse than the smell of

garbage. It turned out that the smell of garbage cooking under a midday sun during the hot season was worse; the worst part about the season, in her opinion. *Well, that and all the deaths by dehydration, heat stroke, and mosquito-borne diseases.*

The entrance to this warehouse was particularly bad. Amidst the usual stench of rotten food and burnt plastic, the acrid tang of human waste told her that the residents had not organized proper latrines.

As she crossed the threshold and her eyes adjusted to the dim, smoky lighting, she realized why. *It's all children.* They were everywhere: running, screaming, sleeping, fighting. She saw babies carried on the backs of six- and seven-year-olds. Older children of nine, ten, eleven years old were already burned and branded huaina. Young teenagers lounged in groups, smoking or playing cards, while others corralled the younger children into gangs or some type of legitimate family—she couldn't tell which. Her instructions suddenly made sense.

"Hey," she asked a girl of maybe eight. "Where's the old man?"

The girl just shrugged, scratching her greasy hair lazily. Sam reached into her basket, pulled out the roll she had been saving, and tossed the girl half.

"I' the corner," she said, mouth full, pointing to the far end of the warehouse.

Holding her bike by the handlebars, Sam picked her way forward. The floor was sludgy from rainwater that had leaked through the roof. Even so, most of the children didn't even have tents, just nests: the nicer ones consisted of a big piece of plastic to keep out the damp and a blanket for warmth.

They should be in school.

Going to set one up, are you?

Not me, but it could be done. They just need a teacher.

Sure. These kids will have great educational outcomes with no books, no slates.

A teacher and school supplies.

And I'm sure the hunger gnawing at their little bodies won't interfere at all with their ability to concentrate. Or the parasites they all undoubtedly have. Or the iron deficiency. Wait, make that iron and iodine deficiency. Don't forget Lyme disease, either. Nothing lasts like Lyme disease.

The light faded from dim to dark as she moved toward the old man's corner. The smell worsened. It clung, sticky, to her hair and clothes. She moved one hand to the center of her handlebars, freeing the other so that she could swat the air in front of her face, which was thick with flies.

She reached the far corner. A few sheets of metal blocked off what looked to be a room of rags: folded rags, balled-up rags, coloured rags, and grey, ripped rags. Some were stacked in piles; others lined the floor. One particularly large pile of grey rags could be a bed, she supposed. For the rest she could imagine no purpose. *Does this man collect rags? What an odd thing to do.*

The large pile of grey rags shuddered and sprang apart, giving birth to a grey-haired, grey-bearded old man.

"You!" His eyes fixed on Sam. "What the jit taow do you want?"

"Er." She pulled out the scroll. "An R44."

She tried to say it with confidence, as though she knew exactly what an R44 was. This whole system of providing codes and numbers but no actual information on the product itself had always struck Sam as extremely stupid. What was to prevent a vendor from taking the pay and giving her some other, worthless object? Fear of the compounds, she supposed, although she did not doubt that there were some desperate enough to take the risk. Even so, the initial secrecy was pointless: she almost always saw the item when she purchased it.

The man's eyes lit up. He dived into a pile of rags, pulling out one box, then another. Eventually he must have found the right one, for he surfaced brandishing a pair of filthy candlesticks, which he waved triumphantly as he waded through the rags toward Sam.

"Um—" Sam started, once she held the surprisingly heavy candlesticks and he the xots.

"Um!" he shouted over her, bulging his eyes and sticking out his lower jaw in the most ridiculous grimace she had ever witnessed.

"Can you give me a box, or one of those rags? These will slip right through my basket."

"A rag?!" the man shrieked. "Bav! Bav! Bav!"

Sam waited patiently for him to calm down, at which point he painstakingly selected a rag and threw it at her, then dove back under a mountain of fabric. As she wrapped the candlesticks in the smelly bit of cloth he'd given her, Sam saw something sparkling amidst the grime. She brought it close to her face and saw a clear, white jewel. It looked like the Vauns might have gotten the better end of the bargain, after all.

Sam turned and hurried back the way she had come. She told herself that it was to make up for the time she had lost. *Liar. You're fleeing the stench.* A shriek pulled her attention to the other side of the warehouse, where yet another child seemed to be in the process of having metal punched through her skin—though in this case it seemed to be her navel, rather than an eyebrow or an ear, that was being pierced.

Behind them, Sam was relieved to see a group of women: young women, but adults nonetheless. Perhaps this mouldy hell had not been entirely abandoned to the tyranny of minors. *Unless they've only stopped in to recruit.*

As she drew closer, Sam realized that the women stood clustered around a very familiar silhouette. She had never come across one of her teammates on mission before. Was he here to check up on her? Had Benison asked him to spy? Sam considered and then immediately dismissed the thought. Benison would have expected her to have left the warehouse over an hour ago, which meant that Jackal could not have timed this overlap. He would have had to have followed her from the import market, and considering the myriad of deserted trails and paths she'd followed that morning, it seemed highly improbable that he could have followed behind without her noticing. *Chances are he was sent here for reasons that have nothing to do with you.*

Judging from their body language, it seemed that these women were well acquainted with Jackal. There was one girl, tall with shoulder-length brown hair, who actually seemed to be scolding him. Could she be a relative, perhaps? It was possible she had stumbled across a personal, rather than a compound-given, task.

"Hey!"

A small hand was reaching into her pocket; it belonged to the same girl that had directed Sam to the old man earlier. She flipped Sam a rude hand gesture and ran off. Sam started to turn back toward Jackal and gave her head a shake. Even accidently running into another drudge while she was working was enough to get her sacked. Besides, she was late.

Sam pushed her bicycle out into the daylight, blinding after the darkness of the warehouse.

"You again." The voice was soft, the tone warm. *Like velvet.* It was also familiar. Sam's eyes adjusted and a backlit figure came into view. Broad shoulders, oiled blond hair, an easy smile.

Maddox. Hunters. Raina. Her heart skipped a beat. This was her chance.

Act natural.

How?

I don't know, start with a normal conversation and lead into it?

"So, did you win anything?"

"I—uh, what?" Sam asked, stupidly.

"At the Dens. Did you win?"

"Oh. Um...nope," said Sam. Maddox's presence seemed to be impeding her ability to think and speak. He might not be the villain that Shale said he was, but he was definitely trouble. Her mind raced, trying to think of something to say.

"Did you...did you win?"

"Me?" He grinned at Sam. "I always win."

"Why, do you cheat?" she asked, without thinking. *Great, insult him. Good start.*

Maddox threw back his head and laughed. "Just lucky."

"Oh." Silence. "Um, actually, the man you were with that night, I need to talk to him." *Oh, very natural. Not abrupt and awkward at all.*

"Duncan?" Though his lips remained curved in a smile, the warmth had disappeared. "Why?"

"Oh, I just..." She wracked her brains for a lie but could not seem to think of anything. "I just need to talk to him, is all. There's coin in it for him. I don't suppose you know how to get in touch with him?"

"Well, I suppose I could arrange a meeting." Maddox winked at her. "For a small fee."

"How much?"

"Oh, nothing much, say, three xot?"

She swallowed, but nodded.

"Where do you live?" he asked. "I'll talk to him and send over a messenger."

Something in her balked. She might not be acting as cautiously as she should be, but she wasn't a reckless person, either.

"Ask him to meet me Sunday at sunset, at the front entrance to the import market." She wanted somewhere public, with lots of witnesses.

Maddox raised his eyebrows. "The day and time I can probably manage, but he's not gonna like being told to hoof it around town. Meet him under the Pike, north end."

She hesitated.

"Or not." He was watching her with a knowing look on his face. "Maybe you'll run into him by chance?"

"Okay," she said. "The Pike it is."

He grinned and held out his hand.

"One now, the other two at the meeting."

He shook his head. "Can't do, lala. I'll take it up front."

His body pressed against hers as he slid past her toward the warehouse, three xots richer. *Too intimate.* She shivered, despite the heat of the day.

It'll be worth it. The Hunters will know something. They will.

29

The North

SAM DIDN'T SLEEP much that week, and when she did, she dreamed of Raina. It was the same dream, though the lens and the colours and the props made it feel more and more like a Seiran film. It always began with Corvus, though he was never alive for her anymore. There was no weapon either, only loss. Black and white and silent. Sometimes she wept and the grief was terrible and raw, and sometimes she was numb.

Down the hallway she inevitably ran, following Corvus or Raina or, more often than not, a hybrid Corvus/Raina, a figure that alternated between the two in whole or in parts. Raina's hair became Corvus' became Raina's over his neck, her neck, their arms. It was as though someone had collected different takes of the same scene and then collaged them all together.

She chased Corvus or Raina or the hybrid Corvus/Raina into the underground city where dramatic torchlight lit stiff background actors in almost life-like poses. More scenery, more art; no plotline.

She kept running and eventually they reached the house, which was now a compound.

There was Raina and sometimes there were the other ex-girl-friends; there were weapons, or drugs, or chains to keep the prisoners subdued; and there were cockroaches, because what was a film about the Barrow if cockroaches didn't play a prominent part? Finlay's presence haunted the rooms, though the man himself never made a cameo. He didn't need to; the audience knew he was there. Sometimes Sam played the role of Sam and rescued Raina and the other women. Sometimes she played the role of Raina and rescued herself. Sometimes she was a cockroach.

In her waking hours she tried to visualize her upcoming meeting with the Hunter, Duncan. In the best-case scenario, she handed over a pile of coin in exchange for detailed directions to Finlay's hideout. In the worst-case scenario, Duncan pulled a weapon and she had to fight her way out. *Which I can do, now that I am once again able-bodied.*

Walking home from the compound on Sunday, Sam hesitated outside of Geo and Jem's door. *You're just trying to hide from Ava. Admit it.* She was, of course. Ava was impossible to lie to, even by omission. She seemed to sniff out secrets. *It'll take my mind off the night's mission.*

It didn't.

Sam sighed, looking down at the book in front of her. It was the third one she'd pulled off the shelf, and for the third time she couldn't seem to get past the first page. She gave up on reading and began flicking through the shelves, half listening to Geo and Jem as they debated a poem.

Focus. You need to focus.

She did. She couldn't.

As she said her goodbyes an hour later, she tried and failed to suppress a shiver of excitement.

"Are you alright, dear?" Geo asked her.

Sam nodded, forcibly relaxing her shoulders, her jaw.

"Do you...do you have a late-night mission?"

"Yes." It *was* a late-night mission; it just wasn't for the Vauns.

"Well, do be careful. We'd like you back in one piece," said Geo. Jem grunted his agreement and thrust a biscuit at Sam.

206

She stepped out into the evening heat. The sky was bright, though clouds covered the sun; the rain had eased from a downpour to light, warm mist.

You should have told someone where you're going. Sam waved the thought away and concentrated on her biscuit. Her friends would have tried to dissuade her from meeting with the Hunter. She could already imagine each conversation in its entirety: their shock, her explanation, their disapproval, her defense. There was no agreement to be had and she did not have time to waste arguing.

Nervous energy coursed through her veins, pushing her forward, onward, faster. She wanted to sing, but all she knew were Southern songs.

Sam arrived before the Hunter did. Wanting to spot him before he spotted her, she crept into one of her favourite mouse holes: an alley filled with the husks of abandoned cars. Small and lithe as she was, Sam knew she could easily lose a larger pursuer in the wreckage.

She waited. The Pike was teeming with huaina tonight. They wandered by, coin or sack or small bundles passing from one set of hands to another like a game of hot potato. A couple of older, heavily tattooed men were playing a game of dice while a younger man, smoking nearby, watched. Teenage girls sporting matching tank tops and hairline tattoos kept arriving in twos or threes. The early arrivals finished two bottles of moonshine in the time that it took for the last girls to straggle in. Whooping and hollering, they left together—the high of perceived invulnerability. They had the numbers tonight, and moonshine. What harm could befall them?

She killed two mosquitoes, though not before the second one had bitten her on the arm. *Hope it's not a carrier.*

She had just killed her third mosquito when a thought occurred to her: *What if he is here, hidden as I am, waiting for me to appear?* Loath though she was to leave her hiding spot, Sam couldn't abide the thought of returning home empty handed.

She walked up to the base of the Pike, giving the smoker a wide berth. Feeling exposed, she dug her hands into her pockets and leaned back against the graffitied concrete of the structure itself.

Sunset faded into dusk. Heavy with disappointment, she was about to leave when a gigantic figure swaggered into view.

He came toward her, a smirk on his face. His eyes shifted from her face downward. Sam fought the urge to fold her arms across her chest. She glared at him instead.

"You the girl Maddox sent?"

Sam nodded.

"What you want?"

"I'm looking to find someone." *Keep it bland, professional.* She wanted to neither encourage nor antagonize him. "If you, or another Hunter, know where he is…I'll pay for information."

"Me or another Hunter, huh?" He leered at her. "What, I'm that replaceable for you?" He stepped closer; too close. "What jit you looking for, anyway?"

"A guy named Finlay, disappeared last summer."

"Fin?"

She saw it, in that split second, knew what was happening, even before he whistled and the two men emerged from the building opposite her. She sprinted toward the alley.

I might make it, she thought, as she made to leap pass the smoker. *I might make it there before they do.*

She was midair when she realized her mistake, saw the smoke fall, the man's fist move forward as though in slow motion.

She lost consciousness before she hit the ground.

30

The North

SAM CAME TO MID-FLIGHT. She flung her arms out, bracing for the fall, and swung forward. *Not falling. Hanging. And now swaying.* She could also only seem to see out of one eye. *No matter. You can see. That's what counts.*

What she could see: a big, empty room; a row of broken windows, high up on the wall; and a rope that bound her ankles to the rafters above.

Sam heard voices and twisted to see behind her. Four men stood huddled, deep in conversation. None of them seemed to be looking her way. Sam glanced up at the ceiling again. Besides the throbbing in her face, she seemed physically intact. If she could make it to the rafters, she might be able to run along one of the large metal beams and jump out a window. She studied the knots that bound her. *How long will they take to untie?*

If it came to a fight, she was in trouble. Four-to-one was not a good ratio, even if she wasn't hanging from the ceiling. They were also likely armed. Was she? Sam wiggled her ankle and felt the hard metal of her baton. Nobody had noticed it shoved down the side of her boot. *A lot of good it will do you, considering they probably have cross-bows.* A thought struck her. She patted the pocket of her jeans, her heart sinking. The small bag of coins she'd been carrying was gone.

Sam looked at her hands suddenly, puzzled. Why weren't her hands tied? They obviously did not consider her a threat. *Are you a threat?* If not, why had they bothered to string her up? To humiliate her, she supposed. *Or for fun.*

"...my deal. I get her first." It sounded like Duncan.

"You get what I give you." Sam didn't recognize the second voice. She twisted around again, and saw that the speaker was a large, heavily muscled man, almost as large as Duncan.

"Of course, Axel, you're the boss, whatever you say. But Maddox—"

"You think 'cause Maddox came to you, you got first rights? Don't think I don't know you would've cut me out, Dunc. If Jayce here hadn't told me—"

"Never!" Duncan sounded indignant. He also sounded like he was lying.

"Here." The smoker who had knocked Sam out was doling out her hard-earned xots. "Double cut for you, boss."

"I'll take Jayce's cut too," the man that Duncan had called Axel said with a wide grin. "You don't mind, do you, you stupid shint?" A fourth man, tall, skinny, and covered head-to-toe in tattoos, just shook his head, his eyes on the floor.

"Oi." Duncan had noticed Sam watching them. "Girl's awake."

Sam watched through her good eye as the four men approached. With a sick feeling in her stomach, she realized that the man she'd thought was heavily tattooed was actually covered in bruises: his face, his arms, his legs. He stopped a few feet away, as did Duncan and the smoker, while Axel continued forward until he was only inches away from Sam. There was nothing in his cold, calculating stare to suggest that he was looking at a human being.

With a smile, he brought his hand up to her face and pressed his thumb gently into her swollen eye. Sam bit back a moan of pain.

"Hey, girl," he said. "That was a lot of coin you had on you.

Thanks for that." Duncan and the smoker roared with laughter. "Now, we're gonna have a little fun with you. But first, you're gonna tell me where that jit Finlay is."

"I—" Sam stared back at him, confused. "But—so you don't know?"

He backhanded her, hard. Twinges of black obscured the edges of her vision. He turned to Duncan. "Thought you said she knew about Fin?" he said, his voice tight with anger.

"Uh, well, she said Fin's name, is all."

Axel turned back to Sam. He pulled out a knife and ran the dull edge across Sam's throat, slowly and lovingly, as though he were seducing her instead of threatening her.

"That shint owes us—near a year's worth of tribute. Tell me where he is."

"I don't know," she said, speaking as slowly and calmly as she could. She needed to think, and to think, she needed to stay calm. *You can take out Axel, maybe, but then what? There are three other men.* She knew that as soon as she demonstrated skill as a fighter, they would bind her hands. And then she would really and truly be out of options. Except...

"I work for the Vauns," she said. "They know where I am, and—"

She was ready for the backhand this time.

"You think we're scared of some compound?" He pressed the point of the knife against her swollen eyelid. "I look scared?"

She returned his gaze with her good eye, not speaking, not moving.

"But Fin, Fin and his shint brother, they know the rules," he said. "We're Hunters till we die, girl. He wants to go work for some compound, he pays tribute. He was lucky we didn't cut him up. Take turns with his girl, like we did to Jayce. Right, kid?" He turned to look back at the bruised man. "Thought you could take more'n your share, huh? You won't do that again." He turned back to Sam and grinned. "Guess if you don't know anything about Fin, though, we can get right to it. Maybe after we've had you a few times, you'll remember something, huh? If not, well, no matter."

He gestured at Jayce. "Tie her hands together and cut her down.

We'll bring her to the back room where your girl's being kept. She's pretty used up, so maybe you'll get to cut her up and—"

Axel faltered, silenced by the knife that had been shoved into his eye. Jayce was screaming, a horrible sound: rage and fear and grief. His hand, wrapped around the handle of the knife, was shaking. He pulled out the knife and stabbed again, and again.

Sam pulled herself upward, grabbing the beam with one hand and untying the rope that bound her ankles with the other. When her feet were free, she swung her legs over the beam and pulled herself shakily to her feet, grabbing a second, higher beam for balance.

"Hey! What about her?" Duncan's voice roared from below.

Sam walked as quickly as she dared along the beam, her eyes on the open window ahead of her. A knife spun through the air, hit the beam above her head, and clattered down to the floor. She was almost at the window when a bolt shot past her face. Hoping fervently that she wasn't several stories up, she dove forward.

The trash pile rose up to meet her, cushioning what might otherwise have been a deadly two-story fall onto cement. Sam swam through bits of discarded plastic, fabric, and food scraps, making her way to the chain-link fence that bifurcated the garbage pile. She reached it and swung herself over just as the door to the building opened with a resounding crash. She thrashed forward, propelling herself down to the ground, and, without a backward glance, took off running into the night.

31

The North

"OF ALL THE STUPID THINGS." Though Ava's voice was shaking with anger, her touch was gentle as she pressed the cold cloth against Sam's swollen face. "Meeting with a Huaina, and down at the Pike! Alone! Gods, Samarra. Are the Vauns trying to kill you?"

Sam stayed silent, offering no correction. Shale arched an eyebrow at her from where she sat atop a crate, but she too said nothing.

"Don't go killing yourself for coin! Finally healed from that stab wound, and you go and do this." Ava stood back and glared at Sam. "Think I wanna lose another girl?"

"But—"

Ava threw up her hands and stalked off to the kitchen. Frank, who'd been sitting in the corner casting her dirty looks, followed.

"Thanks," Sam said to Shale once they were alone.

"Keep your secrets if you want. None of my business." The two girls sat in silent for a moment.

"I asked Maddox," Sam blurted out.

This time both eyebrows went up. "Well, that's your business too. But I didn't peg you for someone who took stupid risks."

"I didn't want to," said Sam. She sounded defensive, and she knew it. "But we were getting nowhere. I didn't have a choice."

"Of course you did," Shale said. "If you weren't so obsessed with Raina—"

"I'm not obsessed!" Sam said, stung. "I just want to help Ava."

Shale nodded, though even with one eye swollen shut Sam could see that the older girl was only placating her.

"I hope it was worth it."

"I—" Sam stopped to consider it. "Maybe. I don't know. I found out that Finlay was a Hunter. They were looking for him too, said he owes them money."

"Finlay was a Hunter?" Shale let out a deep breath. "Well, that explains why he was such a creep."

"It also explains—"

"Why he might've wanted to leave town." The two girls looked at each other. "Maybe the tribute was getting to be too costly."

It was a nice thought: no hiding place; no chains; Raina free and possibly even happy; Finlay not a wolf but a man after all.

Shale's face was impassive, a mask. Sam wondered if she cared, if Raina mattered to her. She'd never asked. *So, ask then. Be Northern.* "Do you miss her?"

"Wasted effort, lover, missing anyone."

"But you were friends, weren't you?"

Shale chewed on the question for a moment before responding. "I looked out for Raina. Not because we had some great connection— we didn't. I did it for Ava."

"You're loyal to her."

"Of course."

"Why?"

Ava burst back into the room carrying some leftover boil.

"I saved you dinner," she said, thrusting the bowl at Sam. "Not that you deserve it. Stupid girl."

Sam grabbed Ava's other hand. "I'll be more careful," she promised, and she meant it.

Ava stared down at her hand. "I know you don't choose your missions," she said after a moment. "Sometimes I wonder if Raina, well... Where did they send her?"

"She—" Sam started, though she hadn't the faintest idea what she would say.

"Anyway, eat before it gets even colder," Ava said. "I've got dishes to wash." She hurried back out of the room.

Sam turned to speak to Shale and found that the crate the other girl had been sitting atop a moment ago was now empty.

With a sigh Sam picked up her boil. She felt hollow, as though someone had come along with a spoon, scooped out her insides, and picked her bones clean. She wished she wasn't alone. She was lucky to be alive. She wished her face didn't hurt. She should be grateful. She wished she'd been left with someone other than herself for company.

32

The North

"ARE you sure she wants a bunch of strangers watching?" Sam asked as she hurried alongside Xenia, whose long legs could travel at an obscenely fast pace.

"I'm not a stranger," Shale said. She gave a coy smile. "In fact, she knows me rather well."

"Well, I am."

"To be honest, darling, she just needs the numbers," said Xenia. "A bride without a crowd of at least thirty women? That's bad luck. And she, well...she isn't always the easiest person to befriend."

"Did you hear what she did to that cult, the blood goddess one?" asked Shale.

"Oh, everyone heard about that." Xenia grinned at Sam. "They kept preaching beside her booth, driving off the customers, see, so she poisoned the lot of them. Didn't kill them, just popped something in their boil that made them puke up blood. And then she told them that since they were now the sick, they had to sacrifice themselves."

She laughed again. "The crazy thing is that they did it! There were bodies everywhere."

"Funny story," said Sam.

"Oh, come on, those jits kill babies! They deserved it."

"Why, are you trying to bail?" Shale asked Sam.

"No, it's just that the rituals are different here. I'm not sure what, you know..."

"Oh, you won't actually have to do anything. We're really just witnesses. I mean, there's the orgy, but that's later," Xenia said. She saw Sam's horrified expression and burst out laughing. "Kidding, darling. Well, I mean, there *is* an orgy, but it's not mandatory or anything."

A night full of strangers, Sam thought with unease. *Why did I agree to this?*

At least the bruising on her face was mostly gone. In dim lighting it wouldn't be noticeable at all, saving her the embarrassment of trying to explain how she'd gotten a black eye. *Run over by a speeding bicycle. Tripped on some trash and fell face first into more trash: hard, eye-bruising trash. Better yet, I'll say I was high and don't remember. Who can argue with that?*

The truth was, she'd needed to get out of the factory, to do something other than eat, sleep, work, and mope. She had no reason for moping, anyway. She'd come as far as she could, tracked down every lead. The logical conclusion to draw from the limited information she'd obtained was that Raina and Finlay had left town. She should feel hopeful. Instead she felt horribly, inexplicably let down.

Oh, but did you expect to find her yourself? Carry her home and dump her at Ava's grateful feet? It was vanity; that was all. *Or maybe you just have to have a mission. Can't just get by—you need a prize to strive for?*

Sam rubbed her temples. She was tired of listening to her own thoughts; they were repetitive and unflattering. A distraction was what she needed.

They found them on a riverbank, in a small glade surrounded by skinny, young trees: twenty-eight women weaving garlands and cutting candles from strips of tallow inlaid with wick. A mountain of dry sticks and herbs stood in the middle of the glade, encircled by stones—fuel for the night's bonfire.

One of the women ran over, threw her arms around Xenia and Shale, and gave Sam a kiss on the lips. From the excitement on her face, Sam figured her for Alina, the bride.

"So glad you're here, we're about to start."

She let out a shriek of excited laughter as one of the other women grabbed her and started pulling her down toward the river.

"Come on," Xenia said, linking arms with Sam and Shale. "I want a good spot."

They made their way down to the water, picking up an unlit candle on the way. Alina was standing on a large, flat rock in the middle of the river, shivering as she removed her clothing. An old woman, a child, and a pregnant woman, each carrying a bag, climbed up onto the stone beside her. Once the bride was completely nude, a fire was sparked, the flame passed candle to candle, and the women began singing.

> *Waters brace*
>> *Steel the blood*
>> *Soon they're wed*

> *Fire burn*
>> *In his eyes*
>> *Light their bed*

The old woman dipped her hand into a pot. Her fingers muddy, she began drawing symbols on Alina's back.

> *Earth to ground*
>> *Rooted down*
>> *Bonded day*

The child pulled out a simple instrument made of reeds and began to play. She didn't follow the melody of the song; her line was singular.

Wind aloft
  From the mud
  Find your way

The pregnant woman dipped her fingers into a different pot. It wasn't mud that she used to paint symbols onto Alina's chest and abdomen, though. The lines came out a dark, syrupy scarlet. *Blood.*

Blood for blood
  Still the flow
  We Pray

The old woman, the child, and the pregnant woman made their way back to the strand, though the child continued playing her reed instrument as the women started the song over again.

Two girls waded into the river toward Alina. One of them gathered the hair on the left side of Alina's head, pulled out a knife, and began shearing it off at the root. The other girl caught the hair and passed it to Alina. When the left side of her head was completely shorn, the song began a third time. Sam found that she was able to join in this time, singing softly at first and then more loudly as she became familiar with the words.

Alina braided the hair into a circlet and slid it onto her wrist.

From down the river a crowd of men was approaching, adding their voices to the song. In the midst of them walked a naked man who had been painted with symbols to match Alina's.

When he reached his bride, the man passed her something he had been holding in his hand. It was so small that Sam couldn't quite make it out. The bride took it, popped it into her mouth, and swallowed.

"The fertility stone," whispered Xenia.

The bride and the groom then took out the hair bracelets they had made and slid them onto each other's wrists.

At this point the crowd stopped singing and cheering broke out, soon joined by whistles and lewd comments as the bride and groom exchanged a less-than-chaste kiss.

"What if they have short hair?" Sam asked, shouting to be heard above the clamor.

"What's that?" asked Xenia.

"What if one of them has short hair? Can they make the bracelets out of something else?"

"It has to come from the body. I suppose they can cut it from... other places," Shale said with a grin.

"What?! No!"

The three of them laughed. "No, they have to grow it on their heads," said Xenia.

"But what if one of them's had their head shaved?"

"Well, they have to wait then."

"But that could take years!"

Xenia let out a yelp and slapped her arm. The squashed mosquito carcass fell to the ground. "Keeps you from taking the decision lightly, I suppose. It's why you see so many folks shearing off after a row though!"

Another mosquito appeared, and then suddenly there were a dozen of them, buzzing, biting, flying at their eyes and mouths. Swatting them away as best they could, the three girls made their way up the riverbank toward the glade, where a line of drummers had already formed.

The beat was fast, mirroring the crowd, which had spread out in a flurry of activity. Candles were being wedged into the ground, and a group of young women and men were setting up food.

A circle of dancers had already formed, and Sam could see Xenia's feet starting to twitch.

"Food?" she asked, to delay the inevitable.

Sam took a piece of potato and some lentils and rice. Xenia found a bottle of something that looked foul and smelled worse. She drank some and passed it to Sam, who took a tiny sip and grimaced. Hoping to push down the revolting flavour of the liquor, she shoved a handful of rice and lentils into her mouth and almost retched. Shale, watching, laughed and grabbed a peach off the table. She bit off a small chunk and wedged it into the bottle.

"Hey, you're ruining it!" said Xenia.

"Sugar, you can't ruin something this foul." Shale added a second and a third piece of peach.

She took a sip, gave an approving nod, and passed it back to Sam. The liquor was just as abrasive as it had been before the fruit addition, but at least the aftertaste had improved.

The bride and groom had lit the bonfire. Sam breathed in the fragrant smoke, wonderfully free of the usual taint of plastic waste and animal dung, and drifted towards the fire. Xenia and Shale followed, still drinking.

Other guests soon flocked toward Xenia and Shale, creating a steady stream of small talk and propositions. Sam was quite happy to chew away, listening to the music and watching the dancers, only half paying attention to the odd bits of conversation floating around her.

"So, I took the kneecap, anyway, because it was way less rank—"

"Oh, I rub it on my breasts every time the moon is full—"

"I said if the baby smells like goat's milk that's no business of his—"

Any of the wedding guests who attempted to approach Sam soon found themselves pulled into Xenia and Shale's increasingly absurd debates and narrations. She was not sure whether her friends were consciously saving her from awkward conversations with strangers, or whether they simply enjoyed a large audience. Either way, she found that she was actually having a nice time. The fire or the smoke or the herbs even seemed to be driving the mosquitoes away. She had more alcohol. The more she drank, the better it tasted.

A short spurt of heavy rainfall turned the dance floor into a swamp. As women and men spun and slipped in the mud, articles of clothing began to gather on nearby branches.

"Okay, darlings," Xenia said, finishing the bottle. "No more denying me what I want."

She pulled off her socks and boots, gesturing for them to do the same. Mud squished through Sam's toes, cool and slimy.

There was no set pattern to dancing in the North; the only commonality she saw from one person to another was a lot of full-limbed extensions and wild enthusiasm.

Xenia spun around, her long, graceful arms shining white against the darkness of the night. Red hair laced across them as Shale swayed past, eyes closed. The drummers sped up, and suddenly everyone was jumping. A chant rippled out across the dance floor. Sam couldn't make out the word.

"What are they saying?" she shouted in Xenia's direction.

"Sykva! Luck to the new married couple. Now they have to kiss."

A group of women hoisted the bride up onto their shoulders, a group of men the groom. They surged forward and backward like opposing waves as the guests holding them tottered and slipped in the mud, until bride and groom collided, arms out, lips meeting at the crest. They continued to kiss as passionately as if they were alone in their bed, instead of floating atop a sea of bodies.

As they were lowered gently to the ground, a woman was thrown up into the air. She fell backward, arms splayed wide, eyes closed. The crowd reached up to receive her, catching and passing her from hand to hand.

Sam felt something at her feet; Shale and Xenia were trying to lift her. Sam grabbed onto their shoulders, pushing down against them.

"What are you doing?" she shouted, yanking her feet free.

They grabbed her by the knees instead and moved to launch her upward. Sam crunched her body down, digging her thumbs into their armpits for leverage.

"It's okay!" Xenia was laughing. "Let go, they'll catch you!"

Someone let loose a howl. All around them, voices echoed back. *I could.* Xenia threw back her head and joined in, Shale just a beat after her. *Maybe I could.*

Before the more practical parts of her could catch up, she tensed her body, springing forward this time as her friends hurled her upward. She flew, for a split second she flew, and then she was falling back toward the waiting hands of strangers. As they passed her along the top of the crowd, she stared up at the moon staring down at her and added her voice to the song.

She was staggering off the dance floor in search of water when she ran into him.

"Uh, uh, uh," he said, wagging a finger at her as she slid into a fighter's stance. "No violence at a wedding. You want these nice people to rip you apart?"

"You set me up," she snarled at him.

"Yeah, and you killed Axel. Impressive." Maddox lifted his mug toward her, as though in congratulations.

"I...? What?" Sam stared at him, flabbergasted. "I didn't kill him! It was that guy he'd had beaten—what was his name, Jayce?"

"Oh." Maddox seemed only mildly interested. "They said it was you."

"Do you know what they were planning to do me?"

"Oh, yeah, sorry. It wasn't personal."

"It wasn't perso—? What is wrong with you?"

Maddox took a long swig of his drink. It was then that Sam noticed that he was swaying slightly.

"I mean, it is personal; it just ain't about you specifically." He grabbed a bottle from a girl who was so drunk that she could barely walk, filled his mug, and raised it toward Sam a second time.

"My compliments to the Vauns."

The drunken girl gestured rudely at him, and then slumped down against a tree trunk and went to sleep.

"For my idiot brother."

Sam watched him gulp down the stolen alcohol. The gears in her brain seemed to be moving in slow motion. Something Axel had said...

"Brother... You're—you're Finlay's brother?"

"I was." There was a definite slur to his words now. "Can't be brothers with a corpse, can I?"

"But the tribute... Axel said... I thought maybe he left town, to avoid—"

Maddox's laugh was high and thin. "You think he'd leave town, leave a compound job because he didn't want to pay tribute? Here." He dug a hand into his pocket, pulled out a couple of xots and waved them in her face. "There's a month's tribute. It's a laugh. Nothing."

"Well, Raina—"

"Who?" Maddox was squinting at her, as though trying to bring her into focus.

"Raina, his girlfriend."

Maddox frowned for a second, and then broke into a leer. "Right. Dark-skinned girl. Those legs..."

"She wanted to go west, so—"

"Good for her. My brother never would have left the Barrow." His mug empty, Maddox threw it on the ground and made to turn away.

Sam reached out and grabbed him by the sleeve. "If he didn't leave, what happened to him?"

Maddox shrugged. His eyes were glazing over. "Ask the Vauns."

"Why?"

"His fault," Maddox said, trying to pull away from Sam. "His fault, not mine. I was there first. Stupid jit. They don't allow connections, one compound to another. It was stupid. What, he thought they wouldn't find out?"

Sam stared at him. *"Fin, Fin and his shint brother, they know the rules,"* Axel had said. *"We're Hunters till we die, girl. You want to go work for some compound, you pay tribute."*

"You're a drudge too," she whispered. "Who for?"

In her surprise she'd let go of his sleeve. Maddox pushed away from her and gestured drunkenly in the air. "You don't need to know." He staggered away from her, toward the woods.

"And, wait." The thought had just occurred to her. "How did you know who I am?"

His high-pitched laugh rang out again. "Saw you with them, at the Hive. Everyone knows them: big and black; the quiet, skinny man; the pretty, dark-haired boy; and the blonde." He licked his lips. "Saw her here. Wouldn't mind a taste. Maybe I will. Don't matter to me, which one of you. All Vaun shints." He blew a kiss to Sam and stumbled, backward, into the trees. Already she couldn't make out his form, only glowing eyes and teeth. Then he was gone.

"I THOUGHT they were gonna follow you home, girl." Shale's tongue tripped over the words.

"Ah yes," Xenia said, sweeping her arms out into an elaborate bow which she directed at a nearby tree. "My fans do hate to part with me, but a girl's got to sleep eventually." She slid one arm around Shale's waist, and slung the other around Sam's shoulders. "I'm knackered, actually, will you dears carry me?"

"What we need is a bike that can pull people," said Shale. "It could be big business, girls. Pay a sack, then lie back and let someone else drive you home."

"Sounds like a horrid amount of exercise."

"Yeah," said Shale, "but we could hire the workers. You see? We supply the bikes, they give us a cut. What you think, little one?"

Sam's head felt as though it had been stuffed with straw. Maddox's words were still ringing in her head. If he was right, if Benison had found out that Finlay's brother worked for another compound... She shuddered to think of it. *But killed? And what about Raina? This has nothing to do with her.* It did, though, and she knew it. Though it wasn't logical or just, in the Barrow you were guilty by association. She thought of what Axel had said about Jayce's girl-friend, and swallowed.

There was something she was missing. Something someone had said once, that hadn't seemed important at the time. If only her brain wasn't so cloudy. *Stupid alcohol.*

"Big business, right?"

"Er..." She squinted for a second. What where they talking about? *Oh right, bicycle carts.* "Roads. I think you need better roads first."

"Oh." Shale sounded disappointed. "Right. Trails like these, a heavy cart would just get stuck, huh."

They heard the laughter first. There were several voices, all male. Sam caught Shale's eye and saw that she heard it too: the ugly under-tone, the stink of cruelty. Sam reached for her baton. Beside her, Xenia was doing the same. Shale had already taken out a pair of knives.

They rounded the corner cautiously, only to find the path deserted. Someone screamed. They followed the sound to the edge of the trail. Sam glanced at her friends. Their eyes were clear and focused. Sam too found that her senses had returned; adrenaline had stripped the haze away.

Together the three girls stepped off the path. The voices were louder now. They made their way past a cluster of trees and saw them: four men, clearly drunk, watching a fifth man on his knees. Sam could see the girl in front of him, sobbing.

"No way," one of the men slurred out, "not more than thirty seconds more, max. Tell you what—closest bet goes next."

Sam was raising her fingers to indicate a countdown when Xenia burst forward, baton out, battle cry cutting through the night air. Sam and Shale raced after her. Sam selected a mark, the greasy, tattooed man standing closest to the rape, whose head was tipped back as he gulped the final dregs of a bottle. She slammed her baton into his stomach, slashed it backward against his neck as he buckled down, and, grabbing his shoulders, kneed him in the face. She turned and kicked the rapist in the head, once to get his attention and then twice more in the time it took for him to fall away from the girl. He landed on his back. She kicked him in the head a fourth time, and a fifth. Her vision was going blurry; she could barely see him anymore. She kept kicking until someone grabbed her shoulders from behind. She spun around, baton raised, and realized it was Shale.

"We got it," she was saying. Her voice sounded tinny, like it was coming through a speaker.

Looking past her, Sam saw the other four men lying prone on the forest floor. The one she had attacked first had been slashed across the throat. Someone had finished him off while she was busy with the rapist. She looked back at him and almost gagged. The mass of blood and flesh above his shoulders hardly even resembled a head anymore. She wondered how much time she had wasted beating a corpse. Not that the other girls had needed her help, clearly. Shale didn't have a mark on her, and Xenia...

Xenia was kneeling beside the victim, a young girl with dirty blond hair. She was skinny, very skinny. She looked up at them and Sam realized with shock that the girl was practically a child, not more than twelve or thirteen years old.

"Back in the bushes there," the girl whispered, pointing back toward the trail.

Xenia nodded. "Can you two look for her clothes?" she asked.

Sam nodded, staggering over to the trees. She bent over suddenly—was she about to vomit? She waited, but the feeling passed.

"Got 'em," said Shale. "You okay?" she asked, placing a hand on Sam's shoulder. Sam nodded, and followed her back toward Xenia and the child.

Xenia helped her dress, the girl moving so gingerly that Sam had to ask if anything had been broken. She shook her head, and Xenia and Sam lifted her slowly to her feet. She leaned on their shoulders, wincing with every step, as they walked back to the trail. They were close to the exit.

"Where do you live?" Shale asked her.

The girl described a factory near to Xenia and Cassio's.

"Shouldn't we get her to a stitcher?" Sam asked quietly.

"What could a stitcher possibly do for her?" Xenia asked, a confused expression on her face.

"Well, is there something else? Somewhere she can get care, at least talk to someone?"

Shale looked at Sam as if she'd grown antlers. "Is there some magic place you know about?"

Sam shrugged helplessly and clammed up. She wanted to take this girl to a safe place filled with doctors, nurses, and therapists. She wanted police—she shouldn't have blood on her hands; it shouldn't be her burden.

Instead they walked the girl home. They brought her to a little bunk in a dirty factory, in a small corner she shared with three other people. Xenia sat beside her, while Sam and Shale hovered above.

"You got family?" Shale asked. The girl shook her head slowly, robotically. Her expression was blank, her eyes glazed over. Sam wondered if this was shock. "Friends any good?"

The girl paused, and then nodded. A shiver seemed to ripple through her, and tears started to pour down her cheeks.

"I'll go look for them," said Shale. "What's your name?"

"Niya," the girl whispered. Shale nodded and left.

Sam knew she should probably go help Shale, but she couldn't seem to move. Xenia reached up slowly and stroked the girl's hair. Niya jumped but did not move away.

"It's horrible, I know," Xenia said in a soft voice. "You'll see it, and you'll hear it, and you'll smell it for a long time." She lowered her voice even further, speaking in a whisper so low that Sam could barely hear her. "But then it will pass, I promise."

"He said...he said he was gonna sell me, after. Said there's a man in a swamp that'll pay for people to cut up and burn." She started shaking uncontrollably.

Something stirred in Sam's memory, something pushed down, deep out of sight, dismissed. *A man in a swamp that'll pay for people to cut up and burn.*

"Shh," said Xenia, still stroking her hair. "They're dead. You saw it. They can't do anything else to hurt you."

Three girls, just as young, burst in and crowded around Niya.

"Can you get a bath in here, and warm water?" Xenia asked. One of the girls nodded and ran back out. Xenia looked at the other two. "Either of you been through this before?"

Of course not. They're children. One of them looked up at Xenia and dipped her head, ever so slightly.

"Well, the one good thing about going through something horrible is that you can help your friends when it happens to them."

"I know," the girl said, reaching up and taking Niya's hand. "We got this." There was steel in her voice, young and high pitched though it was. Sam saw it more often than not in the Barrow: big heads on skinny bodies and old, old eyes. "Thanks for bringing her home. You should go, though. We'll take care of her."

Xenia looked at Niya, who nodded.

Back outside, Shale pulled out a smoke for herself and passed one each to Xenia and Sam. Xenia took hers and wandered off toward an outdoor kitchen fire. The other two watched in silence as Xenia bent down to light her smoke. She walked back slowly, a feigned nonchalance. As Sam held her own smoke out for Xenia to light, Sam realized that both of their hands were shaking. Sam took a drag and then bent forward over her knees again. She felt moisture on her cheeks and realized she was crying.

"She'll be okay," Shale said.

"Why?" Sam asked, trying and failing to keep her voice down. "Why would she be okay?"

"You've never had it happen to you, have you?" Xenia asked.

"No," Sam said, straightening up and taking a shaky drag of her smoke. "Have you?"

Both Xenia and Shale shrugged. Sam froze. "Both of you, like that?"

"If you survive, and you don't get some sickness from the prick who did it, and you don't have to raise his seed, well, I guess count yourself lucky," Shale said. Her voice was tight, her eyes cold.

"Lucky," Sam repeated.

"Yeah, love," Xenia said, her beautiful face twisted up in grief. "If it's only one, lucky again." Sam had never heard hatred in Xenia's voice before. "At least we killed the bastards for her."

"I don't—"

"Just try not to think about it," Shale said.

Sam tried to slow her breaths. She raised the smoke to her face and realized that the light had gone out. Xenia lit it a second time for her.

"Let's just not talk about it, love," Xenia whispered. She took a few steps backward, in the direction of her factory. "We helped someone tonight, girls, good on us," she shouted, her voice breaking. As she turned away, there were tears pouring down her face.

Sam continued to stare at the spot where her friend had been, Xenia's face clear, then grainy in her mind's eye, as though she was looking at a screen. Out of the corner of her eye, she registered that Shale, too, had left, following Xenia.

Scenes flared to the forefront and then faded to pixels, melding one into the other: Niya, her little face frozen in shock; the unnamed men at the Dens, and the snakes; the rage on Jayce's face; the unknown girlfriend, systematically brutalized to send a message. It was sickening, all of the violence.

A man in a swamp. Her mouth was going dry. Ugly remembrance prickled up the back of her neck. *Niya, the men and the snakes, Jayce and his girlfriend.* The images cycled back, repeated, only this time new scenes intruded: a big, broken-down house on a flooded field, the smell of rust, and a little man seated on a dirty chair. The words came back to her too. Hakuund's voice: *"Compounds'll never just throw away an investment. There's always some profit left to be had."*

Niya, the men and the snakes, Jayce and his girlfriend, the house, rust, the little man. She pictured Raina and Finlay, tied up and tortured. *Niya, the men and the snakes, Jayce and his girlfriend, the house, rust, the little man, Raina, Finlay.* She felt like she might vomit. *The house, rust, the little man, Raina, Finlay.* She knew where they were.

33

The South

"...AND when she shot it out of the air? Incredible. When do you think we'll get to try those?"

"What was it Protector Gin told us?" Starling asks, turning to Pipit and me.

"We'll learn hand-to-hand and staff first, then steel, and then projectiles," Pipit says between mouthfuls of sorghum porridge.

"She said if," I correct him, leaning back to answer Finch, a tall girl with dark skin who is seated on the other side of Starling. "If we master one, we are allowed to move on to the next."

"Of course. Fundamentals first. But then someday..." She smiles with excitement.

I smile back and finish off the last of my millet bread, peeking over to where Protector Nem is eating. I am impatient for the day's lessons to begin. My exhaustion seems to have finally faded: my eyes are no longer dry and sore; no headache lingers. I feel more energized than I have in weeks, days, however long I have been here.

We are not the only ones discussing last night's qualifiers.

Throughout the canteen, cadets and protectors talk about the weapons, the feats, and the failures. At our table, the excitement of this shared experience seems to have dispelled yesterday's awkwardness. In addition to Finch, I have met a boy named Lark and a girl named Parakeet.

I look around at the other first years. I know that not all of them can be new arrivals, but try as I might I cannot seem to connect those seated around me with last week's faces. It is as if the memories have been scrubbed clean of any identifying factors.

After breakfast, a fifth-year cadet named Birch shows us which equipment we are expected to use when sanitizing and drying dishes, and where to stack them, as well as where to find materials for wiping tables and chairs and for sweeping and washing the floors.

"You will have lessons every morning," he says, calling back over his shoulder as we follow him down the corridor after morning chores. "We are fortunate here to have many knowledgeable P2s willing to serve as instructors." His voice is loud and clipped, his speech as mechanical as Protector Nem's. Due to repetition, or scripting, I am not sure which.

"Choose a desk and stand beside it," Protector Nem says by way of welcome when we enter the first classroom. "The words of thanks are about to begin.

Once the closing notes have sounded, she gestures and a holodisplay depicting a timeline and a map materializes in front of her.

"You will begin every morning here with me for virtues and health and hygiene, which of course includes sexual and reproductive health.

"You are fortunate to have the opportunity to spend two hours every morning learning mathematics, coding, and cryptography with P3 Protector Lock. Mathematics is the founding block of a strong mind, an effective protector, and a sound society. While P3s are not typically involved in the training of cadets, Protector Lock has elected to work directly with C1s to ensure that all cadets master the basic principles before advancing further. He will also occasionally hand-pick first years for admittance to his advanced seminars.

"For your remaining years as a cadet, your mathematical training will be overseen by Protector Guent, a P2 who is equally valued by the administration for his dedication, consistency, and the clarity of his expositions.

"Following mathematics, you will spend one hour with P2 Protector Drest to expand your knowledge of the history of our great nation. After the midday meal, P2 Protector Hurst will oversee your learning on geoscience.

"As you can see," she says, pulling at the holodisplay with her thumb and forefinger, "the C1 classrooms are all situated in this same corridor. The remainder of each day will be spent here," Ring One flashes on the screen, "with P2 Training Masters Tila and Jheb. Depending on the needs of the other cadets and protectors, some of your training sessions may be redirected to one of the fields located here." She points to two large squares situated south of the compound. "Twice a week P2 Protector Shyli will direct your mechanical training, replacing your morning studies on Day Three and your physical training on Day Six.

"As C1s you are responsible for cleaning the canteen after each meal under the supervision of a C5. You have already met Cadet Birch. Cadet Cedar will take over this role with the midday meal, and Cadet Fir with supper. Following the evening meal each night, you can expect to spend two hours supporting the upkeep and maintenance of our base, either indoors or outdoors. The entire base is grateful to our first years for taking on the largest support role.

"Your free time is limited to holidays and evenings, in the time that remains to you after you have completed your chores and any evening assignments. You are then welcome to socialize, although Ring One will remain open should you prefer to spend your time more productively. Each year your chores will change, with an overall trend toward greater free time, including one free day per week once you have become a protector, and two days per week after five years of service.

"As a cadet you will undergo two rounds of examinations. At the end of year one, you will have the opportunity to demonstrate your progress with a six-hour examination in mathematics, virtues, history, and geoscience, followed by a physical display of your proficiency with first-year weapons. The entire process lasts approximately nine hours and will be overseen by your training masters and professors, Grand Neilem and her seconds, and select, interested P3s and P4s. At the end of your fifth year you will again showcase your mastery of the material, although in addition to the written test and individual martial skills display, there will be an oral exam and controlled sparring. On rare occasions a junior delegate of the Administration may attend for quality control purposes.

"Following your fifth-year examination, you will receive your designation as a P1 or P2, or in exceptional cases, as apprentice to a P3, P4, or even a P5. Once you have received official status, the Administration, along with supporting your daily needs for sustenance and shelter, will provide you with a stipend that you can spend on products of your choosing. At this point you will also receive individual or couple quarters, depending on your preference. Living arrangements may be revised pending submission of the proper forms, which can be requested using one of the many Personal Communication Boxes found in classrooms and public areas." There is a PCB, I realize, located beside the receiver. I wonder that I did not notice it earlier.

"Standard health checks for C1s occur in the medical ward at the start of each month. Your appointment time and date will be provided to you seven days in advance. For female cadets, when you begin menstruating, please submit an immediate request to medical.

"When you wish to begin engaging in sexual intercourse, please request a medical appointment for all sexual partners prior to and following coitus. This process must be undertaken each time there is a new sexual partner. Administration recommends that you do not limit the selection of sexual partners by gender or sex.

"Consent forms are to be filled out ahead of time, although medical staff will walk through the requisite information with you prior to official submission. As a cadet you may only engage in sexual activity with members of your own age cohort. As a new protector, sexual partners may also be selected from adjacent and near-adjacent age cohorts. Age restrictions do not apply amongst protectors aged twenty-one and older.

"If you are interested in changing your assigned birth sex, the interview process can be started by filling out form 8B. To document a pronoun change, please complete form 8C. We will discuss these topics in greater detail beginning in week six of the health and hygiene curriculum."

She gestures at the holodisplay, and the image of a PCB screen appears. She touches the button labeled *medical*, and then selects *requests*. A series of categories appears, including *illness, injury, mental health, menstruation, sexuality, and sexual health*. Under each category is a list of forms.

"Now." She gestures at the corner of the holodisplay and a small timer is briefly magnified. "The remainder of our time today will be spent on virtues. Who would like to begin with the top of the hierarchy?" Every hand, including my own, shoots upward in response.

"Good morning, cadets," a large man announces, striding purposefully into the room. "Welcome to mathematics, coding, and cryptography."

Waves of energy bounce off of him so forcefully that his presence seems to fill the room, floor to ceiling, corner to corner. His hair and moustache, a vibrant blue, only serve to reaffirm his similarity to an electric charge.

"I am Protector Lock. Now, who would like to tell me why mathematics is so important? Let's see...who is Sparrow this year?"

I look around and see a tall boy with wide shoulders and thick eyebrows stand and hesitantly raise a gigantic, fleshy hand.

"You, huh? You look nothing like last year's. She was small and dainty, more like...you," he says, his eyes having landed on Starling. "Who are you?"

"Starling, Protector Lock," she says, jumping to her feet.

"Humph. I wish we would just assign names. Then there could be some kind of classification system, ordering cohorts by size, perhaps, or speed... Not that I am criticizing, of course. But in mathematics we must always strive for two things. Sparrow?"

"Uh." The boy stares blankly at Protector Lock, clearly unable to keep pace with the rapid flittering from one topic to another. The professor does not give him time to ponder.

"You, then, the one who should have been Sparrow."

"Efficiency of time and labour, Protector," she says. "And obedience."

"Hmm," he says, pursing his mouth. "Well, I gave you the first answer. Yes, we seek the best approach, or the greatest output for the least input. As for the second one, you are incorrect. Well, no, you are correct in the larger sense, looking at Seira as a whole. In fact, you are arguably semi-correct if we apply this to the topic at hand. I am looking for something more specific here, though. Anyone? Anyone at all?"

I raise my hand and rise to stand beside my desk.

"Yes, and you are?"

"Sora, Protector."

"Are you now?" he says, eyebrows thrusting up into his disorderly hairline. "Let's see if you are anything like the previous Sora."

"Rules, Protector. We strive to learn the rules that have been tested and proven. This is also why mathematics is so important—it trains the mind. When we follow the process exactly as we should, we obtain the desired results. When we deviate, we fail."

He stares at me for a moment. "Nope, nothing like the last Sora."

I sit down, uncertain of whether to interpret this feedback as positive or negative.

"New Sora is correct. It is not general obedience that we pursue in mathematics, but obedience, or submission rather, to rules. Whether the problem you face is simple or complex, the process is the same: find the rules, find the formula. Otherwise you will fail.

"Now, speaking of formulas, you will recall that the tangent of an angle in a right triangle is equal to the ratio of the length of the side opposite to the angle divided by the length of the side adjacent to the angle. We can use this fact in something called the mathematics of triangulation. It enables one to calculate distance while travelling along, say, a border. Let's suppose that we are looking at a far-away object and want to know approximately how far away it is. What is the first thing we should do? I want to hear from...let's see...who is Quail this year?"

"WHY DID THE NORTH FALL?"

Protector Drest is younger than the other professors. His hair, a blue so dark that it is nearly black, is slicked back away from his face. He speaks with proper formality—none of the odd flippancy that we have just experienced with Protector Lock.

Finch is the first to jump to her feet, along with a boy I have not yet spoken with.

"It is a trick question, protector," says Finch when Protector Drest gestures for her to speak. "All governments fell, in the North and the South, both."

"And why did they fall?"

"The financial burden of climate change. Governments could not afford to respond to all of the earthquakes, tsunamis, tornados, flooding, hurricanes, and the drought."

"It was too expensive. Governments borrowed money until they collapsed under the debt." Protector Drest turns his attention to the boy. "What was different in the South? What did we have that they did not?"

"MWDA, mass desalination, and AME, Protector."

"Minimal water-dependent agronomy," he repeats, nodding his head, "large-scale desalination of previously non-potable sea water, and atmospheric moisture extraction. What else?"

"Cloud seeding and polli bugs, Protector," the boy blurts out before Protector Drest has even finished speaking.

"Cloud seeding, yes. And artificial pollination." Protector Drest looks back to Finch. "And?"

"And synthetic procreation, Protector," she says.

"Critical achievements. Drought, famine, the loss of natural human reproductive capabilities; any one of these misfortunes alone is enough to test a society, especially one driven by emotion rather than reason. The fact that these three disasters struck almost simultaneously, well, our superstitious predecessors believed that it signaled the end of civilization.

"It was not only the rapid advances in technology that staved off extinction. What else was critical?"

We are all standing now, right hands raised, puffed to bursting with the pre-packaged response.

"You," Protector Drest says, looking down at Vireo. I was incorrect; there is one cadet that remains in his seat.

He stands before responding. Perhaps it is my perception only, but I fancy he is moving more slowly than is necessary. This confuses me. Does he want Protector Drest to form an unfavourable impression of him?

"Rapid and efficient organization of existing communities into profession-based units."

"So you knew the answer—then why did you not stand with the others?" Protector Drest asks, though he sounds curious rather than cross.

"Because everyone knows this," says Vireo. I feel the collective intake of breath. Is he being disrespectful?

"What is your name, cadet?"

"Vireo, Protector."

"You may be seated." The professor raises his voice as he looks away from Vireo and addresses the room at large. "Vireo has brought up a critical point. This is the history that you know—that we all know. We know the technologies and the policies that enabled the South to flourish. We know that in the North there was no similar system of organization, and that ninety percent of the population died from disease, disaster, or violence.

"This history is important, and functions as the framework within which we process and analyze new information. Your education from this point forward, however, will venture beyond this broad overview, pulling out specific moments so that we may look at them critically together, and ask ourselves: What made this success possible? Or, what could have been done to avoid failure?

"Vireo, there is a stack of booklets at the back of the classroom; please pass them out. On page sixteen, you will see a detailed account of a battle that took place here on the northern border, not long after the mass re-organization. Read through the passage and then form groups of four. As a group, determine which specific actions contributed to our success, which actions were counterproductive, and why. Each group will report on this verbally tomorrow, so if you do not finish during class time you may assemble and continue working this evening."

PROTECTOR HURST IS STANDING with her back toward us when we file into the geoscience room after the midday meal, her spiky, purple head tipped back as she stares up at the massive screen that covers most of the front wall. She starts at the sound of our footsteps, and waves her hand at the screen. The agricultural plans disappear and are replaced with a plain, olive green background and the title *Geoscience* in large bold letters. Reaching the front of the room, I realize that Protector Hurst is barely taller than I am.

"Welcome, cadets," she says, beaming, as we file into desks. At first, I think that portas have been laid out for each of us, but then I realize that the desks themselves are screens, providing us with a surface that we can work directly upon.

"I am P2 Protector Hurst and this is geoscience. Who can tell me the purpose of geoscience?"

A girl named Quail jumps to her feet. "To help us understand the natural world and the resources that sustain us, Protector," she says.

"Perfect." Protector Hurst picks up a stack of books and begins passing them out. "What is your name, cadet?"

"Quail, Protector."

"Quail, you may read the introductory paragraph on page two."

"Geoscience," she reads, "is the study of the Earth's varied geological systems. This textbook will cover the key advancements that the Administration has made in the creation of systems and technologies to best utilize resources such as minerals, soil, water, and energy..."

My attention is pulled from the lesson to the desk beside me, where Vireo is tapping his finger against the cover of his unopened textbook. The sound is muted, but I can make out a pattern: A single tap, followed by a long pause, and then two taps with almost no pause between them, a fourth and final tap, and then silence. He repeats these four counts, and I find my fingers twitching in response. I count: one, pause, two-three-four; one, pause, two-three-four; one, pause, two-three-four. Perhaps I whisper the count, or tap my foot inadvertently, for Vireo turns to look at me. He smiles, and the spell is broken. I flip my focus back to Quail and the paragraph she is reading, struggling to hold onto the words as she speaks them. I fear the information is passing through me too quickly, coursing through my head without leaving an imprint.

Protector Hurst selects a different cadet to continue with page three, and I wonder whether we will spend the entire hour this way, just reading aloud and listening. Perhaps there will be a quiz at the end. I click on the notebook function and begin jotting down key points as they are spoken, swiping the surface clean when I run out of room. The notes themselves are irrelevant, of course; we all know that it is the act of writing that supports knowledge retention. I can feel Vireo watching me now and firmly subdue the part of my brain that is watching back. To properly absorb information, one needs undivided focus. I have no time for strange people or their quirks.

34

The South

THERE IS one female and one male protector waiting outside the training ring when we arrive. Are they the same training masters from last week? Though I try, I cannot seem to visualize them; not their faces, not even hair colour.

"Welcome, cadets," the male protector says, his long, thin pink braids swishing back and forth as he takes a moment to make eye contact with each of us. The smile on his face is relaxed and friendly. "I am P2 Training Master Jheb. This is P2 Training Master Tila."

Protector Tila looks to be several years older than her training partner, probably closer in age to Protector Nem, with a similar muscled grace. Her hair, coloured a vibrant silver, is tightly plaited and secured to her head in what seems like pointed opposition to Protector Jheb's jaunty braids.

"I will be leading movement, with a focus on cardio and balance, and supporting Protector Tila as she trains you in hand-to-hand combat and staff work. We will start off each afternoon with a pleasant jog around the fields, building strength and stamina, followed by stretching and core balancing exercises. Is everyone ready? Follow me."

The afternoon sun is hot as we circle the grounds. I breathe in deeply, enjoying the taste of the warm, dry air. We run in a tight cluster, Starling to my right and Pipit in front of me. There is a pink patch forming on the back of his skinny neck. I wonder if he is tiring or if he simply missed a patch of skin when he applied his sun-saving lotion.

After movement we return indoors. Instead of Ring One, though, they lead us downstairs to the armoury. Protector Gin's tiny head pokes up from behind a shelf as we file in. She walks around to meet us, waving an arm at a selection of wooden staves.

"They look identical but they are not. Pick up a few, find the one that feels right. If you cannot follow through with the full range of motion, then it is too heavy. Do not go too light either, or you will sacrifice power; you will not be able to block more forceful blows.

"These are yours until you receive your designation. Do not lose them; do not allow them to be damaged." She pauses a moment to glower at us.

"Oh, and take a couple of those too," she says, pointing toward a selection of chest guards. "You are going to need them, little birds."

In Ring One, the older cadets are swinging and jabbing in set patterns. I hear shouting and realize that the training masters are calling out codes. The outcome is musical, of course. What is music but patterns of sound, repeated, altered, and then repeated again?

Our training masters lead us to the far side of the arena, where a strip of ground has been sectioned off.

"You may lean your equipment against the wall and join me here in the center," calls out Protector Tila. I think it is the first time that she has spoken.

I hurry so that I can stand close to her, my heart racing with anticipation. She stands perfectly straight with her hands clasped behind her back as she surveys us.

"Why are we teaching you to fight?" she asks a boy—Lark, I remember that his name is Lark.

"We learn to fight so that we may help keep Seira safe, Protector." The answer is automatic, pre-scripted. This is something that we all know.

"Safe from what?" she asks.

"Northern savages."

"Yes. We guard our northern border, just as our fellow protectors guard the southern wall and the coasts." She pauses, and turns to Parakeet. "How do we fight them?"

"We, uh…" Parakeet looks around the ring, at the wooden staves, the blades. "I'm sorry, Protector, but do we fight them with steel?"

Training Master Tila's mouth twitches slightly. "Your hesitation is correct, cadet. We do not usually fight with steel, or staff, or even crossbows and guns. We have detectors that survey the land approaching our border, detectors that allow us to assess and exterminate a threat before it can come within a mile of our walls. Why, then, do we expect you to master the fighting arts?"

She is looking at Pipit now.

"For discipline, Protector," he says, "and because you should not rely solely on technology or tools that can fail or be taken away."

She eyes Pipit for a moment. "You are one of the four that visited Protector Gin in the armoury yesterday."

"Yes, Protector."

"Hmm." She shifts her gaze back to the group at large. "We teach you the fighting arts so that you are capable of applying these techniques should the Administration call upon you to do so."

She catches my eye, and lifts her eyebrows. "You may ask your question, cadet."

I stare at her, taken aback. "I—I apologize, Protector. I was wondering how often, and in what situations, protectors have been called upon to directly engage with Northerners in the past."

I feel the crowd stir around me and I fight to keep from looking down. I had not intended to ask this aloud, but it is not permissible to conceal your thoughts when questioned. If I wish to keep my thoughts hidden, I must learn to keep them from manifesting on my face.

Protector Tila turns to Jheb.

"Seven years ago," he says, "our detectors alerted us to a group of savages approaching from the north. They relayed this information, and then negated it. It was as though the party had simply vanished. Clearly the savages had found some way of hiding from the detectors. Grand Neilem dispatched a small party of protectors, including myself, out beyond the wall to resolve the situation."

I memorize the words now so that I can process them in length later. I cannot afford to be distracted today—or worse, be perceived as a distraction.

We mimic simple footwork for half an hour, advancing a few steps forward, backward, to each side, and on diagonal. We then move on to blocks. Again, we learn only a few simple moves, which we repeat over and over. Bruises start to form on the blades of my forearms.

By the time Protector Tila calls for us to retrieve our staves, the muscles in my arms and shoulders are heavy, exhausted; they tremble as I lift my weapon from the dirt.

She teaches us cross-body downward and upward strikes; side swings; a forward thrust; the corresponding counter blocks. We file into two lines, working with a single partner as Protector Tila calls out each move. I am paired with Pipit, who seems hesitant, careful with his blows. Despite the growing ache in my arms and shoulders, I intensify my force. Pipit's eyes widen with surprise, but he soon responds in kind, his strikes and blocks coming stronger and faster as he gains confidence. We move on to short, simple patterns, and again I find him wavering, a touch too slow, too soft. I check my stance, my grip, and again increase force. This time it seems to make him more nervous; he flinches. The training master's voice grows louder and I realize that she is directly behind me.

"Stop." She speaks quietly, so that only we can hear. "Swing from your core, not your arms. Also, you need to aim higher. This," she points to a spot three quarters of the way up my staff, "is where you want to make contact."

"Yes, Protector," he says, flushed again. She nods and moves away.

"I suggest that you incorporate additional training into your free time," Protector Tila says, addressing the entire group once the day's training session has come to a close. "The faster you build strength and improve your coordination, the better you will be able to master the basics. These are your building blocks. They must be ingrained into your muscle memory. You will not be able to proceed to the next level until they are."

35

The South

"WE COULD START TOMORROW," Starling says, hiding a yawn behind a hand streaked with dust.

"Putting off until tomorrow—" I start.

"I know, I know. But she said free time. It's already past 2100 hours."

"So it will be a quick session."

The corridor is teeming with first years returning, as we are, from evening chores. A few rush past us looking frantic, history textbooks in their arms.

"At least we finished our assignment," Pipit says, joining us as two hallways merge into one. "I hate rushing written work. What was your task tonight? I was down in the basement, cleaning."

"Fields," says Starling. "And now Sora wants to train. Again."

Pipit looks down at his hands, curling and stretching them a few times. "I think maybe I should too. To keep up with all of you."

Starling and I exchange a glance.

"Okay, okay," she says after a moment. "If it's a team activity, I suppose I'll come too."

There are a handful of cadets and protectors in Ring One when we arrive, though only a single figure occupies the far strip where we trained this afternoon.

"The amount we're running into you, we're clearly meant to be friends," Starling says to Vireo with a big smile.

He lays down his staff, pulls one arm into a stretch and dips his head to the side, neither rejecting nor embracing her explicit offer of friendship. Nonplussed, Starling leans against the wall beside him and begins rolling her neck out.

"Four is better anyway," I say to break the silence. "Shall we pair up?"

Vireo is a good partner, meeting each blow with equal force. My arms begin quaking within minutes. "Do you want to stop and stretch?" he asks. I shake my head. "Thirty more swings."

By the time we break I am pooling with sweat. I glance over at the large arena clock. Two minutes, I tell myself. No longer. Vireo reaches over and takes my staff. I open my mouth in protest, but then stop, biting the inside of my lip. I do not own anything, I remind myself. Everything I hold is the property of the Administration, and any of my classmates is equally entitled to its use. He swings it once, twice.

"Want to go over the footwork?" he asks, handing it back to me.

I look over at Starling and Pipit and the weak, exhausted blows passing back and forth between them and nod. "Footwork?" I call out.

We have to jog to make it back to the dormitory before 2200. "Good to finish off with cardio," Pipit gasps as we turn the last corner.

Starling bursts into laughter, eliciting a confused but pleased expression from Pipit.

I have already changed into my nightclothes and settled into bed when I remember that I have not yet taken my evening sweet. Though the overhead lamps clicked off at precisely 2200, the dispensary screen casts enough light to navigate by.

I tiptoe across the cold, concrete floor. Pipit sees me and jumps out of bed as well.

"Sora," I say quietly to the machine, pulling out the small dish that appears and moving aside for Pipit. There are two sweets in my cup tonight. Both yellow, like Pipit's, although he has only received one. We munch in silence for a moment.

"I think," he whispers to me, "I think that if we do that every night, I won't be the worst for long."

"We'll be the best," I whisper back, earning a hopeful smile from him. It is hard to be sure in the dark, but I think his ears are glowing red again.

36

The North

IT TOOK two days for Sam to feel herself again, for her body to physically process both the alcohol and the trauma of what she had witnessed. Numb and withdrawn, and feverish by turns, she forced herself to move through the daily routine of eating, working, and trying to sleep. There were new nightmares now, in addition to her recurring dreams about Corvus and Raina, and she woke up feeling exhausted. It was as though gravity itself was out of kilter, making the air thick and soupy.

On the third day, her head cleared and her body seemed her own again. The nightmares, she suspected, would continue.

The first thing she did, once she had managed to scrape together the beginnings of a plan, was find Shale.

"You want weapons," Shale repeated.

"Yes. A crossbow and some knives."

"Always good friends to have," she said, looking thoughtful. "I can give you a few names. Or if you can wait until tomorrow I could go for you—I might be able to get you a better price."

"Thanks, but I think I need to go today."

"Of course." Shale gave Sam a sympathetic, knowing smile.

She thinks it's for self-defense, Sam realized. *Because of what happened after the wedding.*

"It might take them some time to get everything for you, but I can lend you knives. I have extras."

"Thanks. Oh, and rope."

"Rope?" Shale's smile faltered.

"Rope," Sam repeated. She was too tired to come up with a believable lie. Shale, ever secretive herself, had never been one to probe. Sure enough, the redhead simply shrugged. Sam wavered for a moment, wondering if it was a mistake to hide her plan from Shale. *Can I count on her to keep it from Xenia, though?* She honestly didn't know. The two girls had become inseparable. It was not that she mistrusted Xenia. In matters unrelated to their work, she felt that she could count on any of the other drudges. What she was about to do, though, was explicitly contrary to the terms of her employment.

In the end, Sam got a name and a location, and set off on her own. *It's safer this way.*

37

The North

THERE WERE no guards stationed outside. In fact, save for the muted glow of a candle behind the curtain of a second-storey window, there were no signs of life about the house or the surrounding property at all.

Hidden within the branches of a tree high atop the hill, Sam waited. The descending sun flared out in embers of red, orange, and yellow, before the sky faded to grey and then a deep, dense black. There would be no moonlight tonight to guide her.

The minutes ticked slowly by and the darkness and the silence both remained unbroken. Only when the mosquitoes became unbearable did Sam abandon her hiding place, climbing down silently and landing with a gentle thud on the dirt below. The day had been strangely, miraculously, dry. In terms of rainfall, anyway. The humidity continued its oppression unabated.

Even with the darkness to cloak her descent, she was reluctant to head straight down the hill toward the bridge, as she had last time. In and out, unseen and unheard: Sam would play the sneak, not the soldier. If she were to be seen...they knew who she was. Sam had no illusions about the consequences she would face if the Vauns found out what she was doing. *So, don't be seen.*

Straying from the direct path would be a bad idea too, thanks to the deadly pits that had been dug into the hillside. From the security of the trees, Sam began picking her way toward the back of the house. Her best chance, though it was by no means a good option, was the cliffs.

Once she'd tethered the rope to the trunk of an older, sturdier tree, she walked to the edge of the cliff, tossed it over, and waited for the gentle thud of rope hitting dirt. There was only silence. *Is it not long enough?* She peered over the edge, but in the darkness couldn't make out the ground below.

Her eyes drifted over to the house and the dark water that surrounded it. Her hands moved from her crossbow to her baton, to Shale's knives, and finally the old hammer she'd borrowed from Ava. All remained securely attached to her person. A small plastic bag containing a few torches and a striker was strapped to her shoulder, where it would hopefully remain dry. *And if I have to swim...*

Sam pushed the thought away. Grasping the rope firmly in her hands, she swung her body out into open space. A split second of horrifying nothingness and then her feet found the knot below her. She slid her hands down to the next knot, and then carefully shifted her feet downward too.

When she was halfway down, the sound of footsteps brought her heart to a standstill. There was someone on the hill, picking their way down to the main entrance. She squinted. The shape was wrong. It wasn't human—just some kind of animal.

After a slow, deep breath, she continued downward. She'd been lucky: the rope ended just a foot above the ground. She dropped into the phragmites, grateful for the cover they provided.

A mosquito circled, buzzing. Sam swatted it away just as another one landed on her shoulder. Her fingers slapped empty skin as it dodged the blow.

Sam pushed her way forward until she came to the edge of the black, greasy water. There was the squelch of her feet hitting mud, and then a gentle splash. She waded up to her shins, then her knees.

It's not an ocean, or a river, or a lake. It's only a bit of rainwater. It cannot be that deep. The water pooled, warm and slimy and reeking of human waste, around her stomach. Sam slowed. *What if it drops suddenly? They might have dug down, like the pits up on the hill.* She forced herself to inch forward, feeling for the swamp bottom with the toe of her boot before transferring her weight. *If it drops, I'll just fall back. I won't have to swim.*

The blast ripped through the night. Sam had the crossbow off her back and pointed at the house before it registered that the sound had come from her left, from the hill where she'd seen the animal. Noise sounded from inside the house. A moment later the heavy metal door opened and light spilled onto the front stoop.

She saw the dog first, its shadow stretching forward, monstrously large. The little man stepped outside a moment later, a torch in one hand, a loaded crossbow in the other.

"Stay," he said to the dog, and Sam was disgusted to hear excitement in his voice. The torchlight detached itself from the house and began bobbing across the bridge. The dog remained at the door, though he kept sniffing the air and growling. Sam was suddenly grateful to be standing in sewage. It seemed to be masking her scent.

The mosquitoes returned. Sam felt one land on her neck and another on her trigger finger. Their little legs crawled along her skin. Sam stiffened, though she did not dare move, not with the enemy so close. *What is the probability that it will bite? What is the probability that it will bite and that it is carrying a disease? What is the probability that it will bite and that it is carrying a disease and that the disease will be fatal to me? The man, the dog, the mosquitoes, the water; what is the probability that I die tonight?* The sweat began to drip from Sam's hairline down her cheeks. *There are two mosquitoes, so I would have to multiply it by two.* A third mosquito landed on her, and then a fourth, a fifth, a sixth.

Staying perfectly still, Sam kept her eyes on the man, who had reached the end of the bridge. She thought of the crossbow in her hand. At this range, she couldn't miss.

A mosquito walked along her lower lip. Another found her earlobe. *What if you're wrong about him?* It didn't matter. Even if she didn't find what she expected to find in his house, she knew that she wasn't wrong about what he was. It would be better for everyone if she shot him.

She took aim and paused. Would she have time to reload before the dog reached her? The thought of fighting in the water brought on a wave of fresh, raw fear.

The dog first, then. She pointed her crossbow back toward the front entrance. *And if the man escapes back into the house?* He'd be inside, waiting for her. *And if he thought you were coming for his captives, what would he do to them in the meantime?*

The mosquitos bit. All of them, as though they'd planned it: the mosquito dance of death. She exhaled, slowly and silently. *Physical discomfort is information. That is all. Information being transmitted from my body to my brain.* Her body disagreed. She ignored it.

Sam looked from the dog to the man one more time and then lowered her weapon. She couldn't risk it.

The man was bending down, picking something up. Several somethings, in fact: bits of an animal. *Land mines,* Sam realized with horror. *He planted land mines.* The creature she'd heard earlier must have set it off.

The man shuffled back to the front door. He tossed a chunk of animal flesh to the dog, who caught it in his mouth before following his master back inside. The door slammed shut, leaving Sam alone in the darkness once again.

A ghost of a smile appeared suddenly on her face. *A man who leaves traps all around his property, who goes outside in his nightshirt to investigate a noise, who brings his dog for protection... That is a man with no guards.*

Another step forward, and another; Sam hit the base of a bank. Steadily she made her way upward, the water relinquishing its hold on her stomach, her hips, her knees, until she crawled, sopping and stinking, onto dry land. She lowered her crossbow gently to the ground, and silently flicked the mosquitoes that still lingered on her skin. The bites had already grown into raised, angry welts.

She was shivering, despite the heat. Too much adrenaline was pumping through her body, overwhelming her senses, goading her to action. With shaking hands, she took out her hammer and knelt to inspect a boarded-up window. She pressed her ear to the rotting wood: silence.

It didn't take long to pry the nails from the boards. Slowly, carefully, she lowered the last wooden panel to the ground. Pulling out her crossbow again, she peered inside. Accustomed though her eyes were to the darkness, she couldn't make out more than the vague outline of a doorway within.

She moved to the side, lit a torch, and tossed it onto the window ledge. After waiting a moment, she poked her crossbow around the edge and peeked inside.

The room was empty. It was also tiny, barely larger than a closet. A bathroom, actually, she realized, spying a crud-encrusted toilet bowl. The seat had been removed, the tank smashed.

Feet first, she slid through the window and dropped down into the room below. Something crunched beneath her boots. She froze, her heart racing, and listened for the sound of footsteps. Seconds passed, and then a minute. The house was silent.

She looked down at her feet and retched. Rusted chains hung down from the wall, snaking around a pile of greasy rags and hair. Not wanting to look, but needing to know, Sam brought her torch closer. The bits of skin that remained, clinging like tissue paper to the bones beneath, looked to have been decomposing for years, not months.

"Not her," Sam whispered.

With a deep breath, she steeled herself and walked toward the door that would lead her farther into the house.

The next three rooms were worse. She found more bodies: chained to the walls; strapped to chairs; piled like rubbish in the corners. She wandered past them, horrified and nauseated.

Some of the corpses were fresher. She stared at hair, skin, faces. It seemed impossible that these grey and black bits of flesh could have once been living, breathing people. It seemed hopeless. Raina and Finlay could easily be here, piled amongst the nameless dead.

255

She reached the dusty staircase and hesitated. If Finlay and Raina were here, they were dead. There was nothing here for her. She should leave.

There was something hanging on the wall. Sam lifted her torch. Knives had been arranged, largest to smallest, in a row. Sam extinguished her torch.

The door wasn't locked. Silently, she pushed it open and made her way down a dark hallway. At the far end of the hallway, firelight flickered. The sitting room, she was sure. She felt as though she was in a dream. Had she dreamed this? Images and sounds plucked and pulled at her. She couldn't remember.

She heard movement and ducked into the nearest room. Her body hidden behind the doorframe, she peeked out into the hallway, her crossbow aimed at the sitting room. There were shuffling steps, and sniffing. It knew she was here.

The blow to the back of her head was enough to stun but not knock her out. She turned and shot into the dark room behind her. A cry sounded. The voice was wrong; too high.

There was no time to reload her crossbow. She threw it down, pulled a knife out of each boot and turned back to the hallway just in time to see the dog's yellow eyes as it lunged toward her. Crossing her arms, she thrust the knives forward.

His body slammed into hers. She felt the impact against her blades as she fell to the ground, his teeth snapping wildly at her throat. Tucking her chin into her chest to protect her neck, she twisted. The dog shuddered and went limp.

Her breath was coming out in gasps now. Sam pushed his body off of hers, pulled her knives out of his chest, and sank into a fighter's crouch. *There's someone else. You shot someone. Where are they?* It took her a moment to spot the body. It wasn't moving. She crept over to it. It was the old woman, the one who had let Sam in when she had visited on mission for the Vauns. Sam felt for a pulse. Nothing.

She waited, uncertain. Where was the man? He must have heard the commotion. After a moment, she wiped the knives on her T-shirt and put them away. They were solidly built, well balanced and newly sharpened, but still a far cry from the quality she was used to. *Crossbow's better.* She retrieved it and loaded another bolt.

The hallway was still empty. Sam crept toward the sitting room, her heart racing. *One down.* She reached the edge of the doorway and listened. She could hear nothing. Was he asleep? Or was he waiting for her?

From behind the crossbow, she peered into the room. There was the bookcase and the revolting dolls, the stained tables and chairs. Where was the man?

Sam turned back to the hallway and contemplated her options. There were three doors left: one open, two closed.

She stepped through the open doorway first and found a kitchen: a normal, functioning kitchen with a fireplace and big bags of grain. It seemed out of place, though even monsters, she supposed, needed to eat.

The next room she knew to be a bathroom by the smell, even before she opened the door. It too was empty.

Back in the hallway she saw it: light flickering under the doorway of the last room. Seconds later, the door swung open and the little man appeared, torch in one hand, a knife in the other.

She did not hesitate. He let out a small gasp as the bolt sank into his chest, and stumbled backward through the doorway behind him. Sam reloaded and followed.

He was lying on the floor when she reached him, his face twisted in pain. His legs were shaking uncontrollably. "Give—"

"What did you do to the other Vaun drudge?" Sam asked. Her voice was calm, authoritative. *A soldier after all.*

He didn't appear to be listening. "Lots, lots of girls." He flicked a white, filmy tongue at her.

"The Vaun drudge," Sam repeated. This time he heard her. His eyes flickered upward.

"It was a gift..." His voice had faded to a whisper. He licked his lips. "Come here."

Sam kicked the blade out of his hand, picked up the torch he'd dropped, and waved it near the ceiling.

She spotted the latch and pulled the staircase down.

"Come here!" His whole body was shaking now, and wet, drowning sounds were coming from his mouth.

Sam climbed the stairs to the attic. It had been decorated like a child's playroom. There was a low, yellow table, set with a teapot and cups. There were more dolls too, though she could only see their backs. They had been turned to face the wall. In the corner near a boarded-up window, there was a bed. A skinny body wrapped in heavy chains lay curled on top of it.

The body moved, and Sam's heart leapt. She rushed to the bed and turned the frail frame toward her.

A young man stared up at her, terrified. He bore the marks of torture: cuts and bruises and burns. The skin on his chest looked as though it had been peeled off and regrown.

Sam stepped back from the bed. She'd dared to hope. *Enough. Get it together.* The man shrank away from her as she reached for one of his chains.

"Where's the key?" she asked him. He merely shook his head at her.

"I'll come back."

He let out a cry as she left, a weak, anguished sound.

Down the ladder and into the room. She poked the little man with the toe of her boot. He didn't move. There was a set of keys on the small table beside his bed. Sam grabbed them and headed back up to the attic.

The man watched numbly as she tried key after key, finally finding the correct one and unlocking the chains that bound his wrists and ankles to the bed.

"Can you walk?" Again, he only shook his head at her.

She didn't talk as she helped him off the bed and down the ladder. Though he was tall, much taller than Sam, he seemed to weigh only as much as a child.

Back in the bedchamber, he stared at the corpse of his captor until Sam pulled him away. He leaned heavily on her as they inched to the front door and down the stairs to the bridge. Slowly they began to trudge up the hill, Sam half leading, half carrying him.

"Are you Finlay?" she asked him when they reached the top of the hill.

He stared at her. "Finlay…I'm Finlay," he whispered. "Who…who are you?"

"I'm Sam. I work for the Vauns. But I'm not here for them," she added quickly, as his look of terror returned. "I was looking for Raina." She swallowed. "I don't know which…I couldn't identify her body."

He looked bewildered. "Raina?"

"Yes, Raina. Your girlfriend." *Is he really Finlay?* She'd given him the name, after all, and he certainly looked nothing like his brother. *He knows who the Vauns are, though.*

"She…" He coughed, a deep, wracking cough. "What?"

"The bodies in the basement, I couldn't tell which—"

"No." He coughed again, shaking his head. "I was alone. She wasn't…wasn't ever here."

Finlay remembered where his brother lived, in a small apartment south of the Pike. The building stretched high into the sky, though only the bottom floors looked to be livable now. Judging from the gutted ruins that remained and the rotted debris that still littered the streets below, it was a tornado that had destroyed the upper stories.

They trudged up three flights of stairs. Maddox wasn't there, but they let themselves in.

Sam helped Finlay into his brother's bed. He lay on his side with his knees pulled up toward his chest, staring at the wall. He did not ask her to leave, nor did she offer. She felt responsible for him, somehow. She sat down near his feet on an unoccupied corner of the bed. They waited side by side in silence for what seemed like hours before he spoke.

"Raina. She's…gone?"

This was not a conversation that Sam had anticipated having. In her mind, Finlay was always with Raina: her lover or her captor or her murderer or some combination of the three.

"She disappeared the night of the solstice." Sam glanced over at him, but Finlay's expression had not changed. He looked frozen. She wondered if he'd even heard her.

She waited a beat, not wanting to hound him for information, but not willing to let the opportunity pass, either. "Do you know where she was, or where she was planning to be, that night?"

Moving stiffly, he shook his head. "I saw her...I saw her that morning. We were gonna meet at a warehouse, later." He left out a rasp that may have been intended as laughter. "Celebrate the solstice."

They lapsed back into silence. Sam wanted to ask him about his ex-girlfriend, the one that had gone missing before Raina. *To what end? The satisfaction of your curiosity? It was a coincidence, nothing more. Finlay is not the wolf. This girl, whoever she is, won't lead you to Raina.*

After a moment, Sam stood up. She didn't want to intrude on his grief, his anger.

"Wait." Finlay was trying to pull himself up. Sam didn't miss the note of panic in his voice.

"I'm not leaving. Does your brother keep water here?"

He relaxed back into the bed. "Outside."

Sam closed the bedroom door, though she wasn't sure why. It only took her a moment to find the balcony. Outside it was still dark, though dawn was not far off. A pot of water sat in a cold fire pit. She found a metal tankard and filled it, but instead of going back inside, she leaned her arms upon the railing and stared at the city streets. The lake beyond it was invisible, part of the black void that stretched outward until it blended with the sky.

It should have been cooler at this hour, a brief respite from the heat and humidity. Instead the heat seemed to be building, hour by hour. She wished it would rain.

She was tired, emotionally and physically both. She was tired of loss, tired of looking for Raina, tired of filth, tired of violence. She was tired of the North.

Don't blame the North. You chose this. You. Raina, Finlay, none of this had anything to do with you.

I just wanted to find her.

Why? What did you hope to gain from all this?

I'm not hoping for anything.

Liar.

It's the right thing to do.

That's not it. You're after something. The cynical voice in her head shrieked with laughter. *You think you can do one good thing one time for somebody else and it'll erase what you did?*

It wouldn't. Nothing would. She knew that.

You're right. You're not. You're nothing.

Something cold and sharp pressed against her throat. "I'm not here to fight," she said dully to the man behind her.

"Bullshit," Maddox said. "Why are you here, then?"

"Check your bed," said Sam. She could feel her eyelids getting heavier.

"What the jit is that supposed to mean?" He was too loud, too aggressive.

"Your brother's back." If only she could sleep.

His hold on her loosened. "What do you... Why..." A beat, and then the edge of the knife dug in with renewed force. "What are you trying to pull?"

"Bring him this." She put the tankard full of water on the railing. "He's dehydrated. Also, tell him to stay hidden. I won't tell anyone he's alive, but if he shows his face on the streets, the Vauns will figure it out before long."

She slid her fingers between the blade and her neck and pushed his knife away. He let her do it. He also let her continue past him, back into his apartment. She paused outside the bedroom door before continuing down the hallway to the door. Finlay's brother could take care of him now. She was done.

38

The North

Six days later, it still had not rained.

Sam hurried home through the trails, sweating in the evening heat and swatting at the mosquitoes that seemed determined to land on her with their filthy, diseased bodies. The light was fading; it would be fully dark by the time she reached the warehouse.

She had kept her word, telling no one, not even Shale, about Finlay. It hadn't been difficult. Benison had kept her working past dusk every night since; she had barely seen her friends.

Too busy working for your kindly employers? Images from the little man's house pushed their way up from her subconscious. Sam wrestled them back down.

You were under no illusions. She had been warned about the Vauns, it was true. *But this?*

Sam pushed these thoughts away too. She would take their coin, use it to buy what she needed to start a life somewhere else, somewhere quiet, and then she would leave the Barrow. That had been the plan all along. *Or did you forget? You've been so focused on Raina...*

Raina. She gritted her teeth as the familiar wave of disappointment crashed through. She had felt so close... *And now you're back to square one. Worse, actually: you've no leads.* It was probably time to let it go. Acceptance: that was what they taught in the North. It rankled, though, the failure of it; like a wound gone septic. *Can you let it go?*

I have.

You still dream of her.

It was true; the dreams hadn't stopped when she'd found Finlay. The content hadn't even changed. She tried to tell her subconscious that the premise was no longer relevant, but it refused to listen. *They'll fade. Eventually.*

The gnarled, rotted tree carcass that marked her exit loomed up in front of her. *Would it be such a bad decision, to stay?* There were dangers in the Barrow, but that was true of any place. She had friends here now; friends that had looked after her when she'd needed it. That was a rare and valuable thing to throw away. *And for what, to hide in a cave, safe but alone? What kind of a life is that?*

She left the trails for the city streets, and the increasingly unbearable smell of refuse.

Breathe it in. You'll get used to it. She was almost at the halfway point. If she rushed, she could be home in twenty minutes. *And what about Frank? I can't just abandon him. He'd be difficult to transport, though.*

Sam realized she was being watched a split second before she heard them.

"That the drudge?"

The words were hushed, but Sam had good hearing. She took a sharp turn into an alley, pulling the baton from her boot as she slipped into the darkness of a doorway. Crouching down low, she thought longingly of the crossbow hidden in her nest.

She'd been warned that it invited trouble, wearing expensive weapons. Popular wisdom dictated that something as noticeable as a crossbow should be saved for special occasions, situations where the benefits were sure to outweigh the risks. The problem with surprise attacks, though, is that they are surprising.

Moonlight illuminated the three women as they turned into the alley. They were young and newly branded, the skin around their neck tattoos still raw and swollen. Two of them carried metal poles, the third an axe.

"Come out, you little jit! We just want to bash your face in!"

One of the other girls giggled, and Sam heard a slap.

"Think it's funny," another slap, "what happened to Axel?"

Sam heard someone spit.

"Taow," the slapper cursed. "You earned this, compound shint!"

They can't be Hunters—no mixed-sex gangs. An affiliated gang, maybe? They were passing her hiding place now, one of the girls so close that Sam thought she could probably take out her knees with one good thrust of her baton.

So she did. One hit to the knees, another straight up into the girl's face. Sam then spun and kicked one of the other girls in the stomach.

An axe hissed through the air. Sam dodged it easily, and slammed her baton into the exposed ear of the girl wielding it. There was a shriek of pain, but Sam did not have time to assess the damage, as the girl she'd kicked in the stomach was already swinging her metal pole at Sam's head. Sam ducked and lashed a foot outward, this time connecting with the girl's kneecap.

They were fighters, clearly, but they had not been trained: all savagery, no technique. As long as they kept attacking her one by one, she was in no real danger. The girl with the axe screamed, rage distorting her face, and swung for Sam's ribs. Sam stepped out of range. The anger in her attacker's eyes concerned Sam more than the axe.

Axel's sister, perhaps, or his lover? Sam lowered her baton a fraction of an inch. "Whatever you heard about me is a lie."

Angry tears welled up in the girl's eyes as she raised the axe a second time. Sam ducked the blow that followed and slashed her baton down on the girl's wrist. The girl let out a cry of pain and dropped the axe.

A blow from behind sent Sam tumbling forward. The first huaina she'd taken down was back in the fray. Thrusting aside the pain in her shoulder blade, Sam spun around, managing to throw up her baton in time to cushion the second strike. She then thrust her knee up into her attacker's exposed stomach, bringing forth a spray of vomit.

An uppercut to the chin and a hook to the temple, and the girl started to collapse. Sam caught her by the shoulders and shoved her toward the other two girls, who were advancing toward her. They pushed the girl aside and continued on toward Sam.

She backed down the alley, giving her head a quick shake to keep the sweat from falling into her eyes. She should have grabbed one of the metal poles—the reach was twice as long as her little baton. A knife or two would have been helpful too—if only she hadn't already returned the borrowed blades to Shale.

Perhaps she could throw something, to distract them. She scanned the ground for a rock, a piece of metal, or even dirt. This end of the alley was amazingly clear of debris. She had somehow managed to find the only lane in the Barrow not covered in trash. She slid back into a fighting stance and waited.

A stone emerged at the edge of Sam's vision, sailing through the air and striking the girl with the axe in the temple. She dropped the axe and lurched sideways into her friend.

Sam was there before the girls had finished falling. Her boot lashed out once, twice, finding a temple each time. One more kick apiece and the girls dropped.

Sam waited a beat, and then crouched down. They were unconscious, but alive.

"It's like the gods *want* us to be friends," a familiar voice said.

Sam leapt to her feet and spun around, flustered. She'd forgotten about the thrower. Adder leaned casually against a nearby doorframe.

Footsteps sounded from the mouth of the alley. Sam spun around a second time, baton up.

"I, uh." Cassio slid his baton back into the side of one of his stylish boots. "You seemed like you needed help." He paused. "But then you didn't."

"I had it under control," she said.

"Clearly." His eyes moved from the huaina lying on the ground to Adder, and then back to Sam. He cocked his head questioningly.

"He's…" Sam hesitated. Adder was difficult to sum up. *An obnoxiously friendly man who once helped protect my bicycle, then carrying a bomb, from huainas? A musician who stole my pastries?* "Adder."

"I'm Adder." He shot Cassio a cheerful grin. "And you're one of the infamous twins."

Cassio nodded, seeming unfazed by his celebrity status. His eyes were still on Sam. "There are a bunch more of these girls with the neck tats up the street. They see this…"

"If you need to exit in a hurry," Adder said, gesturing toward the building at his back, "I can help. Like you said, they should call me Saint Adder."

"Like I…? That's what you—"

"Sam. Listen." Cassio was eyeing the mouth of the alley. She could hear it now too: the thrum of footsteps.

"Right, let's go."

Last to exit, Sam had the door nearly shut when they appeared. A teenage girl at the front of the pack shrieked and ran toward the first unconscious body. As slowly and as silently as she could, Sam pulled the door closed. She needed to get away from the alley, away from the bodies, and away from the rest of the gang that apparently wanted her dead.

Adder was talking quietly to an old man who seemed surprised to find all three of them in his living room. Instead of ushering them to the front door, as Sam expected, Adder led them up a flight of rickety stairs to the second floor and out onto a balcony. They were on the opposite side of the building now, hidden from the alley.

A stack of packing crates enabled them to climb onto the roof, where long, heavy planks of wood lay piled.

"So," Adder said in a whisper, turning to Sam. "Which way, ladkhi?"

"North. About twenty minutes."

He nodded. "Can do."

Together they pushed one of the planks across the open air and onto the roof of the building opposite it, creating a narrow and shaky bridge. On his hands and knees, Adder crawled across. Cassio gave a tiny groan and followed, Sam on his heels. Like the last rooftop, this one too housed a stack of long planks.

"Do all buildings have this?" Sam asked.

Adder shook his head. "Only the ones I need." He gave Sam a wink.

"This is all you?"

"Well...no, not *all* me, but it's not exactly a public route, either."

They crawled to a third rooftop, and then a fourth, at which point Adder indicated that they should stop. There was a latch on this roof. Pulling it open, they were able to drop down into the home below. A teenage girl with a baby on her hip looked over anxiously, but then smiled when she saw Adder.

He waved at her and then ushered them down to the basement, where a pit had been dug into the floor.

"In we go," Adder said cheerfully, lowering himself in.

Cassio peered into the dark hole and sighed. "This was a bad night to come looking for you."

"Looking for me?" Sam asked, following him down into the pit, where Adder was lighting a torch. They seemed to be in some kind of tunnel. "Why?"

"Well, looking for Hak. He was supposed to meet me after work, but he never showed. Thought maybe he'd come by yours."

"He might've done, though I doubt it. He hasn't come by in a while."

"Well, he—Gods, where are we?"

The tunnel had opened up into an enormous hall, properly built with smooth concrete floors and staircases. She saw a booth and what might once have been a vendor's stand.

"Was this an underground market?" Sam asked, her voice echoing off the empty walls.

"It was for trains," Adder said. "Underground trains. People used to take them to work in the morning."

"I heard about this." There was a note of wonder in Cassio's voice. "They closed and sealed them up, not long after the start of the Decline."

A laneway had been dug into the ground. Adder dropped down

onto it, landing with a splash. The other two followed. Beneath a foot of water, Sam felt metal rungs. *Tracks,* she realized.

"Why?" Sam asked. "If people needed them, why close them up?"

"It cost too much to maintain, with all the flooding," Adder said. "And then, well, there was nobody to make sure it got maintained."

"How far does it go?"

"All across the city, apparently. I've gone two hours that way." Adder pointed forward and then backward. "And two hours back that way."

"Ever seen anyone else down here?" Cassio asked.

"Here and there. No huaina."

"Amazing," Sam heard Cassio mutter to himself. They continued along the tracks, the silence broken only by the splashing of their feet.

Eventually they came to another platform. They pulled themselves up and followed Adder up a flight of stairs. Sam heard movement behind her and snapped around, arms up. It was only rats. Massive, Frank-sized rats, but rats nonetheless.

She entered another tunnel, this one so small that they were forced to crawl. A few minutes later they emerged into someone's kitchen. An old woman, busy boiling water, blew Adder a sensual kiss. He mimed catching it, blew one back, and then led the others through another room and down a little hallway to the front door. Stepping out into the street, Sam realized that they were only one street north of the factory.

"Well," Cassio said. "That was...informative. How have I lived so many years in this city and never once stumbled across our giant underground?"

"You can't stumble across what's hidden," Adder said. Sam glanced at his face, but it was hard to make out his expression in the dark.

"Can you only access it through people's homes?" Sam asked.

"As far as I know," he said. "It's the same families keeping watch, you know. Generation after generation guarding the doors, ever since the original entranceways were sealed up and these tunnels dug out."

"So how did you find out about them?" Cassio asked, arms crossed over his slim chest.

Adder smiled. "People like to tell me things."

Cassio raised his eyebrows at Sam, who shrugged in reply.

They parted ways with Adder, though Cassio walked with Sam back to the factory.

Ava's shop was still open for business, though the lady herself was seated on a crate, dangling a piece of string for Frank. The latter gave a loud meow and ran over to greet them.

Sam reached down and petted his soft fur.

"Hi, cat," she whispered. "I missed you too."

He gave a funny sort of squawk, ran back to Ava's shop, plopped down in the corner with his back to the group, and started washing himself.

"Brawling, I see," Ava said, looking them up and down with a scowl on her face. "Piss poor reason to miss dinner, you ask me."

"Right," said Sam, wincing as she reached a hand back and felt the spot where the metal pipe had hit her. *Only a bruise. You're lucky.* "I just love to fight."

Ava was already up and scrounging for a cloth. She dunked it in some cold water and passed it to Sam, who pressed it against her aching shoulder.

"This one looks okay," she said, pointing at Cassio. "What's your problem, huh?"

"I was fashionably late," Cassio said, taking up the string and flicking it at Frank, who was pointedly ignoring him. "Did Hakuund ever come by?" he asked. His tone was casual; the look in his eyes was not.

Ava shook her head. "Nope. He ain't been by in weeks." She turned and began rummaging through one of her cupboards. "Any later, you'd have completely missed out on xeres."

She put three of her most colourful and least dented cups on the counter, and then returned to her cupboard for a small bottle of liquor. She pulled out the stopper and poured three sizable portions.

"A whole year of bad," she said, passing one cup to Sam and one to Cassio. "Would've served you right."

"That makes no sense," said Sam.

"Don't matter if it makes sense or not. We'll have our round of the stuff, just in case. A quick round—tomorrow's early, even for me."

"Tomorrow?" asked Sam, peering at the liquor inside her cup. She gave it a sniff and almost choked. *How much alcohol is in this?*

She looked up to find Ava staring at her, an exasperated look on her face.

"Gods, girl. Thought they hit your shoulder, not that chickpea in your head. Tomorrow's the solstice."

39

The South

"CAN YOU BELIEVE IT?" Starling whispers to me as we sweep the floors in Tranquility Square. "Apparently they have been doing it all year. Fir just didn't catch them until tonight. Can you imagine, just trading tasks like that?"

"What do you think will happen to them?"

Starling shrugs her skinny shoulders in response. "Protector Nem was called, and since Vireo and Parakeet were not at supper I suppose they're still in self-regulation."

"I don't know why we're surprised, at Vireo anyway," I say, frowning at the dust pile accumulating at my feet. "He does stuff like this for fun."

"No, I'm sure he...well... Maybe he didn't know that it was forbidden?" Starling's hopeful words are undermined by the lack of conviction in her voice.

"It's common sense. You receive an order; you carry out that same order. Can you imagine if someone did that during a war? Just decided they would rather do someone else's assignment?"

"Is it so bad, though, if both parties agree to the switch? I mean, two chores were assigned, two chores were completed."

"When we are protectors, it will be up to the P4s or P5s to define our individual roles; they are the ones trained to calculate the strengths and weaknesses of the protectors under them. Switching assignments is like saying that you know better than them."

Out of the corner of my eye I can see that Starling is struggling to suppress a smile.

"What?" I ask.

"You sound like Protector Drest," she says.

I glance around. The C5 supervisor has left the room. I swing my broom at her. Starling blocks it, her grin widening.

"You telegraphed."

Pipit is already at the meeting spot when we arrive, textbooks fanned out in front of him. We are just getting settled when Vireo plops himself down into his usual seat next to me. As one, our three heads turn toward him.

"Long talk," he says, and I am relieved to see a glimmer of shame in his eyes. This relief is short-lived.

"But at least it got me out of mending." He flashes us a wicked grin.

"You're unbelievable," I say, taking out my textbooks.

"What," he says. "You've never broken a rule before?"

An image flashes through my mind: me crawling after Iris through a dusty vent. "Perhaps as a child, but I wouldn't now. Especially the night before the examinations!"

He shrugs. "The examination standards are objective. They can't lower my mathematics or weapons score because of something like this."

"They could take it out of virtues. Or even just make a note in your file. You heard Protector Nem: Everything will be taken into account when they assign our roles."

Vireo waves a hand dismissively at me. "That's four years away. No one will remember this in four years."

I am feeling irritated, a signal that it is time to end this conversation. Opening my geoscience textbook, I flip to the review section at the back.

I am midway through the first paragraph when a slate slides into my line of vision. I decode the dots and lines to read: *Do not be mad, I am not that bad.*

I bite my lip to hide a smile and turn to scowl at Vireo, who looks extremely pleased with himself.

"At least your coding is getting better," is all I say before turning back to my work.

It is a struggle to keep my mind on the material. The truth is that I am studying tonight because I feel that I should, not because I need to. It has been a year since we arrived at the base, and in that year we have studied every day and every night in anticipation of tomorrow's examination. I shut my book.

"I'd rather be training."

Starling and Vireo follow suit, looking relieved.

"You can join us after, if you'd prefer," I tell Pipit, who looks reluctant to leave the comfort of his nest of books. "We'll start with footwork and shadow strikes; we can wait until you join us to pair up."

He shakes his head and begins gathering his textbooks. "I should take advantage of the extra training time," he says. "We all know I need it."

"Don't be so hard on yourself," Starling says, reaching out to squeeze his hand as we make our way back to the dormitory to change. "You've improved a lot."

He looks at her hand in his and brightens, for a moment. Like Vireo's repentance, though, his happiness is short-lived. "I'm still at the bottom of the class."

"Yeah, well, we've all improved a lot too," Starling says with her usual cheery smile. "The point is that we're all better than we were."

"Besides," I say. "It's not as though you're competing against us; we're all being measured against the C1 standards."

"Until fifth year," Vireo says. "Then you're competing against us."

"Oh right." I snort. "As though you want a higher position with all of the added responsibility."

"I don't." He smiles at me. "I just like winning."

Ring One is packed with bodies. Not only first years, although I see a good many of our cohort, but with upper-year cadets and protectors too.

"Of course," Pipit says. "Ring Two is off-limits until after the contests."

The contests. The words loom large in my mind. It is hard to believe that it has been a year since the contest qualifiers. It is harder still to imagine a more impressive display of physical strength and teamwork than we witnessed that night; yet tomorrow's spectacle is bound to be. The qualifiers serve to separate the good from the great. During the contests, when the great are pitted against one another, this is when we will discover who is the best.

Finch and Sparrow wave at us as we make our way over to the C1 strip.

"Busy, isn't it?" Starling says, glancing around. "It must be examination nerves."

Few of the other first years have been training in the evenings as we have. Too many chores and too many assignments seems to be the general consensus. Finch and Sparrow have joined us in the past, but even they are sporadic additions to our foursome.

A group of fifth years crowding around a target catch my eye. I wonder how they are feeling, the night before their own examination. The first-year tests are intended to prepare us for the upper years; all of our professors have said so. The fifth-year examination, though, determines your rank. It is not impossible to rise as a protector, after your rank has been assigned, but it is uncommon. Of course, many cadets seem to be satisfied with the idea of being a P1. Regular patrols on the wall, occasional forays north for excitement; it is a comfortable career, not to mention vital to the safety of our nation.

I wonder, though, if some of them are not more focused on the perks that come with receiving your designation, such as the additional rest day and access to couple quarters, than they are with position or rank. The stipend is another subject oft discussed by cadets, who dream of purchasing off-duty clothing, custom-made weapons, or hair dye tablets.

There are always the contests, in addition to regular training, to keep protectors goal oriented. In addition to C5s the contests are open to all protectors, but I have heard that it is the PIs who most often represent their bases.

We reach our dormitory two minutes before curfew. There is a purple sweet in my cup tonight—a treat in advance of the examination, I suppose. By the time I have changed into my nightclothes, the dispensary has been remotely shut off, leaving us in absolute darkness. Even the window offers little by way of illumination. There must be a dark moon tonight. I try to count lunar phases, but my head feels fuzzy. My eyelids are already beginning to droop. I must not be nervous after all, I realize, for sleep to come so easily on the eve of such an important day. Maybe I am just physically exhausted, as I have been all year. Or maybe I am ready to be tested.

40

The South

THE SECOND YEARS take over our cleaning duties after breakfast, as C5 Birch had told us that they would. It is not to unburden or honour us, he was careful to clarify, but simply a decision made in consideration of the positive correlation between examination nerves and broken dishware.

Protector Nem leads us to a room I do not recognize. It is twice the size of a classroom, the desks spread out. Do they fear cheating, I wonder? I cannot imagine who would risk it. Even Vireo would not dare. I hope.

We are given test after test with only short breaks of ten minutes between them, scarcely enough time for a small cup of prickly pear juice and a visit to the lavatory. At some point a fourth year passes around a midday meal bar, which tells me that we must be two thirds of the way through.

Protector Nem is present the entire day, the only constant as various professors and protectors I recognize but do not know by name flitter in and out. Grand Neilem only joins us in the last minutes of the last exam. I have already finished, and am waiting to hand in my porta.

I wonder if Grand Neilem finds it anticlimactic to move from fifth-year sparring matches to first-year martial demonstrations. Then I wonder if anyone else imagines scales when they look at her. I start counting the fictitious scales, and then look frantically down at my test. Oh right, I have finished my test. I resume counting. I wonder when the others will finish.

"Time," Protector Nem calls out. "Please switch off your portas."

After returning to our dormitories to change clothing and collect staves and steel, we follow a C4 down to Ring One, where we line up below an amplobox occupied by our training masters and a collection of P3s and P4s. Snaking from the upper entrance down toward the box is Grand Neilem, this time flanked on either side by a pair of protectors also sporting the rare alphanumeric code of P5: her seconds. We wait in silence as they enter the box and settle into seats at the front.

Grand Neilem looks down upon us, and smiles. "Congratulations, cadets, on completing the first portion of your examination. Your marks will be posted on the screen in Tranquility Square tomorrow. For the next portion of your examination I—"

The patter of running feet pulls her focus and ours to a breathless C4 scurrying down the stands toward the amplobox, which he enters without first requesting permission, hurrying straight over to Grand Neilem. I wait for the gentle reproach, a calm word about the importance of decorum. Instead, as the C4 whispers in her ear, Grand Neilem's eyes widen; her pale skin turns from white to ashen. She speaks quietly to the C4 and then straightens, her lips widening into a tight smile as she looks back down at us.

"I am so pleased," she begins, her voice unnaturally high. She pauses for a moment, and then continues in her usual register, "to share that a council member has arrived early for the contests, and will be honouring us with his presence during your martial examination today. Please join me in welcoming our nation's chief medical officer, Councilman Naru."

There is a collective intake of breath. We press our hands together in the sign for deference, though I am sure that I am not the only one who is looking past my own hands, straining to see the man walking into the arena.

Seira's chief medical officer is not yet middle-aged. Black lines frame a square jaw, the hair meticulously sculpted and oiled. He is as familiar as my own reflection. With a smile on his face, he waves at us with the same easy manner that he has in national broadcasts.

I wonder how they travel, council members. Do they ride trains as we do? I imagine not. I imagine they have something faster, the speed of travel consistent with the value of their time.

"Thank you! Thank you, Grand Neilem, thank you, protectors, and thank you, cadets." His voice is rich, deep and musical. He claps his hands together once, out of enthusiasm, it seems, and looks at each of us in turn. I suppress a shiver when his eyes meet mine, halfway down the line. The gaze pushes inward, brute force bearable only because the incursion is not hostile. It drags on; he is in no hurry. For all his dynamism he does not flutter, but waits.

I struggle to maintain eye contact, fighting the instinct to shy away. As one of the five council members, he has every right to intrude. My training holds. By the time he moves to Pipit beside me, my eyes have begun to water.

"They suggested I rest after my journey." The councilman grins at us. "I told them: no, thank you. First-year cadets, tested for the first time; the greatness of our nation is founded upon this very energy, this determination. I myself was trained as a cadet and then as a medical P3 before I was recruited to work in Ankev. I know exactly how hard you have been working, and how ready you are to show us what you can do. I look forward to seeing the best of you."

Councilman Naru moves to take a seat, and I find that I have been holding my breath. I have changed my mind; broadcasts do nothing to capture a person.

They split us up into four groups, three of which, my group included, are led back outside by a C4 to wait our turn.

Outside the arena, half of my classmates slump to the floor, while the other half start pacing. I walk down to the end of the corridor and begin moving slowly through an array of stances and warm-up poses.

Eventually they call a second group and then a third, until only five other first years and I remain. I try to keep moving through the poses, though my focus flitters, playing back flashes of the morning examinations and the councilman's speech and then flipping forward to the trials ahead of me. There are a dozen light fixtures in the corridor where we wait. I like the number twelve; I like that it is divisible by six, by four, by three, by two, and by one and itself, of course.

The other cadets are seated in the stands when the C4 finally leads us back to the ring, lining the amplobox on three sides. Three lines of seated cadets, one amplobox filled with evaluators—three sides, but four groups altogether, with six of us on the ground. It all feeds back into twelve again. I breathe deeply and tell the numbers to retreat. Training Master Jheb is entering the ring.

He calls out a series of poses: the more difficult ones that took weeks to master. The minutes stretch on, the counts seeming longer than usual although I cannot say for certain that they are. I see limbs begin to quake as stabilizing feet or hands falter. I keep my eyes focused on a single point in front of me and remind myself that pain is only data, communicated from the body to the brain in case action is required. I acknowledge the information and tell my body to let go of the pain. It works, a little, some of the time.

Training Master Tila enters the ring, relieving Protector Jheb, and hands out head and chest guards. I secure mine and glance up at the crowd, trying to find my friends. The scant light that spills outward from the amplobox is insufficient—I can make out nothing but shorn scalps over shrouded faces.

She pairs us up: Robin and Wren, Phoebe and Quail, and Sparrow and me. Usually in class we are partnered with cadets of a similar height and weight. Sparrow is a foot taller and a hand wider than the average first year; I am an outlier in the opposite direction. I suspect Protector Tila is making a point—the size of our opponent is irrelevant. I am thankful that Sparrow joined our evening practice sessions. If he hadn't—I dismiss the thought. What-ifs hold no sway. We bow to Grand Neilem and the audience, again to our training master, and lastly to one another.

She calls out jabs, uppercuts, roundhouses; Sparrow advances toward me as I dodge or block. His strikes are strong, in force as well as technique. Meaty he may be, but he is not clumsy. Nor is he slow, although I am faster.

By the time she calls for us to switch roles there are bruises forming on my forearms. I give them a shake and use the short break to take stock of Sparrow's dimensions from a striker's perspective. Every cross, every knee, every kick must be angled upward, higher than the strikes we perfected in training. Not higher, though, than the shadow strikes I have practiced each evening. I push the grateful voice from my head and fill my ears with my training master's voice. Now is not the time for self-congratulations.

We move to throws, and then wooden staves, and finally blunted blades. Each time, Protector Tila calls out the strikes, leaving the defensive partner to block or dodge as per their judgment and reflexes. When we finish my arms are shaking.

We bow again, in reverse order, beginning with our partners and ending with the judges in the amplobox.

"Beautifully done, beautifully done by all." Councilman Naru has risen from his seat and stands beside Grand Neilem.

"You honour us—"

He cuts her off. "I wonder, though—please forgive my question but you will remember that I too underwent such examinations, and so I speak with both an insider and an outsider's perspective—whether we are truly testing defensive skills as well as we might."

Grand Neilem swallows, just once. Fear or anger, I cannot tell which, though both of course are perfectly normal emotional reactions to criticism. I frown. I have no right to evaluate the Grand's behaviour.

"Please, Councilman, we would be grateful for your guidance," she says, calm and courteous.

He turns from Grand Neilem and begins walking along the amplobox. "So, as we have it now, the cadets on defense are able to hear the commands given to the strikers." His voice fills the arena; he speaks to all of us—the judges, the cadets in the stands, our training masters, and us. "It's a bit of cheat, in a sense. In a real conflict, no one will be calling out blows before they happen!" He smiles, inviting us to share in the joke. "I am interested in how they perform when they are not privy to this information; how they interpret and respond when they are limited to physical cues. If they are unable to hear the training master's instructions to their opponents, will they still be able to anticipate and block the strikes?"

"Of course, Councilman, I—"

"In fact, I have a blocker on me now. I always carry one when I travel, pacers being so noisy. Could we have a demonstration?"

Without hesitation Grand Neilem nods. "It would be our pleasure. Perhaps Training Master Tila could select—"

"Oh, let's just go with two of the cadets who are still warm. How about the pair in the middle?"

"As you wish, Councilman. May I?"

Grand Neilem passes the blocker to Training Master Jheb, who exits the amplobox and jogs for the exit, appearing below at ground level a moment later.

"Do you have a preference for who is defensive, Councilman?" Grand Neilem asks.

"No, although...actually, I think the female cadet might prove to be a more interesting case study, considering the mismatch in size."

Only when Protect Jheb reaches for my helmet does my exhausted brain connect the demonstration at hand with my person. I feel my heart begin to race, and reach down into a stretch to calm my nerves and keep my muscles from tightening up. I transition into a second stretch, and then a third, grateful for the time it is taking my training master to clip the blocker onto my helmet.

I am familiar with blockers, of course. We spent an entire mechanical class learning how they work. Protector Shyli even allowed each of us to wear the blocker for a few minutes, so the slight buzz I hear when I place my helmet back on is familiar, as is the silence that thickens around me, though the magnitude is not comparable. In class it seemed as though sound had leached from the room. Standing in the arena with dozens of pairs of eyes watching my transition into noiselessness, it's as though walls have sprung up between me and every other person in the ring; they don't exist, only I do, and Sparrow.

Protector Tila passes us our wooden staves. I turn toward my partner, bowing when he bows. Though my partner has not changed, my brain seems to register the boy in front of me as larger and more powerful: as a threat. I feel energy pulsate through my body, pushing out the fatigue that has been clinging to my arms, shoulders, and legs. I move ever so slightly, lightly on the balls of my feet, my eyes on his hips, his shoulders.

There. I catch the downward swing on my staff, already watching for the next strike. The kick, when it does come, is easy to spot, slow even. I evade it effortlessly, as I do the next swing of his staff, and the thrust that follows it.

My fear is receding, my adrenaline augmenting, shifting. I spot the low swing, stepping lightly aside. He telegraphs the lunge—I have time to dodge but instead I block, forcefully, deflecting his staff back toward him. It is more than self-preservation—what I feel now is rooted in something more powerful. I want to advance on him; I want to strike back.

Sparrow lowers his baton and bows to me. I blink, and then follow suit. What was I thinking, wanting to press forward? I shake the sweat from my eyes and the thoughts from my head, turning to bow at our training master and the amplobox above.

I pull the helmet from my head; sound floods down toward me like sand through a funnel. I cannot distinguish one voice from another. Everyone seems to be moving toward the exit.

Protector Tila is in front of me. Her lips are moving. What is she saying? The helmet. She wants the helmet. I pass it to her. She is smiling, a real smile with teeth showing.

I stumble out of the ring still holding my staff, and find myself caught in a stampede of thundering feet and clanking weapons. The rest of my cohort fills the corridor around me. Starling is beside me, beaming. Pipit is there too, talking too quickly. I hear fragments only, though his face is less than a foot away. "...always wondered, but you were spectacular!"

"How did—" My throat is too dry, my voice catches. I swallow. "How did yours go?"

"Good, good, uneventful really, compared to yours. Star's got bloody knuckles."

"But I only missed one, you missed more than me," Starling says, though she is laughing. "Just bad luck the one I missed was steel."

"Do you have to go to medical?" I ask.

Pipit looks at me, surprised. "Well, of course she does. We all do."

Sure enough, when I look around I realize that we are not moving toward the dormitory, as I had supposed, but to the medical wing.

The P3s take charge of us when we arrive, ushering us to curtained rooms. I stand in my small cubicle, wondering where I should put my staff. A P3 bustles in, plops it down on the floor, and instructs me to sit up on the examination table. She checks my vital signs, shines a light into my eyes, ears, and mouth, and tests my reflexes. Have I met her before? I am not sure. She is humming to herself, rather than speaking. I wonder why the examination is so rushed, and then I remember: the contests. The P3 hands me an orange sweet and tells me that I am free to return to my dormitory.

I pick up my staff and join the crowd of cadets leaving the medical ward. Everyone is hurrying. I wonder what time it is. We pass the canteen, and I see that supper is well underway.

In the dormitory is a stack of meal replacement bars and a few jugs of prickly pear juice. Someone has returned my sword. I change into dry clothes, slide both weapons under my bed, and sit on the hard mattress, unwrapping my supper. Even these small tasks seem to demand too much effort. I have not felt this exhausted since the initial assessment. I chew slowly, staring out the small window beside my bed and listening to the excited chatter of my dorm mates.

A body sits down on the bed beside me. "Are you okay?" Starling asks.

"I am well, thank you."

"Right, well, you seem a bit off. Did the medic say anything?"

I shake my head and turn painstakingly toward her. "How's your hand?"

"Good as new!" She beams, brandishing the smooth skin of her knuckles at me. "The contests kick off soon. Want to head down now?"

I nod, and coerce my mouth into a smile.

Starling purses her lips, watching me. "Are you sure you're okay?"

"I'm just tired."

"Are you coming?" Pipit calls from behind us. I turn around and see him and Vireo standing beside the door. Everyone else has already left.

"Of course," I say, hopping off the bed with a show of energy I do not feel. "How did the examinations go for you?" I ask Vireo as we exit the dormitory.

He shrugs. "Fine."

"Fine? His combat technique was flawless," says Pipit.

Vireo winks at me. "I was being modest."

"And the written?"

"Good enough."

I sigh. "Good enough is not something that—"

"I know, I know." Vireo draws me into a one-armed hug. "Don't fuss. I did fine."

"At least it's over," says Pipit.

"And now we get to watch the contests." Vireo grins at me. "What more could you want?"

"Perfect marks," I say, though I am genuinely smiling now. After all, is there anything more exciting than witnessing the contests?

"Sora." A P4 is walking toward me. "Your presence is requested."

"Of course, Protector." I turn toward my friends.

"We'll save you a seat," promises Starling.

I trot stiffly after the P4 as she heads eastward and stops in front of what I have always assumed to be an upper-year classroom. When she opens the door, I realize that it is actually another hallway. At the end of the hall there is a set of double doors. She presses her hand against a small screen and the doors swing open. We have entered the east wing, I realize with a chill, off-limits even to my professors and training masters.

We climb a flight of stairs to reach a door inscribed with the number five. The P4 raps on the door with her knuckles and then retreats back down the stairs. I am wiping my palms on the sides of my shirt when the door opens to reveal Grand Neilem.

I press my hands together over my eyes.

"Come in, please," she says, turning back into the room behind her.

Starlight draws my gaze upward, to a domed ceiling dotted with small skylights. The walls, though dominated by screens, have a similar scattering of windows. There is a desk and a few cabinets, large, heavy pieces. Shimmering light blinks from the desk: a porta. I step onto a plush carpet.

In the corner examining one of the screens is Councilman Naru. "Ah, young Sora is here. Excellent. Thank you, Grand Neilem. I am sure that you are occupied enough with the contests about to begin, so please do not let me keep you."

Grand Neilem presses her hands together across her eyes and exits.

The door closes behind her, leaving me alone with one of the most powerful people in the country. I repeat the gesture of deference.

"Please, come, have a seat here. You must be exhausted."

He seats himself behind the desk while I take the armchair opposite him. My feet do not reach the ground.

"Sora, Sora." The councilman picks up a porta and begins swiping. "I see some very promising things."

He stops swiping for a moment to smile at me over the porta. "Top of your class, for both academics and combat, which is rare. A perfect score in virtues, and I can see that you have been selected for training in advanced mathematics."

"I have?" I blurt out. Immediately I cover my mouth with my hand. "My apologies, Councilman."

"Hmm? Yes, I can see that only two of you have been selected, and actually...hmm, it looks like you are the first cadet to have been chosen in four years."

He swipes the screen a few more times. "No infractions, and let's see...you train every evening, along with three others." He is speaking softly, more to himself than to me.

He places the porta back on the desk and leans across the table, his black eyes watching me carefully. "Your performance today, under

285

pressure, working undoubtedly from reserve strength—it was impressive. How did you find it? Was it unfair, do you think, to ask you to try something new during your examination, in front of an audience?"

"I—It was fair, Councilman," I say. I believe it, too. "We are taught to look for physical tells when we are on defense. If we have been relying on the verbal commands given to the strikers instead of watching for these tells, that is a lack of discipline on our part."

He nods, pleased. "Exactly, exactly what I believe. Discipline, or self-discipline, rather, is the key, always. May I ask you a question, Sora?"

"Of—of course, Councilman." I stumble over the words. The idea of a council member soliciting my permission, even as a courtesy, is absurd. The entire conversation, for that matter, is absurd. I wonder if I am hallucinating. Perhaps I took a blow to the head during the martial display?

"What do you want? After your training, that is, what do you aspire to?"

He smiles at the dumbfounded expression on my face.

"How about a P5, a Grand? Or would you like work in Ankev? If you continue along your current trajectory, it would only be fitting for the administration to support you in achieving your goals."

"I—yes, Councilman, of course, I would be happy to serve the Administration in whichever way my superiors deem best."

"But you have thought about it, no?"

"Yes, Councilman," I whisper, fighting not to look down. "I know that promotion to P5 is extremely rare, but I hoped, maybe, the strategy and leadership positions in P4..."

"Hmm, yes. A worthy ambition, of course, but I do not want you to be hampered by what you *think* you can obtain. I give you permission to aim your sights higher. Yes?"

"I—yes, Councilman, thank you, I..."

He leans back in his chair and grins. "We are having a forthright conversation, child, so please, if there is something you would like to say, say it."

"Thank you, Councilman." I bite back a smile. He speaks like a professor. "I suppose I just feel grateful for your interest in my welfare."

"And curious, perhaps?"

"Yes, Councilman." I cringe at the bluntness.

"Oh, well, you should know this, considering your perfect score in virtues. What is a leader's best trait?"

"The ability to recognize self-discipline and skill in those that serve them, and the willingness to help them to reach their full potential, Councilman," I recite word-by-word from the first-year textbook.

"Exactly! Although it goes beyond that, doesn't it? Just like your professor of mathematics, it is not uncommon for this support to transform into something weightier: mentorship, we call it."

"Yes, Councilman," I say, when the silence stretches between us.

"I will keep an eye out for you, Sora." He rises from his chair and approaches one of the screens. With a flick of his wrist it becomes a mirror. As he adjusts the collar of his jacket, I look past his reflection to the small figure sitting perfectly still on a large chair, feet dangling down. Shaven head, dull green uniform: the one drab spot in an elegant picture.

"I expect great things. Do not disappoint me. Now." He turns back to me, and smiles. "We don't want to miss the start of the contests, do we? Should be great fun."

He strides toward the door, waving at me over his shoulder. "I can expect to see you contending in the future, I hope?"

"I—I hope so," I whisper to the empty room. I sit alone in the stillness for a moment, and then drop my feet down to the carpet. Tentatively I approach the open door, shutting it quietly behind me, and make my way down the staircase. The P4 who accompanied me earlier is waiting at the bottom of the stairs.

"Quickly, the contests are starting. And here." The P4 passes me a small package. "Have a sweet."

41

The North

THE MARKETS CLOSED at noon the following day. Sam pedaled full speed back to the compound, basket packed full of candy, candles, oils, and coloured powder. There were even a few extra bags of candy tucked in amidst the goods she had picked up for the Vauns. Sugar, according to Ava, was important during the solstice, as were gift giving, alcohol, and colour, all of which were said to promote 'good luck', a concept that Sam considered absurd. Cleanliness was also important, Ava had insisted, bullying Sam until she agreed to wake up at four in the morning to dust out her nest and bathe. Not that she would have been able to sleep anyway—the entire factory had been awake for the same reason. Apparently, superstition dictated that the ritual be completed before dawn.

"Why?" Sam had asked.

"Well, it's the new start," Ava had said. "You have to reset."

"Reset what?"

"You can't start fresh with dirty hair, it keeps the bad luck in."

"What if I don't have any bad luck lingering?" Sam had asked, earning a sharp poke to the scar in her side. It was a fair point.

She had to admit that the concept of a reset was appealing. It wasn't just the injury, either; weighing heavier on her mind was what could have happened at the Pike, or the house in the swamp. She hadn't been forced into those situations by Benison—she had sought them out. *And for what? For a girl you don't even know?* She needed to leave Raina behind.

Jackal and the twins were already at the compound when she arrived. Once Benison had combed through the items and doled out her pay, he grudgingly told them to take the rest of the day off.

"You'll come by early?" Xenia asked Sam as they turned to leave. "We can get primped together."

Sam's misgivings must have shown on her face.

"Just come," said Xenia. "I'll decorate you."

Sam wasn't sure that she felt comforted, but she agreed nonetheless. She'd gone back and forth about accepting the invitation. In the end, she hadn't been able to bear the thought of spending the summer solstice like she had the winter one—alone in her nest, feeling like an outsider.

"Oh, and I invited Shale—try to bring her along with you. Thanks, darling." She gave Sam a kiss on each cheek, grabbed her brother by the hand, spun him in a circle, and danced off toward the trees.

Hands sunk deep in his pockets, Jackal made to follow.

"See you tonight?"

He looked back at her and nodded, seeming distracted. Sam bent down and pretended to fiddle with the shoelace on her boot, waiting until he was halfway across the grounds to begin walking. She liked Jackal well enough, but one-on-one conversations remained awkward. It was better to avoid them.

The streets were hot and smoky; smouldering mounds of garbage appeared on every block, as though someone had made it their mission to burn the city clean. *Except that the fumes are worse than the garbage.* The stench of burning plastic followed her into Geo and Jem's.

"Come in, come in." Jem was unusually chipper, though he wrinkled his nose at the smell.

He was dressed for the solstice, with a bright yellow shirt tucked into green slacks and a red knit sweater.

Geo's long white hair had been braided and woven with a violet ribbon. Brightly patterned scarves hung around her shoulders, and dark kohl lined both of her eyes. She gave Sam a kiss on each cheek.

"Solstice blessings, dear. So thoughtful of you to visit today."

Sam passed her one of the bags of candy.

"How kind! Such a nice assortment too. Jem, darling, there are strawberry dulces! They are his favourite." She winked at Sam.

Jem wandered back over and took a peek into the bag. He gave a grunt of approval and patted Sam awkwardly on the shoulder.

"I wasn't sure if you'd come by," Geo called over her shoulder as she left the room. "But I made something for you, just in case." She returned with a long hair ribbon, deep violet on one side and red on the other. Sam stuttered out a thank you.

"Shall I weave it in for you, dear? Unless you'd like to do it yourself..."

Sam accepted with thanks. Seated in a chair, she closed her eyes as Geo gently pulled a comb through her long black hair. She was suddenly very grateful that Ava had insisted she bathe. Geo began braiding the ribbon into Sam's hair, starting at the base of her head and bringing it up around her face. The bulk of the ribbon, much longer than the braid, fell loose over Sam's shoulder.

"Lovely," Geo said, smiling at Sam. "There's a mirror in the bedroom if you'd like to see."

Sam had never been in their bedroom before. She tiptoed in, feeling the trespasser despite Geo's invitation. A rug covered the floor, hand-woven and un-dyed. Sam slipped out of her dusty boots, leaving them beside the door as she stepped onto the softness of the rug. Besides the bed there was only a wardrobe and a small bookshelf. Simple furnishing, but well crafted.

The bookshelf housed a few curios: a glass replica of a piano, and several creatures made of stone, all small enough to sit on Sam's palm. She picked up the stone elephant. It was lighter than she'd expected. Bringing it up to her eyes, she realized that parts of the animal had been hollowed out. She gave it a little shake, and saw a second, smaller animal rattling around inside its belly.

The handheld mirror was on the second shelf. She held it up and peeked at her hair. She liked the way it framed her face, the dark purple blending in with her black hair, the red vivid beside it.

Conscious that she had lingered for too long, Sam placed the mirror back on the shelf, tugged on her boots, and closed the door softly behind her. She could hear Geo and Jem speaking excitedly, and smiled to herself, wondering what they were discussing. *A book, undoubtedly.* Jem did not chat, but he could be vocal when it came to books.

She turned the corner and a knife spun through the air toward her. Flinging her body forward, she landed behind the kitchen cabinet. She sat, stunned, her heartbeat thudding in her ears as her brain struggled to register what had happened. *Breathe,* she commanded herself. A second later, sound kicked back in. Geo and Jem were both shouting, their words mingling with the assailant's, a jumble of incomprehensible sounds. Sam pulled out her baton. It was a sorry match for knives, but it would have to do. Praying he had not hurt Geo or Jem, she sprinted out from behind the cabinet, toward her attacker. Jem had grasped him by the shirt collar, while Geo struggled to twist a second blade out of his hand.

Sam aimed a kick at the attacker's exposed right side and nearly fell when Jem stepped out in front, shielding the man with his body. She regained her balance, keeping the baton between her and...

"Adder?"

The bright blue eyes that glared back at her were furious. "How did you find them?"

She stared at him, bewildered.

"Dear heart, you're all mixed up," said Geo.

"How did I...? I.... I stopped in their doorway, to get out of the—"

"Who ordered it? That jit Benison, or someone else? The Vauns directly? What did they tell you?"

"I... What?"

"She's a drudge," he said, turning to Geo and then Jem. "For the Vauns."

"Yes, we know," said Geo.

He spun back toward Geo. "You knew? You...what, you just invite spies in now?"

"Sweetheart." Geo stroked his hair. "I know when someone is spying on me, and when they're not. She has no idea who we are."

The gears seemed to click into place all at once. "You...you're Vauns," she whispered. Of course they were. It was obvious. Who else would have the things they had, know the things that they knew?

"I was," Geo said. "But not for several decades now."

Sam knew that she was staring, but she could not seem to look away. The Vauns were shadows in her mind: concepts, not people. *Geo, a Vaun? And Jem?* Sam turned toward him. He shook his head.

"Jem was with me in the compound," Geo said, "but..."

"I was property, not family. A domestic." He practically spat out the word.

"And they let you leave?" asked Sam.

Jem's laugh was bitter.

"We fled," said Geo. "So, you can see, of course, why our grandson is suspicious of you. But then, he's always been a bit rash, just like his father."

"Thick-headed too," growled Jem, "to think we'd let a threat into our home."

"Hush. He's just being protective." Geo turned to her grandson. "But you can see, darling, that Samarra is not a spy. If she was, they would have sent their guns in months ago."

"She is hiding something," Adder insisted. "Anyone can see it."

"Well, we are all entitled to our secrets," said Geo.

"Not if it's about..."

"It's not," she said.

"How can you be sure?"

"We're sure." Jem scowled at his grandson.

"Okay, enough." Sam slid her baton back into her boot and turned to Adder, arms crossed. "Put your knives down. You are not going to stab me."

Reluctantly, Adder disarmed.

"Now, you're going to tell me exactly what is going on. Did you come here looking for me?"

"Well, no, I...I came for the solstice," he said.

"You just always keep throwing knives on you."

"Well, yes."

"Oh." Sam frowned at him. "So when we met, that day I was attacked in the marketplace, why didn't you..."

Adder had a rather guilty look on his face.

"Wait." She stared at him, her mouth open. "Did you set me up?"

He had the grace to look ashamed. "I needed an excuse to talk to you—"

"So you hired huaina to set off a bomb in the middle of a—"

"Of course not! How was I supposed to know you were picking up an explosive?"

"I, well—"

"All I knew was that you were the new Vaun drudge."

"And...and you wanted to make sure no one was hunting your grandparents?"

"Oh, darling," Geo said, "they gave up looking for us long ago."

"So why then?"

Geo sighed and looked at her husband. "We may as well just tell her. Adder, dear, would you put on some tea, please?"

The four of them sat around the table, steaming mugs of peppermint tea in front of them. Jem had brought the bag of candy over and was unwrapping a pink one. Sam watched Geo, waiting for her to begin. When the silence finally broke, however, it was Jem who spoke.

"You're born a domestic, see; you're born, you serve, and you die without ever going outside the compound. Same as your parents before you, same as your grandparents, same as any children you have."

"Everyone knows this, Gran—"

Jem's glare silenced his grandson. "We're always there. So we hear a lot of things. After all, you wouldn't care if the furniture learned your secrets, would you? That's all they see us as—furniture."

"Not everyone."

"No, not everyone." Jem's expression softened when he looked at Geo, a look so full of love that Sam had to turn away.

"When I was six, or seven maybe, a bunch of strangers came to the compound for a meeting. I was sweeping around under the table for bits they'd spilled over dinner. They were fixing a price. Colouring mattered, they said, and age. I remember that exactly, those words: colouring and age. They were real excited. I figured that this shipment, whatever it was, was special. Guess that's why it stuck in my mind.

"So for years, anytime a big shipment came in, I looked for something special: something with colouring and age. Liquor, I thought.

"The solstice when I was fourteen, I was pouring wine at the masquerade—"

"The what?" asked Sam.

"A party where everyone wears masks," said Geo. "There is bad blood between compounds. Social gatherings that bring the main families together, well, everyone feels less exposed in a costume."

"And...wait, did you say wine?" Sam frowned. "Grape vines don't grow here. The summertime rot gets them." She looked at Adder, who nodded.

Jem frowned at the interruption. "Well, they got it there in the compound. Don't ask me how, I don't bloody know. Anyway, I was pouring, and we ran out. So, I went down to the cellar to fetch more. Nobody asked me to; I just thought to be helpful. In the cellar were girls, Northern girls, and women, some barely more than children, others older, though none were old. They were all wearing masks. Found 'em lying all in a heap—dead, I thought, until I got closer and realized they were just drugged. Branded, too, with the Vaun sigil. Then someone started coming down the steps and I ran."

"The next morning he told me what he'd seen," said Geo. "We were already close."

"They allowed it?" asked Sam. "Relationships with domestics?"

Geo took a sip of her tea before replying. "Compounds are lonely places. Domestics...they fill the gap. It wasn't a problem until I wanted to marry him."

"I took her down to the cellar that morning, to show her, but the girls were gone. Same thing the next year, and the year after that."

"But this was sixty years ago. Why are you..." Sam's throat went dry. "It's still happening."

Geo and Jem nodded. Adder was eyeing her suspiciously.

"And...and they just disappeared?"

Jem's face darkened. "Mostly. Sometimes a girl or two was moved to the master's quarters."

Her heart was thrumming in her ears now. "And the other girls... what happens to them?"

"We don't know." Adder stood up from the table and started pacing. "Traded amongst the compounds, maybe, or sold to outside buyers as domestics or bed-warmers. Or even, well, there's a rumour that compound doctors are so advanced now they can replace weak or damaged organs. Which means they need healthy ones... But this is all just speculation." He stopped pacing and looked down at Sam. "All we know is that they're taken, and that it happens during the solstice, which is why nobody ever seems to notice. How many folk skip town the night of the solstice? How would we know who fled or moved away, who crossed the wrong huaina, who was taken?"

Sam pushed her chair back from the table and leaned forward, her forearms on her thighs. She felt nauseous. All this time she'd been looking for Raina, and Raina was only one of many. Missing girls, missing women; not just missing—taken by the Vauns. She pictured the little man's house and shivered. *What did they do with the girls? What wouldn't they do, for the right price?*

"It's not just the Vauns, either." Adder resumed pacing. "The strangers Granddad saw, we wondered if they might have come from the other compounds. Anyway, it's taken ages, but we've confirmed that the Estate is working with them." He noticed the blank look on Sam's face. "Very wealthy, very powerful; probably the only compound with more coin and more guards than the Vauns."

"How do you know they're involved?" Sam asked. "Are you watching them?"

"I work for them." He gave her a wry smile.

"So you're a spy and a drudge."

"Well, yes. Technically. The difference is I'm spying *on* them, not *for* them. And I caught one of my team recruiting. He's been meeting with girls, young ones: getting to know them, gaining their trust." He rested his forearms on the back of his chair. "Then one night I'm trailing Maddox and he goes to the Vaun compound, passes something to Benison."

"Maddox." The gears clicked into place.

"You know him?"

"I...I know his brother."

Adder frowned. "I didn't know he had a brother."

Sam swallowed. "Most people don't."

"Anyway, whatever they're planning, it's going down tonight. Except that from what I've seen, he's only been working on six girls."

"Is that not enough?"

Jem shook his head. "There was always at least a dozen."

"Which means someone else is recruiting too." Adder was watching Sam carefully. "Someone on your team."

Sam blanched. "My team." She shook her head. "How do you know it's a drudge?"

"Because it makes sense. If the Estate uses a drudge, the Vauns probably do too. Plus, there's no one else on the outside." He straightened until only the palms of his hands rested on the back of the chair. "Look, I can take care of Maddox. There's a big blowout tonight at a factory near the Pike. I know he's going, so my guess is he'll lead the girls from there to the Vaun compound. I know who he is, I know where it's going down. I can handle it. If I don't know who it is on your side, I'll have to stake out the compound itself, wait for them to show up. But if we could avoid confrontation, well...confrontation is risky for everyone, and it would expose the drudge."

"Which you don't want...because if you know who it is, you can muck it up next time too."

"Exactly."

"So what exactly are you asking of me? And wait, you don't like confrontation but you just threw a knife at me?"

"Yeah, that wasn't planned. It was just, you know, seeing a threat around my family..."

"I am not a threat."

"Well, I realize that now. Anyway, here." He passed a small bag to Sam. "Do you know where your team will be tonight?"

Sam nodded.

"Watch them. See who's acting off. If you figure out who it is, slip this into their drink. It'll knock them out for the rest of the night. The Vauns won't be impressed, but they won't get suspicious the first time, or probably even the second time."

"Still," Sam said. "It's a temporary fix."

He shrugged. "You got a better idea?"

"Why not just tell people this is happening?"

Adder snorted. "What, you want to knock on every door in the Barrow before nightfall? Not that anyone would believe some drudge they don't know. They'd think you were high on dust or trying to scam them."

"So...either I stop them, or..."

"Or I stop them."

42

The North

HE DIDN'T ANSWER on the first knock, or the second. Sam was wondering whether she would have to break in when the door finally opened a crack. Maddox's wary expression softened when he recognized her. He stepped out into the hall, shutting the door gently behind himself.

"He's sleeping." Maddox leaned back against the wall, crossing his arms over his chest. For once he was neither trying to charm nor threaten her.

"Good. How's he doing?"

Maddox shrugged. "He's alive. That's what counts."

Sam nodded.

"Did you want to see him?"

She shook her head. "I'm here to talk to you."

The suspicious expression returned. "About what?"

She decided on the direct approach; she didn't have time for anything else. "Your brother's girlfriend, Raina. Do you know what happened to her?"

Maddox raised his eyebrows. "Why would you think—"

"I know you kidnap girls for the Estate."

Maddox's lips curled into a snarl. "You don't know shit. Who the—"

"I'm not here to talk about it. I just want to know if you took—"

"Think you can come here, talk to me like this?" He straightened up and took a step toward her.

"You owe me."

He started to say something, but then stopped. She'd won; she could see it even before he spoke.

"You'd have to be stupid, to mess with another compound's drudge," he said finally, settling back against the wall.

"Did you do it on their orders?"

Maddox eyed her for a moment, and then shook his head. *Is he lying?* She didn't think so, but she couldn't be sure.

"Look," he said. "My brother, I wouldn't..." She waited, but he left the sentence unfinished.

"So there is one person you wouldn't screw over, then."

He flashed her a crooked smile. "Everybody's got one."

43

T he North

"YOU'RE QUIET TONIGHT," Shale said as they walked to Xenia and Cassio's factory. Sam raised her eyebrows. "Don't you play me, girl. Something's going on."

"I'll fill you in tomorrow," she promised. *As soon as I know it's not Xenia.* It was laughable, the idea of Xenia being complicit in the abductions, but she couldn't afford to rule anyone out. It wasn't just about Raina anymore. Sam had done the math. Even with conservative figures—supposing the Vauns had only managed one shipment a year, and that it had only been going on for sixty years—it still amounted to over seven hundred missing girls.

"Darlings!" Xenia greeted them with kisses and tall cups of sikera. She had already painted her own face: black and white contouring with a skeletal effect. Her fine blond eyelashes were purple and sparkly, and there were streaks of blue in her hair. Silver paint twined around her bare arms in vines.

"You gruesome beauty," Shale said, "you look like some kind of solstice goddess. Should we be paying tribute to you?"

"Just wait 'til I'm done with you." Xenia barred her teeth in a grin. "Love this, by the way," she said, reaching out and stroking the leather choker Shale wore. "Let's start with you, ladki. Sam, darling, will you cut the yellow string into strips? About three feet a piece should do it."

It felt wrong, as though she was going off mission. *I'm not, though.* Adder's plan demanded stealth, not confrontation. Sam started measuring out string. *I have to wait, and watch.* Xenia showed her how to wind it around small sections of Shale's hair. *I'll stay with Xenia for now; if she tries to leave, I'll follow her. If I determine that it isn't her, I'll go find Cassio, Hakuund, and Jackal.*

Sam fell into a rhythm, her fingers moving more and more quickly. The simplicity and repetitiveness of the task was calming. They didn't speak, though Xenia sang softly to herself as she worked. It was as though they were inside their own tranquil bubble. The party sounds permeated through the cracks in the walls, only to fade into nothingness before reaching them. The last few hours started to seem like a dream, and the night's assignment absurd. What if Adder was wrong, or mad, or a liar? It was a comforting thought.

Once Xenia was satisfied with Shale's appearance, the two women advanced on Sam. "Close your eyes, lala," Xenia said, her nose an inch away from Sam's, an old paintbrush held between her long fingers like a smoke.

As Xenia painted, Shale rubbed goop onto her arms. Sam closed her eyes, and the world shrank to the sound of Xenia's voice, the pull of Shale's hands, and the regular stroke of the paintbrush caressing her face.

She had no idea how much time had passed when Xenia stepped back, staring critically at her for a moment before nodding in somber approval and digging out a bit of mirror. They had painted her face to match theirs, with the modification that Sam's skeletal mask combined white with a deep, dark purple. Her arms were coated in shimmering gold dust.

"I truly am gifted," Xenia said.

"'We', honey, you mean 'we'."

Xenia rolled her eyes at Shale. "Always raining on my party," she said with a pout, and reached for her heretofore forgotten drink, which she downed in one long gulp. With a mad giggle, she grabbed a container of sparkles, flung it in Shale's face, and sprinted outside.

"Oh, she is going to get it." Shale growled as she picked up a second container and stalked out after her.

Sam waited a moment. *Are they going to come back?* She took a small sip of her drink, and then put it back down. Alcohol was the last thing she needed tonight.

"Alcohol, right." Sam felt her back pocket, reassuring herself that the small bag was still securely stowed away. "Time to drug one of my friends."

44

The North

AS SHE EMERGED FROM THE TWINS' apartment, something hit her in the face. A woman she didn't know was trying to shove a piece of cake into her mouth. Sam threw up an arm to defend herself, but it was unnecessary: the woman was already attacking someone else. It wasn't just her, either; there was cake everywhere. With half of the crowd dancing and the other half rushing madly about, little of it seemed to be connecting with the targeted mouths. Asphyxiation aside, it was not a bad dessert: fluffy and light, with a hint of lemon.

A flash of red hair caught her eye. Sam started off after Shale, only to be blocked by a line of drummers. She turned, looking for an alternate route, and realized that she was surrounded. Sweaty, shirtless men and women pounded drums and sang, all working within the same overarching rhythm. Was it planned, practiced? Perhaps it was unavoidable, musicians pulled along with the dominating beat like minnows in a river.

To her right, someone let loose a war cry. An arrow flew into the rafters above, piercing an inflated plastic bag. Pink powder rained down. Two more arrows followed, showering the crowd in blue and then purple. Sam tried to shake the powder from her hair, and only succeeded in transferring it from her head to the rest of her body.

She spotted an opening and leapt through the line of drummers, nearly colliding with a girl with long, copper-coloured hair: a girl who was most definitely not Shale. Sam steadied herself and scanned the crowd. It was hot and sweaty, and there were too many people. Painted faces floated like ghouls in a mess of colours, everyone dancing, writhing, shouting. It was too much. She needed a direction, any direction.

Sam followed a convoy of girls snaking their way toward the center of the factory, which turned out to be a dance floor. Sam skirted back toward the safety of the closest wall, almost tripping over something short and scruffy in her haste. A small black dog, unnaturally striped with silver paint and pink sparkles, stared up at her.

"Uh, sorry," Sam said, squeezing around him.

She had ended up near the stage, which was packed with painted dancers—*naked* painted dancers. Just then a puff of yellow powder rained down from the ceiling. In unison, the dancers each reached for the closest face and shared a wet, sloppy kiss. One of the men caught Sam's eye and beckoned her toward him, the antlers he had strapped onto his head bouncing along with him. She waved but kept walking. She did not have time for naked, painted antler men; she was on a mission. Farther up, a cage was swinging, the two women inside sharing a passionate kiss. Sam walked past it, stopped, and backed up to take a closer look. *Well, I can probably cross Xenia off the list.* Xenia looked to be much more interested in Shale than in compound plots and kidnappings. *Unless...is Shale only one of six?*

Xenia reached a hand up and stroked Shale's hair, pulled her in closer. The intimacy of it made Sam want to look away. She didn't. She waited for them to surface.

After a few minutes Sam glanced around, then back up to the cage, where Shale and Xenia were still locked together. It was as though nothing else existed for them. *I remember that feeling.* The knot in Sam's stomach loosened ever so slightly. *On to the boys, then.*

"Love test!" a voice cried out. "Newlywed love test!"

An older woman was blindfolding a teenage girl as men formed a line, their backs toward her. An excited young man waited impatiently until the others were more or less assembled, and then wedged himself into the middle of the group. Giggling, the blindfolded bride started walking down the line, grasping each backside in turn. She lingered on her lover's rear end for a moment, before continuing on to the next buttock. At the end she turned and slowly made her way back to him, clutching each man she passed. When she reached him again, she gave a big, two-handed squeeze, and threw up her arms.

Sam turned away. Her teammates were not here. Fighting her way past the crowd that had gathered to watch, Sam ran into the dog again. Except that this dog was brown, and it had been painted with polka dots instead of stripes. *Gods, how am I going to find anyone in the middle of all this?*

She found a table and stepped up onto it, scanning the factory around her. Someone was whooping. It seemed to be getting louder. Sam turned her head toward the sound and saw a woman soaring toward her on a swing. She made it off the table just in time. The woman sailed past her and into a crowd of people who were waiting, arms outreached, to receive her. The woman emerged a moment later and grabbed one of the spectators, kissed him hard on the mouth, and began staggering back across the factory. *For another ride, perhaps?* Sam abandoned the table and began pushing her way forward through the crowd. She didn't fancy ending the night with a concussion.

Somewhere ahead of her a man howled in glee, loud enough to be heard over the madness. *Hakuund?*

Sam followed the voice to the far wall, where mobs of people were craning their heads toward something she couldn't see. Not sure anymore where the voice had come from, she chose a direction at random, and ended up following the line. It led to a curtain, in front of which stood a table draped in gold fabric and covered with lit candles. A man was kneeling in front of it, his head hanging over a low, wide basket. A woman and a man stood over him, chanting. They wore nothing but flower garlands and were covered head to toe in glittering gold paint. The woman pulled out a pair of long metal blades, and for one horrific moment Sam thought that she was about to witness a human sacrifice. Instead, the blades were used to shave the man's head. Accepting a smaller blade from the woman, he nicked the ends of his thumbs, squeezing a drop of blood from each into the basket. The two gold figures then lifted him to his feet and gestured for him to pass behind the curtain.

The next person in line was a woman. She tossed two sack into the basket and knelt. As they began to shave her head, Sam circled around the curtain, where she found a mess of bodies interlocking, moaning and groaning in a shorn, paint-smudged orgy. Four golden bodies hovered above the bacchanalian frenzy, chanting "for the gods!" over and over.

Hakuund was not here, nor was Cassio or Jackal. She was wasting time. *Or perhaps you don't actually want to find them?* She frowned, but she couldn't dismiss the thought. *Maybe I don't.* It wasn't her fight, not really. She didn't have to go along with Adder's plan; no one had ordered her to do this. *You know now, though. Can't pretend you don't. And what about Raina?*

As she made her way past the ritualistic fornicators, excited shouting began to drown out the chanting. *Is it shouting? Perhaps it is meant to be singing.* Sam drifted toward them.

> *They called bullshit on the warnings*
> > *They cried wolf, he said, cried wolf*
> > *Dancing in the moonlight*
> > *Like they'd never see the mornings*
> > *Anyway, hey hey*
> > *They cried bullshit on the day*

They were seated around a rough-hewn table, a huge tankard of brew clutched in each hand. At the end of the verse, the men hit their mugs twice against the table and then took a large swig. As they drank, the women followed suit, although they rapped their mugs against the table three times instead of twice. A group of onlookers clapped to the beat, shouting at them to drink more, drink faster.

The winds came to the islands
    Dry came to the heat
    The seas the seas were rising
    Still they sucked the oil teat
    Hey, hey
    They cried bullshit on the day

Rap, rap "DRINK!"
Rap, rap, rap "DRINK!"

Hey hey, hey hey
    They threw us all away
    Hey hey, hey hey
    In the end of the day

Fires hit the prairies,
    Tremors took the coasts
    Waves wiped out the little towns
    The rich were never coming down
    To see
    Hey hey
    They cried bullshit on the day

Rap, rap "DRINK!"
Rap, rap, rap "DRINK!"

Hey hey, hey hey
    They threw us all away
    Hey hey, hey hey
    In the end of the day

Two shirtless men shared a heated kiss as the crowd whooped and cheered. The larger man broke away from the kiss, downed both his drinks, and brandished the empty cups with a roar. The crowd stomped and shouted their approval. Covered as they were in body paint, with antlers on their heads, it took Sam a moment to realize she had been watching Hakuund and Cassio. As Hakuund staggered toward Cassio for a second kiss, Sam knew that they, too, could be crossed off the list. They looked far too drunk to be on mission tonight.

She sighed, felt for the pill in her pocket, and peered around the factory. She knew who she needed to look for. She had known all night.

45

The North

IF I WERE JACKAL, where would I be? After first scanning the airways for people on swings, she stepped up onto a sparkly crate that was clearly intended for naked dancers, and looked up at the second floor balcony. There he was, directly above her, speaking with two girls. Sam hopped off the crate and began making her way toward a ladder.

On the way, she tossed a sack to a man serving moonshine and grabbed two tankards. Hidden beneath the base of the ladder, Sam pulled out the powder that Adder had given her and dumped it into one of the drinks. It disappeared instantly, colourless. *What if he lied? What if it's toxic?* She didn't know Adder very well, after all. *What about Geo and Jem? Don't I trust them?* Clutching the handles of the two cups in her left hand, she climbed one-handed up the ladder.

Sam recognized one of his companions as the girl she'd seen scolding Jackal at the warehouse. She was tall, with shoulder-length brown hair. The other girl was new. She was very pretty, with tanned skin and high cheekbones. Both of the girls were beautifully dressed, with long strips of sheer fabric draped over one shoulder and bare midriffs. Their eyes were lined with black kohl and sparkles shone brilliantly off their faces and arms. They each carried a large, burlap sack over one shoulder. They also looked sober.

Jackal nodded to her as she approached. "Shya, Dot, this is Samarra." Sam forced a smile, unsure of which name belonged to which girl. The one with the short brown hair returned her weak attempt of a smile with a friendly grin.

"Solstice blessings," she said, reaching out and giving Sam a kiss on each cheek. Her friend followed suit.

"Solstice blessings," Sam repeated, and then turned back to Jackal. "I saw you up here and thought you could use a drink," she said, passing the drugged cup of moonshine to him. He took the tankard, stared at it with a curious expression on his face, and then gave her a long, searching look. He turned to the other girls, speaking to them in a low voice. They nodded and turned away, melting back into the crowd.

Oh, bav. The crowd pressed against her back, pushing her closer to Jackal; she had no hope of slipping away, or even shifting into a better position. Tight spaces were not her favourite, particularly in situations where her opponent outweighed her by so much. Sam rolled her weight to the balls of her feet, readying herself to spring as he stepped forward and leaned his forearms on the railing. His eyes moved to the crowd below, his back and side left undefended. Puzzled, she watched him.

"Do you want to tell me why you're drugging me, or do you just want me to guess?" He sounded tired, she realized with surprise. Tired, and there was something else there too. She opened her mouth to speak, and then closed it. Was this a trick?

He gave her a long, hard look, and she had to fight the urge to look away. He was still the enemy, and it was never a good idea to take your eyes off the enemy.

"Are you following compound orders?" he asked her. Bewildered, she just stared at him. He nodded and looked back down to the crowd. "I didn't think so." There was a faint smile on his face. "That would have been a letdown."

Something on the ground floor seemed to catch his eye. He

straightened and looked at her. "I got something to show you, if you care to see it."

He turned and began making his way back through the crowd, upturning his mug and tossing it into a corner. Though she didn't quite know why, she followed him, down the ladder and into the pulsing chaos below.

It had somehow become even louder, rowdier, sweatier. They passed two brawls and at least a dozen prone bodies—drunk, she hoped, not dead. Another orgy had sprung up, this one with an audience. Staggering, a painted man pushed his way between her and Jackal. Sam tried to scramble around him and felt herself being pushed even farther back as a second body wedged itself in front of her. She craned her head, trying not to lose sight of Jackal. He looked back, slowed a step, and took her hand. A shiver ran from her palm up her wrist to her shoulders. She gripped him back, his hand warm and callused and solid in hers, and he tightened his hold.

When they finally burst out into the night, Sam sucked in a lungful of hot, smoky air and coughed. She took a second breath and let it out with more control.

"Can you run?" he asked her.

"I can run."

Together they sped through the dark streets. *Toward what, though? How have you gone from hunting this man to following him?* He had neither defended nor explained himself. Why was she suddenly convinced of his innocence? *It's illogical,* argued the voice in the back of her head. She did not bother disagreeing.

They were heading to the compound, she realized after several minutes. *Toward a trap? Maybe he's going to lead you into a wolf pit and then double back to the party.* It was possible. She kept running anyway.

They barely slowed when they reached the woods. The canopy overhead was sparse and moonlight shone down, lighting their path.

Jackal stopped when their trail met with two others, the three paths converging into one. Gesturing for Sam to follow him, Jackal stepped off the path and into the cover of the trees.

Sam wiped the sweat from her forehead. Squinting at the black and white patches on the back of her hand, she suddenly remembered her face paint. *Not black; purple.* She glanced up to see if Jackal had noticed and found him looking down at her, a slight smile on his face. He was also standing very close to her. Or perhaps she was standing very close to him. She couldn't be certain. Conscious both of his body next to hers and her smudged face, Sam looked out towards the trail. As one, their breath slowed. Sam hugged the silence close, listening for footsteps.

It was a quarter of an hour before she heard them: female voices laughing and calling out to one other. They came into sight, seven girls in masks. At the head of the group a figure led them, equally masked but still unmistakable. With his tall, broad frame and smooth black skin, Hakuund always stood out in a crowd.

Even with his face hidden, it was clear to Sam that Hakuund was drunker than she had ever seen him before. He stumbled, knocking into one of the girls. She threw back her head and laughed, and then lifted one of his brawny arms and slung it across her shoulders. Their masks knocked together and this time they both laughed.

The group passed by the trees that shielded Sam and Jackal from view and were almost out of sight when Sam heard it, footsteps pounding down the path toward them. Crossbow in hand, Adder sprinted into view. Up ahead, Hakuund was about to turn the corner, placing him directly in Adder's sightline and easily within bowshot.

Jackal hurtled out of the bushes and tackled Adder to the ground. Adder was quick, but Jackal was faster, and stronger. He pinned Adder, grabbed the bow from his hands, and pointed it at the smaller man's throat.

"Enough," Sam hissed, following Jackal out onto the path.

Adder's head snapped around. "You told him?"

"I told him nothing," she said. "He led me here."

"Because he's involved!"

"You don't wanna shoot Hakuund," Jackal said, so quietly that he almost sounded calm.

"I really do."

"And what then?"

"I—What?"

"What about the girls they've already taken?" Something had changed in Jackal's voice. Sam found herself taking a step back. "I need to know what happens next."

The two men stared at each other, until something shifted and the tension eased. Jackal climbed off Adder.

"New recruit, Jack?" The two girls he had been speaking with earlier had somehow snuck up on them. Jackal passed Adder's crossbow to the tall girl with light brown hair.

"You can go home, or you can go with Dot. She'll fill you in," Jackal said to Adder.

She grinned down at Adder and offered him her hand. "We got a plan."

For a moment Sam thought he was going to refuse. Then Adder took her hand and allowed her to help him up and lead him toward a side trail. The other girl followed silently behind them. Adder turned around once. He eyed Sam, and then Jackal.

"Anything happens to them, that's on you," Adder said, and turned back around and jogged after Dot. "Hey, can I have my crossbow back?"

He's not wrong, thought Sam as she watched them disappear into the woods. Jackal had already started walking, following the trail that Hakuund and the masked women had taken.

I could go home. I should go home.

What about those girls, walking into a trap? You're complicit now. Sam shifted uncomfortably. *And Raina. All these months searching for her, and you've finally stumbled upon the real story. Gonna walk away, are you?*

Down the trail, Jackal had stopped. He looked back at her, questioningly.

I should go home.

"Do we need to hurry?" she asked, jogging up to him.

He shook his head. "Not anymore."

46

The North

NEITHER OF THEM spoke again until they reached the compound.

Torches had been bound to the fence, ringing the compound in fire, and music drifted out onto the grounds, not drumming or homemade string instruments but real violins, even a piano. As they drew nearer, she was surprised to see only two guards on duty, one of which was disappearing around the corner of the building.

Jackal followed her sightline. "They've got outsiders visiting tonight, from the other compounds. Most of the guards—"

"Are inside," Sam finished for him.

He nodded, and then gestured for her to hang back. She watched as he approached the remaining guard, a young man leaning against the base of an otherwise empty tower. The guard greeted Jackal with an easy smile. Sam watched with growing unease as the two men clasped hands through the bars. *Did I miscalculate? Is Jackal about to sell me out while I stand here, politely waiting?*

Jackal reached inside his pack and pulled out a small package, which he passed to the other man. The guard stared at it for a long moment, and then grasped Jackal's hand a second time. He pulled him forward into as much of a hug as the fence would permit, and whispered in his ear. Jackal's response prompted the guard's eyes to flicker over to Sam. Sam wondered what kind of range his gun had. *Is it more or less than the crossbow strapped to his back? It is so nice that they have options.* She expected that crossbows were encouraged for minor threats—much more cost efficient. He would have to be very unlucky or very unskilled to miss at this range, whichever weapon he selected. After a moment's hesitation, the guard pulled out a key and unlocked a section of the fence. Jackal stepped through, waving at Sam to follow.

She stared at him wide-eyed for a moment, and then stepped forward. *If they mean you harm, well, you're already caught, aren't you?* The guard signaled for them to follow him into the base of the tower. An enclosed staircase took them upward; each floor they passed was walled with parapets, complete with crenellations.

It stuck in her mind, the sight of the guard unlocking the fence for them. She'd always thought of the compound as a prison. If guards could leave—and they did venture into the Barrow on occasion, when the compound ordered it—why didn't they? *Fear, definitely; money, probably.* She considered it a moment. The Vauns probably didn't send guards out into the Barrow or give them keys when they first signed on with the compound. Maybe it took years. Maybe by the time they did get those privileges, they were just accustomed to following orders. *Obedience is a tricky habit to shake.*

When the staircase ended, the guard pulled on a latch, revealing a ladder up to the roof.

He nodded to them. "Should be starting soon."

Jackal grabbed the guard's arm before he could leave and passed him a bottle. The guard's face lit up. He took the offering and disappeared back down below, a huge grin on his face.

Sam followed Jackal up onto the roof. It was the tallest of the three towers; Sam estimated they were probably close to a hundred feet up. She crawled over to the edge of the roof and looked out.

A maze of buildings stretched before her, connected one to the other by covered walkways. The tips of trees hinted at green spaces even within the compound. Directly below them, in a paved square, were several large carriages. Craning her head, Sam spotted the portcullis.

Light drew her eyes over to a large frosted glass window. Ringed with the steady white halos that could only come from electrical light bulbs, colours and shapes flashed by, distorted by the opaque glass—hints of the party within. Outside the hall, a bonfire danced in a brick-lined pit.

Sam turned toward Jackal and realized that he was staring at the roof of the building below. Solar panels. The compound was covered in them. Sam had not seen a solar panel since arriving in the North. In the Barrow, it was fire or darkness. Did Jackal even understand what he was looking at?

"Now what?" she asked him.

"Now we wait," he said, pushing back from the ledge to settle at the center of the roof, where they would be all but invisible from the ground.

They sat in silence. The music slowed, stopped, and then began again. It grew louder; someone must have opened a door or a window. She kept expecting the air to cool, but the night remained hot and humid. And still it didn't rain.

Sam watched Jackal out of the corner of her eye. He was shrouded in darkness, as always, from the hat that hung low on his forehead to the dark stubble that covered his square jaw. Something had lightened in his eyes, though. Something buzzed tonight.

"What did you give him?"

"Something from his wife and kid."

"He has a family, and he chose this?"

"He has a family, and some bad habits. You know how much money you get, when you sign on to be a guard?"

Sam shook her head.

"Five years' pay, up front. If you got someone who needs that, well." He shrugged and let the sentence hang.

"Five years' pay. What happens after the five years?"

"They get a bit every month; not much, but it's something to send home. The guards get taken care of, of course." He caught sight of her face, and the corners of his mouth twitched. "Don't waste your pity. They live better than most. So do the domestics."

Sam thought about it for a moment. "That might depend on who you work for."

"They get fed, they get real stitchers."

"If the compound says so."

They relapsed into silence.

"What do you know about that guy?" he asked.

"Who, Adder? Nothing, really. I met him a few times by chance, and then I found out tonight we have friends in common."

"Friends that know about the abductions?"

Sam nodded.

"What do they know?"

"They say the girls are brought into the compound, that they're drugged, and then...they're gone. They don't know what happens to them either." She found that she was staring at the window again. Light, real electric light—something she had not even realized that she missed. "Who was..." she started, and then stopped. She had no right to pry.

"My sister," he said. "Three years ago, tonight."

"You know for sure she was taken?"

"For a long time I thought she was dead." He stared at the window too. "Anna wouldn't have skipped out. She cared about...well, everything. People. And they...they just kind of followed her around." He chuckled. "Dot called her the girl with a thousand friends. Community, she said, and family, was what we needed to stop kids joining gangs. I thought maybe huaina went after her. Winter solstice that year, Shya—the girl you just met—she and Anna were always together, and Dot. Well, she was at a factory, and some guy told her he could get her into a compound party."

"Hakuund?"

He shook his head. "Someone else. He must have left or been

axed or something pretty soon after, since I never met him. He gave them some drug but it made her sick instead of high, because she got lost—guess he didn't notice, probably too stoned himself—and woke up the next morning in the woods. Couple of days passed and she realized that all the girls she was with that night were gone. She came and found me, told me what happened. I had her walk me through everything she remembered, show me where she passed out. From that I figured it was probably the Vauns' they'd been heading to."

"Which is why you wanted to work for them."

"Lucky I can read and write."

"So for the past two years, you've been, what, spying?"

"Waiting, making friends." He nodded toward the base of the tower, where the guard who had let them in was busy drinking himself into a stupor.

"Did you know it was Hakuund?"

He shook his head. "Not until the end. For a while I thought it was you."

"Oh." She started to ask why, and then stopped. It wasn't as though she had been honest with her friends; could she fault him for seeing that she was hiding something?

"Think Cassio knows about Hakuund?" she asked instead.

Jackal turned his gaze down to the courtyard, where a group of women and men dressed in white had appeared. They were carrying a box of dirt. A child followed along behind, a basket of colourful sticks in his arms. "I don't think so."

They dropped down to their stomachs and moved closer to the edge. The domestics placed the box on the ground and began laying carpets and arranging chairs. The child took out one of the sticks and pressed it into the soil.

Guards soon filtered out of the hall, some of whom Sam recognized, many of whom she didn't. She shouldn't have been surprised, seeing as she only ever saw the guards stationed at the front entrance and towers.

A string of familiar notes pulled Sam's attention to the back corner, where a trio of young women had begun playing the violin. *Violin Sonata No.1 in G minor*. Disturbed by the strength of her nostalgia, she turned away from the musicians, fixing her attention on the door to the hall.

The people who were emerging into the courtyard now were dressed in beautiful, vibrant clothing. The women wore form-hugging dresses with thin straps in blues or greens or golds, the men flamboyant trousers and light shirts. Their hair was clean and shiny and often curled or twisted into elaborate knots. Gold shimmered from the elaborate masks they wore.

Once the guests had settled into their seats, domestics handed out drinks in glass goblets. Sam cringed as a little boy dropped his, shattering glass on the ground. The child's father just laughed and called for another drink. One domestic ran to obey while two others knelt down on the ground and picked up the shards of glass.

Jackal pointed toward the box of dirt, where a domestic was setting fire to one of the colourful sticks. With a sound like gunfire, a green ball of light shot twenty feet into the air and exploded, gold mingling with the green in a sphere of light. The sparks faded away before they hit the ground.

Fireworks, that's all. They were pretty, though nothing exceptional compared to what Sam had seen in Seira. She snuck a glance at Jackal and was surprised to see him staring up at the display with an unguarded smile on his face. It occurred to Sam that she'd never seen him look joyful before. As the sky lit up with purple, blue, red, and silver, Sam found that she couldn't take her eyes off his face.

When it ended, the children clapped and shouted, and the spell was broken. Sam shifted her gaze downward again.

After another round of drinks, torch-laden domestics led the guests back inside, guiding them through the turbid air and then returning to collect chairs, carpets, and glassware.

Sudden movement drew her eyes eastward, where domestics were loading boxes into carriages. Jackal leaned forward, staring intently at two men who were carrying out a large wooden chest. They placed it in the foremost carriage and returned inside. Several minutes later a squad of guards emerged with a young family. The guards helped them settle into that same carriage, and then stepped up onto the platform at the back of the carriage, guns positioned skyward.

"Watch for any more that size," Jackal whispered, and slid to the opposite side of the tower, away from the compound. As the Vaun guards raised the portcullis, Jackal slipped a red scrap of cloth from his pack and lowered it discreetly over the edge of the tower. After a beat, he re-joined Sam at the center of the roof.

"You think it's one of the girls in there?" she asked.

He nodded.

"And...and you have people waiting. An ambush?"

He nodded again.

"But all the guards, the weapons... These carriages aren't built of wood, they're metal. How do you expect...?"

Jackal gave her a small smile.

"Fine, don't tell me how." Sam furrowed her brow. "Is it an explosive? They had a child with them, and the guards..."

Jackal merely raised his eyebrows in response. Exasperated, Sam sighed and turned her attention back to the remaining carriages. Jackal was not a proponent of unnecessary violence, she knew that much. Murkier, however, was what he might consider necessary in this situation.

"Anything?" Jackal asked.

"No." They continued watching for another hour, until it seemed all of the packages had been loaded, none of them near large enough to conceal a person. They waited a half hour longer, until the courtyard was silent, the carriages all gone.

"They must have...they must be shipping them out tomorrow then," Jackal said. Sam didn't miss the note of worry in his voice.

"The girls—or at least most of the girls—they're always gone by morning."

"The friends you talked about say this?"

She nodded.

"They sure about this?"

"Yes, but their information is old. Really old."

Jackal glanced at her sharply just as the door to the roof swung open, revealing the guard who had let them in earlier. He was swaying slightly and reeked of alcohol. As they followed him back down the tower, Sam tried not to imagine what would happen should he be called upon to use a weapon in his condition. Perhaps sobriety was not a bad practice for compound guards.

Luckily the yard was still empty, allowing Sam and Jackal to slip through the fence without incident. They jogged back to the woods in silence, not slowing until they reached the cover of the trees.

Panting, Sam leaned against a tree. They had not been followed. She felt uneasy, though; she felt as though she was being watched.

There was rustling above them. Sam was reaching for her baton when Dot appeared, swinging down from a tree branch. Adder landed nimbly beside her. They were both wearing crossbows now.

"What happened, Jack? I mean, we got the one girl. She's okay. Drugged, but that'll wear off." Dot passed Adder a burlap sack, and he began packing their crossbows and bolts away. "It went down pretty smooth too. Couple of the Estate guards got injured, but no deaths. Well, the carriage, I guess. But what about the others? If the Vauns are keeping them—"

"They're not," said Jackal. "Sam's got a source says they'll be gone by morning."

Dot blanched. "But—but if they didn't ship them out, and they don't keep them there..."

Nobody said the words aloud, but Sam knew what the others were thinking. Images from the house in the swamp flashed through her mind.

"Great plan," Adder said, turning on Jackal. "Really great plan. Those girls just—"

Jackal had turned to stare at the compound. "We'll get 'em back," he said, more to himself than to Adder.

"Yeah? How? You gonna go knock on the fence, ask politely?"

Sam stepped toward Adder. "This isn't helpful," she said. "What we need is to sit down with everyone and come up with a new plan. Your grand—"

Adder was still glaring at Jackal. "Absolutely not."

"Well, it's that or go home," she said.

He was silent for moment, and then turned to her and let out a growl.

"Fine. But they don't come."

"You need all the help you can get."

Adder let out a second growl and stormed off down the trail. Dot looked at Sam, eyebrows raised. Sam shrugged and followed Adder. A few minutes later, two pairs of footsteps caught up with them.

47

T he North

"WELL, THIS IS A BIG GROUP," said Geo.

"At a late hour." Catching a stern look from his wife, Jem grumbled out a "solstice blessings," before heading into the kitchen to put on the kettle.

"This is Jackal," Sam said, "and Dot, who was—*is* his sister's friend."

A look of understanding flashed across Geo's face. "Your sister is one of our missing women then."

Jackal nodded.

"We had a plan," said Dot, "we thought—"

"Come, dears, have a seat. Jem's making tea. Adder, will you light the candles on the table please? Let me fetch some biscuits."

"We're on a bit of a clock, Grandmother."

"Yes, and you look like you've been through the wringer. What do I always say about problem solving?"

"Calm minds, clear plans."

"Exactly. Ah, here, these are gingerbread, Adder's favourite." Geo pulled out a tin of biscuits from the cupboard and placed them on the table. "Darling," she said, when her grandson turned to glower at her, "not everything is a deep, dark secret. Tea?"

Once everyone had tea and a biscuit, Geo turned to Dot. "Now, since I rudely interrupted, why don't you start?"

"Basically, we're stuck," Dot said, once they'd run through the night's events. "We got the one lead, with the carriage that Jack scouted, but for the rest of the girls, we got nothing."

"Is it even a lead?" Adder asked Dot. "So the Vauns gave the Estate one girl, probably as a gift. New bed warmer, big surprise. Doesn't tell us what's happening to the others." He looked at Jackal. "Besides never having seen anyone who looks like your sister, the guard we questioned was useless."

"And the other guards?"

Dot shook her head. "They were *fast*. It's like they practiced for this. They left everything, just grabbed the family and ran. The one we got, he stayed behind, shooting at us from behind the carriage. Kept us real busy."

"You know, if you had just let me take out your friend before—"

"Enough, my love," Geo cut her grandson off. "What's done is done."

Jackal took off his hat and laid it on the table. "Maybe it's time," he said to Dot.

She stared at him, hard, for a minute, and then nodded. "Will your friend help? Get us in, even?"

Jackal shook his head. "He's not disloyal, he's...obliging. Going back again, there's no way."

"Time? What's time? Time for what?" asked Adder.

"To do something really, really stupid," said Dot.

"I, well, that's not...wait—are you going to attack the compound?" Adder looked from Dot to Jackal, his mouth hanging open.

"We've been stockpiling weapons for years," she said. "And there's almost twenty of us now. If everyone recruits just one other person, that would—"

"It's not enough," said Jem. "You got, what, knives and crossbows? They got better ones, and real guns, and towers to shoot from."

Geo reached out and took one of Jem's hands. "Let's say you did get in," she said to Dot. "There are a lot of innocent people in there: children, domestics, men and women who know nothing about the kidnappings. What happens to them, if you go charging in with your weapons?"

Dot looked taken aback. "We wouldn't hurt them!"

"Accidents happen," said Geo.

For the second time that night, Adder started pacing the kitchen. "An accident *might* happen. But if we do nothing, those girls *will* be gone by morning. And we'll have nothing more to go on until the winter solstice."

"If we just knew more." Dot rubbed a hand across her eye, smudging the kohl onto her cheekbone. "I feel like we've been doing this blind. If we just knew what they're doing with them..."

Adder laughed. "Yeah, a magical peephole into the compound. That would be swell." He took a sip of his tea.

Geo glanced at her husband. Sam could see the question in the air between them, just as she could see that Jem was passing the decision back to his wife.

"There is one, of course," said Geo.

There was a sputtering sound as Adder choked on his tea.

"It's not without risk, but you'll be able to see what's going on inside without being seen yourselves."

Adder looked livid. "How have you never told me this? I would have gone ages ago!"

"Yes," said Geo, placing a hand on his shoulder. "By yourself, and if you heard something you didn't like you would have raced in and forced a confrontation. And I would have lost my grandson."

He glowered at her, but said nothing.

"So, we'd actually be able to get into the compound?" asked Dot. "Not just look around, like you said, but actually get inside?"

"Well, yes. It's how we managed to escape ourselves. Few inside the compound know about it. Nobody told me, even; I found it by accident."

"So if we find the girls, we can get them out..."

Geo shook her head. "It's too dangerous. Guards patrol the halls day and night."

Dot frowned and seemed about to say something, when she gasped. "But...but this passage, this must be how they're moving the girls! We can—"

"Impossible," said Jem. "Barely space to crawl in there. Couldn't drag a bunch of bodies through if they tried."

"I suggest you use the hidden passageway to gather information, nothing more," said Geo. "I would like your word on this, actually."

"So, what," said Adder. "We should give up on the girls they've taken? Watch while they sacrifice them to the blood goddess, or whatever?"

"I don't know what you'll find. But I do know that knives and bolts aren't a match for guns. And even if that wasn't the case, I won't have you turn the compound into a warzone. Promise me."

Jackal and Dot nodded, then Sam.

Adder let out a grunt of frustration. "Fine. We'll spy on the wolves and watch helplessly while they slaughter the sheep. Happy?"

"Don't joke, lad." Jem glared at him. "Think you could talk your way out, if they found you? These guards shoot on sight."

Though Geo's face remained impassive, her left hand began to fiddle with the collar of her robe, pulling it more tightly around her neck. "There is an older man to watch for. His name is Eli. If he is still alive, I suspect he is the one in charge of the abductions. Eli, he...well..."

"He used to go for the girls," said Jem, not bothering to hide the anger in his voice. "The young ones. Said it was his right."

"He has children; if he's gone, he may have passed the task onto them. They were just babes when we left, so for all I know they are normal, decent people. Or they're like him."

Geo pulled Sam into a hug as they were readying to leave.

"We'll see you in the morning," Sam said. "To plan the next step."

"Be safe, please, darling. And keep Adder safe. I'm counting on you." Sam could hear the fear in her voice.

"We'll stay hidden," she promised, and she meant it. The plan suited her perfectly. A reconnaissance mission she would happily help with—it thrilled her, the idea of seeing into the compound—but she had no intention of putting her life in danger.

"Sam!" Xenia was loping down the street toward her, Shale following along behind. "Have you seen Cass? He's gone crazy looking for Hakuund."

Adder grabbed Sam's arm as she started toward Xenia.

"We don't have time for this."

She stared at him and he pulled his hand away, running it through his black hair in a show of exasperation.

"We've been looking for, what, an hour already? I can't find him anywhere." Xenia sounded close to tears.

"I'm sure he's fine," Sam said. "Uh, is there somewhere he usually goes when he's upset?"

"Anywhere that's dark and quiet; so basically the whole damn Barrow. He hides from me, even though I always find him. Why does he hide from *me*?"

"Uh, hmm." Sam turned back to her companions. "So, I think we're all headed the same way, actually."

48

The North

"THIS HAS gotta be how they're moving the girls," Dot said as they waded along the flooded tracks, her voice reverberating off the crumbling walls.

"*If* they're moving the girls," said Adder.

"You don't really think...I mean, blood sacrifices?"

"No. Probably not. But who can say? Living your whole life inside a couple of walls, who knows what they believe."

"You'd think your grandparents would know."

"If the Vauns believe in blood sacrifice? If so, they never said. But they left decades ago; their info's kind of outdated. Besides, my grandfather said the passage from the compound to the tunnels is too small."

"What if there's another passage?" asked Dot.

"This whole story is insane," Xenia called out from behind them. "For the record, I'm only looking for my brother. I don't believe any of this."

"Is it?" asked Shale. "Seems to me it's the same damn story over and over: women treated like animals. The Vauns, they already have slaves. What part of this is a surprise?"

Xenia stopped walking and turned to face Shale. "The part where nobody noticed that some sicko's been stealing girls! The part where one of them got packed up in a box like a bottle of xeres. The part where my friend is...whatever he is."

Shale slid an arm around Xenia, who tipped her head back to the darkness above, and let out a deep, shuddering breath.

"I know, baby. I know," Shale whispered.

Up ahead, Adder and Dot came to an abrupt halt. Walking slowly back toward the other four, they gestured at them for silence. Sam held her breath. If compound guards did use the tunnels, this would be a bad spot for a fight. There were no platforms to shoot down from, no crumbling walls to hide behind. To say that they would fare poorly against them was an understatement. Sam glanced down at her baton and swallowed, picturing the automatic rifles and state-of-the-art crossbows the guards carried.

When the water swilling around their feet stilled, she heard it: something clattering against the concrete. *Is it a pattern?*

Xenia straightened, shrugging off Shale's arm. She let out a small gasp and took off running down the tunnel, toward the sound. Without thinking, Sam followed. It wasn't until she drew neck-and-neck with Xenia that her brain kicked in. She slowed for just a moment. *What am I thinking? It shouldn't be automatic; there's a choice to make.* With a snarl of frustration, she lowered her chin and pushed forward.

They rounded the corner and the thin flicker of a dying torch reached out to greet them. Sitting on the platform with a bottle in one hand, a shadowy figure rapped a rock against the concrete and then threw it at the water. It skipped twice before sinking down to the tracks below. Xenia leapt up onto the platform and threw herself at her brother.

"Arrrrg, geddoff, Xen," a familiar voice slurred.

"Cass, you jit, you had me panicked!" Xenia was hugging her twin, ignoring his feeble attempts to push her away. "Yeeesh, you stink. What the gods are you drinking?" Xenia took a sniff of the bottle he was holding and gagged. "Even for you that is foul. Are you actually trying to drink yourself to death?"

Cassio mumbled something incoherent.

"Well, it's not just about you, my love, actually there's something going on, something big." Xenia picked the torch up off the ground and wedged it into a crack in the cement, illuminating the tunnel.

Cassio looked up and noticed the rest of the group for the first time. "Hey guys," he managed. Then, seeing Adder and Dot, he turned back to his twin. "Who are they?"

"I'm Dot, this is Adder." She gave a wave.

Adder moaned with impatience and gave Sam an exasperated look. She ignored him and took a few steps down the tunnel, thinking.

"What is it?" She had not even heard Jackal approach.

"I'm thinking...I'm thinking that we could use some backup," Sam said. "In case we're followed out. The entrance should be just up ahead, and this is a good spot, lots of cover. A few well-placed fighters with crossbows could take out a lot of guards."

There was silence for a moment while he considered it. "Agreed."

"Adder!" Sam called out. "New plan."

"You sure you're okay with this?" Jackal asked again.

Xenia nodded, testing out Adder's crossbow. "I want to help."

"Besides," Shale said, settling down behind a broken wall, Dot's crossbow at her side. "It's less crazy down here than up there. It'll keep us out of trouble."

Jackal nodded absently. "And Cass?"

"He needs to sleep off the drink," said Xenia. "I guess here's as good a place as any."

"If he wakes up...will you tell him?"

She nodded. "I don't keep things from him. Besides, he's got a right to know."

"Want one?" Dot asked Sam, holding out Shale's array of knives. Sam selected one of the ones she had borrowed before. It felt good in her hand, like an old friend. Dot passed her a small piece of leather, which Sam folded around the knife before tucking the weapon into the top of her left boot. If they were lucky, and the passageway was empty, she wouldn't need it. *If it's not, well, better to be prepared.*

"Remember the rules," Adder called out. "No—"

"No domestics, no women, no children, nobody who doesn't want to fight," Shale cut him off. "What do you think we are?"

"Even guards, shoot but try not to kill," he continued. "You'll have open shots on anyone that walks through here. Compound stitchers can fix almost anything—as long as you leave them a live body they can work on."

Adder looked expectantly at the other three.

"Yup, yup. Espionage only," Dot said, tossing and catching one of the knives. "Priorities are the cellar and the old man."

"We'll give it an hour," Adder said. "And then meet back at the first fork. If we've still got nothing, we'll do a second round. Ready?"

Dot gave him a mock salute, while Sam and Jackal nodded.

First, though, they had to find the entrance. The four of them spread out, two on each wall, and began running their hands along the concrete. Geo and Jem had said that when they'd emerged from the passageway to find themselves in the underground tunnel, they'd been just a few inches above the waterline. Which side of the tunnel, they'd forgotten.

Eighty paces from the platform Sam stopped and turned around. From Geo's account, she should have found it by now. *Unless...* She lowered her fingertips an inch below the surface of the water and walked back toward the platform. Midway, she felt something jutting out, and stopped. It was a handle. She pulled it upward, revealing the entrance to the passageway.

"Of course the water has risen," Adder muttered to himself, walking back toward her and crawling into the dank, stone passageway. Dot followed, then Jackal, with Sam bringing up the rear.

49

The North

HER HANDS BUMPED into Jackal's feet once, twice, and then they fell into a rhythm. Water sloshed into her boots and up the legs of her pants, wet and oily and loud. The sound made her cringe: every noise was amplified.

Something must have caught Adder by surprise. The curse he let out ricocheted off the walls, growing in volume and reach until it was all Sam could hear; so loud it seemed the ceiling would crack and dump a city's worth of roots and concrete onto their four sorry, fleshy frames. They waited, frozen, straining to hear the click of readying weapons, the thud of combat boots on concrete.

One second passed, and then another, and then the paralysis dissipated in a long, collective exhale. No one had heard them; no one was coming. The group began to move faster, emboldened by the realization that they were probably alone after all.

Just as her wet knees were starting to chafe unbearably, Sam heard a thud up ahead. Adder and Dot called out at the same time, making it impossible for Sam to understand what either of them were saying.

"What?" It was too late. Before she knew what was happening, the ground disappeared beneath her. As she pitched forward, a pair of hands caught her and deposited her carefully on her feet.

"Thanks," she whispered as someone lit a torch. Firelight danced across Jackal's face, running along his jawline to his mouth. He was smiling, so slightly that she wondered if she was imagining it. Glancing upward, she caught his eye briefly, accidentally, and looked away. His hands dropped and he stepped back, then turned and followed the others farther into the passageway.

They soon reached a fork. Wordlessly Sam and Jackal veered to the right, Adder and Dot to the left, Dot stopping only long enough to tuck the torch into a crevice in the cement floor.

They proceeded in absolute darkness. Sam waved one hand protectively in front of her and dragged the other along the wall. When their passage split a second time, Sam kept right, while Jackal took the passageway on their left.

Sam's path led steeply upward. After a moment it turned sharply, and a glimmer of light flashed, blinding after the darkness of the passageway. She advanced toward it, and found, as Jem had promised, a tiny peephole.

Peering though, Sam spotted a bedchamber, empty except for a young boy with curly black hair who was building a fire. He looked tired but healthy, with a certain plumpness to his face that Sam did not usually see among Northern children.

He stood up, gazed at the small fire in satisfaction, and began to tidy the vials and jars that had been left scattered across a vanity. Sam pushed back away from the wall, giving herself a mental shake. *How long was I watching? Two minutes? Five?* The hour was counting down.

She continued down the passageway until she spotted another speck of light. This peephole also looked into a bedchamber, this one filled with heavy, dark furniture. Several bottles of liquor were arranged on a shelf.

She heard sounds coming from the bed, and jerked back. *Don't be silly.* Sam forced herself to look back through the peephole. The woman was probably in her early thirties, the man not much older. She had smooth, unmarked skin and white, straight teeth, and from the expression on her face, the sex was consensual. Sam turned away. This was not one of their missing women.

The passage split again. She chose the path that led downward. *Falling, falling; all the way to the cellar, I hope.*

Another sharp turn and the passage leveled out. Disappointed, Sam approached the first of two peepholes that had been cut into the left hand wall. The room was dimly lit. Squinting, she eventually made out a set of small beds surrounded by bars. A young infant slept in one, a toddler in another. Soft music was playing from a box on the dresser.

A woman's laughter sounded from the next room. Sam moved to the second peephole. There were two tables: women were seated around one and men around the other. The men were playing with cards, the women some kind of game on a wooden board. Three young female domestics stood waiting along the back wall, hands clasped meekly in front of their starched white skirts.

An old woman beckoned and one of the girls hastened to fill her glass with scarlet liquid. The woman smiled at her and whispered something into her ear. The girl covered a grin with one hand before returning to her post against the wall.

A small girl draped in fabric tripped over her costume and tumbled to the floor in a tangle of chiffon. A woman came over, scooped the girl up, and planted a kiss on her forehead.

"Now are you tired?" she asked. The little girl smiled and shook her head, bopping her nose gently to the woman's.

Sam felt a pinch in her throat and turned away. *The cellar, I need to find the cellar. The cellar or the old man.*

She came to another fork, but neither path sloped downward. She chose one at random and found herself taking another sharp turn. *How much time is left?* She was losing track.

A light glimmered up ahead, the last before a dead end. She quickened her pace. She would reach the end of this passage and then she would turn back.

It was a parlor, or perhaps a meeting room. She could see only the edge of a large, heavy wooden table and one low cabinet that ran the length of the far wall. Above the cabinet, which was well stocked with alcohol, a succession of men glared disapprovingly from within elaborate black picture frames.

The room was empty, she thought, until a hand reached into her line of sight. It grasped for a glass bottle, missed, and knocked the bottle on its side. As amber liquid pooled over the table and onto the carpet, someone stood up and walked unsteadily to the cabinet.

Hakuund took out another bottle and stumbled into the closest chair. It looked as though he had started to wipe the paint off his body, but had given up halfway. There were large streaks and smudges across his chest and along his arms, and tracks of red paint ran down one side of his face. His eyes were bloodshot. *Drugs, maybe, or could it be tears?* His antlers lay on the table in pieces, his mask discarded on the floor. The big man, the sad clown.

A large, curved blade lay on the middle of the table. Hakuund reached out and slapped the handle, watching it spin around and around. Eventually it slowed to a stop, the blade pointing away from him. To allow him inside their home, unguarded and carrying a weapon—the Vauns trusted him, Sam realized.

The minutes were ticking by, but she found that she could not turn away. She didn't know why he had agreed to kidnap these women, but it wasn't for pleasure; of that she was certain. He bore the unmistakable signs of a man whose self-hatred ran deep.

It didn't matter, of course. *We are measured by our actions,* she had been taught. She believed it too. And yet, she could not just leave him here alone, like this.

Something crashed against the door. Sam ducked, before remembering that she could not be seen. She peered through the eyehole again, and realized with horror that the figure stumbling into the room was Cassio.

"Babe." His voice was slurred.

Hakuund lurched to his feet. "What...no, no, you have to get out of here."

"Sure, yeah, just, after you tell me what's going on." Cassio pushed past Hakuund into the room. "Kidnapping girls, lover?"

"No. No, I'll tell you later, but you have to get out of here, they'll shoot a drudge on sight." Hakuund was shaking, his eyes not on Cassio but the door.

"So, you, you're what, then? Besides a selfish coward, I mean."

"I, you—"

"And who is this beauty?" Cassio wandered over to the table and picked up the knife. "You've been cheating on me." He turned back to Hakuund. "I don't know who you are." His mask of indifference sputtered and dropped.

"I am one of you, I swear. Not to start, maybe, but now. When they ask me, I make shit up, I don't tell them anything!"

"Oh, so you abduct girls *and* spy on your friends? When did this happen?"

"I—I'm not..."

"When?" Cassio pressed his forehead against the wall. "I loved you," he said, so quietly that Sam could barely hear it.

"My whole life." Hakuund started to reach out a hand toward Cassio, and stopped. "It's not my fault, I—"

Sam pushed away from the peephole. She had to get Cassio out of there. She ran her hands along the wall, frantically searching for a catch, anything to indicate a doorway into the room beyond. She pulled her one torch from her back pocket and lit it. *Last resort,* Adder had said, *in case the smoke or the light attracts attention.*

She raced up and down the passageway. Nothing, there was nothing. *How did he get in?* If there was an entrance, one of the others must have come across it. She would find them, and they could all go in after him.

A voice inside the room sent Sam's heart up into her throat. She looked back through the eyehole.

"Just come back with me," Xenia was saying, her voice quiet and calm, although Sam could see that the hand that was gripping Cassio's arm was trembling. "We can sort this out tomorrow, on the outside."

"He's a domestic, a compound spy!" Cassio pointed at Hakuund with the knife.

"Sssh, Cass, keep your voice down, we—"

Sam did not even see the guard; she just saw the bolt. She saw the bolt and watched Xenia crumple to the ground. He stepped forward into the room, bending down toward her. Faster than Sam would have thought possible, Cassio lashed out sideways, plunging Haku-und's knife into the guard's neck. He shoved the guard's body aside, falling to his knees and pulling his sister toward him.

"Xen, Xenia, you're okay, you're okay, honey…"

Her body was limp in his arms. Cassio cradled his sister's head, sobbing and stroking her hair. "Xen, Xen, wake up, Xenia, please."

50

The North

Sam stepped back. She had to find Jackal. She turned and sprinted down the passageway. Something wet dripped onto her collarbone and she realized that she was crying. She kept running.

The meeting place was empty. "Jackal! Jack!"

Dot stepped into view. "Sam, what—"

"Where's Jackal?"

"No idea, we came—"

"Did you find a way in?"

"Yes, but—"

"Where?"

"Down the left fork, then take the first right, it will lead you to—"

Sam was already running. She could hear Dot shouting something behind her, but her ears didn't bother making sense of the words. She thought she heard Shale's voice as well, but it may have been her imagination.

The walls of the passageway flashed by. She turned a corner and ran straight into him.

"Sam." Jackal held her up by the shoulders. "What happened?"

She felt herself starting to cave. *Later.*

"Cassio went in to find Hakuund, Xenia followed. She's hurt." She paused. "Maybe dead." She sounded calm—hollow, but calm. Jackal was staring at her. "They killed the guard. We need to extract them."

"They're with Hakuund?"

"Yes. I don't think he'll be any help, though."

"Okay," he said. "Okay. Come with me."

Sam followed him as the path twisted and turned, eventually arriving at a doorway.

She crouched down and pressed her ear to the door. The thud of her heartbeat was deafening; she pushed it down, her breathing as well. Silence. Perhaps the room was empty. Of course, the door might be soundproof, or the room full of guards but void of conversation. She looked at Jackal, who looked as uncertain as she felt.

In the end, what else could they do? As quietly as she could, Sam turned the handle.

The room was dark. It was an office, or a library of sorts. The entrance they'd come through was hidden; a section of one of the bookshelves had been built onto the door itself.

They crept through the room, nudged the door open, and peeked out into the empty hallway. As Jackal started to pull the door farther ajar, Sam grabbed his arm, gesturing for him to wait.

Placing a finger on the wall, she traced the routes she had taken from the meeting place to where she had found Hakuund. It had seemed a long way when she was exploring room by room, but retracing her steps had taken no time at all. What about elevation? She had gone up, and then down, a similar vertical distance both times. What about from the meeting place to finding Jackal, to arriving at the entrance? *Flat.* They should be on the same floor. Actually, she realized, they had to be close, for Cassio to have stumbled across Hakuund before any guards stumbled across him.

She beckoned to Jackal and turned right out of the room, creeping slowly down the hallway. All of the doors were shut except for one, which stood halfway ajar, filling the corridor with firelight. Silently they approached it.

Sam pulled out her knife and angled the blade so that she could see into the room. There were two men sitting in armchairs, one elderly and the other middle-aged, a sofa between them and the doorway. Jackal pointed to the ground, and she nodded. They dropped to their stomachs and crawled forward.

At the end of the corridor they turned right again. The first two doors were ajar, though the rooms themselves were dark. Jackal saw the handle move on the third door before Sam did, and shoved her into the closest room.

There was a woman on the bed. Sam had her knife out before she realized that the woman was asleep. They waited until the footsteps faded away, and then crept back into the hallway.

Jackal quickened his pace, forcing Sam to jog to keep up. Their path ended, forcing them to turn down another hallway. *Where are all the guards?*

A young child burst into the hallway. He giggled at them, and then tottered back into the room he had come from, pulling the door shut after him. Without a word between them, Sam and Jackal sprinted forward, quietly, on their toes.

Another fork: they turned left down a small hallway with two closed doors and a dead end. Sam walked to the last door and crouched down low. She could see a body lying on the other side.

She stood up and opened the door slowly. "Cassio," she whispered. "It's Sam." She pushed the door open a little farther.

She had known from the way Xenia was hit, from the way her body collapsed on the floor. She had known, but she had hoped anyway. The sight in front of them left no doubt. Cassio had not moved. He sat on the floor, encircled by a pool of dark red blood, holding his sister's head in his lap. He looked up at Sam and Jackal. "She's not breathing."

"We need to get you out of here," Jackal said.

Cassio nodded, but then looked helplessly at Sam. "I can't leave her."

"I know," she said. "But we have to. More guards could come at any second."

"There's no more," said a voice. Hakuund was sitting with his back against the wall, a bottle in his hand.

"What do you mean?" asked Jackal. "Where are they?"

Hakuund gestured upward. "Upstairs. Or outside. Unless there are visitors, he doesn't like to see them."

"What about the Vauns, and the domestics?" asked Jackal. "Are they armed?"

Hakuund took a long swig. "They got weapons, dunno if anyone is carrying theirs around."

Jackal walked forward, crouching down to look Hakuund in the eye. "Where do they take the girls?" His voice was calm and quiet.

Hakuund's hands started shaking. "Dunno," he whispered. "Sometimes, sometimes they keep one, or two, but the rest...I dunno where they go."

"Did they keep one this time?"

He shook his head. "No."

"You sure?"

"Not enough girls this time. And the ones from before." Hakuund licked his lips nervously. "He—they didn't last."

"There was a girl, three years ago. Long, dark hair. Skinny. Her name was Anna?"

"Don't know an Anna." Hakuund buried his head in his arms. "Don't remember an Anna."

Jackal nodded and stood back up.

"Wait." Sam looked at Hakuund. "What about Raina?"

His right hand jerked, giving him away.

"Was she here?"

"She, she... It wasn't me. She was here but it wasn't me."

"We need to go," said Jackal.

"It was Fin's fault, he told me. Why would he tell me?"

"Sam, we have to go," said Jackal. He reached for Cassio's arm.

"I can't leave her," Cassio said again, his eyes frightened and pleading. Jackal sighed and turned to Sam. "You help him, I'll carry her."

She forced herself not to look away as Jackal picked up Xenia's body

341

and draped it over his shoulder. Xenia, who was light and motion. *To see her so still...* Sam shook her head. *Later.* She helped Cassio up, and slid her arm around him. Together they followed Jackal back into the hallway.

"I didn't...I'm sorry," Hakuund called after them, sobbing. Not one of them looked back.

Each time they turned a corner she expected to see armed men: domestics with clubs, guards with guns and crossbows, Vauns with knives. Hakuund's words floated around her, insubstantial. It wasn't that she thought he'd lied, she just thought he might be wrong.

They passed down dark, quiet hallways filled with dark, quiet rooms, and nothing stirred. They made it to the office.

Cassio and Sam stepped into the passageway first. Jackal passed Cassio his sister's body, and stepped back into the office.

"I—there's something I need to do."

He shut the door behind them, leaving Sam in darkness, her arms around Cassio as he held his twin and sobbed.

51

The North

SHALE FOUND THEM, Sam was not sure how much later. She appeared with a torch, the light blinding after the darkness. "I left Adder and Dot to guard the exit to the tunnel," she said in a whisper. "Did you find..."

She stopped abruptly, shock rippling through her body. Her hands must have started shaking, for the light from the torch began to shimmer, pulsing against the walls. Like the drumming, Sam remembered, the heart of a building. She watched as Shale crouched down over Xenia's body, moving so slowly, so carefully, as though to avoid disturbing the other girl. She took one of Xenia's hands and held it to her lips. *The heart of us.*

The three of them sat frozen until Dot came upon them, breaking the silence. "We got the—oh." She stopped, realizing what she was intruding upon. "Is she...?"

Sam nodded.

"Oh gods. And Jackal, is he also...?"

"He went back in." Sam's voice was hoarse, as though she had not spoken in several days. "I should go see if he needs help." She was so tired she could not even muster the energy to feel worried.

"I'll come with you."

Sam shook her head. "The more of us are in there, the more likely we are to be seen."

Dot nodded, though she looked uncertain.

"You should tell Jackal there's a second passageway." Shale's voice was flat, robotic. "A big one. They came out...so we got the girls. But they saw us. We weren't going to shoot to kill, but...it's a mess."

Sam nodded, climbing stiffly to her feet. She glanced down at Xenia one more time, and then slipped through the door after Jackal.

Sam stood in the dark office for a moment. Her eyelids felt pinched, as though she was fighting to wake from a dream. *Jackal. I need to find Jackal.* Where would he have gone? *The cellar? Maybe.* She knew that the girls were no longer there, but he didn't.

Stairs, then. We'll find stairs. Silently, she crept out of the room and turned left. A long hallway led her to a T-junction. To the right, she heard voices, punctuated by the harsh dissonance of metal utensils clanking off pots clanking off pans. Her ears picked up a lone set of footsteps. They were growing louder.

Sam scrambled back down the hallway and ducked into an open doorway. In the darkness she grabbed hold of the only solid thing she could find. Hands gliding along the smooth wood, she slipped behind the door seconds before the footsteps followed her in. They veered left, moving deeper into the room and away from Sam.

She pressed an eye to the crack of the door. A small pool of light cast by a single candle illuminated rows of long, unornamented tables: a canteen. A man, bent low over his food, was dining without so much as a book for company. He raised his head up to take a sip of water, and Sam felt her heart begin to race, stricken by a sudden, illogical fear that he would sense her presence, sniff her out like a wolf downwind of prey. She waited for his eyes to narrow, his lip to curl. She waited, but he only stared at the grey emptiness in front of him, chewing mechanically. Stripped of his sneer, his condescension, he seemed to have shrunk; the remains were pitiable.

Feeling a voyeur, she watched him finish his meal, gather up his dishes, and smother the light. As he passed her, unknowingly within arm's reach, her nose filled with the smell of rot. Benison always smelled of rot.

She waited for the sound of his footsteps to fade away, and then she waited some more. When she was certain the hallway was empty, she struck out from her hiding place, turning quickly left: once, twice. The second hallway ended at the top of a staircase.

A few steps down, it curved sharply. Not wanting to come face to face with a guard here, where she could so easily be trapped, Sam pulled out her knife and angled it so she could see around the corner. It was empty.

Sam hated blind corners in confined spaces. That was twice the blade had doubled as a mirror. Her mind flickered back to the first time, earlier that night, and the two men she and Jackal had passed. It was strange, wasn't it, choosing to spend the solstice alone, in silence, when the rest of the family was celebrating together.

She slid the knife into its sheath and took a step down. One of the men had been old, as old as Geo. *And Jackal, he's not after the girls. He wants information.* She took one more step and then turned and jogged back up the other way.

Sam was certain it was the same room. Someone had since closed the door, but firelight still flickered through the gap. She pressed her ear to the door. It was faint, and she could not make out the words, but she certainly knew the voice.

Quietly, Sam cracked the door an inch and peered inside. Jackal's head jerked up, his right hand snapping back, ready to throw the blade in his hand. His eyes caught hers, and he lowered his knife back toward the person seated in front of him.

Closing the door quietly behind her, Sam skirted around the sofa and two large cabinets. Reaching Jackal's side, she looked down at the tiny old man seated in an enormous, padded armchair.

"We're being overrun by trash tonight, it seems. At least this one can be...enjoyed." He leaned toward Sam. "Not my type, but I might as well use the flesh before I peel it off."

Jackal pressed the blade to the old man's throat. "Enough."

"And you," he spat at Jackal. "I don't know what you hope to accomplish, vermin. My son will be back in a moment."

"Your son just took a domestic to bed. He ain't coming back. Now, tell me what you do with the girls."

"You know what I do with them," he said, a sick grin on his wasted face. "And after we feed them to the pigs."

"Bullshit," said Sam.

The grin widened. "Well, only *some* of them. The little ones. They want them mature, so the young ones, well, those are for me."

Jackal leaned in closer. "Who wants them?"

Silence.

He touched the tip of the knife to the old man's neck. "Tell me what you do with the rest of them."

"You cannot order me, trash!" the man screamed, his eyes bulging out, spit dribbling down his face, not realizing or not caring that the motion had pushed the tip of the knife into his throat. A thin line of blood trickled out as Jackal wrestled the man's jaw shut.

"Get me something to gag him with," he said to Sam.

"It's too late, someone will have heard that."

He ignored her, and started ripping fabric off a pillow.

"Jackal, we have to go!" Sam grabbed his arm.

"No," he said, frantic for the first time since Sam had known him. "You will tell me," he said, stuffing the fabric into the man's mouth. "Or you'll lose a whole lot of body parts before you die." Footsteps sounded above them, heavy boots thundering down a staircase.

Sam pulled out her knife and sunk it into the man's throat. Jackal stared at her, wide-eyed.

"Run!" She shoved him toward the door.

They stumbled out of the room and down the corridor, turning the corner just as voices sounded in the hallway behind them.

They made it back to the office. As Jackal closed the door closed behind them, Sam yanked the hidden door open and dove into the passageway. Jackal crawled in after her and pulled the door shut. They waited, breaths held, weapons out, as footsteps thudded past the room.

As quietly as she could, Sam turned and walked back down the passageway. Jackal seemed to hesitate a moment, but in the end he followed her.

52

The North

SHE SAW them as soon as they arrived back in the tunnel: three men, presumably guards, lying face down in the water, bolts protruding from chests, stomachs.

Adder dislodged himself from the others and hopped off the platform, walking over to meet them. Dot followed closely behind him.

"Were you followed?" he asked.

Jackal shook his head.

Sam looked past Adder, and then back toward the guards.

"We moved it past the first corner," said Dot. "Just in case someone else came out." She gestured down the tunnel, past the passageway. "It's just right there, the other passage. They left it open when they came through, so Cassio, while we were busy fighting the guards, he, well..."

Jackal nodded, his attention already shifting to the group huddled on the platform. Sam followed Jackal as he walked over to Cassio and Shale, Dot and Adder trailing behind.

"Hey, man." Jackal laid his hand on Cassio's shoulder. "Where you thinking?"

"There's..." Cassio cleared his throat. "There's this clearing she likes, overlooks the city." His voice broke on the last word.

"Of course."

Dot and Adder had caught up. "We should hide the cart and the bodies," said Dot. "If they don't know we used the tunnel..."

"We can try again come June," Adder finished for her. His eyes flickered over to Cassio. "We can help with her...or maybe you want to be alone. We could come by after. Whatever you want. We should move, though, in case someone thinks to check the passage."

Jackal and Cassio carried her body, followed by Sam and Shale. The two outsiders brought up the rear. They turned the corner, and Sam froze.

She'd always thought it was funny, how her memory held onto small, unimportant bits of information: something seen once and remembered forever. How much room did these images or sounds or smells take up in her memory? *A metal box painted brown, tall and narrow, with large wheels covered in black rubber.*

Adder opened the back door, revealing six unconscious women packed onto metal grills—

"...like meat in an oven. It's disgusting."

Along the top, another six slots lay empty.

"How long do you think, until they'll wake up?"

It was too loud. She couldn't think.

"Sam." If only everyone would stop talking.

"Sam."

"What?" Everyone was staring at her.

"Did you hear me?" Jackal looked concerned. "I said we should split up."

She nodded numbly.

Jackal, Cassio, and Shale left, holding Xenia's body between them. Sam sat alone with the cart. What was she waiting for? She couldn't remember.

Dot appeared. She was carrying a gun and a crossbow, which she loaded into the cart.

"Wait. Where's Adder?" asked Sam.

Dot looked at her quizzically. "He's taking care of the bodies."

That makes sense.

Once they had finished loading the dead guards and all of their weapons, they began rolling the cart forward. It was easier to move than Sam had expected.

The girls still had not woken up by the time they reached the entry point. Sam stared dully up at the platform. *When we thought it was reconnaissance only. When Xenia was still alive.*

And she still would be, if you hadn't brought her along.

I know.

And for what? For Raina and the nameless hundreds? They're probably dead. You sacrificed living, breathing, beautiful Xenia for nothing. For ghosts.

I had to try.

For what, for pride? To solve the puzzle that nobody asked you to solve? There's no victory here. You think that if Raina goes home, you can too?

Sam closed her eyes.

You're a child. A selfish child.

"So we just leave it here?" Adder was looking dubiously at the cart.

"We can hide it better later," said Dot. "After we deal with them." She pointed at the six unconscious forms they had lifted onto the platform.

"We have to wait for them to wake up anyway."

"This is fine, though. It's far enough away from the Vauns that they won't find it unless they really look."

"They might look this far, you don't know."

"Is another five minutes really going to make a difference, then?"

"It might."

In the end, they decided that Sam would stay with the girls while Dot and Adder pushed the cart farther into the tunnel.

Sam was glad when they left, grateful for the silence. A crossbow in each hand, she settled down on the cold concrete floor, her back against the wall, her eyes closed. Even the dim light cast by the torch Dot had left seemed too bright.

She was almost asleep when she heard the rustle of fabric. Someone let out a faint groan, which turned into a whimper, and then a scream of rage.

Sam muscled her eyes open. A tall, full-bodied girl, her face tight with pain, was clutching the outside of her forearm. On the soft skin above her wrist, a large 'V' bulged out from a bed of inflamed skin.

She caught sight of Sam and snarled. "What did you do to me, you shint?"

"The Vauns drugged you."

"I'll kill you!"

"Stop shouting." Sam adjusted her grip on the crossbows. "Please." She was far too tired to fight fair, should one of them attack her.

Luckily the girl got the message. She settled down to wait with her back against the wall, though her eyes never left Sam.

Dot and Adder returned before the next girl awoke. Sam closed her eyes again. Let the others explain what had happened. All she wanted to do was sleep.

"...remember was the party. Where's Hakuund?" The girl sounded young and scared. "He wouldn't do this to me."

"Well, he did."

"Bullshit!" She started crying, though whether from pain or shock, Sam wasn't sure.

An hour later, all but the smallest girl was awake. Dot led the way out, Adder followed, carrying the unconscious girl over his shoulder. Sam took anchor, walking several feet back behind the girls, who were casting her and her crossbow dark looks.

They emerged into the pale light of early dawn.

"Anyone know where this one lives?" Adder asked.

One of the smaller girls nodded. She looked to be about thirteen years old. She also looked vaguely familiar, though Sam couldn't place her.

"Okay, we'll follow you then," he said. "The rest of you okay to get home?"

The girls had been tensed, readying for a fight. At his words, a change came over them. Suspicion and anger gave way to shock. Two of the girls started shaking; another bent forward and retched.

She was one of Niya's little friends, Sam realized, the little girl that had been raped in the woods. She seemed to have recognized Sam, too, for she gave her a tiny smile.

"Sam."

She turned to Adder.

"We'll get her home. Go be with your..." He didn't seem to know what to call them. "Go be with them. We'll find you after."

She nodded and turned to leave.

"You're just going to carry that crossbow?"

"Yep." If huainas jumped her, then they jumped her. She was too tired to worry about it. She had a bag of bolts, a baton, and Shale's knife. *Let them come.*

53

T he North

S<small>AM</small> <small>FOUND</small> the entrance to the trail that Cassio had described easily enough and followed it steadily upward.

Finally, silence. Then the thoughts came flooding in: thoughts and the memory of a cart. *A metal box painted brown, tall and narrow, with large wheels covered in black rubber.*

She should tell them. She couldn't, though, not without revealing who she really was. *Really, does it matter? Would anyone care?* Ava's fears seemed overblown. What lynch mob would appear and string her up for being a Southerner? Where were the Seiran spies, paid to sniff out runaways and drag them back to Ankev? She imagined spending the rest of her life lying to her friends and felt exhausted.

The clearing was small, just a break between a few young trees atop a hill. The Barrow was spread out beneath them, obscured by the early morning fog and the smoke from fires burning.

They had laid Xenia beneath one of the trees. Cassio sat at her head, stroking her hair. Shale, sitting by Xenia's feet, was silent. Jackal was walking toward Sam, into the woods.

"Where are you going?" Cassio asked, his voice hoarse.

"Dry branches."

"I don't think...I don't want to watch her burn up."

"I know she still looks like herself now," said Jackal. "But soon she won't."

"I know."

"What about the old way?" asked Jackal. "We can lay her in the ground."

Cassio thought about it for a moment, and then nodded.

Wordlessly, Sam joined Jackal. They would need hardwood or stone to break the soil.

We stopped the shipment this year. She came across a flat rock and brought it over to the clearing. Someone had outlined the shape of the grave in the dirt. *They can do it again next summer and the year after.* It was possible that they would not even need to intervene again. Eli was dead, as were the guards involved in transporting the girls. No one had followed them into the passageway, so it was possible that Eli had kept everything a secret from his household: the passageway, the abductions... It could already be finished. *The son, though...the son knows something. Benison, too. He would have been giving Hakuund instructions.*

And Raina...what about Raina? And Jackal's sister? What about the hundreds of women that have already been taken?

Jackal appeared with two sticks. He passed one to Sam and started digging into the rocky ground.

Despite her exhaustion, the simplicity of physical labour felt good. She tried to empty her mind, but thoughts and images kept popping in uninvited: Cassio's face when Xenia fell; Eli spitting with rage; the women packed into the cart. *Like meat,* someone had said, *and they were right.*

The sun was fully up by the time the grave was deep enough, though the light was trapped behind thick clouds. Sam wished the rain would start. The sky was tense with waiting.

Shale had washed the paint off Xenia's face and arms. Sam thought she looked oddly naked without it. She wanted to cover her with flowers, but there weren't any in the clearing, only leaves and branches and long grasses.

Sam untied the ribbon from her hair and began winding it around one of Xenia's wrists. A moment later Shale unfastened her woven leather choker and tied it around the other wrist. Cassio's silver ring was too large for any of his sister's fingers, so he placed it in the palm of her right hand and folded her arm over her chest so that hand and ring lay pressed against her heart. Jackal, unadorned, watched silently, hands deep in his pockets. A moment of silence, heavy with words hoarded, and then they began to cover her with dirt.

54

The North

THEY WERE SITTING SILENTLY around the grave when Adder and Dot appeared. They hesitated at the edge of the clearing, reluctant to tread upon their grief.

Cassio waved them over, breaking the stillness.

"How are the girls?" Cassio asked.

"Awake. Pissed off," said Dot.

"You go by Shya's?" asked Jackal.

"Yeah." She brightened. "Everyone's still running high from last night. I tell you we hit the spokes? It was Charis' idea, last minute. So next time—"

"They'll have more guards," said Adder.

"Or maybe they'll decide it's not worth taking a girl."

"It's a temporary fix," said Adder. "It's always been a temporary fix. We're just patching the same hole over and over."

"Well, it's still the best plan we got," said Dot, "at least until we know more. We can spy through the passages again next solstice— even the weeks leading up to it."

"She's right," said Jackal. He leaned back on his hands, his eyes on the fresh grave in front of them. "It's all we've got. We don't know where they're shipping them to, who's buying…"

"I know where they're going," said Sam, her voice barely above a whisper. She looked down as five sets of eyes turned to her. *No going back now.* "South. They're going south."

"What, Kylai?" asked Adder, naming a town south of the Barrow. "What's the name of the compound there, again?"

"No. I mean Seira."

It was Dot who finally broke the silence. "What?"

"Did you hear something last night?" Adder asked. "Why didn't you tell us?"

"The cart. I've seen it before."

"That makes no sense," said Dot. "How did—"

Sam was too tired to lie and too sad to care about the fallout. "I'm Seiran."

"Yep," said Jackal.

Sam lifted her head.

"Yeah, we figured that out, what, a month after she started?" Cassio looked at Jackal for confirmation.

Jackal nodded. "'Bout that."

"What? How?"

"It's obvious," said Cassio. "Also, we're actually from Kanlan, so we knew your stories were bullshit."

"Did you know?" Sam turned to Shale, who shook her head, though she didn't look up from the mound of dirt in front of them. Sam bent forward to look at her and wished she hadn't. It was too intimate, the pain on Shale's face. She had no right to witness it.

"I said you were hiding something!" said Adder.

"What, you want a prize? Leave the girl alone." Dot turned to Sam. "Okay, they go south. Why? Some rich nutter have a thing for Northern women?"

"All I know is that the border guards are told to let them pass."

"Well," said Jackal. "Guess I'm going south."

"What, alone?" asked Adder. "That's insane. What are you gonna do, knock on the wall and ask them to let you in, please?"

"We'll go together," said Dot. "We'll find a weak spot, fight our way through if we have to."

Sam shook her head. "The weapons they have, and the tech... It's impossible."

"Sneak through?"

"You don't understand; they have equipment that will see you approaching from miles away."

"We got the cart," said Dot, frowning. "They don't know who's coming, right? Just that it'll be a bunch of girls and a guard or two?"

"There was paperwork for six girls," said Adder. "Why, you want to re-kidnap a bunch of women so we can follow the trail?"

"You wouldn't need to. Six girls? I can get five volunteers by nightfall, easy."

"I'd rather go alone," said Jackal. "Don't need them risking their lives for this."

"Uh, they risked their lives last night when they took on a compound carriage. And it's their decision. Five girls is nothing; I could find you twice that."

"Four," said Shale, though if Sam hadn't seen her speak she might not have been able to identify the speaker. The usual velvet had been stripped from her voice, leaving nothing but a dry rasp. Sam wondered if it was the first word she'd uttered since they left the passageway.

Dot and Jackal raised their eyebrows.

"Well, I'm going," said Adder cheerfully, when it was clear that Shale was not going to elaborate further.

Sam found that her eyes kept drifting back to Cassio, who didn't seem to be following the conversation. He was rubbing his thumb against the knuckle where his ring used to be, a vacant expression on his face. It took her a moment to notice Jackal watching her.

When the inevitable question came, though, it didn't come from him, it came from Adder.

"Why'd you leave?"

"I..." Sam swallowed. They were watching her. She needed to say something, anything. "I...I just, I didn't want to be guilty of what they were guilty of." *Not again, anyway. Not anymore.*

You are, though, aren't you? Sam looked at the grave in front of her. *She'd be home safe right now, if it wasn't for you.*

And the abductions: you know, now. Can't un-know it. Every solstice, more girls. It'll be on you. And whatever Raina's going through in the South, and Jackal's sister, that's on you, too. If they're still alive.

It wasn't what she wanted. There was no chance that this would end well.

And yet. And yet.

No. Enough.

They'll die without me.

Then they'll die. And you will too. Is that what you want?

No.

It won't bring Corvus back.

I know.

Even if you find Raina. Even if you die. Even if you save a life or a hundred lives or a thousand.

I know.

And it won't absolve you. Scales can't be balanced, it doesn't work that way.

I know.

There is no redemption here.

I am not the hero of this play. I am not the hero of any play I could be in. Except a play I wrote.

You're an idiot.

"You know, we'd stand a way better chance if you came," said Adder. "Since you know so much about the South and all."

She sighed and rubbed her temples. "You don't have to persuade me. I'm not going to sit up here eating apple loaf while you all die in the South."

She thought she detected a shadow of a smile on Jackal's face, buried somewhere beneath the rind.

"Peachy." Adder actually rubbed his hands in anticipation. "How far are we from the wall?"

"Fifteen, twenty days maybe. It'll be more with the cart," said Sam.

"So...we probably want to make their timeline."

Adder looked at Dot. "Think you can get three other girls by tonight?"

"Watch me," she said.

"Well then," said Adder after nobody had spoken for a minute. "I guess we should pack up and head out for sundown."

"Well, some of you." Jackal turned at Sam and Cassio. "Hakuund, he's their puppet through and through. They'll know by now that it was us. There'll be a watch out."

"We can get your stuff," said Dot. She looked at Cassio. "Are you...?"

He shook his head.

"Well, even if you're not coming...like Jack said, there'll be a watch. But I can bring you what you need or move your stuff somewhere safe."

"Just a change of clothes," he said. "And there's a couple bags of dust hidden in the extra cooking pot. Wouldn't say no."

For some reason it hurt Sam to think of the twins' beautiful apartment being picked over, all of their curios stolen or pawned off. What was it Xenia had called her brother that night? A dragon. She'd laughed about it: a dragon with his treasure.

Adder, Shale, and Dot turned to go.

"Wait," Sam said, looking at Shale. "Tell Ava, tell her...nothing, I guess, in case someone from the compound questions her. Just tell her I'll try to come back." *And that I'll bring Raina back with me.* She didn't say it, though. She knew their chances weren't good. "Oh, and ask her to take care of Frank."

"You know she will."

"I know, but ask her anyway. This is a bad idea," Sam called after them.

"Yup," said Dot, without looking back.

"A really bad idea."

"Yeah, we know." Adder's voice floated back to them from the edge of the woods.

"We're probably all going to die for nothing."

"Yeah, got it. We'll see you soon." Dot waved a hand back at them.

Sam, Jackal, and Cassio watched until the others had disappeared beyond the hillside.

"Cass—" Jackal started to say.

"I think I just need to be alone with her," he said, a tremor creeping back into his voice.

Jackal nodded, and pulled his friend into a one-armed hug. When Sam approached, Cassio placed his hand on the back of her neck, bringing his forehead in gently to rest against hers. Sam struggled for something to say but could not seem to land on the words. She didn't know how to say sorry, and Northerners did not believe in goodbyes.

They would need to find somewhere to hide out the day, Sam supposed. After all, she couldn't go home to the factory. Even if she wasn't leaving, it was over; her time in the Barrow was done.

Sam looked back once, as she and Jackal began their descent. The sky had brightened, and raindrops were starting to fall. Standing beside the mound of dirt, his eyes pointed downward, Cassio did not seem to notice.

ACKNOWLEDGMENTS

I am so very grateful to the people who supported me in writing and self-publishing my first novel. I would not have gotten here without you.

If you enjoyed this novel at all you have my editor to thank. Through some magic she was able to see past the awkwardness of early drafts to the story's true potential. Each question she posed led to a dozen new idea, new developments, new complexities. Melissa Frain—thank you for your insight, your brilliance, and especially your enthusiasm.

Thank you to my designer, Dan Van Oss, who took the images in my head and melded them into the perfect cover.

I am immensely grateful to the great John Patrick Shanley for permission to quote *The Big Funk,* and more generally for writing some of the world's most beautiful plays. Along those same lines, thank you Margaret Atwood for writing *The Handmaid's Tale,* Aldous Leonard Huxley for *Brave New World, Yevgeny Zamyatin* for *We,* and *Tamora Pierce* for *The Song of the Lioness* and *The Protector of the Small.* All of these works inspired and influenced me, and I humbly pay tribute to their genius.

Thank you to Dr. Barry Smit of the University of Guelph, expert in climate change, environment and resource use and global change, for taking the time to speak with me about possible climate change scenarios. Thank you as well to Russ Foxx, body piercing and modifications expert, for answering numerous questions on the subject of branding.

Salal McConnell, Sarah Christie, and Cat van Ruyven, thank you for making it through painful early drafts and for sharing your feedback. Also to Jane Ford, for helping me navigate the stark and terrifying terrain of self-publishing, to my sister Megan Lee for support with marketing and to Helen Blackmore for early artistic conceptualizations.

To everyone who was supportive of my earlier writing experiences—you helped give me the confidence to try my hand at a novel. In particular, from my days as a CIDA intern, thank you to Miek van Gaalen and Hazel Postma for your early guidance, and to Richard dal Monte of the Tri-City News for publishing my columns. Also, to my friend and honorary auntie, the late Dorothy King, who at ninety-nine years old had thought that my blogs were funny enough to download onto her tablet and read to her friends over tea.

Thank you to my mom Diane Lee for teaching me to love books and for reading numerous drafts of *The Wolf and the Rain*. Your feedback and encouragement made all the difference. And to my dad Andrew Lee for holding the baby so I could write, and for a lifetime of being in my corner.

And most of all, to my husband Andrew for his unwavering support. For reading countless revisions. For getting up early with the baby so I could work all night. For being my muse, listening agreeably while I debated and ranted my way to a solution. I truly couldn't have done it without you.

Lastly, to every reader who decides to pick up *The Wolf and the Rain*, a new book by an unknown author. Thanks for taking the gamble. I hope it pays off.

EXCLUSIVE BONUS CHAPTER

But wait...**there's more!** One more chapter, in fact, set six months before *The Wolf and the Rain*. Go to eepurl.com/dwhIhT to join my mailing list and I'll send a downloadable link right to your inbox. It's **free**, of course!

I'll also let you know as soon as new books or audiobooks come out. I may even send you a photo of the real, live Frank...

If you have any trouble with the link, you can also request the form via the contact page at Tanya-Lee.com

ABOUT THE AUTHOR

Tanya Lee holds a B.A from the University of British Columbia in literature and political science, and an MSc.(Planning) in international rural planning and development from the University of Guelph. With a focus on international development and human rights, Tanya has worked on counter-trafficking, safe-migration, and maternal and child health projects in India, Nepal, Mexico, and various countries in Africa. She also acts in independent films, particularly those with a focus on human rights and gender equality.

She currently lives in Toronto with her husband, her two young children, and a belligerent 23lb orange tabby named Frank. *The Wolf and the Rain* is her first novel.

Visit Tanya's website at: Tanya-Lee.com

 twitter.com/the_tanyalee
 instagram.com/tanyaleeofficial
 facebook.com/thewolfandtherain

BOOKS BY TANYA LEE

The Wolf and the Rain

The Thief and the Waste